THE GRANVILLE AFFAIRE

Una-Mary Parker

severn
House

This first world edition published in Great Britain 2005 by
SEVERN HOUSE PUBLISHERS LTD of
9–15 High Street, Sutton, Surrey SM1 1DF.
This first world edition published in the USA 2006 by
SEVERN HOUSE PUBLISHERS INC of
595 Madison Avenue, New York, N.Y. 10022.

British Library Cataloguing in Publication Data

Parker, Una-Mary
      The Granville affaire
      1.   World War, 1939-1945 - Social conditions - Fiction
      2.   Domestic fiction
      I.   Title
      823.9'14 [F]

      ISBN-10: 0-7278-6303-7 (cased)
                      0-7278- 9146-4 (paper)

Printed and bound in Great Britain by
MPG Books Ltd., Bodmin, Cornwall.

PART ONE

Shadows of Destiny
1939–1940

One

Henry Granville sat at his desk, his eyes unseeing as he stared blankly at the beautiful gardens of Hartley Hall on this mild September day. The blow had fallen two hours ago, predicted for years but nevertheless shattering in its intensity now that the official announcement had been made by the Prime Minister that Britain was at war with Germany. Henry's best and oldest friend, Ian Cavendish, who worked in the Foreign Office, had been telling him since 1935 that war was inevitable.

'If Hitler goes ahead with his plans to invade Poland, that's when we'll be forced to declare war on Germany,' Ian had said. 'And France will back us, mark my words. If they don't there's no hope for any of us.'

Henry sighed deeply as he continued to gaze at the gold-tipped trees of an early autumn. Ian had been proved right. In spite of two warnings from Britain, the *Wehrmacht* had stormed into Poland two days ago. The Third Reich was now prepared to take on the rest of Europe.

'Dear God,' Henry murmured to himself. 'We've barely recovered from the Great War. How many young men are going to be killed this time?'

Henry had brought Liza and their five daughters down to Hartley several weeks ago, because Ian had predicted that London would be razed to the ground within the first twenty-four hours. With them had come Parsons, the butler, and all the other servants, who, with extreme diplomacy on all sides, were managing to work and live alongside his mother's staff albeit it in cramped conditions. Not that they'd have to for much longer. With the exception of Mrs Fowler, the elderly cook, they'd all be called up and he and Liza were going to gave to 'do' for themselves in future.

Parsons entered the library at that moment. 'A telegram has arrived for you, sir.'

3

Henry snatched the brown envelope off the silver salver, fearing the worst. His third daughter, Louise, who was only fourteen, was on holiday in Brittany with his sister and her daughter. They should never have gone. He'd said so at the time, but Candida had assured him they'd be fine. 'We can catch the ferry home if there's any trouble,' she'd said airily.

Now he couldn't bear to even contemplate what would become of Louise if she was stranded on the continent. Visions of prisoner-of-war camps filled his fevered mind.

Scanning the message, his hands shaking, Henry suddenly sank back into his chair with a cry that sounded like a sob.

'Oh, thank God! They've landed at Southampton. Louise is safe.'

'Yes, sir. Cutting it fine, sir,' Parsons ventured, drily.

Henry jumped up and charged into the hall. 'Louise is safe. Liza!' he shouted up the stairs. 'Mother! They're all safely back!'

Doors flew open all over the house. His mother, Lady Anne, came out of her private sitting room, her face pale. His youngest daughters, Amanda and Charlotte, came running in from the garden, shrieking with delight.

'Thank God,' cried Liza, hurrying down the stairs from her bedroom, tears of relief stinging her eyes. She flung her arms around Henry's neck, while Lady Anne looked on quietly, murmuring, 'Our prayers have been answered.'

Then the servants burst into the hall through the green baize door, breathless with excitement, followed by Nanny and the nursery maid, Ruby.

'What a tale she'll have to tell,' Ruby exclaimed. 'I wonder if she saw any German soldiers?'

'When will they be here?' Lady Anne enquired.

Henry read the telegram more carefully this time. 'Candida says: LANDED SAFELY AT SOUTHAMPTON. ALL WELL. GOING STRAIGHT HOME. WILL BRING LOUISE TO YOU TOMORROW. CANDIDA.'

'Why aren't they coming straight here?' Liza asked fretfully. She'd had sleepless nights worrying about Louise, combined with pangs of guilt for ever allowing her to go.

'Candida only lives ten miles from Southampton. It's obvious they'd go to her house first,' Henry pointed out.

'We can phone her this evening and find out how they all are, can't we?' Lady Anne suggested.

4

'Of course, Mother.' He felt light-headed for a moment with sheer relief. War or no war, at least Louise was safe. 'I'll postpone returning to London until Monday morning. I want to find out why on earth they didn't come home before. I could murder Candida for putting us all through the agony of the last few days.' Suddenly he felt angry. He'd *told* Candida not to go abroad at this time. It was madness and he blamed himself for letting Louise go, even if St Malo was only just across the Channel and could be reached by the ferry in a few short hours.

'Bloody selfish of her, that's what I call it,' he added, stomping back into the library.

There was an awkard silence in the hall and a feeling of anti-climax. No one knew quite what to do next.

'Shall I proceed with the tea, M'Lady, Madame?' Parsons asked Lady Anne and Liza, in his usual formal manner.

'Proceed away, Parsons,' Lady Anne replied, laughing gaily. 'It's too cold for the conservatory, don't you think, my dear?' She turned to Liza, who nodded automatically, used to her mother-in-law running Hartley Hall.

'Yes,' Liza agreed, politely. 'I think we might have it in the drawing room, Parsons.'

There were times when Parsons found it quite tricky to keep two mistresses happy. It required a certain *je ne sais quoi*, he reflected, as he fastidiously set out the Minton cups and saucers and put them on the silver tray, with the Georgian silver teapot.

Hartley Hall really belonged to Henry and Liza, but as Lady Anne had come here as a bride, and it had always been her home, Henry insisted she remain, running the estate for them, as they lived in London during the week. Liza hated the country anyway so this had been the perfect solution since Henry's father had died.

But now, Parsons reflected darkly, they were stuck here for the duration of the war. Mother-in-law and daughter-in-law, cooped up together with the three youngest of the five sisters, while the master of the house was away in London from Monday to Friday, as Chairman of Hammerton's Bank.

Parsons sniffed delicately as he took some silver teaspoons out of their velvet lined case. How long was it going to be before they were all at each other's throats?

*   *   *

5

In London, Juliet stretched luxuriously, her pale limbs gleaming as she lay on the bed, while daylight filtered through the curtains of Daniel Lawrence's little house in Chelsea.

The night had been hot and humid, and she and Daniel had thrown the bedclothes onto the floor as they'd made love as if they could never have enough of each other.

Daniel lay beside her now, dozing. His skin much darker than hers, his head indenting the pillow. Juliet had never realized before just how much she loved him.

She'd intended to return to her husband in Scotland the day before, but she couldn't resist Daniel when he persuaded her to stay until Sunday evening.

'What shall we do if I stay on?' she'd asked, teasingly.

His hungry eyes had devoured every inch of her exquisite face. 'Do I have to spell it out?' he'd whispered. 'D'you know something? You grow more beautiful every day.'

'That's because you make me happy.'

She'd recently had her hair cut and it hung to her shoulders in blonde waves, falling seductively over one side of her face when she leaned forward. Every day she looked more and more like a Hollywood film star, and less and less like Juliet Granville, the second daughter of Henry Granville, an ex-débutante with a shady reputation and now the wife of a Scottish duke.

Cocooned with her lover in the bedroom of his little house, they made love again as soon as Daniel awoke. He was filled with fresh desire and so was she, wanting each other so much there were moments when Juliet thought her heart would stop beating and she'd die with ecstacy as she lay in his arms and felt him thrusting inside her.

Suddenly a piercing wailing sound, rising to a high-pitched screaming note, shattered the peaceful Sunday morning.

Daniel was out of the bed in a flash. 'Quick!'

He grabbed Juliet's wrist.

'What's happening?' Naked, except for a soft blue satin eiderdown which she wrapped around herself, she followed him down the stairs to the ground floor. The penetrating unearthly wailing continued to whoop up and down, with ear-splitting intensity.

'Air raid siren,' Daniel shouted abruptly, above the din, as he lead her down another flight, to the cellar.

Fear impaled her heart. 'Are we going to be bombed?'

Without answering, Daniel pushed her into a windowless

6

room, and, switching on a central light, followed her, closing the reinforced door behind him. The low-ceilinged old wine cellar had whitewashed brick walls, and was furnished with a bed, a stack of blankets and, on a card table, a hurricane lamp, candles, matches, some brandy and a wireless.

'When did you do all this?' Juliet asked, looking around as she sank on to the bed.

'As soon as I bought the house.' Daniel looked at his wrist watch. 'Let's find out what's happening.' He turned on the wireless.

'. . . I regret to announce we are now at war with Germany.' intoned the quavery voice of the Prime Minister.

'Oh, my God!' Juliet sat up, her eyes round with shock. 'When did this happen?'

'I was expecting it.'

'I knew there was going to be a war, but not so *soon*.'

Daniel, deep in thought, didn't reply. Handing her one of his sweaters, he said, 'Darling, put this on, or you'll catch your death.'

It nearly reached her knees. She curled up on the bed like a child and looked up at the arched ceiling, almost as if she expected it to fall in on them.

'So this is it, then,' she said, appalled. 'Are we being invaded? What's it going to be like, Daniel?'

'Bloody awful. It's going to involve women and children, as much as the armed forces. When the bombing really starts . . .' He reached for the brandy, and poured the amber liquid into two tots.

They drank in silence. Juliet turned to him, looking deeply into his eyes. 'If I'm going to be killed I want to die with you. I couldn't bear it if you were to . . .' she broke off, unable to continue.

Startled, as if from a deep reverie, Daniel looked back at her. 'Oh, my darling, my darling.' He wrapped his arms around her, pulling her to him, climbing on to the bed and covering her with his body. 'I love you, Juliet . . . Never forget that.'

She looked back at him unwaveringly. 'I want you . . . I want you, so much . . . I want you now . . .'

The fear of dying suddenly made her feel rapacious, desperate to be close to him, wanting to be impregnated by him, locked in passion as if they only had minutes to live.

7

He entered her swiftly, pumping his life and his love into her, as if he would never be able to assuage his desire.

At that moment the All Clear sounded.

Afterwards Juliet couldn't stop laughing. 'Talk of a climax and an anti-climax happening at the same moment,' she giggled.

'That may have been a false alarm, but you ought to go back to Scotland right away,' Daniel told her.

'Oh, no! I can't bear the thought. Especially now. I want to stay near you, Daniel.'

'But God knows where I'll be?' he replied worriedly. 'I want to know you're out of harm's way. In that fortified castle of yours in the Highlands, you'll be safe from the bombs, and an invasion, too.'

Juliet frowned, knowing what he said made sense, but not wanting to have to spend maybe months away from him. Especially not stuck in Glenmally Castle with Cameron and his old witch of a mother.

'Daniel, what are you going to do?' They never talked about his family or his home on the South Coast, or even what he did for a living, so wrapped up were they in each other during the brief hours when they were together.

'I must go home to Kent,' he said, stiffly. 'That's where the Germans will land; I must get my family away.'

His wife. And his three children. Juliet looked away, trying to hide her anguish.

'Of course,' she murmured automatically. Most of the time she managed to put the existence of his wife and children to the back of her mind. Now it seemed they were foremost in his thoughts; that was why he wanted her to return to Scotland.

'Shall I come with you?' Gaston asked, loading Louise's suitcase into the boot of Candida's car.

'Absolutely not,' she replied, appalled. 'My family know nothing about you, and the shock might kill my elderly mother. When I return, Gaston, we will have to sit down and have a talk. I'm sure you appreciate this is a difficult situation?'

Gaston nodded sullenly, and shrugged. 'If you say so.'

'I'll be back this evening,' Candida continued. 'Cook will give you luncheon and anything else you want. You must be tired, especially as you cycled all the way from Amiens before we even left St Malo.'

'I wish I had my bicycle now.'

'Perhaps we can find you another one. We'll look in the garage tomorrow.'

Gaston looked at her sulkily and without another word, turned and went back into the house.

'Louise,' Candida called to her niece. 'Come along. It's time we left.'

A moment later Louise appeared and got into the car, pretending she hadn't overheard the conversation between Aunt Candida and this sullen Frenchman they'd been forced to bring with them as they struggled on to the last passenger ferry back to England.

'Are you all right?' Candida asked, as she pulled out of the drive of her Georgian house, in her old Bentley. 'Had a good sleep last night? I bet you jolly well needed it.'

'I'm fine,' Louise replied, longing to get back to Hartley now. 'Is Gaston going to stay with you?' she asked carefully, keeping her tone neutral.

'I hope not but I could hardly leave him at Southampton. I suppose now the war's started, there'll be plenty of work about, though not necessarily for a writer,' she added with a trace of sarcasm.

'Is that what he is?' Louise asked, trying to sound innocent. 'Has he only got his mother? Is his father dead?'

'Yes.'

'No other family? No brothers or sisters?' she pressed on, wishing her aunt would tell her the truth about Gaston, because she was finding it a great burden to keep this terrible secret to herself.

'No.' Candida kept her eyes firmly on the road ahead.

'Poor thing,' Louise said sadly. 'He must be very lonely.'

Candida didn't reply. Instead she said, 'You'll definitely be staying down at Hartley, now, won't you? I suppose your Papa will have to go up to town to the bank every day, or perhaps he'll stay at his club, during the week?'

Louise sounded anxious. 'I heard there was an air raid in London, yesterday.'

Candida grinned at her, as if relieved the conversation had taken a different turn. 'False alarm, apparently,' she said briskly. 'The All Clear sounded fifteen minutes later.'

*   *   *

9

Rosie, returning from shopping in the village, with both Sophia and Jonathan in the big pram, found Charles standing in the hall, staring at the letter in his hands.

His face was drained of colour and he looked sick.

'What's the matter? Another bill?' Rosie asked, wearily, hauling her shopping bags into the kitchen. The cottage was too small. There was nowhere to put the pram. There was nowhere for the children to play. Disgruntled, she dumped bags of potatoes, runner beans, tomatoes, and a pound of sausages, wrapped in white butcher's paper, beside the earthenware sink.

This wasn't the life she'd planned, she reflected angrily. As the eldest of the Granville girls, and Mummy's pet, she'd taken it for granted she'd marry a rich man with a title, who lived in a big mansion, and had pots of money. But thanks to Juliet, who should not have been allowed to Come Out the same year, all she'd been left with was Charles Padmore, a drunken gambler, who might be a lord, but who couldn't even hold down a simple job.

They'd had to leave London because she couldn't afford to keep up with her friends; she couldn't even afford to keep up with her *mother*, because Liza would have been horrified and upset if she knew Rosie's dress allowance went to pay all the bills.

And now here she was, stuck with two children in a tiny cottage in the village, a quarter of a mile away from Hartley Hall, too proud to admit failure, pretending instead to want 'the simple country life that is so good for the children'.

Charles had followed her into the kitchen. His voice was hollow.

'I've had a letter from my mother,' he said, aghast. 'She says I must join my father's regiment immediately and not wait to be conscripted.'

'She's right, isn't she? After all, you're only twenty-six, and able-bodied; which was your father's regiment?'

'The Guards.' Charles chewed his lower lip and looked miserable. 'But I'm not cut out for the Army,' he said petulantly.

'No, I realize that.' Her tone was acid.

He threw his mother's letter down on the table. 'Oh, this bloody *bloody* war . . . !'

Sophia started wailing. She always did when the atmosphere became tense.

'You'll manage,' Rosie said slowly, as it sank in what Charles joining the army would mean. He'd was away from home. Earning regular money. Being forced to work. And no longer a liability and a thorn in her side. She picked up a knife and started peeling the potatoes for lunch.

'I wonder how I can get out of it?' Charles wailed, stricken. This was the most horrific thing that had ever happened to him; worse even than being sent to boarding school when he was seven.

Rosie looked at him askance. 'Perhaps, instead of joining the Army, you can volunteer for the Navy or the Airforce?'

'That would be even worse. I get terribly seasick, and I don't like heights.'

'You're going to have to do something, unless they find you medically unfit; which you're not,' she said cruelly, and then realized how unfeeling that sounded.

'What am I going to do . . . ?' He grabbed her hand, though it was wet and muddy from the potatoes, and she felt a wave of revulsion; he was like a frightened child, clinging to its mother.

'I think your mother's right, Charles,' she said slowly. 'Join up before you're conscripted. Everyone is having to join up, women too, unless they've got small children; you wouldn't want anyone to think you were a conscientious objector, would you?'

'No.' His voice broke on a sob, and he turned and fled from the kitchen.

As Rosie stood at the sink, hot tears trickling down her own cheeks. Her immediate feelings of relief that Charles would be away for a long time now gave way to feelings of guilt. A sense of shame overwhelmed her. Was she wishing him *dead*? He might be killed. He might never come back. And for the rest of her life she would be haunted by her wickedness at wishing him gone for good.

Sophia tugged at her skirt. 'Mummy?'

Wiping her hands on a tea towel, Rosie swept the little girl into her arms and hugged her close. At least she had her babies as a result of her disastrous marriage, and she'd never let anything happen to them.

But suddenly she realized, it was not going to be as easy to say goodbye to Charles as she'd thought. She'd be on her own, with no one else to blame if anything went wrong.

'Goodness . . . !' exclaimed Liza, reading the new edition of the *Tatler*, dated September the sixth. 'Listen to this, girls. "The crisis robbed Deauville of many of its most regular supporters before Grand Prix day, yet there was still a good attendance for a very exciting day's racing." Imagine that? I wish we'd been there.'

The thought of living in the country permanently was making Liza restless.

Juliet, instead of returning to Scotland immediately as she'd planned, had decided to drive down to Hartley for a few days, to say goodbye to the family. With a war on, she now had no idea when she'd be able to come South again.

'That was probably written weeks ago,' she pointed out. 'It takes them ages to print the magazine, so it's bound to be out of date.'

Liza looked crushed. 'It says here, Queen Mary has gone to stay with the Duke and Duchess of Beaufort, at Badminton, for the duration of the war. She's taken sixty-three servants with her!'

Parsons came on silent feet into the room. 'There's a telephone call from His Grace, for Your Grace,' he announced grandly to Juliet.

Juliet left the room to take the call.

'Hello, Cameron?' she said, putting on a bright voice. 'How are you?'

'Fine, dear. But when are you coming home?'

'At the weekend. It's all a bit hectic down here. Charles is joining the Guards, so I've had to stay and comfort Rosie and her babies. Daddy's in London and Granny thinks we should try and squeeze in a few evacuees, but Mummy won't let her. Says we'll all get nits and lice . . .' Juliet chattered on, in an effort to cover up what she was really feeling; that life without Daniel, who she hadn't seen since Sunday, was unbearable.

'When at the weekend?' Cameron asked, as if he hadn't heard a word she'd said.

'I'll let you know. Probably sometime on Saturday.'

'You've been away for a long time.' He sounded sullen and reproving.

'Well, it's been very chaotic. I've been shopping for clothes and silk stockings before they're rationed. I've bought some furs because fuel is going to be rationed, too, and you know how cold Glenmally can get . . . Oh, yes – and war broke out! Quite a busy week in fact,' she added sarcastically.

Walking restlessly in the garden the next morning, Juliet met Louise, who'd been asked by her grandmother to pick some chrysanthemums and dahlias for the dining-room table.

'What's wrong?' Juliet asked. 'You look miserable.'

'Juliet, can I talk to you?' Louise indicated a wooden bench set under a cherry tree. 'Can we sit down for a minute?'

'Yes, of course. What is it?'

'There's something I must tell you; I must tell someone, or I'll burst,' Louise blurted out.

'What is it?' Juliet asked sharply, looking at Louise apprehensively.

'It's a secret. A *terrible* secret. You must promise faithfully not to tell a soul,' Louise beseeched.

Juliet's heart stood still for a moment. If what had happened to her had now happened to Louise, she'd kill . . . She forced herself to sound calm. 'Sounds serious,' she said, trying desperately to keep her tone light. She sat down on the bench and looked in the sweet young face of her sister. 'Now, what's it all about?'

'When we were in Brittany . . .' Twenty minutes later Louise finished telling Juliet all about Gaston being Grandpa's illigitimate son.

'The thing is,' Louise concluded, 'Aunt Candida doesn't realize I know that he's Daddy's half-brother. She's making out she was doing Madame St John Brevelay a favour by letting her son come to England with us, to escape the Germans.'

Juliet felt quite weak with relief. Louise was all right. That was all that mattered. What she'd heard was a tale of adultery that had taken place forty years ago and now the pigeon, or should she say cuckoo, had come home to roost.

'What shall we *do*?' Louise implored.

'I'll think about it, darling,' Juliet promised, feeling almost light-headed. 'Don't worry any more about it.'

'You'll never let on I told you, will you?' Louise still looked pale with the strain of keeping this explosive knowledge to herself. 'It might kill Granny if she knew Grandpa had had a lady friend.'

Would it kill Daniel's wife, if she found out about me? Juliet wondered, cynically. But still she couldn't dredge up even an iota of guilt or feelings of pity for this other woman, with whom she was supposed to share Daniel.

'Ian and Helen are coming next weekend,' Henry informed everyone at breakfast the next morning. 'He's up to his eyes in work at the Foreign Office, and this is probably the last time they'll be able to get away for a little break.'

Liza brightened. Everything was so gloomy at the moment, it would be nice to do a little entertaining. 'Shall I invite a few other people for dinner, darling? Or Sunday lunch?'

'Don't count me in, I'll be back in Scotland by then,' Juliet remarked firmly.

'Oh, darling, do stay until next Monday,' Liza said. 'Ian is your godfather; you haven't seen him for ages. Not since your wedding, in fact.'

'I must get back to Cameron. I've been away too long as it is.'

Henry stared at her, puzzled by her vehemence. Lady Anne spoke in conciliatory tones. 'Cameron must be missing you.'

Juliet ignored the remark. Daniel had banished her nightmares. The demons that still caught her unawares at moments, filling her with panic, had abated. And she didn't want them to recur.

'Uncle Ian's such a darling,' Rosie remarked. 'It'll be nice to see him again.'

'Why do you call him "uncle"? He's not a relative,' Juliet snapped.

Rosie looked confused. 'We've always called anyone Mummy and Daddy's age uncle or aunt,' she protested.

'For God's sake, that was when we were children. I call all older people by their first name now.'

'Well, I'm still going to call him Uncle Ian. I think it's such a shame he and Aunt Helen have no children of their own.'

'You seem to think children are the be-all and end-all of life, Rosie,' Juliet retorted with mounting anger. 'Some people should never have children.'

Henry looked pained. 'You're being very harsh, Juliet,' he observed. 'I believe it's been a great sadness to Ian and Helen.'

14

There was an awkard silence around the table, broken after a few minutes by Liza, who was nervous of silences.

'Well, Henry darling, who else shall we ask? We really should make an effort . . .' she rattled on, but no one was listening.

Henry looked at Juliet closely, wondering what had caused her outburst.

Lady Anne, however, was sure she knew the cause. Juliet's irritable outburst suggested she was pregnant herself, though she might not yet realize it.

Juliet found the old dowager lying on the library sofa, suffering from a sprained ankle. Dressed in tartan, she looked as if she was resting among the well worn rugs of a dog's basket. Hairs and the odd spray of biscuit crumbs lurked in the folds, amid the hot sweaty smell of sleeping labradors.

'So you've decided to come back, have you?' Iona Kincardine asked querously.

'This is my home,' Juliet replied spiritedly. 'How are you feeling?'

'I'm in pain, but why should you care?'

'Can I get you an asprin or anything?'

Iona looked at her sourly. 'Cameron's looking after me.'

'Of course,' Juliet smiled sarcastically. 'I'm sure he is.' Iona moved restlessly, trying to prise herself into a sitting position. 'What on earth were you doing in London all that time?'

'I wasn't in London *all* the time. I was staying with my family. Where's Cameron?'

Juliet had telephoned to say she'd be arriving at noon, but there was no sign of him anywhere.

'Seeing to things on the estate,' Iona replied, averting her eyes. It was the answer she always gave.

Juliet looked out of the window at the view. The mountains were hazy mauve with heather, and tumbling grey clouds obliterated their peaks. In the foreground, a bleak lawn stretched to a forest of pine trees. The melancholy atmosphere of the landscape was almost palpable; she felt it closing in around her, paralysing her with its slowly choking grasp. Robbing her of the desire to do anything, except creep into a corner and hibernate until she could get away again. Glenmally was oppressive and, worse, it had an evil atmosphere.

I'll go out of my mind if I have to stay here for ever, she thought with a flash of desperation. She wanted to be back in the little Chelsea house with Daniel. She wanted to hear the gentle roar of the traffic, and see the crowds jostling along the pavements. She wanted to know that five minutes away were cocktail bars, and places to dance, restaurants galore, and amusing companions.

The awful thing was she'd only been back at the castle for a few minutes, and yet she already regretted returning.

Aloud she said, 'I'm taking the dogs for a walk. Come along, boys and girls.' At the command, there was a mass disturbance of black fur on the hearth, as the dogs leapt to their feet, jostling to be first out of the door. The dowager glared balefully at them for deserting her side with such alacrity.

Juliet set off briskly, her mind in turmoil. This is not what I'd planned to do with my life, she reflected. Cameron had led her to believe they'd divide their time between London and Scotland; why else would he have bought the Park Lane house?

She had not expected to be isolated in a fifty-roomed castle either, with no one to talk to – except for an old witch of a mother-in-law, and a desultory husband who was out all day, and who only occasionally came to her room at night. She was about to be twenty-one, and already her life seemed to be over.

As she stood stock still under the pine trees, this seemed like a defining moment in her life, as the dogs scurried about, and she considered her future.

Saddest of all was the thought that she and Cameron had been good friends before they'd married, but now they weren't even that. It made her realize, even if she took Daniel out of the equation, that she'd reached for the most valuable card in the pack, grabbing its riches, its position, and its power, only to find it had turned out to be the Joker. And now it seemed as if the joke was on her. What a stupid, meaningless prize she'd sought so cleverly. And what a hollow vessel it had proved to be.

Juliet walked on, searching for answers. The onset of war had already provided Rosie with a perfectly acceptable reason to be separated from Charles; why shouldn't it provide her with the perfect exit from Glenmally, too?

She would volunteer to do something; maybe train to be a nurse? Or drive an ambulance. She wanted to do something that was dangerous, in the thick of things, because she was no longer afraid to die. Why should she be – when life without Daniel wasn't worth living?

'So how was London?' Cameron asked genially, as he poured glasses of sherry before dinner that evening. 'Is the house all right?'

'The house is fine,' she replied, smiling amicably. There was no need to get Cameron's back up before she'd laid her plans. The house he'd bought in Park Lane was a vital factor for her future. 'London's ready for a bombardment. And at night there's a complete black-out of course.'

Cameron nodded, frowning with concern. 'I read about that in *The Times*.'

'Look what I've got!' She held out an identity card, a ration book and a book of clothing coupons. Then she went over to a table, piled high with books and picked up a square cardboard box. She pulled out a black rubber gas mask, with a round nozzle to cover the nose and mouth, and a clear panel across the eyes.

'I look like a black pig in it, with a great snout,' she joked, 'and it smells horrid.' She stuffed it back into the box.

'What are we going to do now there's a war, Cameron?'

He blinked, bemused. 'Do?'

'We're both going to have to volunteer to join up,' she continued cheerfully, testing the ground with deliberate flippancy, indulging in a fantasy to watch his reaction. 'I rather like the idea of joining the Women's Royal Naval Service; gorgeous navy blue uniform with brass buttons. And black stockings! Really terribly sexy! What about you? Will you go into the Army, like Charles?'

Cameron shifted from foot to foot, looking uncomfortable.

'I'll have to stay here, running things,' he replied, rather too quickly.

'Stay here? Surely you'll be called up?'

'I'd never be accepted, because of my bad back.'

'Since when have you had a bad back?' she asked incredulously.

'Since I was ten,' he said stiffly. 'I was thrown from a horse. My spine was damaged.'

'You've never mentioned it before; are you joking?'

He flushed angrily. 'Of course I'm not joking. Why should I be joking? You've got to be A1 to get into the forces; I've already been told I couldn't qualify.'

17

'Not even for a desk job?

'What is the matter with you, Juliet?' His hand shook as he put his sherry glass down on the table. 'You're acting as if you don't believe me.'

She shrugged. 'It's just so . . .' – she nearly said, 'convenient', but changed it to – '. . . so surprising. I've never heard you complain about your back. Personally, I can't wait to do something.'

'I don't think we'll be much troubled with the war up here.' His manner was cold now, and wary.

'So you're going to stay here, all safe and cosy in this fortification, letting everyone else in the country get on with it? Fighting the Germans for you?'

'I'm not a conscientious objector, if that's what you're inferring?' he retorted angrily.

No, just a Mummy's boy, Juliet thought in disgust, but decided if she wanted to get her own way, insulting him wouldn't help. 'I never said you were, but I'm told there's likely to be an invasion. We can't sit back and do nothing.'

Cameron gave her a strange look. 'You seem almost excited at the prospect of war.'

Juliet didn't answer. She'd no experience of war. Couldn't visualize the reality of it. But whatever happened it was going to be an experience, a new adventure, being a part of history in the making . . . and a way of escaping from her husband.

'Of course I'm not excited, but I can't bear to be out of things,' she admitted at last. 'I also think it's our duty to defend our country.'

The only sound in the room was the chink of glasses as he topped up their drinks, and the whisper of the logs, as they crumbled into red hot ash in the fireplace.

'I need you here, Juliet,' he said, breaking the silence.

'What for, darling?' she asked lightly, adding mockingly, 'you have your mother to look after you; what more do you want?'

He turned and stared, unblinking, into her eyes. 'I need a son.'

'One day, yes, but what's the hurry? In fact, I think it would be better to wait until after the war, when everything's settled and things are back to normal, don't you? Would it be fair to bring a child into the world, in the middle of a war?'

'I want a son, and I don't want to have to wait until you

feel like it, Juliet. I think you owe it to me.' He walked over to his desk, and dropped heavily into the chair behind it, distancing himself from her, taking up a position of power behind his heavy silver topped ink wells, and framed family photographs. Almost as if he were her employer.

'I've given you everything you ever wanted, Juliet, and I think it return you should try and give me the one thing I want, the only thing I want; an heir to carry on here, after I'm gone.'

Juliet looked at him, with false coquetry. 'And to think I thought you'd married me because you couldn't resist me!'

He looked away, unamused, not answering.

'I'm only here for breeding purposes, then. How charming,' she remarked drily. 'I'm glad you think my pedigree is good enough.' There was a cold savagery in her tone now. 'Why didn't you marry the daughter of one of your ducal friends? Or a foreign princess? It's a pity our royal family have no young women wanting to make a "suitable marriage",' she mocked.

Daniel . . . Daniel . . . This was not how Daniel asked her to have his baby. His heart-throbbing words of wanting to impregnate her because he loved her had aroused her then, as the memory of them aroused her now.

She sat looking down at her hands, twisting her emerald and diamond engagement ring, feeling physically sick.

'There's no need to put it like that,' Cameron said uncomfortably. 'You have to admit you're not exactly welcoming when it comes to . . .'

'Fucking?' she demanded coarsely.

He blinked again, shocked and startled. 'Really, Juliet . . . !'

'That's what it is to you, isn't it? Or perhaps you'd prefer to describe it as rutting, like your deers on the hill.'

'You knew it was a part of marriage; I do have conjugal rights.'

'Then I wonder why you're so reluctant to exercise them?' she flashed back. 'All I'm saying is I don't think this is a good moment to have a baby. We've plenty of time, Cameron. I really think we should wait until after the war.'

He stared at her across the vast expanse of his desk, his expression appalled. 'Do you know how long the Great War lasted? Four *years*! This war could last even longer. I'm telling you I want a son right away. Why should we wait? Now that you've returned from your gallivanting,' he sneered as he said the word, 'I want you to stay up here, and try to get pregnant.'

'It's going to be difficult on my own, Cameron,' she replied, brittle as pork crackling, 'unless you're hoping for an immaculate conception?'

He turned an ugly shade of red. 'Perhaps if you were more enticing . . .' he began.

'. . . And perhaps if you were more interested,' she cut in harshly.

The butler came into the library at that moment to announce dinner. In silence they left the room and walked across the stone flagged hall, its walls bristling with antlers, until they reached the dark panelled dining room, where a polished table that seated twenty-four had been ceremoniously laid for two.

They ate in silence. The only noise was the ticking of the clock on the carved mantelpiece, and the soft footfalls of the servants as they served dinner. Juliet studiously avoided looking at Cameron, adopting a haughty air and drinking a lot of wine.

When dinner ended, she left the dining room without a word, and made her way up to her suite of rooms, walking along shadowy corridors hung with tapestries, past narrow windows overlooking the bleak mountains that loomed darkly in the distance.

This was the most godforsaken place she'd ever known, and she was stuck here – but for how long?

Juliet awoke with a start, feeling hot and sticky, her stomach in turmoil. Sliding carefully out of bed because her head was pounding and she felt sick, she staggered to her bathroom.

Cursing the rich dark venison she'd had for dinner – something at the time had warned her it tasted odd – she was violently sick, kneeling on the cold floor in front of the lavatory, feeling so ill she wished, for a moment, she was dead.

She was normally never sick. Never ill. How long, for God's sake, had that meat been hanging around the cave-like old-fashioned kitchen of Glenmally?

Tottering unsteadily back to bed, she wondered how Cameron had fared – and Iona, whose supper had been sent up to her on a tray?

Almost immediately she fell into an exhausted slumber, and did not even hear when her lady's maid brought in her morning tea and placed it on the bedside table. It was cold when she awoke two hours later, feeling much better. Well enough to get up and have a bath and get dressed to go downstairs. Hungry now, wanting some breakfast.

'How is the Duke this morning?' she asked Ferguson the butler, when she ordered fresh coffee to be made. 'I was very ill, earlier. The venison was off. Please tell cook to see it doesn't happen again.'

'His Grace is fine, Your Grace. So is Her Grace the Dowager Duchess,' he replied, almost reproachfully. 'I'll mention it to cook, of course, but no one else has been ill, and it was served in the servants' hall as well.'

For a fleeting moment Juliet wondered if she'd been poisoned. She knew she was being ridiculous. But why was she the only one who'd been affected? Then she decided it was an absurd thought. She was becoming paranoid. It was time she pulled herself together.

After breakfast, and having ascertained Cameron was out and his mother still in her room, Juliet shut herself in the library and dialled the number of the cottage to see if Daniel was there. She craved the reassuring sound of his voice, was desperate to have him say he loved her. The phone rang and rang, while she prayed for him to be there to answer it.

'Been sick this morning, I hear?'

Juliet started with fright, quickly crashing the receiver back on to its cradle. She spun round and saw Iona standing in the doorway, watching her.

'The venison was off last night. It made me very ill.'

'There was nothing wrong with the venison!' Iona's smile was sly, showing grey teeth. Her manner was sweetly cloying. 'It looks to me as if you have an announcement to make.' She lifted her hand and waggled a knowing finger at Juliet.

The shock of her remark, and the implication of her meaning, thundered through Juliet's head like an explosion. For a moment her memory tried to grapple with it. When was the last time Cameron had come to her room? Three weeks ago? Four weeks? No, longer . . . She remembered having had her period two days after the last occasion. So . . . the colour rushed to her face; if she was pregnant, it certainly wasn't Cameron's baby.

'There no need to blush,' Iona wheedled. 'Have you told Cameron?'

'I . . .' The words stuck in Juliet's throat, she felt so over-whelmed with mixed emotions. *Both* Daniel and Cameron were going to be thrilled when they knew, but how did she feel about it, herself? How was she going to handle this situation?

In her mind, having Daniel's baby had been a beautiful, romantic fantasy. But she hadn't thought it through. If it meant she was going to have to stay permanently at Glenmally, pretending the child was Cameron's, then it was a horrifying prospect. On the other hand if she insisted on living in London, she'd have to give Cameron a good reason for her decision.

Unless, of course . . . she admitted the baby wasn't his?

'Are you all right?' Juliet heard Iona ask, as a cloud of black spots seemed to envelope her and she broke into a sweat.

'I feel . . .' she staggered, reaching out to a chair for support, as her legs gave way.

'Ferguson,' the dowager shouted urgently. 'Come quickly.'

The butler came hurrying into the room.

'Your Grace?'

'Fetch a glass of water. My daughter-in-law feels faint.'

Juliet sat slumped, her eyes closed. She felt sick again. And utterly dazed.

Ferguson rushed off to get the water, but before returning with it he popped his head round the kitchen door, where the cook and several scullery maids were preparing luncheon. Making a thumbs-up gesture, he mouthed, 'She's expecting!'

Cameron came hurrying back from wherever he spend his days, as soon as he got the message from his mother. He looked jubilant.

'Well done, my dear,' he said to Juliet, who was resting by the library fire, which was the warmest room in the house. All animosity was forgotten as he kissed her warmly on the cheek, and asked if there was anything he could get her.

'Nothing, thank you,' she replied meekly, realizing that now she could do no wrong.

'Are you feeling better? Mother said you fainted. Shall I call the doctor?' He fussed around her like an old woman.

'There's no need. I just feel a bit tired.' She couldn't help feeling a pang of guilt.

'Don't you think the doctor should have a look at you. Make sure everything's all right?'

'Everything's fine.' Juliet realized the need to be careful. Cameron, who was no fool, would realize they'd last had sex at least seven or eight weeks ago; he probably thinks I'm two months pregnant, she thought. Instead of which . . . She knew with certainty now that she'd conceived on September the third. In the air raid shelter in Daniel's cottage, when the siren had sounded and they'd expected the fearful outcome of being bombed. A doctor's examination might reveal she was only two or three weeks pregnant.

'I'll see my own doctor, next time I go to London, Cameron.'

'You can't go to London now, with the war and everything.'

'Nonsense,' she said firmly. 'I've been to our family doctor since I was a child; I'm not going to anyone else.'

'I can't allow that.' Suddenly he was being obstinate, in an effort to appear dominant. 'The journey could be very bad for you, and the bombing might start. Anything could happen. I can't allow you to put my child's life in jeopardy.'

'If you think I'm going to some local doctor up here, you're mistaken,' she snapped.

'But . . . but . . .' he became flustered and agitated. 'The baby's got to be born here, so you might as well see our family doctor, now.'

'Born *here*?' she echoed, with genuine horror. She sat up, her expression indignant. 'I'm not going to have it here. I shall have it at home, in London. My parents can come and stay with me, and I'll be fine. Let's not argue about this, Cameron. My mind is made up.'

He screwed up his face in misery, not knowing how to handle Juliet. 'I was born here, so was my father and grand-father and . . . we've *all* been born here.'

She looked at him coldly. 'Then let's have a break from tradition, shall we? Anyway,' she continued craftily, 'if anything were to go wrong, it's essential to be near a good hospital; that's why Mummy had all of us in London, instead of at Hartley. St George's Hospital is only a few minutes away from Park Lane, so let's have no more talk of subjecting me to endure childbirth *miles* away from civilization.'

Realizing he was beaten, and wondering what his mother was going to say, Cameron nodded slowly. 'Very well, then. Have it your own way. I'm going to telephone Hector; invite him to dinner tonight. Do you feel up to a little celebration?'

With the broker of our marriage? she thought intuitively. 'Yes, certainly,' she replied smoothly, 'and when you've done that, I'll phone my family.' *And the baby's father.*

Toasts had been drunk, a feast of locally caught lobster had been consumed, and Iona and Juliet had retired to bed for the night, leaving Hector, who'd been persuaded to stay until the next day, alone with Cameron in the library, consuming rather large quantities of best malt.

Hector raised his glass for the umteenth time. 'This really is splendid news.'

Cameron beamed, raising his own glass again. 'Yes, isn't it? I was beginning to think it would never happen.'

Hector nodded sagely. 'Better late than never.'

'I hope to God it's a boy.'

'There's time enough for that. You'll surely have more than one child?'

Cameron looked doubtful. 'I think one will be enough, as long as it's a son.'

Hector let it pass. 'Your mother's over the moon, isn't she?'

Cameron's smile widened and he gave a chuckle. 'She's thrilled.'

'You'd no doubt like my help, setting up a trust fund for the wee bairn when he's born?'

'I was going to talk to you about that. Do you think I should make over Glenmally to him right away, to avoid death duties?'

'Gang away with you, man!' Hector burst out, lapsing into his native accent. 'You'll no be worrying about dying, yet?'

'Accidents can happen. I'd like to make sure the estate remains intact when I die.'

'I'll look into it, Cameron, and if you do have a boy, we can discuss the matter again, but you've no need to rush things.'

'Thank you, Hector.' Cameron took another swig of whisky, his eyes brimming with sudden emotion. 'I don't know what I'd do without you. You've been like a second father to me.'

'You hardly had a first one,' Hector remarked drily. The old Duke had been a brutal bully, treating Cameron shamefully when he'd been a boy. Whipping him for being slow, unathletic and too sensitive. He'd locked him in his room when Cameron was five, because he'd wept when he saw his father killing a trout he'd caught, by slamming its head against a rock.

'That's what will happen to you if you don't buck up,' the old Duke had thundered. 'You're a weakling. You've no backbone. We've got to make a man of you, somehow.'

Iona had done her best to protect Cameron from his father's profound loathing, but that had only made things worse. When the old Duke had died from a sudden heart attack at the age of fifty-eight, there were few who mourned his going.

'Juliet seems very well,' Hector observed conversationally, as Cameron refilled their glasses.

'She does, doesn't she? She goes down to London a lot, though,' he added critically.

'Cameron, the best thing you did was to buy that splendid house in Park Lane. Not only is it a good investment, but I knew it would appeal to Juliet. Anyway, surely her being away gives you some breathing space, doesn't it?'

'That's right. The deeds of the house are in my name, aren't they?' Cameron asked, with sudden suspicion.

Hector's tomb-stone teeth showed as he smiled. 'Give me credit for having some sense, man. Everything, down to the cups and saucers, is in your name.'

'Good.' Cameron continued to sip his whisky contentedly. The logs crackled in the hearth. The dogs snored gently at his feet, two of them twitching their legs as they dreamed of some canine excitement. It wasn't that he distrusted Juliet on her trips to London. He knew she'd never risk having an affair, because she had too much to lose if she did. Money, position and power were all that mattered to her. And she was no more interested in sex than . . . well, than he was, with her. A lot of women were like that, he'd heard, so really they were well suited.

'So . . . everything else all right?' Hector asked carefully, breaking into his thoughts.

Cameron nodded, without replying. He didn't like Hector prying too closely into the details of his private life.

There was still no reply from the cottage in Bywater Street. Juliet thought of writing to Daniel, but she so badly wanted to tell him the news in person, see the delight on his face, feel the comforting warmth of his arms around her, that she felt quite desperate with frustration and longing.

'I'm going to London, on Tuesday,' she announced the next evening, when Iona had gone to bed, and she and Cameron were alone. 'My mother says I should see her gynaecologist,' she added, Liza having said no such thing because Juliet hadn't told her family she was pregnant, yet.

'Would you like me to come with you?'

Oh, God, he's trying so hard to be nice, she thought despairingly. 'There's no need, sweetie,' she said, smiling. '*You* don't need to see the gynaecologist.'

Cameron reddened, and rubbed his hands together in embarrassment. 'Well, no . . .'

When Juliet went up to her room a little later, she was struck by the loveliest of thoughts. Now she was pregnant, there was no need for her to sleep with Cameron, ever again.

Everywhere Juliet looked, the majority of people seemed to be in uniform. Had every man in London joined up? Surely there must be some civilians around?

Silver barrage balloons swayed, high up in the sky, like surreal drunken elephants. The traffic was much lighter, because petrol rationing had been introduced. Posters stuck on hoardings warned TALK COSTS LIVES. Air raid wardens in tin hats patrolled the streets. The city had an air of waiting for something to happen.

She greeted the housekeeper briefly, ordered some iced tea, and then went straight to her bedroom, where she'd had a telephone installed.

There was still no answer from Daniel. She was beginning to feel frantic with worry now. Suppose something had happened to him?

When the housekeeper came to tell her that the butler and all the maids had left to join up or work in munition factories, and that she, too, was leaving to work in the NAAFI, Juliet was too distracted to care.

'Very well, Mrs Johnson,' she said vaguely, only half listening.

'I expect you'll be closing up the house for the duration, Your Grace?'

Juliet looked at her blankly. 'I've no idea,' she replied, surprised. Confused because she hadn't thought through her future, she hadn't considered what having Daniel's baby was going to mean. Was she going to remain in London in the grand six-bedroomed house Cameron had bought?

By late afternoon, when there was still no answer, Juliet

decided to write a letter to Daniel, telling him she was in town and that she needed to see him. She didn't tell him why. Nothing was going to rob her of that magical moment of seeing his delight at her news.

Jumping in a taxi, she told the driver to take her to Bywater Street. When she got there it was obvious there no one was in. The cottage had a sad and deserted air, and the roses in the front garden had withered from lack of rain. Her spirits plunged. She decided to ring the bell, just in case Daniel was there, but in her heart of hearts, she knew he wasn't.

The taxi took her back to Park Lane, having driven to the Embankment first, only to find the houseboat was also deserted.

What was she going to do now?

London had changed overnight, and there was nothing for her here any more. The giddy débutante who had gone to five parties a night had gone.

In her place was a pregnant woman with a husband and a lover; a woman who had allowed herself to conceive a baby by Daniel, but had not considered the consequences. Supposing she did have a son? Would it be right to pass him off as Cameron's heir? Could the baby, half Jewish by birth, become the next Duke of Kincardine?

She'd told Daniel in her letter that she'd be going down to Hartley the next day, and she'd given him the telephone number. All she could do now was wait and pray.

'Granny, that was Juliet on the telephone,' Rosie informed Lady Anne, who was feeding Tinker, Brandy and Whisky in the pantry. 'She's travelling down with Daddy, this evening. They'll be here in time for dinner.'

In recent weeks, Rosie had moved back to Hartley, where Nanny could look after Sophia and Jonathan, while she helped in the house, as the only staff left now were Mrs Dobbs, Warwick, the old butler whose feet caused him great suffering, and Spence, the gardener, who'd been turned down by the armed forces because he had asthma.

'Juliet? Down here again?' Lady Anne's surprise veiled a certain concern. Weren't her trips south rather too frequent for a supposedly happily married woman? 'How lovely. Is she well?'

'She seems fine; no doubt spending another small fortune

on clothes,' Rosie added tartly. She scooped Jonathan up in her arms as he started crawling towards the cupboard where Warwick kept the china.

'Not that way, my precious,' she cooed, nuzzling his neck. 'We can't have you breaking the Wedgewood.' Jonathan gave a rich milky giggle, and grabbed the string of pearls around her neck.

Lady Anne watched them, an indulgent smile on her face.

Rosie looked so much better these days. She'd put on weight, her skin was glowing and her eyes were bright again. For the first time in ages she seemed content, once more ensconced at Hartley and surrounded by the family.

Juliet arrived looking rather gaunt and tired. 'Are there any telephone messages for me?' she asked immediately.

'Not that I know of,' Rosie replied. 'Now that Parsons has joined up there's no one to take proper messages.'

'Are you sure no one has called me?' Juliet persisted, edgily.

'No one has rung for you, darling,' said Liza, coming out of the drawing room to greet her. 'Who are you expecting? Cameron knows you're here, doesn't he?'

'Of course he does,' Juliet snapped, taking off her sable coat and discarding it on a hall chair.

'It's lovely to see you,' Louise said shyly, giving Juliet a kiss. 'What a gorgeous coat!'

'What sort of fur is it?' little Charlotte asked, stroking the glistening pelts.

Amanda eyed it critically. 'It must have cost a lot of money.'

'Pounds and pounds,' Juliet retorted lightly.

Henry put his arm around her shoulders. 'Juliet has something to tell us all.' He sounded proud and pleased.

There was an expectant silence. Then Liza eyed her daughter searchingly. 'You're . . . ?'

'I'm having a baby,' Juliet admitted, smiling.

Amid shrieks of delight, she found herself being kissed by everyone, even Rosie.

'When did you find out?' Liza asked, jealous that Henry had been the first to know. It was always the same with Juliet; she told Henry everything first.

'Give me a chance,' Juliet laughed. 'I only knew myself a few days ago.'

'So when is it due?'

Juliet had already done some calculations, to make sure it seemed like Cameron's child. 'Around April,' she replied vaguely.

'A spring baby,' Lady Anne said fondly. 'Darling Juliet, I couldn't be more thrilled for you.' Seeing Rosie looking miffed, she added hastily, 'That will bring the number of my great-grandchildren up to three! Won't that be fun for Sophia and Jonathan, Rosie? They'll be great playmates for each other.'

Mollified that she was back in the picture, Rosie smiled.

'I think this calls for champagne,' Henry announced, leaving the room to help Warwick.

'Come and sit down and tell me all about it,' Liza coaxed Juliet, patting the place beside her on the sofa. 'Is Cameron thrilled? He must be so delighted . . .' she prattled on, but Juliet's thoughts were miles away; in a small cottage in Chelsea, with the man she loved and so badly wanted to be with at this time.

Liza insisted on giving a Sunday luncheon party to celebrate her daughter's pregnancy, although it was the last thing Juliet wanted.

Mrs Dobbs grumbled, too. The only help she had now was a girl from the village and even she was about to join the Women's Land Army.

'*So* inconsiderate!' Liza lamented. 'What are we supposed to do without staff?'

'Let's keep the luncheon simple,' Lady Anne warned.

Liza gave her mother-in-law a withering look. 'Not *too* simple, Mama. We'll manage somehow. Warwick can lay the table, and I'm sure Mrs Dobbs can roast a side of beef, with lots of lovely vegetables, and one of her splendid puddings. Henry can look after the drinks.' It was not known what she would do – except look pretty.

Candida, with her children, Marina and Sebastian, were the first to arrive, followed by Dr Musgrove and his wife, the Reverend William Temple and Mrs Temple, and James and Audrey Bethell, who were Lady Anne's generation, and great friends of hers.

Juliet was the centre of attention, as usual.

Candida was effusive in her congratulations. 'Good for you, old girl!' she said, slapping Juliet on the back as if she'd been one of her mares, 'when are you expecting to drop it?'

Juliet laughed for the first time in days, and Henry thought it was hilarious, but Liza looked po-faced. Such talk, she felt, was 'not nice'.

It was half-way through a convivial lunch when everyone was conversing animatedly that Warwick hobbled over to Lady Anne and said something quietly in her ear.

She looked non-plussed. 'Who?' she queried. 'Do we know him?'

'What is it, Mother?' Henry asked.

Juliet's heart lurched in her rib-cage; perhaps Daniel had come down to Hartley to see her. She half rose in her chair, trembling with excitement, when her grandmother spoke.

'Liza, did you invite a Monsieur Gaston St John de Brevelay to lunch? He's in the hall.'

With a shriek Candida jumped to her feet, while Juliet sank back into her seat, quenched with disappointment.

Louise flushed so deep a shade of red, her eyes brimmed with tears. Then she caught Juliet's eye. Her sister pursed her lips, indicating she should remain silent.

'I'll deal with this,' Candida almost shouted, rushing out of the dining room and into the hall.

Louise sat paralysed with misery as Henry rose to go after his sister. She longing to stop him, prevent him from the shock that awaited him, but what could she do?

'What's going on?' Liza asked. 'Louise? What's the matter? Do you know who this man is?'

'No, Mummy. At least, well, he . . . he travelled home with us from St Malo. Aunt Candida asked him to stay.'

'Then we must ask him to join for us lunch. Warwick, could you lay another place for our unexpected guest . . . ?' In spite of the lack of proper staff, Liza slipped into her hostess performance without missing a beat.

From the hall they could hear an angry roar of abuse in a man's voice, followed by an even angrier and louder roar of filthy expletives in French, as Candida told him exactly what she thought of him.

Warwick hovered uncertainly, while everyone sat spellbound, straining to listen while shifting their food around their plates.

'I had no idea,' Lady Anne remarked mildly, 'that Candida spoke such fluent French.'

The loud clamour of voices receeded and then they heard the study door slam, and the sounds became muffled.

Liza, who didn't understand much French, was still eyeing Louise suspiciously, desperately curious to know what was going on. She couldn't press the matter, though. Not in front of the local clergyman and doctor.

'How *dare* you follow me here!' Candida told Gaston, her fists clenched.

Henry, gazing grimly at his double, was as white as candle-wax. 'You must leave before my mother sees you,' he told the younger man, his voice cold with fury. 'What is it you want? Money?'

'I am part of this family,' Gaston raged arrogantly. 'We are brothers. I want to be accepted. I want to take my rightful place in the family.'

'Over my dead body.' Henry growled, horrified. 'It would kill my mother to know about you.' Henry turned to Candida. 'What in God's name made you take him in in the first place? You should have abandoned him at the docks.'

Candida thrust out her ample chest. 'Don't be silly, Henry. The poor bugger had never been to England. It was only supposed to be for a couple of nights, anyway. His mother told me he had enough money. Don't worry, Henry. I'll get him out of here. Come along, Gaston.' She dropped a heavy hand on his shoulder and man-handled him towards the door, as if she were pushing a horse into its stable.

Henry unlocked a drawer in his desk and pulled out a wad of five-pound notes. 'Take this and get lost,' he commanded roughly, thrusting the money into Gaston's hand. 'And never, *ever*, come back here again. D'you hear me?'

By the time Henry resumed his seat at the table, they heard the thunderous revving of an engine as Candida started her car; it sounded like a aircraft about to take off.

'Sorry about that, everyone,' Henry said lightly, and with forced joviality. 'It was just some wretched French refugee who Candida unwisely befriended.'

They all made polite acquiescent noises, except for Louise and her grandmother. Louise hung her head, her appetite gone, while Lady Anne looked greatly aged as she sipped her wine and remained silent, guessing exactly why Gaston had come to the house.

After the guests had left, and Warwick had cleared the coffee cups from the drawing room, Lady Anne turned to Liza, Henry and Juliet, the others having gone for a walk. Her voice was quiet and calm.

'That was Frederic's son, wasn't it?'

Liza have a sharp little shriek of shock.

Henry spoke reluctantly. 'Yes, Mother. I'm sorry, but I'm afraid it was.'

'Papa's *son*?' Liza exclaimed incredulously. She'd been very fond of her late father-in-law; saw him as a sweet old English duffer, kind, harmless and really rather dull, but an absolute gentleman.

'Frederick had an affair over forty years ago,' Lady Anne continued, without rancour. 'She was a French girl called Margaux. I found out at the time that she was pregnant. I know Frederick offered her money. She returned to France and that was the end of that. We never spoke of it again.'

'I'm so sorry, Mother,' Henry said again, in distress. She was too old for a shock like this. He felt badly shaken himself, so he couldn't imagine what she must be feeling.

Lady Anne smiled wanly, her hand fiddling with the ropes of pearls around her neck. 'It was such a long time ago, Henry. And I forgave him. Everyone is allowed to make a mistake, and providing it never happens again, it is stupid to make too much fuss about it.'

Juliet gazed thoughtfully out of the window; her pregnancy hadn't been 'a mistake' but a deliberate effort to have Daniel's baby; would Cameron be so philosophical if he ever found out?

Candida came blundering back at that moment, looking mortified. She shot Henry a hunted look.

'Mother already knew about Pa's affair,' he said briefly.

'Oh, Mother darling,' Candida exclaimed, going to Lady Anne's side, flinging an arm around her mother's shoulders, almost crushing her. 'I'm so, *so* sorry. I wouldn't have had this happen for the world. We booked into this hotel and I got friendly with the owner . . .'

'Margaux?' Lady Anne cut in. She was looking at her daughter as if she felt sorry for her, for finding out what had happened so many years ago.

Candida looked stunned. 'You knew her? We got talking . . .' – she decided to omit the occasion years ago when Margaux had joined her and her father for lunch – 'and then it all came out when I told her my maiden name,' she added quickly, to make her story sound more plausible. 'I got a terrible shock when he turned up at the hotel and she insisted I take him back with us back to England. But what could I do? He'd have been killed or interned when the Germans invade France. I only intended to put him up for a couple of nights, until he got his bearings. Then it turned out he didn't have a penny on him.'

'Dear girl, there was nothing else you could have done,' Lady Anne said gently, and without emotion. 'I'd have been ashamed of you if you *hadn't* taken him under your wing. None of this is his fault. Have you taken him back to your house now?'

'No, I put him on a train to London,' Candida retorted stoutly. 'I'm sure he can find a job there.'

Lady Anne looked anxious. 'But has he any money?'

Henry spoke. 'I gave him plenty of money, so he'll be all right.'

'I wouldn't have had this happen for the world, Mother,' Candida said, her usual ebullience gone. 'I wish we'd never gone to Brittany, now.'

Liza looked around, thankful the three youngest children were out. This was a family secret that, thank heavens, could be contained. The last thing they wanted was this scandal known to the outside world.

'Telephone for you, Juliet,' Rosie shouted from the hall. 'Some man, said he was the treasurer of something or other. Why does the telephone always have to go when I'm near it? I'm sick of answering it.'

But Juliet wasn't listening to Rosie's grumbles. Her heart had jumped up to her throat, nearly choking her, as she ran down the stairs to take the call.

'Hello?' She didn't even recognize her own clipped and cool voice.

'Juliet.' Daniel said her name warmly and intimately, as if they'd just made love. 'I found your note, darling.'

'So what's going on?' she asked, suddenly angry, wishing to God the only instrument in the house wasn't in the main hall. 'We haven't had a meeting for weeks. How am I supposed to help this charity, unless it gives me support?' she added, as her mother emerged from the drawing room to place some letters on the hall table, for Warwick to post.

He gave an amused chuckle. 'I gather you're not alone?'

She was so relieved to hear from him she felt like exploding with fury. 'You're right. I'm not, but that doesn't alter the fact that you haven't been in touch. Not a word. What am I supposed to think after nearly a month?'

How dare he play fast and loose with me, she fumed inwardly, causing so much pain and misery? If he thought she'd come running . . . !

'You could have telephoned,' Juliet whispered, becoming overwrought, 'or even sent me . . .' – Rosie walked past her from the kitchen, and went up the stairs – '. . . even sent me the charity's accounts.' Her voice wobbling dangerously.

'Listen, Juliet,' Daniel said calmly, 'There's a war on. I've had to move my family from Kent to Devon, because of the threat of an invasion. They were in a very vulnerable position. I have to take care of them,' he added sternly.

'So your wife and children are safe, but I could be in the middle of a battlefield for all you care,' she hissed, enraged.

There was a long silence on the line, before he spoke again. 'Juliet, why are you behaving like this?' His deep voice, grating with anger, sent a shiver through her; half-thrilling her with his dominance, half-scaring her with his lack of feeling towards her.

'You know perfectly well why,' Juliet retorted. 'I've tried and *tried* to get hold of you; couldn't you at least have let me know what was happening? Why didn't you contacted me? Or is that asking too much?'

'It was impossible. What with my work and the family I haven't had a moment to myself since I last saw you. Anyway, you were up in Scotland with your husband,' he growled indignantly. 'What are you complaining about?'

'It's obvious you don't care what the hell happens to me,' she said accusingly, her hand cupping the mouthpiece as she spoke. 'I *needed* to see you. You're *never* there when I need you.'

Juliet was beside herself with jealousy and frustration now. She'd waited for what had seemed an eternity to see him again, so she could tell him the exciting news, and now he was spoiling it all.

'Juliet,' she heard him say, clearly and slowly, as if he was talking to child, 'we are talking about the safety of a three year old boy, and two girls aged five and seven. I knew you'd be perfectly safe, so why are you behaving like a spoilt brat?'

'You can't talk to me like that,' she gasped, shocked.

'I'll talk to you like that if you insist on getting hysterical,' Daniel retorted. 'What's this all about? I found your note when I got back to Bywater Street, saying you needed to see me urgently. That's why I'm phoning you now. Is there someone in the room with you, or can you tell me what this is all about?'

The moment she'd so looked forward to had been ruined; spoiled by his attitude and nastiness.

'Why should I bother?' she stormed, tears of vexation blinding her eyes. 'It's obvious you have, and always have had, pressing family matters that exclude me . . . so get on with it. Go back to your family and leave me alone.'

'You don't mean that.'

'Yes, I do,' she said wildly.

'I cannot believe how selfish you're being, and childish.' His anger was ice cold now, his tone patronizing. 'If you object to my caring about what happens to my children, then we *are* finished. You're too used to getting your own way, you know.'

'Go to hell, you bastard . . . !' Juliet crashed the receiver back on its cradle as sobs wrenched her throat and she became overwhelmed with grief. Rushing up to her bedroom, she slammed the door, and she flung herself on the bed, crying until she felt physically sick.

She was consumed with jealousy towards the woman who was his wife, safely tucked up in Devon now with his children, all of whom he obviously adored. Loved so much, in fact, he'd forgotten all about her. And the poor little baby she was carrying. If Daniel didn't want her, he wouldn't want their baby either, so there was no point telling him she was pregnant now.

Stuffing a handkerchief into her mouth to deaden the sound of her sobs, she wept as much for herself as she did for her baby who would never know his real father.

How could Daniel behave in this uncaring way towards her . . . when they'd been so much in love? she asked herself, over and over again. Perhaps he'd never loved her? Was sex all he'd wanted? Had she just been a bit on the side, while his real devotion was confined to his family?

She eventually fell asleep, worn out with emotion, and crushed by heart-broken disappointment.

As soon as she awoke, some hours later, the memory of

their conversation came flooding back. Fool! she thought. What a bloody fool I've been! Why did I go off the rails like that? Of course I don't want to finish with him, in spite of what I said. What's the matter with me? Juliet felt as if being pregnant was turning her into another person; a pathetic clinging hysterical woman, when she'd always been so independent, and so unemotional, thinking with her head and not her heart.

Except, perhaps, where Daniel had been concerned.

Staggering over to the wash-basin in a corner of her room, she sponged her swollen face with cold water, feeling ill and wretched, half-wishing she'd never gone back to Daniel after she'd found out he was married, regretting now she'd let her temper get the better of her. Should she call him back at the cottage and apologize? Or wait until he cooled down, when he would surely phone back, and apologize to *her*?

Pride made Juliet decide on the latter strategy. He needn't have been so brutally hurtful. Needn't have called her a spoilt brat. But as she applied fresh make-up to hide her blotchy face, her insides ached with a tender longing for him. I love him, she thought. I love him and I need him. And so does our baby.

'I'm going back to Scotland tomorrow,' she informed the family, two days later.

Rosie looked at her strangely, guessing something was wrong, but said nothing.

'You must be missing Cameron,' Liza said eagerly. 'Are you doing up a nursery suite at Glenmally?'

There was an edge to Juliet's smile. 'I haven't thought about it,' she said evasively. What was she going to do now she was sure she'd lost Daniel? There'd been no phone call of apology from him, and in desperation she'd phoned him herself, several times, but there'd been no answer. Now was the time to play her cards carefully. To run away from Cameron right now would be stupid. She had no intention of leaving this marriage empty handed. She had to plan her future, and that of her baby, very carefully.

'How nice that you're back so soon,' Cameron said in welcome, when Juliet arrived at Glenmally the next day. 'Did everything go all right? Is your doctor pleased with you?'

'Everything's fine,' Juliet replied in a small tired voice. She felt defeated, and as if she'd surrendered something special in her life. 'I'll need to go for regular check-ups. He says it will be perfectly all right for me to have the baby at home, in London. I've also got a list of agencies, for a monthly nurse, and then a proper nanny.'

'You seem very organized.' He sounded doubtful. 'I still wish you'd have the baby here.'

Juliet was prepared for that. 'He said that with a first baby it was vital to be very near a hospital, just in case anything were to go wrong,' she replied glibly.

'Nothing went wrong with my mother, when I was born.'

'Then she was lucky, wasn't she? But look at the poor Queen. Both Princess Elizabeth and Princess Margaret had to be born by Caesarean at the last moment.'

There was no answer to this, but Cameron stuck out his bottom lip and looked mutinous.

However, and perhaps because the Dowager had a few tricks up her witch-like sleeves, the following few weeks were unlike any Juliet had known since she'd got married.

Iona's manner towards her was sickly sweet, like molasses; the brood mare had conceived and Juliet could do no wrong. In the circumstances she allowed herself to be pampered, having her favourite food prepared for her, resting alone in her private suite as much as she liked, with the latest novels to read, and accepting generous presents from Cameron.

Nothing assuaged the pain she felt, though, or the sense of terrible loss at her break-up from Daniel, but somehow taking everything she could from the Kincardines seemed like a delicious form of revenge; if Daniel wasn't prepared to look after her, then she'd show him that at least Cameron was more than willing.

As if he sensed her unhappiness, though she suspected he put it down to her being pregnant, Cameron was kindness and consideration personified.

He spend more time with her than before, taking her for gentle walks, showing her around the estate, which she realized was very beautiful, and constantly advised her to get 'plenty of rest'.

It was all very pleasant, and Juliet made the most of it, but she wasn't fooled. It was the son and heir her husband wanted, not her, and she didn't doubt that once the baby was born, he'd ignore her again, and the old witch would start weaving spells.

But she planned to be long gone before that happened.

First, though, she wanted the Park Lane house put in her name. From the moment she'd seen the imposing cream stucco building, with its colonnaded front which supported a Regency style glassed-in veranda, she'd fallen in love with it. Nine French windows led on to this veranda, from magnificent reception rooms which overlooked Hyde Park. It was, Juliet felt, like a town house set in the country; sophisticated, elegant, yet palatial and peaceful.

Anyway, she reckoned the place bore her stamp, and had always been hers in a way that it had never been Cameron's, and she was determined to keep it.

Two

Juliet gazed out at the glistening white blanket that covered everything for as far as the eye could see. They'd been kept like prisoners in Glenmally for the past week as the snow fell relentlessly, muffling sounds and making Juliet want to scream with frustration.

Roads were impassable. Lakes were frozen. The cattle and sheep had been herded into sheds. Only Cameron left the castle every day to 'see to everything', while Juliet and Iona were forced to remain indoors.

'You mustn't go out,' Cameron told Juliet. 'The ground is treacherous and very slippery. You mustn't risk a fall.'

And lose Daniel's baby, she thought despairingly. As if Daniel would care if she did. There'd been no word from him and she had no intention of getting in touch. Time was hardening her feelings towards his attitude, increasing her anger. She was still reeling with hurt and shock, but if that was the way he treated people, then she was better off without him.

At times she hoped she'd never see him again. But then there were moments when she ached for him so deeply, she hurt all over and her arms had never felt so empty. There was no one like Daniel and there never would be.

But how was she going to survive the next five, ten, twenty years without him? Without his smile and the deep vibration of his voice? Without his touch and his tenderness. Without the laughter and the love?

'You haven't forgotten tonight is the tenants' and staff Christmas party have you?' Iona broke into her thoughts as she marched into the library, once again as active and interfering as ever.

Juliet *had* forgotten, so absorbed was she with her own troubles.

'Of course I remember,' she lied, turning away from the window. She and Cameron and his mother were expected in the servants' hall at eight o'clock, resplendent in evening dress, to hand out presents from under the Christmas tree, drink a noggin and dance a couple of reels before slipping diplomatically away.

'Good,' Iona replied, eyeing Juliet suspiciously. 'Are you feeling all right?'

Juliet shrugged. 'I hate being cooped up indoors.'

'If you're bored, why don't you so something useful?'

'Such as?'

'Well, I don't know . . .' Iona floundered. 'I've never suffered from boredom in my life. You need to take more interest in Glenmally.'

'You know Cameron won't let me do anything. He doesn't even tell me what he's doing. Hector McKenzie seems to be the only one who knows what's going on in Cameron's secret private life,' she added bitterly.

As soon as the words were out of her mouth Juliet had a strong presentiment that she'd triggered something that was going to be unstoppable.

When they returned shortly before eleven o'clock from the ball, Hector, who had escorted Iona, managed to manoeuvre Juliet into a corner of the drawing room, as they had a final nightcap.

'I hear, my dear, that you think there are secrets in Cameron's life that only I know about? Is that right?' His manner was oily and patient, as if he were coaxing something out of a child.

I wonder why I'm not surprised by this approach? Juliet

thought as she looked back at him, her pale blue eyes scrutinizing his lined and ruddy face.

'Doesn't everyone have secrets in their lives?' she parried airily.

'But what could be secret about Cameron's life? I can assure you he's like an open book, my dear. This is a big estate you know. He works tremendously hard to keep everything going, in a financial climate that is not kind to land owners. Especially at this time.'

'I'm aware of that.' She paused. 'You know that old stone house, that overlooks Loch Glascarnoch?'

Hector paused, frowning, as if searching his memory.

'There's a long narrow drive that leads to it,' Juliet continued impatiently.

His brow cleared. He smiled thinly. 'That would be his office, my dear.'

'That's not what he told me when I asked him,' she challenged. 'Cameron told me it belonged to one of his tenants.'

Hector shook his head. 'That must be another house you're referring to. There are nineteen houses on the estate. And the Menzies, who own the adjoining land, have several properties by the loch, too.'

Juliet arched her thin eyebrows and smiled, like a cat that's succeeded in cornering a mouse.

'Maybe,' she said languidly, as if she were bored with the subject. Hector had obviously been prompted by the old witch to find out if she knew anything, and now he'd made her really suspicious. What did Cameron do all day, in that bleak stone house by the water's edge?

'A happy New Year!' Cameron said a week later, as he toasted his mother, Juliet and Hector. The grandfather clock in the hall was striking midnight in croaky, weary tones, as if its days of chiming were also drawing to a close. 'Let's hope 1940 is better than 1939.'

Juliet raised her glass. 'Happy New Year,' she murmured tight-lipped, wishing she'd insisted on giving a party. The presence of other people would have diluted this gruesome little group, who hung together as if bonded by something dark and ugly; but she knew not what.

At Hartley it would be all gaiety and laughter, as her family gathered in the drawing room, as they did every New Year's Eve, kissing and hugging, and toasting each other over and over again with champagne.

Lady Anne would be misty-eyed with emotion, and Charlotte, who was being allowed to stay up for the first time this year, would probably be over-excited and slightly out of control by now.

In the kitchen, Mrs Dobbs, Warwick, Spence and Nanny would be having their own celebration, and talking over the good old days when Parsons, Mrs Fowler, Ruby and all the other servants would have been there, too.

'Here's to the coming arrival!' Hector declared, drunkenly waving his glass in the direction of Juliet's stomach.

Juliet instinctivly placed her hand across her front, as if protecting Daniel's child.

'To the new arrival!' Cameron and his mother chorused, looking gleeful.

'I must telephone my family,' Juliet said, rising and leaving the room before her vulnerability showed. Was it pregnancy that was making her so tearful these days?

Her hand hesitated for a moment as she picked up the receiver before dialling the Hartley number. Should she ring the little house in Bywater Street, just in case Daniel was there? The temptation was strong. If he answered it would mean she'd hear his deeply thrilling voices once more. Maybe he would want to see her again? Impulsively her finger started dialling CHE for Chelsea, and then 1475.

An icy rush of anticipation flowed through her veins as the number started ringing. Her heart was thundering in her ears. Would he answer?

But the phone rang and rang with the hollowness of a house she knew was empty. Stupid to try, really, she thought dispiritedly. She might have known he'd be at home or at a party on a night like this.

The snow thawed slowly at first, breaking up into watery crystals on the re-emerging heather and ferns. Then it melted very quickly and was suddenly gone overnight, without trace, leaving the ground soft and springy and the banks of Loch Glascarnoch brimming.

By March, spring had arrived but Juliet had been confined

41

to the castle with a heavy cold and cough for several weeks, agreeing to stay in bed, but refusing to let Cameron call the local doctor, who would realize her pregnancy was less advanced than it was supposed to be.

At last she was better now, and thankful to get out in the fresh air. Wrapped up warmly, she went for a walk with the dogs. They were the only living creatures at Glenmally that she liked, and in return they showed their devotion by following her around, to Iona's jealous fury.

Today there was a purpose in the route she took. She wanted to take a closer look at the house that Hector had maintained was Cameron's office.

Planning to knock politely on the front door when she arrived, she walked down the side of the house past a window that was partly curtained. A central light hanging from the ceiling illuminated the interior.

Juliet glanced casually into the room and then froze, transfixed. What she saw was so shocking, so horrifying, she stood as if paralysed. Then she started to tremble violently.

At that moment she understood everything about her marriage.

Afterwards, Juliet could only vaguely remember stumbling away from the house, half blinded by tears, wanting to be sick, wanting to get back to the castle, wanting to return to London, wanting to get away from this damned place at all costs.

'What are you doing?' Iona asked, as Juliet hurried into the hall, throwing off her coat and hat.

'What do you think I'm doing?' Juliet retorted furiously. 'I'm leaving and I'm not coming back.' She turned and charged up the wide staircase, one hand holding her stomach.

Iona blanched, her eyes wide and scared looking. 'What's the matter?'

'Now I know why you're so happy with the way Cameron is,' Juliet shot back, over her shoulder. She paused, gripping the bannister. 'This way you get to keep your precious son for ever, don't you? This way you don't have to fear that another woman will ever take him away from you because it's only men he wants to sleep with.'

The old Duchess had managed to gather herself into a bundle of plaid fury. 'How dare you talk to me like that?'

'You're as perverted as he is,' Juliet shouted down from

the landing. 'Now I understand why he can't join the armed forces. He's a bloody pansy, isn't he?' She slammed the door to her suite of rooms with a resounding slam.

In the hall below, surrounded by antlers and family portraits, Iona Kincardine leaned heavily against the table, and, picking up the receiver, dialled the number of Cameron's private abode, where Skelly, a crofter's son, lived in great comfort, awaiting the daily visits of his lover.

'Come back at once,' she urged frantically when Cameron answered.

'I can't.' He sounded desperate.

'You've got to. She's having your child for God's sake. That's what this is all about. This is why she's *here*! She's upstairs. Threatening to leave. You've got to stop her, at least until the baby's born.'

'I can't face her, Mother. Not just yet . . .'

'Cameron, I'm warning you . . . !'

'It will still be my son, even if she does leave.'

'She might prevent you having anything to do with him.'

'Hector wouldn't allow that to happen.'

'You've got to face her sooner or later, Cameron.'

'Oh *God* . . .!' he groaned.

'I told you to be discreet; then this would never have happened.'

'I *have* been discreet. I don't know why she came here. It was just wretched bad luck.'

Iona felt a pang of guilt. Perhaps she shouldn't have repeated Juliet's remark about Cameron having secrets to Hector? Perhaps Juliet hadn't meant anything by that remark. Perhaps she was just bored and frustrated because Cameron was out every day, leaving her on her own.

'If you come back now, Cameron,' Iona continued nerv-ously, 'I'm sure you can persade her that nothing untoward was going on.'

'Nothing untoward . . . !' he yelped. 'She caught us, Mother. Red handed. Poor Skelly is petrified.'

'I don't think it's "poor Skelly" you should be thinking about. Poor Skelly, as you call him, is unbalanced for a start. He *shot* you. Have you forgotten that? He could have killed you, Cameron, because he was jealous of you seeing that young boatman, down by the loch. I'm telling you, if Juliet leaves now you'll never see your child. And after all the trouble we've been to, to find you a suitable wife.'

'Suppose she goes to the police?' Cameron was in a panic now. 'Skelly is only nineteen. We could both be sent to prison. This could ruin me.'

'I know,' Iona said grimly. 'That's why you must come back and talk to her before it's too late. She's a sophisticated girl, Cameron, and very ambitious. Offer her money to keep her quiet. *Anything*, Cameron. At all costs. Juliet must be silenced.'

There was a pause. Then Cameron spoke in a flat voise, laden with doom. 'All right. I'll come back.'

Spring had arrived suddenly in London, taking everyone by surprise after a hard winter. By April, the pink and white blossom was out in the park, and the daffodills were nodding merrily in the breeze.

The Season had started again, albeit in a very low-key way compared to previous years. But after all the warnings about the city being bombed and razed to the ground within days of war being declared, nothing had happened since the false alarm on the morning of September the third, and everyone was carrying on, more or less, as usual.

The press were calling it the Phoney War. There might be rationing, but theatres, cinemas and restaurants were open as usual, and hundreds of children, who had been evacuated to the country the previous August, were returning in droves to the city and their welcoming families.

'Why don't we open up the house again, darling? Everyone's returning to London.' Liza coaxed, bored out of her mind by living at Hartley.

'What's that, dear?' Henry asked absently, picking up the evening newspaper he'd brought down from London with him.

'I think we should return to Green Street,' she said brightly, ignoring his exhausted manner. 'I had an invitation from "Chips" today. He's asked us to a dinner party he's giving for the Duke and Duchess of Kent. We're missing out on so much, Henry. Soon we'll lose all our friends.'

'You know we can't return to Green Street,' he replied dismissively. There were dark shadows under his eyes and his cheeks were hollow. As Chairman of Hammertons, he was now doing the work of three people. Long hours, worrying conditions and the war crisis all added to the burden he carried. Thoughts of socializing were the last thing on his mind.

He continued firmly, 'All the good furniture and paintings are in storage. Anyway, we have no staff now.'

'Then let's get a nicer flat than the tiny one you've got, which is so dark and dismal,' she wheedled longingly. 'I miss being with you, Henry. And I miss London and all our friends. The children can remain down here with your mother and Nanny, but there's no reason why both of us shouldn't stay in town during the week.'

'It's not a good idea.'

Liza looked mutinous. 'But nothing's *happening*! There are no bombs, no air raids and no sign of an invasion. Even the King and Queen have remained at Buckingham Palace.'

Henry sighed deeply. It was true. Against all prophecy, there'd been no direct strike from Germany, but that didn't mean it wasn't going to happen.

'Let me think about it,' he said to mollify her. 'Where's Mother? And the girls? Are they all OK?'

'Everyone's fine,' she snapped, and everyone was, except for her. She was bored. And she wanted something really exciting to do. Her friend, Lady Sarah Spencer-Churchill, was actually working in a munitions factory. Lady Courtney was at a Knightsbridge Fire Station, (answering the phone, Liza imagined, not putting out fires). And the famous beauty, Mrs Charles Sweeney, was reported to be 'rolling bandages'. Others were giving cocktail parties to 'raise money'; though the gossip columns didn't specify what for.

As she climbed the stairs to say goodnight to Amanda and Charlotte, who, unlike Louise, were too young to stay up for dinner, she heard Nanny singing at the top of her voice.

'*Who do you think you are kidding, Mr Hitler?*' she warbled lustily, as she folded the bath towels and hung them over a mahogany rail.

Liza stopped and listen, smiling to herself. Thank God for Nanny, who was over sixty, and would remain with them for ever as a retainer. Not for Liza the supreme sacrifice made by the Marchioness of Tavistock, whose war effort was to 'manage without a nanny' for the duration.

Henry, alone in the study, going through the stack of post

on his desk, was ruminating about Liza's desire to go to London to see her friends.

Ian Cavendish had taken a large basement flat in a block in Campden Hill. Helen, his wife, had gone down to Dorset, to look after her elderly parents, so he was mostly there on his own. It struck Henry he might try to do a deal with Ian; offer to pay half the costs of the flat, if he could share it with him, and have Liza stay for the occasional night.

'This is getting like a home for geriatrics,' Rosie giggled, bumping into Henry as she came out of the kitchen with Jonathan tucked under one arm, and Sophia hanging on to her skirt.

'Does that include me, darling?' he laughed. He loved having her at Hartley again, and the babies were an endless source of amusement.

'Oh, Dads, don't be silly!' she retorted, hitching Jonathan higher. She dropped her voice. It bubbled with suppressed laughter. 'Warwick has just asked me to lay the table for dinner because his bunions are killing him, and Mrs Dobbs . . . did you know he calls her Betty? . . . said could I pick up a sack of potatoes from the larder floor, because her back's bad. Then this morning Nanny was complaining about the rheumatism in her hands; said it's come on since Ruby left because she used to do all the children's washing! And just now Spence grumbled that he's too old and his chest is too bad to do the heavy digging.'

Her short blonde curls quivered as she shook her head. 'It's hysterical, Dads,' she laughed, 'I'm the only *young* adult in the place!'

Henry raised a quizzical eyebrow. 'Are you calling your grandmother geriatric? If so, for God's sake don't let her hear you.' He laughed again. 'What a decrepit collection of humanity we are. We should all be put out to grass!'

'Oh, *Dads*!' Rosie gave him a hurried kiss on the cheek and then dashed off to change Jonathan's nappy.

Henry smiled to himself, realizing how she'd changed since Charles had joined up. She positively glowed these days, radiating cheerfulness and high spirits as she bustled around the house, looking after the children, making the beds, and giving a hand with the cooking.

He dreaded to think what was going to happen when the

war ended, and Charles came home again. Henry didn't approve of divorce. He was a strong believer that vows made before God should not be broken, and that having made one's bed, one should lie in it. But surely, he reasoned, there were extreme circumstances that at least permitted a couple to separate, legally if need be, because it was impossible to carry on?

Ian Cavendish instantly agreed to have Henry share the flat with him.

'I'll be glad of the company, old boy,' he said warmly, as they conversed on the phone. 'Why don't you move in right away? I'll leave a set of spare keys with the caretaker. I'm not sure it's up to Liza's standard of glamourous perfection, but it's warm and jolly comfortable. Being in the basement of the block, it's as safe as an air raid shelter.'

'That's useful. Isn't it odd that everything's so quiet at the moment?' Henry commented.

'It is very quiet,' Ian agreed, 'but don't let that fool you. Sorry I can't say more, but we'll talk when you move it.'

'Great, old chap. Thanks awfully.'

Liza received the news with delight. 'That's wonderful, Henry. Clever old you, thinking of Ian's place.'

'Cheaper than the Dorchester when you come to town, too.'

'Do let's have drinks there, though,' she suggested. '*Everyone* who lives in London has gone to live in hotels, rather than be bombed in their own homes. The Dorchester, the Savoy, the Ritz are full – I'm told it's like a continuous cocktail party.'

Henry rolled his eyes. '*Everyone?*' he repeated with a touch of sarcasm.

'You know what I mean,' Liza retorted crossly. 'All the people we know are in hotels.'

Henry leaned over and kissed her. 'Never mind, we'll see this through together, won't we, darling?'

'Of course, as long as I can be with you, Henry,' she replied, grateful to him for indulging her so generously.

'I'm going to be spending a couple of nights in town, with Daddy,' she excitedly informed Louise, Amanda and Charlotte, as she did her own packing. Oh, how she missed Miss Ashley to do this sort of thing for her!

'Mummy, you don't need all those clothes if you're only

going to be away for two nights,' Amanda pointed out, critically. 'And how ever many pairs of shoes are you taking?'

'I thought I might leave a few things at the flat,' Liza replied, looking hurt. Really, Amanda never said anything to make her feel better. 'I don't want us to be invited somewhere terribly smart and then find I have nothing to wear.'

'Why?' Amanda sat on the edge of her mother's bed. 'People are being killed all the time. Why do you want to go to parties?'

'Really, Amanda, don't be so churlish. There's nothing wrong with meeting one's friends and . . .'

'It's a waste of time. If you and your friends put as much effort into war work as you do in to going to parties, the war might end sooner.'

Liza looked at her child as if she was a stranger. So alien, that she might have been a changeling. Why was Amanda so different from her? Different even from her sisters?

'It's not a waste of time,' she said defensively. 'Meeting people keeps up one's morale. There no point going around in sackcloth and ashes and looking on the gloomy side of life.'

'I didn't say that, Mummy.' Her tone was argumentative. 'But instead of spending money having a good time, you should be helping other people. What about all the refugees that have landed from Gibralta? They've got nothing.'

The train drew into Euston in the early morning, and the car Juliet had ordered was there to meet her, but it was one of the loneliest moments of her life. She hadn't told her parents what had happened; they didn't even know she was returning to London.

Leaning back against the soft cream leather seat, she closed her eyes, exhausted by the experience of the past two weeks. At least the pretending was over. The marriage had ended. In return for her silence, and the promise she would not go to the police, the London house and all its wonderful Art Deco furnishings she'd chosen so lovingly were hers. She'd also been able to keep all the jewellery, except the Kincardine family heirlooms, and her valuable collection of furs, plus the wedding presents from her side of the family.

Within a few days her clothes and personal possessions would be packed and brought down from Scotland by Carter Patterson.

Provision was to be made for the baby when it was born.

Finally, she'd received a settlement of a fortune larger than she could ever have expected, providing the grounds for divorce were 'desertion'; hers, not his, on the grounds of 'incompatibility'.

Juliet had been amused by this last diktat. The fact that, in spite of his personal activities, Cameron didn't want to besmirch his good reputation by looking like the one who had done the deserting struck her as really bizarre. However, it suited her. She had no wish to appear as a woman anyone would *want* to desert; that had, and always would be, her privilege.

And now here she was in London, with the whole hideous episode behind her, and she still hadn't told Cameron the baby wasn't even his. He'd talked nervously about shared custody, but she'd parried his remark by suggesting the matter could easily be discussed when the child was born. In truth, she wanted to get away from Glenmally before he found out. If that was cruel, she reasoned, his tricking her into what she presumed would be a normal marriage was even more cruel.

In fact, Juliet relished the thought of bringing up the baby on her own. Daniel's child, whom she would love with all her heart, no matter whether it was a boy or a girl. If only Daniel was around, life would have been perfect.

Since her last trip to London Juliet had taken on a ex-batman, called Tom Dudley, who was too old to go back into the army. She'd engaged him to look after her and the house, between his shifts as a Fire Watcher.

Dudley was on the front doorstep, standing to attention and practically saluting, when Juliet's car drew up outside the house. The agency had told her he was immaculate and that was certainly true. In dark striped trousers and a black coat, his white collar gleamed and his black lace-up shoes shone with polish.

'Good morning, Dudley.'

He stepped forward to open the door, bowing his head as he did so. 'Good morning, Your Grace.' His face was small, round, and reminded her of a garden gnome, with twinkling eyes and small mouth.

Juliet loved all that bowing and scraping and she took to him at once.

'It's so nice to be back in London.' She glanced around her sparkling black, white and silver hall. Dudley had obviously used a lot of spit-and-polish around the place and she nodded approvingly. There was even an arrangements of white lillies on the centre table.

'I'd like some tea, please. In my bedroom. I have a lot of calls to make and I'll answer any in-coming calls myself.'

'Yes, Your Grace. Will His Grace be joining you?'

Much too soon to say anything, Juliet thought. 'I'm afraid my husband can't get away, Dudley, so it's just me. I'll be going down to Surrey tomorrow, for a few days. Then I'll be back and, if food rationing allows it, I want to give a few dinner parties in the coming weeks. Maybe a cocktail party, too.'

Dudley was mesmerized by this dazzling, glamorous young Duchess, with her crimson nails and lips, and her *chic* sky-blue coat with its blue fox collar and cuffs. She was like a Hollywood film star, and there were not many Duchesses in Britain you could say that about.

Life in Park Lane was obviously going to be tickety-boo, and he'd secured himself a wonderful billet, he thought happily, as he went to put on the kettle and lay a tea-tray with the best china.

Juliet drove herself to Hartley the next day; keeping the Rolls coupé Cameron had given her had been part of the deal.

Liza, whom she'd phoned earlier to say she was coming to stay, rushed into the drive to meet her, drawing her to one side, whispering, 'Why are you down here again, on your *own*? Where's Cameron? Is anything the matter?'

'Can I just get my coat off and sit down for a moment?' Juliet remonstrated in exasperation. 'My back is killing me.' She headed for the drawing room, where Henry was reading *The Times*.

'Hello, Dads.' She went to kiss him.

'How are you? Are you all right? Have you come down to see the doctor?' Liza fussed. 'There's nothing wrong, is there?'

'I've left Cameron,' Juliet said simply.

Liza and Henry had been reluctantly getting used to the idea that Rosie might get a separation from Charles one day, but it had never crossed their minds that Juliet would leave the charming, eligible Cameron.

'*What?*' Liza jumped as if she'd had an electric shock. '*Left* him? Oh, my God, Juliet, you can't do that! What on earth are you thinking of? And you're having a baby. For God's sake . . . ! You must get on to him, right away, to . . .'

'There has to be a reason,' Henry butted in, looking penetratingly at Juliet, 'and I hope it's a good one, darling.'

Juliet opened her mouth to explain, but Liza was off again, criticizing her daughter for her flighty ways, her previous scandals involving men, Alastair Slaidburn's suicide because she rejected him, – 'I thought that would be brought up, sooner or later,' Juliet remarked.

'Why are you so self-destructive?' Liza wailed, wringing her hands. 'You had everything! A title, a castle, land, money . . .'

Henry looked at his wife, coolly. 'I do think Juliet should be allowed to explain what's going on,' he said grimly.

'I will. If you give me a chance,' Juliet said, her voice small and tight. 'I now know the marriage could never have worked, no matter what I did. Cameron is a homosexual.'

'Homo—?' Liza's voice rose into a screech.

'Mother, please keep your voice down,' Juliet said sharply. 'Cameron and I have parted as amicably as it's possible under these circumstances, and I've promised to keep it quiet. He could go to prison if this gets out.' No need to tell them that he'd broken down and sobbed his heart out, saying he wished things were different, apologizing for misleading her into thinking she was marrying a normal man, begging her to stay, and when she said she couldn't, begging her not to tell anyone the reason for their break-up.

'Oh, Juliet.' Liza spoke sharply as if it was all Juliet's fault. 'What are you going to do now? What about the baby, for God's sake?'

Henry spoke. 'Calm down, Liza. If Cameron is a queer, there's no way Juliet could have stayed with him.' He turned and looked sadly at his daughter. 'How did you find out, darling?'

Juliet told them, in blunt terms.

Henry blanched, and reached for her hand. 'I'm so sorry, sweetheart. It must have been a terrible shock for you. Is there anything I can do?'

She shook her head. 'I was never really in love with him, so it's not as if I'm heart-broken.' Not the searing, aching longing for Daniel, that filled her days and nights, she reflected.

'We certainly mustn't tell anyone,' Liza affirmed. 'It would not be very nice for people to know you were married to a man like that. And he seemed to *charming*!' she added in bewilderment.

51

Juliet and her father exchanged looks.

'He is charming, and he didn't choose to be like that,' Juliet pointed out, suddenly feeling sorry for Cameron. 'In fact he's devastated about it. I think he really hoped he could make a go of marriage.'

Lady Anne came into the drawing room at that moment. 'I thought I heard voices. How lovely to see you, Juliet darling,' she exclaimed, kissing her granddaughter warmly on both cheeks.

'Well, I'm here to stay, Granny,' she replied softly, taking Lady Anne's hands in both of hers. 'I've come down to break the news to you that Cameron and I have parted.'

'Oh, my dear, I'm so sorry,' Lady Anne looked sad but not entirely surprised. 'Why have you broken up?'

Liza spoke nervously. 'We've got to keep it quiet, Mama,' she explained. 'Apparently Cameron picked up some nasty habits at Eton, and so of course Juliet couldn't possibly remain married to him.'

'You mean he's a homosexual,' Lady Anne said bluntly. 'Poor chap. And poor you, too,' she added, looking into Juliet's eyes. 'That must have been very hard for you. I imagine you'll keep the baby, when it arrives?'

'I certain will.' Juliet replied, with a return of her former breeziness.

Rosie was astounded when she heard Juliet's marriage was over. 'How *could* you?' she asked. 'How could you throw everything you had away? I'd give my eye-teeth to have all that money. And Mummy says he's letting you have the Park Lane house? It simply isn't fair. You behave so badly, and yet you always come out on top. And what about depriving your baby of its father?'

Juliet looked at Rosie's face. She'd put on weight and at the moment she resembled an angry, podgy cherub on a Victorian grave stone.

'You shouldn't be so judgemental,' Juliet told her sister, sternly. 'Things are rarely as they seem, and this is one of those occasions.'

'You would say that.' Rosie tossed her head. 'The trouble is, you don't know how lucky you are. You had as much money to spend in a few hours as Charles gave me in a year. Yet you chuck it all away on some whim. You ought to be ashamed of yourself.' She picked Jonathan out of his play pen, and rested him against her shoulder. 'You're so *spoilt*, Juliet.' She was almost shouting now, eyes blazing with vexation.

Jonathan started whimpering, unnerved by his mother's angry voice.

'You're upsetting him,' Juliet pointed out mildly. 'Would it make you feel any better if you knew that Cameron actually didn't want *me*?'

'Every man seems to want you.'

'Well, this one didn't. We couldn't go on living together, under the circumstances. It isn't very nice when your husband doesn't want to touch you with a barge pole.' Juliet turned away, hoping she hadn't said too much, hoping that Rosie, who was very naïve about sexual matters, wouldn't guess the truth. Juliet agreed with her parents and grandmother that nobody else should know about Charles, especially as Rosie was inclined to gossip.

'We were just totally incompatible,' she added lightly.

'Like I was . . . I mean, like I am, with Charles?' Rosie asked.

Juliet nodded vaguely. 'That sort of thing. The trouble is, you were a virgin when you married Charles . . .'

'. . . Of *course*.'

'. . . And although I wasn't a virgin, I wasn't experienced. I imagined it would be wonderful with all men.' She gave a little sigh. Daniel had taught her what love-making was really like; she doubted if any other man could match that first experience. 'I bet if you'd slept with Charlie first, you'd never have married him.'

'But girls can't be experienced, because then no decent man would want to marry them.'

'That's what Mummy drummed into us; now I think it's nonsense. Would *you* buy a dress without trying it on first?'

Rosie looked profoundly shocked. 'You can't mean that?'

'I do. If I'd spent one night with Cameron, I'd have known – I'd have known we weren't suited,' she added carefully. 'It's not just us, either. I know three girls who married around the same time as we did, and they're terribly unhappy. They'd no idea what sex was all about: thought it would be wonderful, like in romantic novels. They were all desperately disappointed.'

Rosie nodded. 'I know the feeling.'

'If I have a daughter,' Juliet continued, 'I'll encourage her to have sex with her boyfriend, before she decides to marry.'

'Will you? Oh God, I wouldn't want Sophia to do that.' Rosie shook her head. 'It was so nice being pure and untarnished on one's wedding day,' she added dreamily.

Juliet looked away, a sudden bitterness etched on her features. 'Some of us never had that luxury,' she said abruptly.

The traditional Sunday lunch was in progress, and once again the Reverend and Mrs Temple were guests, joining the family after Morning Service.

Now that she was ten, Charlotte had been allowed to join the rest of the family, sitting between Rosie and Henry, who was at the head of the table. Conversation was of a general nature, and Charlotte longed to contribute to the chatter, because it would make her feel more grown-up. The talk was mostly about the war, growing one's own vegetables, and always carrying a gas mask, all of which she found very boring.

That was until she heard Juliet mention to Mrs Temple that she would be living in London in the future.

Charlotte brightened, seizing her big moment. 'Yes,' she announced brightly, 'Juliet's going to be living in London, because she's found out her husband's a bugler.'

For one scintilla of a moment there was a terrible silence.

Then Juliet took a quick deep breath. 'And I just can't stand music,' she remarked, looking smilingly around the table, at the circle of stunned faces.

As soon as luncheon was over, Liza dragged Charlotte into the library, away from the rest of the party who were having coffee in the drawing room.

'Why did you say that . . . about Cameron?' she demanded furiously. 'You won't be allowed to join us for Sunday lunch again. Little girls do *not* speak at grown-up parties, far less air their views. That was terribly naughty of you.'

Charlotte burst loudly into tears. Henry and Juliet, followed by an intrigued Rosie, came into the room at that moment.

'What's going on?' Henry demanded, glaring at Liza.

'I didn't do anything wrong,' Charlotte sobbed. 'I heard Daddy say to you that Cameron was a bugler.'

Juliet stepped forward, and wrapped her arms around her little sister. 'You didn't do anything wrong, sweetheart,' she said softly, 'and no one's going to be angry with you.' She wiped Charlotte's cheeks with her handkerchief. 'Don't cry any more, darling. Maybe, though, you should remember that it's not a good idea to repeat other people's conversation, because sometimes they can say something very rude.'

'I didn't know,' Charlotte wailed, burying her face in Juliet's shoulder. 'Why was it rude to call Cameron a bugler?'

'Because it *is*!' Liza snapped, ignoring Henry's looks.

But Juliet spoke with care, refusing to tell an outright lie because, as she knew from experience, that that can confuse a child more than ever. 'It *can* mean someone who doesn't like being married, you see, and as I was married to Cameron, that's not very nice for me, is it?'

Charlotte raised her head and looked earnestly into her older sister's face. 'No,' she agreed. She gave a hiccuping sob. 'I'm sorry.'

'My darling, it's all right. As long as you never say it again, there's nothing to worry about.'

'I promise.' Charlotte crossed her heart with her small hand.

Juliet hugged her close again and kissed her. 'You're such a good girl, and I love you madly. Now, why don't we put on our gumboots, and warm coat and go for a walk? Maybe Amanda and Louise would like to come too. Why don't you go and ask them?'

'Yes-s-s!' Charlotte crowed, and dashed off happily, all smiles again.

'Well done, Juliet,' Henry commented. 'You handled that perfectly.'

'But the Temples will know what she meant,' Liza fretted anxiously, overcome with the shame of the situation. That a son-in-law of hers should be . . .

'Bugger the Templers,' Henry snapped angrily.

Rosie's eyes widened in sudden understanding. 'So that's what Charlotte meant? You mean Cameron is . . . ?'

'Yes,' Juliet said. 'So you see the break-up wasn't my fault, after all.'

Rosie sank heavily on to one of the much worn brown leather sofas. 'Oh, my God.' She looked up at Juliet. 'I'm sorry I said those things. It must have been terrible for you?'

'It wasn't exactly jolly,' her sister commented drily.

Liza looked despairingly at her two eldest daughters. What

55

had gone wrong? They were both beautiful and charming. They'd had every opportunity.

Instead of which, here they were, back at home, with Juliet getting divorced, and Rosie wishing she was.

Within a few weeks Juliet was back in the swing of things, and in spite of being pregnant, she was going out most evenings armed with a flash-lamp, its light subdued by a black chiffon scarf, because the black-out was all encompassing. Windows were totally darkened and anyone showing a light could go to prison; there were no street lights, headlamps were shielded downwards, even traffic lights were shaded.

Juliet found it all rather thrilling. It was hard to believe there was a war on; in fact she sensed an atmosphere of adventure in the air. And anticipation, as everyone groped their way about the London streets.

Archie Hipwood was on leave from Cumbermere Barracks, at Windsor, and both John Bandon and Edward Courtney were stationed at Knightsbridge Barracks. When they had twenty-four hours leave, they all wanted a good time to relieve the tedium of Army life.

'Come along, old girl!' they chortled, dragging Juliet off to the Mirabelle for dinner, or Quaglino's, where the much-lauded black singer, Hutch, brought tears to her eyes as he sang 'A Nightingale Sang In Berkeley Square'.

'It makes me feel really sad,' Juliet confessed, 'as if those carefree days are over, for ever. As if our youth has gone.'

'It'll all come back, sweetie,' Edward reassured her, with more conviction than he felt. 'Let's go on to the Four Hundred.'

So they managed to find a taxi in the dark to take them to the fashionable Leicester Square club. Next door to the Four Hundred, the Odeon cinema, once a neon-strip extravaganza of different hues, was lit tonight only by a 'Bomber's Moon', as Archie explained knowledgeably.

'Enemy planes would be able to spot every bloody building in London tonight, with a moon like that.'

Juliet looked up at the clear night sky. So far there had been no German planes, and no bombs either; perhaps there never would be. She felt the baby kick, as if in agreement. She patted her stomach reassuringly and wondered what Daniel was doing at this moment.

PART TWO

Aspects of Austerity
1940–1942

Three

Juliet awoke with a start. Something was terribly wrong, and for a moment she lay there wondering what had happened. Through the chink in her curtains the first glimmer of dawn filtered into her room, making the posts of her silver bed gleam.

Then she tore back the bedclothes and screamed, as she looked at the fatal darkness staining her sheets.

'Oh, no! No . . . Oh, God!' She reached for the bell and pressed it several times. She was losing the only part of Daniel she'd got left. She pressed the bell again. Something must be done before she bled to death.

'Dudley . . . !' she shouted as loud as she could. A moment later he was knocking on her door. 'Ring for an ambulance,' she told him with feverish anxiety. Her precious baby's life was slipping away. A violent spasm of pain shot through her body, making her gasp in agony. 'Quick! It's urgent . . . and when you've done that, bring me towels.' Tears were streaming down her face now. Daniel – I need you now like I've never needed you, she thought, frantic with fear. But Daniel didn't even know she'd been pregnant so why should he be here?

Juliet didn't remember much after that. Everything was a blur as she swung between consciousness and oblivion, and when she finally awoke that evening, tucked up in bed in St George's Hospital, she felt confused at first.

'How are you feeling?' a kindly nurse asked, holding her wrist as she took Juliet's pulse.

'What's happening?' The pain had stopped. She felt weak and woozy.

'The doctor will be along to see you in a minute.'

A few minutes later a man in a dark suit came to her bedside and looked down at her. He smelled clean and fresh and his eyes were filled with compassion.

Then she remembered. 'I've lost the baby, haven't I?' she whispered hoarsely, suddenly trembling all over.

'I'm afraid so,' he said gently. 'I'm so sorry. There was nothing we could do.'

'Why? Why did it happen?' Juliet wept.

'These things do happen, without any particular reason. It doesn't mean you won't be able to have more children, though I know that's no great comfort to you at the moment, but I do understand how you feel.'

He pulled up a hard wooden chair and sat down beside her, looking sympathetically into her distraught face.

'You've lost a lot of blood, I'm afraid, so you must stay here for a while, until you get your strength back.'

'I don't think I can bear this . . .' she sobbed, turning her face to the wall.

'We contacted your husband when you were admitted, and told him what was happening . . .'

'My husband?' Oh God . . . Cameron! She felt deeply shocked. She'd forgotten all about him. It was natural, though, for Dudley to have contacted him; no one, apart from her family, knew of her impending divorce.

'He's not coming down from Scotland, is he?' she whispered.

'I expect he will,' the doctor assured her warmly. 'He'll be just as disappointed as you, I'm sure. Fathers can take the loss of a baby just as hard as mothers.'

Cameron *was* going to devestated, she realized, because he still thought the child was his. 'Was the baby a boy?'

'A little girl, actually. Perfect in every way; just too small to survive, I'm afraid.' He pushed back the chair with a scraping noise. 'Now, try and get some rest. We'll give you a sleeping pill. You'll feel much stronger in the morning.'

'Thank you,' she said automatically.

'I'd like to go up to town today to see Juliet,' Rosie announced the next morning. 'I can't imagine how awful she's feeling. If anything had happened to Sophia or Jonathan when they'd been born, I've have died from misery.'

'I might come with you,' Lady Anne suggested. 'I've saved some petrol so we could go in my car. We could take her an orchid plant from the conservatory, and a jar of Mrs Dobbs' bottled raspberries.'

'And we could do some shopping,' Rosie continued. 'I'll

run and ask Nanny to look after the babies for the day, and I'm sure Spence can pick the children up from School. Perhaps we could meet Mummy for tea at the Ritz?' she added hopefully, as Liza was spending another few days in Town.

An hour later Lady Anne set off in her beloved 1929 Austin Seven. Beside her in the passenger seat, Rosie preened herself, looking smart in a red coat with a little feathered hat perched over one eye and matching lipstick. On the back seat a basket of carefully chosen goodies for Juliet nestled next to a pot plant.

'I hardly ever go to up to town these days,' Rosie remarked, but she was not really complaining. The fact she had two healthy children made her realize, compared to Juliet, how lucky she was.

'I feel happy that I don't have to go at all, except for a very good reason,' her grandmother remarked, foot down on the accelerator. 'Juliet's had such a hard time lately, and now to lose the baby must feel like the last straw for her.' Then she continued, 'God moves in mysterious ways, you know, and we have to accept what He decides. Maybe He had a reason for gathering that little baby's soul before it was ready to be born. A child needs two parents, and Juliet is now on her own. It's not the best start for a child. There's the war, too. None of us know what's going to happen next.'

Rosie looked at sharply. 'We're safe at Hartley, though, aren't we?'

'Darling, in this war I don't think any of us are going to be safe, no matter where we are.'

Juliet awakened as she felt a hand take hold of hers. Thinking the doctor had returned to see her, she smiled before opening her eyes.

'Hello, Juliet. How are you feeling?'

Her eyes flew wide and she struggled to sit up.

'Lie down. You must rest,' said Cameron. 'I gather you've had a very bad time.'

'I didn't know you were here.' She gazed up into his face. He looked as if he'd been crying.

'I rushed down as soon as I heard.' He bowed his head. He seemed crushed. 'This is a great loss – to both of us,' he

61

lamented in a low voice. 'I know you had a little girl, but it would still . . . still have been something.'

'A greater loss than you'll ever know,' she replied quietly.

'Juliet,' his voice broke. but with an effort, he pulled himself together. 'Juliet, I'm so sorry. Sorry for everything.'

'You couldn't help this happening,' she said gently.

He turned agonized eyes on her. 'I *might* have done. The shock you had of finding . . . the upheaval of moving south . . . the end of our marriage; it might all have contributed to losing the baby.'

'The doctor assured me that one can have a miscarriage at any time. For no particular reason. It was just one of those things, Cameron. Stop torturing yourself.'

'Would you consider . . . ?'

She shook her head. 'It wouldn't work. And it wouldn't be right to bring a child into the world when its parents have already broken up.'

Tears streamed down his cheeks. 'It would have been wonderful to have had a child, even a girl.'

Juliet realized at that moment that not in a hundred years could she ever tell Cameron the baby hadn't even been his.

She squeezed his hand. 'You know what you should do, Cameron?' she suggested, her voice gentle. 'When our divorce goes through, find yourself a woman in her late twenties or early thirties. Maybe a war widow, not some young flighty bit like me. And explain to her fully what marriage to you actually means. Tell her it's a semi-business arrangement, because you need an heir. Then there'll be no disillusion. No disappointment. She'll get a grand title and home to live in and you'll get a son.'

A glimmer of hope shone through the tears in his eyes. 'You might be right.'

'I know I'm right.' For a moment Juliet looked like her old self, before she sank back against the pillows, exhausted. 'One other thing, Cameron.'

'What's that?'

'Haven't you got a Dower House on the estate? A comfortable home your mother could live in? Believe me, no wife of yours will be able to call Glenmally home whilst your mother's still living there.'

'Don't you think so?' Cameron asked, surprised, as he mopped his face with a silk handkerchief.

'I know so. Where are you staying in town?'

'At the Dorchester.'

She nodded, glad that he hadn't gone to the house. Her house now. 'What did you tell Dudley?'

'I told him that what with food rationing and all that, it was easier for me to go to an hotel.' He leaned forward and kissed her on the cheek. 'I'd better go now, but I had to come and see you. Apart from anything I really wanted to say I'm sorry. So sorry, for everything.'

'Thank you, Cameron.' She closed her eyes, too tired to do or say any more.

'I'm going back to Inverness this afternoon . . . so I probably won't see you again.'

'No.'

'Take care of yourself. Get lots of rest.'

She nodded, keeping her eyes shut so Cameron wouldn't see her own tears. Were they for him? Or the end of her dreams? Her marriage? Or the loss of her baby, which compounded the loss of Daniel? In a way she realized they were probably for all those reasons, so she kept her eyes shut until she'd heard the door close quietly.

Then they flowed once more because she'd never felt lonelier in her life than at that moment.

Henry looked worried when he returned to Hartley, after another long week in town.

'They're coming closer, Mother,' he said to Lady Anne, as he joined her in her sitting room, for a glass of sherry before dinner. 'The Germans are over-running France. At this rate, Paris will be seized within the next couple of weeks.'

Lady Anne looked grave and put down her knitting. 'Then they'll invade us next?'

'I had a quick lunch with Candida today.' His sister now worked in the Cabinet Offices as one of many secretaries to Winston Churchill, who was now Prime Minister of a coalition government that had been formed on May the tenth. 'Our troops in France are being pushed towards the coast. As long as Marshall Pétain doesn't surrender to the Germans and we can beat them back, then we'll be all right.'

'You don't sound very certain, Henry,'

'I'm not, Mother. I think we should be prepared for any eventuality. And that includes an invasion.'

'I'm fed up with sitting around doing nothing,' Juliet exclaimed, swinging her tanned legs over the side of the hammock and standing up. Since her miscarriage she'd spent most of her time at Hartley, hoping the peace of the countryside and the presence of the rest of the family would alleviate her depression. Now that she felt strong again, she had decided she would join the Voluntary Aid Detachment.

'What's that?' Louise asked, looking up from where she lay on the lawn.

'A VAD is a Red Cross nurse. I want to be attached to an ambulance unit.'

'Darling, won't that be rather gory?' Liza asked.

'It probably will be, but I'm not squeamish.'

'I wish I was young enough.' Lady Anne declared. 'Nursing is a very noble form of helping the less fortunate.'

Henry looked admiringly at Juliet. 'Did you say you want to work on an ambulance?'

Juliet nodded. 'A friend of mine works twenty-four-hour shifts at a First Aid Post, in the garage underneath Kingston House. At the moment they mostly deal with road accidents; people who have been knocked down in the black-out and that sort of thing.'

'Isn't Kingston House that block of modern flats in Knightsbridge? Facing Hyde Park?' Liza asked.

'Yes. I could walk to work across the park, from my house. It would be ideal. Laura said she'd put in a good word for me.'

Henry looked deeply into his daughter's eyes; the daughter with whom he felt a deep affinity. 'Help to erase some of the pain?' he suggested softly, while the rest of the family had gone on to chatter about other things.

'Perhaps.' She gave him a little smile. 'No good sitting and moping. I might as well do something before I'm conscripted.'

After a moment's thought he said, 'Why don't you shut up your house for the duration? It's an awfully big place for you to rattle around in, on your own. There's a spare room in the flat in Campden Hill Court, you know. I'm sure Ian would be happy for you to stay there, and I'm there during the week.

Sometimes Mummy, too. What do you think? It would save you having to . . .'

A sudden change came over Juliet. She stiffened. The blood drained from her face. 'I couldn't possibly leave Park Lane,' she said brusquely. 'I must have my own home for entertaining. Thanks all the same, though.'

Henry looked faintly hurt. 'Right. I just thought you might like to be with Mummy and me, and as the flat's in the basement it serves as a very good shelter.'

'I've got a basement, too, Dads. Dudley has already fitted out his little sitting room as a shelter for us, with emergency rations and candles and bedding.' *Just as Daniel did in his cottage*, she reflected, remembering with a stab of pain that it had been in his shelter, during what they thought was a air raid, that their baby had been conceived. Sadness fell on her face like a shadow.

'Well, as long as you're all right,' Henry remarked equably.

But she wasn't all right. Her health might have been restored, but the nightmares had returned, and she thought about Daniel constantly; missing him, wondering where he was and what he was doing; regretting bitterly their quarrel. Now he'd never know they'd nearly had the baby she'd promised him.

Ian was grey and strained-looking. 'Can't stay,' he shouted to Henry, who was making himself some breakfast. 'I've just come home for some papers I left behind yesterday'

'Have you been at the FO all night?' Henry asked incredulously, seeing Ian's unshaven face and crumpled clothes.

'Yup! The balloon's gone up.' He was scrabbling frantically among the papers on his desk. 'Where the hell . . . ?'

'What's happened?'

'The Germans have reached the French coast. There're half a million British and French troops stranded on a beach at a place called Dunkirk. We've lost everything. All out tanks, weapons; and our army.' Ian's voice broke. Then he grabbed the paper he'd been searching for and looked straight at Henry. 'This is a monumental catastrophe; we could lose the war. See you tonight. Maybe.' The door of the flat slammed and he was gone.

So much for the Phoney War, Henry reflected, his appetite

gone. If the Germans had managed to reach the French coast, it wouldn't be long before they landed in England.

Juliet bumped into Edward Courtney outside the Royal Academy in Piccadilly. She hardly recognized him at first.

'Eddie . . . !' she called out, shocked by his gaunt face and haunted eyes.

'Oh, hello, Juliet.' His polite greeting and wan smile were forced, as if he didn't want to emerge from some protective carapace he was sheltering behind.

'Eddie, are you all right?' She grabbed his arm impulsively. Where was the merry young man with whom she'd once had such fun, getting drunk, dancing all night, and flirting outrageously? She knew he'd joined the Irish Fusiliers' and from the pips on his shoulders, she saw he was now a Captain. A very young Captain.

'I'm back from Dunkirk,' he replied hollowly.

Juliet's hand flew to her mouth, aghast. 'Oh, my God!'

He nodded. His eyes were filled with pain.

'I saw those dreadful aerial shots in the newspapers; all those thousands of soldiers stranded on the beach, hoping to be rescued by boat.'

He nodded again, unable to speak. She noticed his hands were shaking.

'You need a stiff drink, Eddie. Why not come back to my place?'

'Thanks. That would be marvellous.' His voice was still tight and clipped.

In the taxi, Edward smoked quiveringly, silently distracted, while Juliet recalled the details of the most humiliating defeat the British Expeditionary Force had ever suffered.

For the first time in her life, she had seen her grandmother weep at the plight of the British and French armies.

Henry had murmured, 'Unless there's a miracle, we've lost the war.'

That had been on June the third, but a miracle *had* happened. By June the seventh, the majority of the troops had been rescued and brought back to Dover by a motley flotilla of ships, from little sailing boats to merchant ships, from pleasure cruisers to destroyers. On the BBC news it was reported that 'for five days the Channel was as calm as a mill pond, enabling the crossing to and fro of all the rescue boats to continue unabated.'

Lady Anne, always a deeply religious woman, declared: 'That was the hand of God, who stilled the waters and made it possible.'

It was now June the twentieth. Juliet glanced at Edward's profile and slumped shoulders and felt great concern; he reminded her of a beaten dog.

'Dudley, will you bring whisky and glasses up to the drawing room?' Juliet asked, as soon as they arrived at her house. 'And I don't want to be disturbed. If anyone telephones, please say I'm out.'

'Yes, Your Grace.'

Juliet opened the French windows and settled Edward on the deeply cushioned white sofa over-looking the park. She sat opposite him and they sipped their drinks in silence for a few minutes, while she waited for him to start talking, which she was sure he'd do when he was ready.

Instead she saw a silent tear slide down his thin cheek and drop on to the lapel of his uniform.

'Oh, Eddie darling.' Without hesitation she moved to his side, wrapping her arms around him, holding him close. When she'd lost the baby, all she'd wanted was for someone to hold her tightly. There'd been no one who really understood how she felt, though, and she didn't want Edward to feel like that.

'It was terrible,' he burst out, sobbing. 'You've no idea. We prayed for the boats to rescue us. And they did but for many it was too late. It was ugly. *Ugly*.'

He couldn't continue. Juliet stroked his face and kissed his cheeks, and topped up his glass. Then she held his hand, her other arm still around his thin shoulders.

After a while he seemed calmer and gave her a watery little smile.

'Who would have thought it, eh? You, the most glamorous débutante of the year and me . . . the dashing stockbroker! And look at us now.'

'Older and wiser, darling. But still the same, inside.'

'I don't know about that, Juliet. I'll never be the same, and I can't talk to my mother and father about it because it would upset them so.' He paused, the pain returning to his eyes.

'When you see your tanks and motor vehicles burning . . . and your friends, burnt to death inside them; and when you *watch* decent men, men you've worked with and trusted with your life, stamp on the faces of their friends in the water, in order to secure a place on one of the boats . . .' His voice trailed off.

'I read you were all caught on the hop because the French Government surrendered to the Germans, without warning?'

Edward shook his head. 'That was British propaganda, to hide the fact that we were disorganized and very badly led. Communications broke down. We were uncoordinated in both our defensive measures and offensive tactics. And we weren't strong enough or in the right position to fight the Germans.' He paused, taking a deep breath. 'In truth, Juliet, it was a catastrophic fuck-up. Thanks to Winston Churchill, it's been turned into what sounds like a heroic episode. He's still even saying we're going to win the war.'

Juliet felt her heart plunge icily. 'And you don't think we will?'

'I believe there's much worse to come.'

'How much more leave have you got?'

'Another twenty-four hours.'

'Would you like to spend it here? With me?' she asked softly.

He looked into her eyes, those pale-blue sparkling eyes he'd been attracted to for years.

'With you?' he croaked.

Juliet smiled her wicked smile. 'In a silver Maharaja's bed.'

'Yes,' he said slowly, 'but are you sure you want to do this?'

For answer she raised her mouth to his, kissing him hungrily, bridging in that instant the gap between friends and lovers.

For the next twenty-four hours they remained in her bed, eating the delicacies and drinking the champagne that she'd ordered Dudley to leave on the table outside her room.

By the time he left to go back to his barracks, Edward's spirits were soothed and his body sated. He'd also fallen in love with Juliet.

In the months that followed, Juliet worked hard to get her First Aid and Home Nursing certificates, attending all the lectures and demonstrations, and by August she'd passed all her exams.

She was now qualified to be part of a nursing team on an ambulance, under the direction of a doctor. Enrolled in the Red Cross, her friend, Laura Walker, whom she'd met when they'd both been débutantes, had even managed to get her on to the same ambulance unit, at Kingston House.

Then her divorce came through, but this time the scandal was swept off the front pages of the newspapers by epic news of the Battle of Britain. There was just a two-inch column on an inside page stating the bald facts of her deserting the Duke of Kincardine.

Juliet decided it was time she reinvented herself. She had her hair cut short, to comply with her uniform regulations; make-up was not allowed either, nor nail varnish. Removing all jewellery, she even took off her wedding ring, never to wear it again. In her plain blue cotton dress, white apron and starched cap she was ready to report for her first twenty-four-hour shift.

'I'd never have believed we'd be here, doing this, when we met,' Juliet laughed. 'And look at us! God! We're not going to appear in the *Sketch* or *Tatler* as glamorous girls now, are we?'

It crossed her mind that Daniel might have seen the short report about her divorce and she wondered if it might encourage him to contact her, knowing she was single once more.

But there was not a word from him, and as they had no mutual friends, she couldn't even find out what he was doing.

At first she wondered if she'd find her shift dull and monotonous. The underground car park was vast and bleak, and even the brightly lit partitioned sections at one end, did little to cheer the place up.

There were cubicles for treating minor injuries, an area for sitting in whilst on duty, a kitchen, a supplies room and a cluttered little office, occupied by the Commandant-in-Chief, a forty-year-old fattypuff called Miss Stafford. Sitting at her desk like a broody bad-tempered hen, in her scarlet cotton uniform dress, she endlessly worked out 'duty charts'.

'How many more times do we need to practise bandaging someone's head, for God's sake?' Juliet whispered to Laura in exasperation.

They were told to practise their bandaging skills on each other. It was only after a week of wrapping and un-wrapping lengths of grubby crêpe strips around heads, arms, chests and legs, or fixing slings and splints, or applying tourniquets until limbs turned blue, that Juliet twigged that it had more to do with Miss Stafford's lesbian tendencies than looking after a patient who might have been knocked down by a bus. She took the opportunity to watch and touch as she selected her 'favourites', and having made her choice, she then became nasty to all the other nurses. Juliet, was fervently thankful not to be a 'favourite', but nevertheless, refused to submit to the type of bullying that included scrubbing the concrete floor which had taken them a total of six hours.

'That woman is a bitch,' Juliet told Laura, as they came off duty the next morning.

'But what can we do?' Laura was timid compared to Juliet, and hated unpleasantness. 'Perhaps we can get put on the other shift, when she's not on duty? She could make life hell for us, if we kick up a fuss.'

'What's this then? Heaven?'

Saying good-bye to Laura, who lived in Kensington, Juliet walked home briskly through the park. It was the end of August, but there was something in the air that made her realize how soon it would be autumn.

In a few days' time the country would also have been at war for twelve months.

As she neared Hyde Park Corner, she could never resist glancing through the trees at St George's Hospital, her eyes searching for the window of the room where her baby had been delivered. And her tender dreams of motherhood had died.

Today, tired after a long night sitting on a hard chair doing nothing, tears blurred her vision, and a feeling of desolation swept over her, as she stood still for a moment, gazing up at the window.

'So you're a sister-of-mercy now, are you? That's a new rôle for you.' The voice was deep and sardonic. The tall, strong-shouldered man raised his trilby as he spoke, revealing coal black hair.

Juliet spun round, shock rendering her speechless. She stood rock still, looking up at him, her pale blue eyes bright with tears.

'Planning to care for the walking wounded now?' Daniel's words seeped poison and his dark eyes were unfathomable.

70

Juliet suddenly flared with anger, almost hating him at that moment. 'As a matter of fact, I'm stationed at Kingston House, on the number one ambulance unit. I can't see what it's got to do with you, though. I see you aren't even in uniform,' she added spitefully.

Daniel cocked his head on one side and regarded her coldly, saying nothing.

They stood staring into each other's eyes, adversaries who had loved each other once, known each other intimately, but who also now had the capacity to hate and destroy each other. Their whole relationship hovered in the balance, and Juliet realized it could go either way.

Then Daniel spoke. 'It's a pity you're so damned selfish, Juliet.'

'What do you mean, selfish?' she flashed furiously, taking a step back from him.

'You resented me putting my children first. You don't know what it's like to have children. They were in danger. I had to take them to Devon and *that* was why I couldn't get in touch with you, but would you listen?' he blazed. 'No. All you could think about was yourself.'

'You could still have let me know. I was worried about you,' she stammered, wounded beyond words at him saying she didn't know what it was like to have children.

'No, you weren't,' he snapped coldly. 'You were worried about yourself, as you always are. You're the sort of person who would hurt anyone, as long as you got what you wanted. I could never do that to my children.'

'What about your affair with me, then?' she raged. 'Wasn't that hurting them? When you should have been with their mother?'

Daniel looked at her steadily. 'However much I loved you, I would never have hurt them, because they'd never have known about you. I read about you leaving your husband. No one man is enough for you, is he?'

Something in her head snapped. 'That's not true! You don't know anything about it. You don't know anything about me either. You don't know . . .' she paused, stricken, a part of her wanting to tell him about his baby, but another part not wanting him to know this way, while they were fighting. 'Don't you *dare* talk to me like that!'

Daniel looked down at her. His expression told her they had no future. A part of her understood why; it was true she'd been jealous and selfish over his children, because she'd been frightened of losing him. But another part broke inside her, split and drifted away, leaving her empty and defeated. She averted her head so she wouldn't haven't to look at him.

'The trouble is, Juliet, you have no heart,' he said heavily. Then he turned and walked away, down the avenue of plane trees, where the leaves were already tinged with gold.

Rosie heard the Austin Seven coming up the drive.

'Granny, where have you been?' she asked, rushing out of the house. 'You said you were only going to the village to do some shopping, and that was hours ago.'

'I'm sorry, I was longer that I meant to be, but I had a most enlightening afternoon.' Lady Anne stepped calmly from the car.

'The shopping's in the boot, darling. I managed to get some sausages, by the way. Mrs Dobbs might be able to make us toad-in-the-hole for supper, if the hens have laid some more eggs.'

'What were you doing?'

'You know Piltdown Court? It used to be a boys' school?'

Rosie carried the week's rations for the household into the house. 'I know where you mean.'

'It's been turned into an Army convalescent home. The butcher told me about it, and how the young men like visitors, so I popped along.'

Rosie looked at her in amazement. 'What? Just like that?'

Lady Anne nodded, taking off her straw hat and putting it with her handbag on the hall chest, before fluffing up her white hair. 'I asked to see the matron; such a charming woman, and then I talked to some of the boys. They *are* lonely. Most of their families live miles away and it's getting so difficult to get about these days. I told them I'd send you along to cheer them up.'

'*Me?*' Rosie looked horrified. 'I wouldn't know what to say to them.'

'They'd rather talk to a lovely young woman like you than an old woman like me. Some need help with writing letters home, if their eyes or hands have been injured. Others like being read to. Mostly, though, they just want a good chin-wag, and an opportunity to talk about their families. Visiting is every day from two o'clock until six. Piltdown Court is only three miles away, darling. You could cycle there in no time at all.'

They'd reached the kitchen and Rosie dumped the shopping on the table. 'You've quite made up your mind I'm going to do this, haven't you, Granny?'

'Why not? Nanny has nothing to do during term time, so she can look after Sophia and Jonathan, who have a nap in the afternoons, anyway. It'll do you good. Get you out of the house for a bit.'

'Should I take anything with me?' Rosie asked nervously.

Lady Anne shrugged. 'Books, magazines, writing materials; I gather those sort of things are very welcome.'

Rosie still looked doubtful.

'Look, my dear,' said her grandmother. 'You can't do proper war work because you have the babies to look after, but this would be a big contribution. I wonder if Liza .... ?' She paused, thinking about her fastidious daughter-in-law having to deal with those who had lost limbs or were horrifically burnt. 'Well, no, maybe not,' she concluded, drily.

Filled with trepidation, wondering if she should dress up and wear a little make-up or not, Rosie finally set off the following afternoon, her bicycle basket filled with some fruit from the garden, a few paperbacks and a couple of bottles of cologne that Charles had been given last Christmas, but refused to use.

Piltdown Court had originally been a Georgian squire's house built in 1732, of soft pink brick and cream-coloured stone. It was the sort of house Rosie had always imagined she'd live in one day, with its solid proportions, symmetric rows of windows and imposing facade.

'My grandmother suggested I come and visit the patients,' Rosie told the matron, blushing slightly as she spoke.

The matron nodded. 'You must be Lady Padmore? Lady Anne cheered up a lot of the chaps yesterday, and she said she'd send you along. Why don't you go into Ward B, to start with? Many of them have families who can't get to visit them and they are rather lonely.'

'Very well.'

The matron opened double doors into what had originally been the school common room, on the ground floor. Beds were arranged down both sides and there were long windows overlooking the estate's park.

'There you go,' she said robustly, giving Rosie a gentle shove.

Rosie suddenly felt horribly shy, her face red as she giggled and walked nervously towards the nearest bed. 'Hello! How are you feeling?' she asked the young man, even younger that her, who was propped up against pillows. In a flash she realized his left pajama sleeve was folded up with a safety-pin.

In the circumstances, her remark sounded stupid and banal to her ears and her heart sank. She wasn't going to be any good at this.

'All the better for seeing you,' he retorted, admiringly, his eyes skimming her slender figure in its pretty printed cotton dress, and her white wedge-heeled shoes. 'Whatcha got there, luv?'

Glad of having something to do with her hands, Rosie picked out some plums and peach from her basket. 'Do you like fruit?' she asked diffidently.

He grinned cheekily. 'I'd rather have some chocolate. Or a packet of fags, 'cept we're not allowed to smoke in this bloomin' place; fire hazard they say.'

'How about something to make you smell nice?' She turned crimson as soon as the words were out of her mouth.

''Ere!' He turned to the other men, twenty in all, who were gawping at Rosie. 'She thinks I don't smell nice! Bloody cheek!' Then he guffawed. 'OK, luv. Let's have a sniff. Watcha got? I 'ope it ain't essence of bloomin' violet?'

Everyone started laughing. This twenty-year-old with one arm was obviously the ward's wag, liked by all, and cheery in spite of everything.

Rosie started wending her way from bed to bed, wishing she'd brought something for each of the men. She couldn't get over their bravery; one had even lost an eye, and another had a badly disfigured face. When she finally left, to a shower of cat-calls and appreciative whistles, she shouted over her shoulder; 'See you all again, soon! And I'll try and bring some chocolate next time.'

Hearing the cheery noise, Matron came out of her office.

'Very kind of you to give your time, Lady Padmore.'

'Not at all,' Rosie replied with sincerity. 'It's the least I can do. Can I go and see the patients in Ward C? My grandmother said they could do with some cheering up.'

The matron narrowed her eyes as she looked at Rosie closely. 'These boys have only minor injuries compared to the ones in the other wards. Do you think you can manage?'

Rosie nodded.

'Right-o! Come this way.' Stout and steady in her starched uniform, she led the way up the grand staircase to a large, high-ceilinged room on the first floor.

'Ready for this?' she asked briskly.

'Yes,' Rosie replied firmly. The fact that Juliet was a nurse on a London ambulance had made her determined to prove that she, too, could be brave, and not flinch from hideously gory sights.

'Here's a young lady, come to say hello to you all,' Matron announced, in a loud voice.

Rosie took in the room, and the twenty beds, at a glance, managing to smile in a face frozen with horror. Several of the men had a part of their face blown away, the scarring not yet healed. Other's lay swathed in bandages, covering their eyes. Others lay still and flat, hardly breathing, only just alive and too weak to even notice her presence. One young man sat propped in a bath chair; he'd lost both legs. Another had lost both arms, and was being spoon-fed by a nurse. There were faces contorted with pain, and boys, not yet men, who were screaming in pain and moaning, 'Morphine! For Christ's sake . . . gimme more morphine!'

For a moment Rosie felt hot and sick, and she thought she was going to faint; from the sights, the sour smells of death and decay, the sheer mutilation of men no older than herself, and the horror of witnessing the reality of war.

Again she reminded herself of what Juliet was doing, and she was damned if she was going to let her younger sister show her up as feeble and squeamish. She took a deep breath, fighting against the terrible odours and smiling bravely, as she went from bed to bed, lingering for a few words if the patient was conscious, stroking the hand or shoulder of those who weren't. She felt enormously maternal as she made her way around the large ward; these men had once been little boys, like Jonathan, and God forbid he'd ever have to go through anything like this.

When she got to the last bed, she saw the patient was a very handsome looking young man, propped up on pillows. He looked up at her and, as she caught his eye, Rosie felt an unexpected jolt of attraction. Then she noticed, by the flatness of his blanket on one side of the bed, that he'd lost a leg.

'Hello,' he greeted her pleasantly, sounding like a younger edition of her father.

Rosie went to his bedside. 'How's everything going?' She was trying to master the art of what to say when first approaching a patient.

'Can't grumble, Rosie,' he replied. 'Not that I'll be able to ask you for a dance any more,' he added drily.

Rosie's brow puckered in concentration. 'Have we met?'

'My name's Freddie Newport; I came to your splendid Coming-Out Ball, in Green Street.'

Her hand flew to her mouth in sudden recollection. 'Freddie! Of course I remember you.' He'd been a regular in the Irish Fusiliers and they'd danced together several times. He'd been a bright and breezy young man, with exceptional good looks, 'but no money,' Liza had told her acidly. 'I asked him because we needed *extra* young men.' Rosie blushed now at the memory of her mother's words.

'So when did all this happen?' she asked, purposely putting on a matter-of-fact manner, as she made a sweeping gesture with her hand.

'A few months ago now,' he replied abruptly, as if he didn't want to talk about it. Then he smiled again and she realized how he'd aged in the past five years.

'How's your family? I've read a bit about Juliet, in the newspapers.'

Rosie made a little *moue*. 'Oh, she's fine,' she said casually 'I see you like reading?' She went to pick up the book lying by his side, as he, too, reached for it. Their hands touched. A strange tingling sensation shot through her. She looked up involuntarily, and as their eyes met something disturbing shifted and melted within her.

'I like a good thriller,' he admitted.

76

'Then the next time I come, I'll bring you a few,' she said, her cheeks flushed. 'Do you like Conan Doyle?'

Freddie nodded. 'And I'd love to have a few magazines. I hope to be moved to another ward downstairs in a few days so maybe they can push me out into the garden. You will visit me again, won't you?'

'Of course I will, Freddie.'

He immediately reached for her hand and, because he looked so vulnerable and almost child-like in his desire to be comforted, she sat on the edge of his bed and let him cling on to her hand.

'Tell me about yourself, Rosie. How are your family?'

'I'm married, with two children. Charles is in the Guards, stationed Somewhere In England, as they say. I'm staying at my parents' place, just a few miles from here.'

'You married Charles Padmore?' Freddie asked, thoughtfully.

'Yes,' she replied brightly.

'Are you happy?'

'Of course. And Sophia and Jonathan are divine. How long do you think you're in here for?' she added hurriedly.

'A while yet. Then I'll get a false leg and be out of here as fast as I can.' He squeezed her hand. 'And you'll come and see me again?' His eyes penetrated hers, making her heart lurch pleasurably. It seemed such a long time since even Charles had put his arms around her and she longed to be held close and loved.

'I must be getting home,' she exclaimed, jumping to her feet. 'The children will be wanting their tea.'

'But you'll come again? Promise?'

'Yes,' she said gaily. 'Of course I will.'

'See you soon, Rosie,' Freddie said softly, his eyes never leaving her face.

As she pedalled furiously along the winding Surrey lanes, Freddie's face was at the front of her mind, and his voice, so like Daddy's, filled her ears. There was something vital and exciting about Freddie that she'd never noticed when she'd been eighteen; or was it her mother's remarks about his lack of money that had caused her not to look at him, at *all*?

The blitz started at the beginning of September, the only warning a siren that sounded at eight o'clock in the evening.

Juliet's ambulance unit, consisting of a doctor and five nurses, was on stand-by. Four times they were called out to incidents in central London, while the bombardment went on relentlessly around them as they did what they could to help the injured before taking them to the casualty department in whichever hospital was the nearest.

As soon as she came off duty at ten o'clock the next morning, she stripped off her dirty blood-stained uniform and climbed into a bath, while listening to the BBC news on the radio.

'. . . Two hundred German Messerschmitts attacked London last night, in an air raid that lasted several hours,' announced the newsreader. 'Many buildings were demolished and the death toll is as yet uncertain. Rescue operations, in conjunction with the Fire Services, were able to save the life of many, by digging them out of rubble, while fleets of doctors, nurses and ambulances attended the scenes of disaster. It is feared the Luftwaffe may strike again . . .'

On impulse, because after last night she now knew that death stalked the city and each day could be her last, Juliet dialled Daniel's number. She needed to hear his voice, even if he was unkind. More than anything she wanted to feel his arms around her, safe and protective.

'Hello?' a man's voice answered.

Juliet nearly dropped the receiver with shock. She hadn't really expected him to be at Bywater Street.

'Where else would I be?' His deep-timbred voice sent wave after wave of desire through her.

'I j-just wondered,' she said falteringly. 'It was pretty bad, wasn't it?'

'Not as bad as it's going to get.' He sounded impersonal. She might have been talking to a mere acquaintance.

'Really?'

'Yes. Really.'

Why didn't he want to know how *she* was? Why didn't he ask where *she*'d been?

'We were called out several times,' she told him.

'Many casualties?'

'Hundreds have been killed, the rest have horrific injuries. I've just come off duty . . .' How wonderful it would be if he suggested coming round to see her, she thought with longing.

There was a silent pause on the line. 'Right then,' he said, sounding business-like.

'Daniel . . . ?' she ventured. What was the matter with her? She was the one who was usually in charge. She was a woman who took control of situations; why was she simpering like a girl of sixteen?

'What is it?' His voice sounded harsh.

'Nothing,' she replied quickly. 'I'd better go. I'm off to Hartley in a few minutes. Thought I'd have twenty-four hours' peace and quiet down there before I go back on duty.'

'OK, then. Good-bye.'

Juliet said good-bye and hung up as if she were surrendering a lifeline. Tears of exhaustion and disappointment washed her cheeks. But what the hell had she been expecting? A 'darling-I-love-you-when-can-I-see-you' conversation? Daniel was finished with her; he probably had another girlfriend by now, anyway. It was time she forgot all about him.

'Darling! How lovely to see you.' Liza greeted Juliet when she arrived in time for lunch. 'How are you?'

'Bloody awful,' Juliet replied succinctly, throwing down her overnight case on to the hall floor. Then she strode over to the stairs and went up to her room.

'Oh, *dear* . . . !' Liza looked after her. 'I wonder what's wrong?'

'I think we'd better leave her alone, for the moment,' said Lady Anne, who had been standing in the doorway of her sitting room, ready to greet Juliet, too. 'She may have had to go out with the ambulance last night.'

'Why?'

Lady Anne tried not to look as infuriated as she felt. 'Because there was a very bad air-raid,' she said severely. 'Tons of bombs were dropped on London. All the docks were on fire, and . . .'

'Oh, my God! When did you hear about this? I must telephone Henry to see if he's all right.'

'If you'd listened to the eight o'clock news on the wireless, you'd have heard about it, too. And they're expecting another raid tonight.'

'Oh!' Looking rather lost, Liza tottered off, feeling as if she were moving at a different speed to everyone else. Everyone

79

else seemed to be busy, knowing what they were doing, and *au fait* with what was happening. Even Amanda and Charlotte were busy looking after the hens, ducks and rabbits, collecting eggs, cleaning out the huts and watering the vegetable patch, when they came back from school in the afternoon. Louise was helping in the soup kitchen every weekend, serving lunch in the village hall to the evacuees and going from house to house collecting old pots and pans and metal scrap to be sent off and melted down to make armaments in the munition factories.

Then there was Rosie, cycling over to that convalescent home with suspicious regularity; surely she couldn't have become enamoured of one of the patients? And Lady Anne, a one-woman knitting factory; and now Juliet . . . !

'Henry, are you all right?' Liza clutched the receiver, her voice quivering, her eyes brimming with a mixture of fear and vexation.

'I'm fine, darling. You don't sound too good, though?'

She tried hard to control her emotions. 'I'm all right. It's just that . . . that everything's happening so *fast*. Everyone is doing something, they all seem to be a part of the war . . . and I'm feeling left behind. And I don't know what to *do*.' She was sobbing now, overcome with sadnes at losing the life she'd so enjoyed. She knew she was being selfish; it didn't take her mother-in-law's attitude to tell her she was being useless, but she felt as helpless as if she'd found herself in a strange foreign country.

'Don't get upset, dearest,' Henry told her sympathetically. 'You don't actually have to *do* anything.'

'But everybody else is doing something, even the children. The way Juliet just spoke to me made me feel . . .'

'. . . You've seen Juliet?' he cut in, sharply.

'She came back here a few minutes ago.' Liza could hear Henry give a deep sigh of relief.

Then he spoke. 'Thank God for that. I've been trying to get hold of her to see if she's all right. I think she was on duty last night.' He'd been torturing himself with the thought that something might have happened to her, because there'd been no answer to the phone in Park Lane.

'I should have known she'd go to Hartley,' he continued. 'How is she?'

80

'She's gone to her room in a huff.'

'Tell her to telephone me later, will you, dearest?'

'Of course,' Liza replied sulkily. She didn't doubt that Juliet would want to talk to her father. Those two had always been close, she thought resentfully.

'I think I'll come up to London, again, Henry.'

'Don't, darling. Now the bombing's started, we're expecting it to be continuous. I like to think of you, safe in the country.'

'You mean you're having more fun without me? You and Ian, in your batchelor pad?' she retorted angrily.

'Now you're being extremely silly, Liza. Look, I've got to go. I've got meetings all day. I'll see you on Friday evening, dearest.'

Henry turned out to be right. In those first three nights of the blitz, the docks were virtually demolished, parts of central London destroyed and twelve thousand people killed.

For the next sixty-eight consecutive nights, there were heavy air raids, but Londoners carried on, day after day, with phlegmatic stubborness, refusing to give in, as they contined to carry on as best they could.

Four

Rosie cycled lazily back up the drive, after her afternoon visit to Piltdown Court. Juliet, off duty for twenty-four hours, looked up. Her sister's face was glowing, her eyes sparkling.

'What have you been up to?' she asked curiously.

'Oh, nothing,' Rosie replied airily, as she propped her cycle up against the garden wall. Then she strolled over to where Juliet was sitting.

Juliet eyed her disbelievingly. 'You don't get *that* look from exercising. What's all this about you visiting wounded soldiers?'

Rosie was so longing to tell someone, even Juliet, that she

burst out, 'Do you remember Freddie Newport? He came to our Coming-Out Ball?'

'So did a hundred and fifty other young men,' Juliet pointed out drily, stretching her arms above her head. If it wasn't for Hartley, which she escaped to for the day as often as she could, she thought she'd go mad.

'Freddie is devastatingly handsome. I danced with him that night. He sounds just like Daddy when he talks.' A shadow fell over her face and her eye became troubled for a moment. 'He's lost a leg. That's why he's at Piltdown. He recognized me the moment I went into the ward.' She smiled. 'Today . . . today he told me he was in love with me,' she added tremulously.

Juliet raised her fine eyebrows mockingly. 'You do pick them, don't you Rosie? First Charlie and now a one-legged invalid.'

Rosie flushed angrily. 'That's terribly unfair. Freddie lost his leg when a land mine blew up. He hopes to get a job in the War Office as soon as he's got a new leg.'

'And you're in love with him?' Juliet teased.

'How can I be? I'm married!' Rosie retorted bitterly.

'Being married doesn't stop one having feelings for other people, and I should know. I had no feelings for Cameron.'

'You must have had some feelings; you and Cameron were having a baby. In spite of everything, that must have been a bond between you? I feel bonded to Charles, even though I don't like him very much.'

'She wasn't Cameron's baby,' Juliet said quietly.

'She wasn't . . . ?' Rosie looked dumb struck. 'Don't tell me you were still carrying on with that married man?'

'Not immediately. But when we did, we wanted a child together more than anything, and I promised him it was only his baby I'd have.'

Rosie looked stunned. 'What did he do when the baby died? Was he with you?'

Juliet took a deep breath. 'He didn't know I was even pregnant, because we'd split up.' The pain in Juliet's voice, forbidding further talk, was chilling. 'He still doesn't know.'

They sat in uneasy silence, each immersed in her own thoughts.

'Did you tell Cameron the truth?' Rosie asked eventually.

'There was no point.'

'Do Mummy and Daddy know all about it?'

'No.' Juliet looked at her sister. 'Please don't tell them, Rosie. I don't want anyone to know.' She remembered how harsh Daniel had been when they'd met in Hyde Park. His words – 'you have no heart' – echoed in her mind. If it was true that she had no heart, why was she sick with misery now; why was she hurting as if she'd never be happy again?

But Rosie felt blissfully happy, yet scared. She *was* in love with Freddie. There was no doubting it. She'd never felt like this before and certainly not with Charles. But what could happen between them? Charles came home on leave occasionally and they put on a together-act for the sake of her family and Sophia and Jonathan, but there was no longer a spark between them. Merely an endurance of what was, and what would always be.

Louise slipped into Hartley through the back door, hoping no one would noticed she'd got home from school much later than Amanda.

'Where have you been?' Mrs Dobbs asked immediately, cup of tea in one hand, biscuit in the other, as she sat in the rocking chair by the old wood stove in the kitchen. 'They're all having tea.'

'I've been checking to see if there were any more eggs,' Louise lied, flushing guiltily. 'Then I got talking to the rabbits and I didn't realize how late it was.'

She scuttled past the Mrs Dobbs, hung up her school coat in the hall cloakroom and checked her reflection in the mirror above the washhand basin. She *felt* different; did she look different?

Today was the first time Jack had spoken to her properly. He'd obviously been waiting for her outside the village smithy, knowing she walked past it every day on her way home from school. It had been an awkard, stilted exchange, but it had lit a flame in her heart, which was already full of fantasies about him.

Jack Scovell was a boy of fifteen, the same age as Louise, who had been evacuated from his home in the East End of London, to live with his aunt, in the village. Although he was a bit older than many of the other children, he mixed with them and had his lunch at the soup kitchen every day.

At weekends, he always wangled it so that Louise was the one who served him and took his sixpence.

Tall for his age, he stood out from all the others because of his stunning good looks. His blond hair, bright blue eyes and pale clear skin meant Louise wasn't the only girl in the village who looked at him twice.

They'd eyed each other with interest at first, as she dished out a plate of watery stew and potatoes and handed it to him.

After a while they'd said 'Hello', and grinned shyly, as he queued up with the other kids, but somehow always managed to land right in front of her.

For several weeks now, Louise's heart had started to flutter as soon as she saw his him, head and shoulders above the rest. His shabby shirt and darned jacket made her feel so tenderly towards him, she felt a pang of sweet pain in her heart. But, she noticed, he was always very clean, almost polished, with his hair neatly combed and his nails cut short.

At night she lay in bed and day-dreamed about him rescuing her from a burning building, or comforting her because one of the dogs had died. It made her dizzy to imagine him holding her hand in one of his strong ones, or putting his arm around her shoulders.

In the back of one of her old exercise books she'd started writing poetry.

This afternoon she'd been thinking about him – did she think about anything else, these days? – when he'd stepped from the shadow of the smithy and spoken, almost taking her breath away.

'Off 'ome?' he'd asked chattily, and she'd loved him for his cockney accent; it was so genuine, so honest. There were no false airs and graces about Jack.

Louise had nodded, her throat jammed with such a feeling of excitement, she couldn't speak. She knew she would replay this moment, again and again, when she was in bed tonight. And every ending to her day-dream would be different.

'Where d'you live?' Jack asked, hands in the pockets of a pair of very worn flannel trousers.

'Ummm . . . er . . . Hartley Hall,' she stammered and instantly felt ashamed. Now he'd thing she was a toff and that was the last thing she wanted.

His bright eyes widened. 'That's the big un, up the 'ill, ain't it?'

Louise nodded, her face scarlet. 'It really belongs to my Granny,' she said defensively. 'We've been evacuated from London.'

'And wot d'yer do? Up at that great place?' He sounded interested, and surely he wouldn't have done if he'd thought she was a snob?

Louise listed her most menial chores with relish, ending with, '– and fetching wood for the stove.'

'See ya, then,' Jack said, giving her a little wave, as he strolled off.

'Yes. OK.' Clutching her school bag, Louise wished she hadn't been in her school uniform. She also wished she'd washed her hair the previous night.

Louise didn't go straight home, but dawdled in the orchard, thinking about Jack, going over what he'd said and how he'd looked. She felt so elated by the encounter that she couldn't wait until she was in bed tonight to day-dream about him again. Would he be rescuing her from . . . drowning? No, she was a good swimmer. Save her from the Germans when they invaded? Yes! That would be a lovely fantasy. She'd be wearing her pretty flowered summer dress . . . and he'd pull her away from an advancing tank . . . and they'd hide in the woods . . .

'Bread and butter, darling?' Lady Anne was offering her, as they sat in the elegant drawing room.

'Oh . . . !' Louise started and blushed. 'Yes, please.'

'Who buttered this bread?' Amanda asked.

'Mrs Dobbs, of course,' Liza replied, sipping a cup of precious Lapsang Souchong. God knows when they'd be able to get it again.

Amanda peered myopically at the slice on her plate. 'Then who scraped it all off again?'

'Do you know how much butter we get each week?' her grandmother asked, trying not to show her amusement.

Amanda shook her head.

'A piece the size of a match box, per person. Two ounces. And two ounces of cheese, lard, tea, and four ounces of bacon.'

'Then why don't we buy a cow? We'd get pounds and

pounds of butter and we could make some of it into cheese, and if we had a pig, we could have *pounds* of bacon,' Amanda pointed out in critical tones. 'People make such a fuss about rationing. If we had a cow, we could eat her, too!' She put her head on one side, wondering how the sweets rationing of two ounces a week could be improved.

'Well, don't suggest we start trying to grow sugar cane, or you'll give Spence a nervous breakdown,' Lady Anne laughed.

'You can have my bread and butter, if you like,' Louise offered Amanda with her unusual generosity.

'Thanks.'

'Don't you want it yourself, Louise?' Liza asked.

She gave her mother a dreamy smile. 'No, thank you. I'm not hungry.'

'I hope you're not sickening for something. Those wretched evacuees are always coming down with some hideous disease. I wish you'd stop working in that soup kitchen.' Liza smoothed her skirt fastidiously, as if there might be germs lurking in the tweed folds.

Louise looked down, keeping her secret tightly to herself. Never in a million years must her mother know that she was love with Jack Scovell, because she simply wouldn't understand.

Juliet picked up her bedroom telephone, dialled a number she knew by heart, and a minute later a male voice answered.

'Peter? Oh, I'm so glad I caught you before you went out. Listen, I'm having some friends round for drinks tonight; can you come?'

Peter Osborne worked at the Air Ministry and she'd met him at a dinner party on one of her nights off. He was forty, divorced and a devil-may-care type, fond of drinking, dancing and sex. As an antidote to distract Juliet from her broken heart, he fitted the bill perfectly. His cheerfulness helped to raise her spirits, his technique in bed was excellent, even though he would never be her soulmate.

He was also game for anything.

'Yup!' he replied, without hesitation. 'What time, sweetie?'

'Six-ish?'

'Okey-doke! How about dinner at the Berkeley, afterwards?'

There was dancing at the Berkeley, and the food wasn't bad. either. 'Lovely, darling,' Juliet drawled. 'See you later.'

She made several more calls, rounding up whoever was in London from amongst her friends. Outside, a cold bleak November day shrouded the naked trees in Hyde Park, where anti-aircraft artillery guns lay in trenches, shrouded in camoflaged netting, like slumbering beasts who would awaken at night, to fire on enemy ourcraft overhead.

Juliet got up, walked around her bedroom, went to the window, walked back to the bed again, and buzzed for Dudley.

She seemed to hum with nervous energy, her body thin and taut. Her high cheekbones had become more defined, making her pale blue eyes seem larger than ever. With her blonde hair styled in soft curls, her slim neck rose from 'salt cellars', as her grandmother described the hollows above the collar bones, it all added to her air of fragility. She was jittery. Living on nervous energy, gin, cigarettes and less than half her food rations.

She'd been out in the ambulance every alternate night and on the nights she'd been off-duty, she painted the town red, in order to obliterate the dreadful scenes she'd witnessed, the injured people she'd helped, and the dead people whose faces she'd covered, with their eyes still staring at her.

Most nights, whether on duty or off, she managed only four or five hours sleep.

Dudley tapped on her bedroom door. 'You rang, Your Grace?'

'What's our supply of gin like, Dudley? And have we still got some Dubonnet? I'm having a dozen or so people for drinks tonight; can you rustle-up some cocktails? And a few cheese straws, perhaps?'

Dudley, who had black-market contacts in a city now riddled with crime and looting, nodded confidently. 'Certainly, Your Grace. What time are you expecting your guests?'

Juliet smiled to herself. Only she, in the midsts of a world war, could somehow still manage to live like a Duchess – with the help of the redoubtable Dudley.

'Six o'clock,' she replied, reaching for a cigarette, and feeling more cheerful. 'Thank you, Dudley.'

'Will you lunching at home today, Your Grace?'

'No. I'm meeting friends.'

Quo Vadis, in the heart of Soho, was packed with people

enjoying the maximum five-shilling set luncheon, as decreed by the government.

Gerald Knight, one of her earliest swains, was already at the table, in his naval uniform. He'd brought along a friend, who was also on his ship, called Hugh Armstrong. They rose as Juliet sashayed her way across the room, turning heads as she made her way around the tables, wearing her wild mink coat over a dusty rose pink woollen dress.

'Juliet darling . . . !' Gerald rose and enveloped her in his arms. 'You're looking terrific – as always, of course. Let me introduce . . .'

Hugh Armstrong looked mesmerized as he gazed at Juliet as if he'd never seen anyone like her before.

'How about a pink gin, darling?' Gerald suggested, as Juliet slid into her seat. Hugh offered her a cigarette.

'Lovely,' she said lightly. 'Is Henry Willis joining us?'

She rather liked Henry. He flirted outrageously, promising to propose to her as soon as the war ended, so that he could get her into bed, now. Of course he didn't mean it, and she hadn't slept with him so far, nevertheless . . . may be one day she would; if she felt like it.

'He'll be along in a minute,' Gerald assured her. Drinks were ordered, the menu studied.

'I'll have a carrot salad,' said Juliet.

'Sweetie, you'll fade away,' he teased. 'End up all skin and bones.'

She fluttered her mascaraed eyelashes. 'But *what* skin! *What* bones,' she said provocatively, her scarlet mouth tipping up at the corners into her wicked smile.

At that moment, Henry Willis arrived, broad and blond and handsome in his naval uniform.

'The fleet's certainly in town!' Juliet crowed flirtatiously. The three men laughed, all of them enamoured by this fascinating creature, whose attractions seemed miraculously to have increased since she'd experienced the horrors of war.

They all raised their glasses to her and she laughed with pleasure. Then she stopped, as if a switch in her head had been turned off. She stared white-faced at the couple who had just entered the restaurant and knew, with a dreadful certainty, that the woman accompanying Daniel was his wife. Daniel was looking straight at her, taking in the scene of three naval officers waving glasses of pink gin about as they toasted her, and then he deliberately turned away, and asked the head waiter for a table on the other side of the restaurant.

'I say, old girl, are you all right?' Gerald asked, concerned. Juliet seemed to have wilted and shrunk in that moment and she drew on her cigarette, as if it were a lifeline.

'I'm fine,' she said harshly and promptly called to the waiter to bring another round of drinks.

'You look as if you'd seen a ghost,' Hugh remarked, jokingly.

Her mouth was tight, her jawline white and sharp. 'Perhaps I did,' she said, her voice low as she struggled to control her emotions.

As if drawn by a magnet, her eyes kept going over to where Daniel and his wife sat. She was dark haired, with olive skin and a gentle expression, and she was gazing lovingly into Daniel's face. She wasn't smart. Her skirt and blouse outlined a plump and slightly sagging figure. Her hair was rolled into a loose knot at the base of her neck. The word 'motherly' came into Juliet's mind, followed instantly by an agonizing thought; would *she* have looked motherly, if the baby hadn't died?

Juliet proceeded to drink and smoke her way through lunch, picking at her salad, laughing too loudly, and telling risqué jokes.

Theirs was the noisiest and most uproarious table in the restaurant and several people turned to look at them. Including Daniel. Juliet happened to be looking his way and for a split second their eyes locked. It reminded her of her wedding reception when he'd had stood in Hyde Park, looking at the proceedings through the window. They'd held each other's gaze then. But this time it was different. Instead of adoration, Daniel's expression seemed to say whore. Harlot. Jezebel.

Juliet lay under Peter Osborne as his groans of pleasure filled her bedroom. It had been a long day and a long evening, but nothing had assuaged her pain. Not the hours of flirting with her admirers, not the amount of alcohol she'd consumed or the food she'd picked at, not the wild dancing to the Ambrose Band at the Embassy, before going on to smooch at the Orchid Room; none of it had made her feel any better.

Her heart was broken afresh, and she couldn't get over the way Daniel had looked at her in the restaurant.

'God, you're so beautiful . . .' Peter murmured in her ear, as the noise of bombs screaming down around them exploded with earth-shattering thuds, making Park Lane rock and shudder.

Julian knew they should be sheltering in the basement, but she no longer cared whether she lived or died. What was life, anyway, without Daniel? The ACK-ACK guns in Hyde Park had opened up with a roar of cannons, splitting the night air with their deafening cracks. The Luftwaffe droned menacingly overhead flying so low they barely seemed to skim the London chimney tops.

Juliet wound her arms around Peter's neck, moving with him, as the violent cacophony of noises seemed to merge together, clashing and screaming, tearing at Juliet's nerves, growing stronger, louder, building inexorably until it reached an unbearable climax of explosions that caused her to cry out, a lonely voice in the darkness.

A few minutes later, Peter rolled off, exhausted. It flashed through Juliet's mind that making love during a blitz was like being right at the heart of Tchaikovsky's '1812' Overture. Drums, cymbals, percussion, explosives, artillery, reverberation, shudders . . . what was the difference? It was all deafening. Frightening. Exciting. Terrible.

Juliet swung her legs to the ground and, naked, groped her way in the darkness across her room to the window. She pulled back the heavy silk curtains, which were lined with black-out material, and looked out.

Buildings were on fire. Searchlights probed the sky with long silver fingers. The guns spat like fireworks in the grass. The hellish noise of bombardment went on.

Juliet closed the curtains again and went back to bed, sickened with her life and everything around her.

Rosie found Freddie being pushed in a wheelchair around the grounds of Piltdown Court by a nurse. He was well wrapped up with a rug over his leg, but the young nurse looked frozen.

'Shall I take over?' Rosie asked, parking her bicycle.

Freddie beamed with delight and the nurse looked grateful.

'Could you really?' she exclaimed, rubbing her purple hands together.

'Of course.' Rosie bent to kiss Freddie on the cheek. 'Where do you want to go?' she asked.

'There's a pretty copse, over there, on the right,' he replied, pointing. 'It's out of the wind.'

As Rosie pushed the chair with one hand, she rested her other on his shoulder and he immediately placed his hand over hers.

'God, Rosie. It's good to see you. I was hoping you'd come over today.'

'Were you?' She leaned forward, placing her cheek next to his. 'I don't think I can bear to stay away,' she murmured.

When they reached the secluded and sheltered copse, Freddie told her to stop by a fallen tree trunk, so she could sit on it, and he could talk to her, face to face.

'That's better,' he said, putting his arms around her and kissing her on the lips, tenderly and diffidently at first, but as she responded, holding on to him tightly, his kisses became more passionate.

'I've missed you so much, Rosie,' he breathed, gazing into her eyes.

'I've missed you, too, but we shouldn't, you know. I'm married to Charles,' she said weakly. 'But I do love you so terribly, Freddie.'

'My darling girl.' He was kissing her again, probingly, demandingly, one of his arms holding her tightly. With his other hand he grabbed her hand, held it for a moment, and then with a swift movement, guided her inside his trousers, which were unbuttoned.

'Oh-h-h!' Rosie gasped, pulling back, trying to extricate her hand, but he held it fast by the wrist. 'Please, darling,' he begged. 'Oh God, please, darling, I love you more than life itself. This isn't wrong, sweetheart. You're not being unfaithful to Charlie by doing this. I promise you.' He moved her hand gently up and down, and closed his eyes in ecstasy. 'I love you, I want you, Rosie. I'd like to spend the rest of my life with you. Wanting, wanting you . . . oh, Christ, darling . . .'

For the first time in her whole life, Rosie was filled with gut-wrenching desire. She wanted him too. For a mad moment she thought of ripping off her clothes so that he could give himself to her, completely, utterly. She closed her own eyes, letting her hand give him the release he craved, wanting him to be happy, and satisfied. It was the least she could do for a man she loved so much.

91

When she heard him draw a sobbing breath of pleasure, she instinctively arched her own back and a wondrous sensation grabbing at her insides made her cry out, too.

'Rosie, Rosie,' he whispered in delight, turning his head from side to side, 'Oh, Rosie, you're so wonderful.'

'So are you,' she murmured, her lips hovering above his. Then she kissed him deeply, taking the initiative, as she'd never wanted to do with Charles, as the sweet clutching sensation echoed once again through her body.

'We're made for each other, aren't we?' Freddie said, dreamily.

'I think we are,' she replied, feeling dazed. What *was* that sensation? Was it what Juliet had alluded to after her trip to Paris with that boyfriend of hers?

It was growing dark when Rosie pushed Freddie through the portals of Piltdown Court.

'When will you come to see me again?' he asked eagerly. 'I'll soon have a false leg and we could go out.' His eyes were filled with meaning; he was thinking of all the things they could do, if they were to book into a hotel.

'Tomorrow, if I can,' she said softly. Her face glowed. Her eyes were sparkling, but at the back of her mind was the thought of Charles; what on earth was she going to do about him?

Rosie didn't even remember cycling back to Hartley. Her mind was in a whirl, her emotions in turmoil. She felt sick with excitement and paralysed by dread. That night she skipped dinner, pleading a headache. But once in bed she lay awake all night, unable to skeep.

Freddie had awakened her sexuality and taken possession of her mind and her heart and she was desperate for him.

The next morning she drifted around the house in a daze, unable to concentrate. When Sophia nagged her to tell a story, and Jonathan cried because he couldn't reach the toy he wanted, she snapped at them angrily for breaking into her lovely reverie.

'What's the matter with that girl?' Liza grumbled to Lady Anne. 'She forgot to bring in the logs, and she hasn't even made her bed yet.'

Her mother-in-law was thinking the same thing; and Louise also seemed a bit off-colour these days, as if she found it hard to concentrate,

'I wonder if they're getting enough to eat?' Lady Anne

suggested, her serene face over-shadowed with worry. 'This rationing really is very meagre. The equivalent of two lamb chops a week isn't enough for a growing girl, or a busy young mother. We're going to have to grow more vegetables. And fruit. I'll have to speak to Spence; we may have to sacrifice the lawn and turn it into another kitchen garden.'

'We could get extra things on the black market,' Liza said, lowering her voice.

'Never!' Lady Anne said firmly. 'That would be totally unpatriotic. There's no reason why we should get more than the rest of the country, just because we have the money to pay for it.'

Liza looked mutinous but said nothing. Henry and his mother were so *correct* in everything they did. Why shouldn't they cheat a little? Masses of people did. One of her London friends was even able to get clothing coupons on the black market. Liza longed to get some too; it was so boring not to be able to have a new wardrobe for the summer and another new collection for the winter. She didn't dare, though. If Henry ever found out he'd be incandescent with anger. In fact he'd already told her to follow the example of everyone else and 'Make Do and Mend' as the popular slogan said, and pass on her coupons to Louise, Amanda and Charlotte, because they were growing so fast.

'I *hate* this war,' Liza burst out pettishly. 'Henry won't even allow me to go up to town any more, yet I've got lots of friends who are staying on, sheltering in the basement of the Dorchester every night and having a really good time. All the theatres are full every night, too. So are the restaurants. It simply isn't fair to leave me stuck down here, with nothing to do and nowhere to go.'

Lady Anne regarded her daughter-in-law with quiet, grim resignation, and for the umpteenth time she wondered why Henry had married this shallow little thing.

Liza didn't seem to care that thousands of civilians, both in London and in provincial cities around the country, had been killed, and thousands more were holed up every night in stinking shelters, or sleeping on the platforms of the London underground. Didn't Liza realize, as she swanned around Hartley, that a quarter of a million people were now home-less?

'Liza,' Lady Anne said stiffly. 'You should take stock of how lucky you really are. You have neither a husband nor a son in the armed forces. You have five healthy daughters and, pray God, they will all remain so. Count your blessings, for goodness sake, instead of behaving . . . behaving like a spoilt child,' she added, her voice rising with cold fury.

'I won't be talked to like that,' Liza retorted tearfully. Then she stalked out of the room, slamming the door behind her.

Jack was waiting for Louise by the smithy again, and when she saw him her heart gave a leap of joy. It had been a month since he'd first stood waiting for her, there. Since then they'd met two or three times a week.

'Got you a Chrissy present,' he mumbled, cheeks flushed, as he shoved a package, wrapped in old and rather crumpled brown paper, into her hand.

Thrilled, but embarrassed because she hadn't got him anything, she stammered her thanks, and mumbled, 'Christmas is still two weeks away,' as if to suggest she was going to give him a present nearer the time.

'I know,' he replied. 'It don't matter. Y'know that book wot you lent me?'

'*Treasure Island*?' Her eyes sparkled. 'Did you like it?'

'I 'aint finished it yet, but it's OK.' He fell into step beside her, as they walked slowly along the lane in the direction of Hartley.

'I'm so glad you're enjoying it.'

It had been on their third meeting that Jack had scoffed at the number of books she was always carrying.

'Some of them are school books, but I've lots of real books at home. Do you like reading?'

'I'll read anyfinck,' he replied, his bright blue eyes earnest. 'Even the labels on jam jars. Me auntie gives me tuppence a week to buy a comic, but she ain't got no books in 'er 'ouse, so I don't get much of a chance.'

'I could lend you some of mine.'

'I don't want to read no romance,' he retorted, looking faintly indignant.

'I don't read romantic books either,' she said sturdily. 'You'd like *A Tale Of Two Cities*, by Charles Dickens. It's really exciting. I *think* you'd like *The Secret Garden*. It's absolutely my favourite book of all.' He reminded her of Dickon, the nature-loving brother of one of the maids.

'Can I have a read of it, then? When I've finished *Treasure Island*?'

'Of course you can.'

'Ta.'

They reached the little bridge that crossed the stream, and, after standing around shuffling their feet for a few awkard moments, sat down on the wall, side by side.

'Are you an only child?' Louise asked.

Jack nodded. 'Me Ma died when I was three. She wos 'aving another babe, an' they both died.'

'Oh!' Louise put her hand to her mouth in horror. 'I'm so sorry. How dreadful for you.'

He shrugged. 'Don' they say you never miss wot you never 'ad?'

'So you were brought up by your father?'

'Nah. 'e were banged up for GBH mos' of the time.'

Louise looked perplexed. 'G-B-H?' she repeated slowly.

'Yup. Grievous Bodily 'arm. 'e beat up a night-watchman, when 'e was robbin' a factory,' Jack's tone was matter-of-fact.

'*Really?*' Louise's eyes widened with fascination. She'd never met anyone whose father had been in prison. It made Jack seem a more romantic figure than ever. A boy without a mother and a father 'banged up'.

''E's out now,' Jack continued. 'Lost an eye, during a fight in porridge, so e's workin' in a garridge. 'e sent me down 'ere when war broke out, though.'

Louise nodded slowly, trying to take it in. 'Porridge?' she said doubtfully.

Jack flashed her a warm smile, his full pink lips framing even white teeth. 'Slang for prison. You don' know much about real life, do you?' he asked kindly.

'Not *much*, I suppose,' she admitted reluctantly. 'Will you tell me more about it, one day?'

His grin widened. 'If you tells me wot it's like up at the big 'ouse? Posh, 'aint you? Probably got servants, an' all that?'

'No,' Louise swiftly. 'Not now. They've left to do war work.'

''Oo does the cleanin', then? An' the cookin'?'

'We all help,' she replied with prim modesty. The light was fading swiftly. She jumped to her feet. 'Goodness, I'd better go or they'll be wondering where I am.'

Jack rose too, unconscious of the natural grace of his long legs and slender body. 'I'll walk you to the gates. It ain't safe for a young lady like you to be out in the dark.'

'You don't have to,' she said shyly. No one had called her a young lady before.

'I know I don't, but I wanna.'

They walked side by side, up the steep lane on the other side of the bridge, and turned left at the top. A few yards further on were the imposing wrought iron gates of Hartley Hall.

'It's bloomin' grand, 'aint it?' Jack said with sudden wistfulness.

'The house might be grand, but I'm not,' Louise replied, 'and thank you for the present.'

'That's OK. See ya soon.'

She heard the clatter of his lace-up boots going down the lane again, and then there was silence. The countryside had closed down for the night. There was no one about, and it was almost dark. But inside Louise's head, birds sang, music wafted on the gentle breeze, she could smell the summer roses, and peeping, she saw Jack had given her a bookmark as a present. Could life be more perfect?

'I've got the most marvellous news,' Rosie said, rushing to Freddie's side, as he sat in the wheelchair, by his bed. Her cheeks were ruddy from the icy wind, and as usual she had a basket full of goodies.

'Kiss me first,' Freddie said, grabbing her arm.

'Oh, Freddie . . . people will see,' she protested laughingly.

There was already a barrage of friendly whoops and catcalls from the other patients.

'Let them see,' he said gaily. 'I've nothing to be ashamed of.'

'No, but I . . .' she pecked him lightly on the mouth, 'I have, Freddie. A husband who says he's going to come home on leave quite soon.' There was a strained look in her eyes at the mention of Charles.

'I'll be out of here by then.'

'That's what I wanted to tell you. I've got a long lease on a cottage in the village, but I moved out, so I wouldn't be alone with the children when Charles joined up. Well, I've been there and opened it up again, it's really very cosy and sweet, and I wondered if you'd like to stay there for a while, when you leave here?' She sat on the edge of his bed, looking triumphant.

Freddie's face was a study. 'You mean it? Really?'

Rosie nodded. 'You're on leave for a while, when you get out of here, aren't you? To get used to your new leg? A sort of rehabilitation time? So what could be more perfect?'

'That's marvellous,' he said slowly. 'That's bloody marvellous.'

'Isn't it?' she agreed ecstatically. 'It's got two bedrooms, so I thought I'd tell my family that I'm going to put up patients when they first leave here, to ease them back into normal life. Isn't that a brilliant idea? Then I can pop down to be with you every day,' she added with a knowing look.

Freddie's eyes swept over her long legs and up to her breasts. 'I can hardly wait, darling.'

Rosie could hardly wait either. Today was New Year's Eve. Tomorrow would be the start of 1941. Whatever the future held, she would be able to spend more time with Freddie; never the nights because of her family, but long afternoons, in bed. The sort of afternoons she'd expected to spend with Charles, before they'd married.

Rosie peered out of the cottage window, and then drew back sharply, half drawing the curtain so she wouldn't be seen from the street.

'What is it?' Freddie asked lazily, from the warm bed she'd just vacated.

'It's Louise,' she said, frowning.

'What about her?' Freddie hadn't met any of Rosie's family because she kept him hidden, her secret lover, her all-consuming passion, but he knew all about them.

'She's with someone . . . they're walking hand and hand.'

'What? A boyfriend? Good for her.'

'No Freddie, I mean, yes, it's a boy, but it's a village boy. One of the evacuees. What on earth is she doing?'

'Maybe on her way to do what we've been doing?' he laughed.

'Freddie, she's still only fifteen!' Rosie sounded profoundly shocked. 'I've seen that boy before. He can't be more than fifteen either. Oh, my God. This is dreadful. Mummy will kill her if she finds out.'

'Come back to bed and kill *me*, darling, with love,' Freddie pleaded. 'I want you again.'

Rosie dragged her gaze away from her sister, and looked over her shoulder at Freddie. 'You're insatiable,' she laughed.

'And you're not?' His eyes drilled hers, his smile mischievous. 'Come on. Get back into bed, or I'll start without you.'

'*Freddie!*' She glanced out of the window for a last look. Still holding hands, Louise and the boy were turning the corner going towards the bridge. She'd have to talk to her, later. Much later. When she and Freddie had exhausted themselves, and she felt happier and more fulfilled than she'd ever been in her whole life.

'Are you warm enough?' Jack asked anxiously, as they took their normal perch on the side of the bridge.

'I'm fine.' Nothing in the world was going to get Louise to admit she could no longer feel her feet, and her fingers pinched with pain. She dug her hands deeper into the pockets of her overcoat. 'Are you all right?'

'The cold don't bother me,' Jack replied easily. For Christmas she'd given him a warm scarf; it was one of hers, because she had neither money not clothing coupons, but she'd never worn it. Jack had kept it muffled around his neck, ever since. But his jacket was thin, and his wrists poked out of the sleeves, and the cheap fabric strained across his back. She wondered if she could get hold of one of her father's old jackets, as long as Jack wasn't offended.

'What do you wish for the New Year, Jack?'

He thought about it for a long moment. 'I wish I was old enough to join up,' he said at last. Then he looked straight into her eyes. 'An' I wish I thought we could always be together.'

Louise was so moved her eyes filled with tears.

'Wot's that for?' he asked incredulously.

'It's such a nice thing to say.' She was smiling and almost

weeping at the same time. 'We *can* always be together. If we want to.'

He turned his head to look in the direction of Hartley Hall. 'I don' think they'd like that, up there. Your posh family.'

'It's up to me who my friends are,' she replied indignantly.

'Even so.'

'They'd like you if they met you,' she said rashly.

Jack didn't answer. He wasn't a fool. People like the Granvilles looked down on the likes of him. ''adn't you better be gettin' back? They'll wonder where you are.'

Louise sighed. These snatched few minutes in the afternoons, when she told the family she was 'going for little walk', were a sweet agony. Every day she looked forward to seeing Jack, and then in no time at all, she had to say good-bye to him.

'I suppose so,' she agreed, depressed.

In sad silence, they walked up the lane to the gates of Hartley. 'G'-bye, then,' Jack said.

On a sudden impulse, she reached up and kissed him on his cold cheek. 'Good-bye, Jack.'

For a moment he looked taken aback. Then a grin spread across his face.' 'appy New Year.' He waved as he turned back down the lane.

'Happy New Year,' she called after him. 'See you tomorrow.'

'If you see that boy again, I'll tell Mummy,' Rosie warned.

'But we're just friends,' Louise pleaded, desperately. 'There's nothing wrong with him. He's the nicest person I've ever met.'

'But can't you see he's unsuitable? He's a common boy from the slums. What were you thinking off, Louise?' Rosie had cornered Louise in the pantry after dinner that night, determined to put a stop to her sister acting so unwisely.

'I don't care,' Louise retorted. 'He's kind and he's interesting. We talk about books. And he wishes he was old enough to fight in the war. There's *nothing* wrong with him.'

'There's *everything* wrong with him,' Rosie said fiercly.

'You're getting just like Mummy.'

'What do you mean?'

'You're a snob. Just like her. Talking about people being "suitable" and "unsuitable". And look where it got *you*. How important is it being a titled lady, if you're not happy with your husband?'

'But . . .'

'And look at Juliet. Married a Duke – and now she's divorced.'

'Louise. Really . . .'

'No, Rosie. Stop living in Never-Never Land. I'm going to have the friends I want . . .' Louise was scarlet in the face with anger. And also fear that Rosie would tell their mother, who would most certainly forbid her to see Jack again. 'If you tell Mummy, then I'll tell her you put a wounded soldier into Speedwell Cottage, and that you spend every afternoon with him.'

Rosie turned white, her eyes widening with horror. 'How did you know . . . ?' she stammered.

'I'm not a child any longer.' Louise raised her chin, suddenly feeling quite grown-up. 'I'll lead my life, and you can lead yours, for all I care.' Then she stalked off across the empty kitchen, feeling as if she'd scored a major victory over the rest of her family.

February brought stinging rain and bitter winds to the countryside. Lady Anne, confined to the house with a heavy cold and cough, watched the comings and goings of the rest of the household with puzzled interest.

Rosie, Louise and Amanda suddenly seemed very interested in having afternoon walks. Rosie, however, never took her children, but left them with Nanny, saying it was too cold for them. When questioned she said she was either visiting the patients at Piltdown Court, or checking up on the chaps who apparently stayed for a few days at a time at her old cottage.

Louise and Amanda, who'd never been particularly close, now set off together, at weekends, for a 'long walk', yet returned to the house separately, an hour or so later.

When the new term started, Charlotte who had joined her sisters at Ingram House School, came back with Amanda, while Louise arrived later, preferring to walk, 'for the exercise'.

Their grandmother wasn't a fool, but decided to say nothing for the moment. It was all probably completely innocent; Louise and Amanda were still children, anyway.

Then Rosie got a telegram that was to change everything.

'Charles is coming home on leave next week,' she announced at dinner that night.

'That's lovely, darling,' Liza enthused, 'we must give him a big welcome. When does he arrive?'

'On March the third.'

'Will he still be here for his birthday, on the the eighth?' Henry asked.

Rosie nodded. 'He's got ten days.' She gazed down at her plate of pale watery mince, and wondered what they were going to do with themselves for ten whole days. The weather was appalling, there wasn't enough petrol to drive around and go anywhere, the local cinema only seemed to show old films, and as Charles wasn't interested in books or music, it was going to be pretty hellish.

Especially as she wouldn't be able to see Freddie, or dare go near Speedwell Cottage.

'Charles will probably be glad of home comforts, won't he?' Henry suggested. He knew *he* longed for nothing more than to get back to the peace and quiet of Hartley at the weekends, always providing he wasn't on ARP duty, in the city.

'Why don't you go up to London?' Liza asked, brightening at the very idea. 'You could stay at the Savoy. All the theatres are open you know; there are some great shows.' Her voice took on a tinge of longing. Henry didn't encourage her to stay with him while the bombing continued, and she was really pining for the bright lights. 'Restaurants are packed, too. You could have a really lovely time.'

'I know what I *could* arrange,' Rosie said thoughtfully. The worse thing was the dread of being alone with Charles. They had nothing to say to each other. But as long as there were other people around, it helped dilute the agony of deathly silences.

As soon as dinner was over, she went to the hall, having put on her fur coat first, because of the whistling draughts that flowed freely through window frames of the old house, which they could no longer heat owing to fuel rationing.

'Juliet? What a bit of luck. I was afraid you'd be on duty, or something.'

'I'm giving a dinner party; it's my night off.' There was the sound of music and laughter in the background.

101

'I've a favour to ask you,' Rosie explained. 'Charles is coming home on leave, at the beginning of March, and as there's nothing happening down here, and it's his birthday on the eighth, I wondered if we could stay with you for a few days. We'd bring our own food, of course.'

'Yes. OK. But don't bother about rations. Dudley looks after all that side of things, including booze. I won't be here that much, you know, and . . .' Juliet paused to flip through her diary, 'I'll actually be on duty on the night of the eighth, but you can go somewhere nice, can't you? The Café de Paris is great at the moment, and there's always the Four Hundred.'

'That would be terrific, Juliet. Thanks a million. Is everything OK? Presumably your house is still standing?'

'Yes. Listen, I must fly. We're just about to have jugged hare; God knows where Dudley got it from. Let me know when you're arriving. And Rosie . . . ? Is this a second honeymoon?' she added teasingly.

'No, thanks,' Rosie replied crisply, although there was laughter in her voice now. 'The first one was *quite* enough.'

Charles looked better and fitter than he'd done before the war. His face looked healthy and tanned, his body was still lean but muscular now, and his eyes shone blue and clear; an indication, Rosie hoped, that he was drinking less.

'How are you, Rosie?' he asked, rather awkwardly, as if she were a stranger he was supposed to know.

'I'm fine.' She kissed him lightly on the cheek. 'You're looking very well?'

'I'm OK. Glad to be home.'

At that moment Sophia came running into the hall, followed by Jonatham, swaying uncertainly on his little legs.

'Hello there!' Charles exclaimed, crouching down and opening his arms wide to them. Then he scooped up first Sophia and then Jonathan, hugging them close, kissing first one then the other.

Watching them together, Rosie felt deeply touched. The children were giggling and Charles was smiling like a carefree young man, and anyone seeing would think they were a happy little family.

Then Lady Anne and Liza appeared to greet Charles, the former with gracious warmth, the latter with girlish excitement.

'You look so handsome in uniform,' Liza gushed, patting his shoulder. 'Doesn't he look marvellous, Rosie?'

Rosie nodded, smiling. 'Uniform certainly suits you, Charles.'

They took the children for a walk after lunch, with Sophia splashing in puddles in her new red gumboots and Jonathan swathed in layers of shawls and blankets in his push chair.

'What do you do with yourself, down here?' Charles asked, hunched in his greatcoat. 'There can't be much going on.'

'I visit the patients at Piltdown Court; Granny comes too, if there's enough petrol,' Rosie replied, managing to keep her voice steady. 'Some of them have been terribly badly injured.'

'That's nice of you. I suppose the children keep you busy?'

'So does housework, and shopping, and helping with the washing up. I never realized that cooking meals for nine or ten people every day is so *relentless*. Thank God for Mrs Dobbs, and for Nanny. Things have changed so much since the war began. Sometimes I wonder if we'll ever get back to normal.'

'It depends what you mean by normal,' Charles observed. 'They'll never get back to the way they were.'

She turned to look at him, wondering if he was joking. 'Why ever not?'

'There won't be the money. And now the servant classes have realized they can have a good life and get employment without being domestic minions, they'll be off. Getting jobs on the buses and trains, or in shops, factories and offices. They'll never to back to being servile to the likes of us.'

Rosie felt quite shocked. How were her parents going to run the house in Green Street without at least six servants? Not to mention a butler, like Parsons. 'What will we do then, Charles?'

'We'll have to do the work, ourselves. The days of running big houses are over, Rosie. Most people will live in flats if they stay in town. It's all going to be different.'

'Goodness . . . !' In the last few moments her vision of the life she'd been born into and had always known had vanished, as if a conjurer had waved a wand and made it all disappear.

He picked up Sophia, because she'd begun to tire and lag behind. 'Want a piggy-back?' he asked.

'Yes! Yes!' she cried excitedly, clinging round his neck.

Rosie felt quite disorientated. She'd believed the war was merely a horrible blip in their lives, but that as soon as it was over, everything would be as before.

Breaking into her thoughts, Charles spoke diffidently, 'Would you mind very much if I spent the next couple of days with my mother and Henrietta? In Cumbria? I'm going to be posted abroad any minute now, and, well, you know . . .' His voice faltered and faded.

'Of course,' she said, suddenly and unexpectedly feeling depressed. She hadn't been looking forward to having him home on leave but now he'd decided to spend some time with his family and not her, it was as if he already recognized their marriage was over.

'Where will you be posted?'

'I'm not sure, and if I knew I'm afraid I wouldn't be allowed to say.' His smile was slightly sheepish as he glanced at her, almost as if he expected her to explode with anger.

'You'll be back for your birthday, on the eighth, won't you?'

'Absolutely.'

'Good. Because I've arranged with Juliet that we can spend a few days days in London, staying with her. I thought we could go out on your birthday?'

'Great idea!' He sounded delighted with the arrangement. 'Why don't we meet up in London, then, when I get back?'

'Make yourself at home. Dudley will get you anything, within reason, you want,' Juliet told Charles, when he arrived from Cumbria, a few hours before Rosie.

'Thanks, Juliet.' He put down his haversack and took off his greatcoat. 'You've got an amazing place here, haven't you?' He glanced around her fashionable hall with admiration.

'I designed all the decorations myself,' she said proudly. 'Let's have a drink before lunch. I've been on duty all night, so I need a little pick-me-up.' As she spoke she led the way into her white and silver drawing room, where the lamps were switched on and a coke fire burned in the black marble fireplace.

'Rosie was telling me all about your being a nurse. It must be pretty tough.' He looked at her seachingly, but she looked as immaculate as always in a pretty royal blue dress, with her hair and make-up perfect.

Juliet returned his gaze. 'Unspeakable,' she said succinctly. Her face had tightened, her eyes looked stricken for a moment. 'Let's not talk about it,' she said, forcing her voice to sound light, 'except to say I've banned raspberry jam from the house, for ever.'

'Oh!' Charles's eyes widened. 'Oh! Yes. I see.'

'Pink Gin? Dry Martini? A Manhattan? Name your poison. It's all here.' She waved hand to an Art Deco mirrored cocktail cabinet. 'I'll ring for some ice.'

Charles went and stood with his back to the fire. 'How do you do it, Juliet?' he asked, bemused. 'The moment I walked into the house, it was as if there was no war. No Blitz. No conflict, anywhere. Nothing but five-star luxury.'

'That's the atmosphere I have to create, whilst I'm doing this job,' she said quietly. 'Otherwise I'd probably go insane.'

'As bad as that?'

She nodded, while Dudley came on silent feet into the room, with a little silver bucket of ice and a plate of home-made cheese straws.

'Is there anything else, Your Grace?' he asked.

'That's all for now, thank you, Dudley. We'll have lunch as soon as Lady Padmore arrives.'

'Very well, Your Grace.'

While she mixed their drinks, she said in a strained voice, almost as if she was talking to herself, 'An incendiary bomb fell on a pub last night. In Chelsea. About twenty people were sheltering in the basement. All the spirits in the bar caught fire, and the bottles were exploding like hand grenades. They were all trapped beneath this blazing building and the only exit was blocked by débris.'

The room was silent. She dropped an ice cube into a glass with a plopping clink. Charles stood watching her, chilled by what she was saying.

'I'm the thinnest person on our unit, you see,' she continued, brittle voiced.

He frowned, wondering where this was leading.

'So they lifted the cover of a manhole in the pavement outside, and I was able to squeeze down, through it. The doctor gave me hypodermics, and masses of morphine. They were all badly injured, you see. Trapped. There was no way they could be rescued. The building above them was ablaze, "Tell them," the doctor said to me, "that you're giving them an injection that will ease their pain, until we can get them all out."

Juliet lifted her glass to her lips and took a long swig of neat gin, tinted pink with a dash of angostura bitters.

Charles's jaw slackened and dropped. His skin prickled. His mouth was suddenly dry. 'Christ!' he muttered under his breath.

Juliet sat on the sofa, by the fire. 'Did I murder twenty people, Charles? Or save them the pain of being burned alive?'

He crouched down in front of her, and took her hand. 'What you did was absolutely right, Juliet,' he said firmly. 'You're a heroine. You risked your own life, in the first place. That was the bravest thing I've ever heard.'

'You think so?' Her lips drew back but she wasn't smiling. 'So you can understand why I need . . . all this.' She looked around the room. There were even sweet-scented lilies in a vase, and a box of expensive chocolates on the coffee table. 'I never thought I'd be able to do it. I hope to God I never have to, again – but how can one tell?'

'I take my hat off to you, Juliet,' Charles said humbly. 'I always thought you were flighty but you've got real guts.'

She smiled. 'You've changed, too, Charles. Army life seems to suit you.'

'Have I? I suppose I like the structure Army life gives one. Out of the way of temptation,' he added wryly. 'Rosie seems to have changed a bit, too. Not as much as you, though. But then, living with the rest of the family at Hartley, she's not really seeing much of the war. Her life is still very protected, isn't it?'

Juliet said nothing. She'd seen Rosie slipping into Speedwell Cottage at weekends, without the children, and then returning to Hartley a couple of hours later, looking flushed and rather *distraite*. Making her own contribution to the war, no doubt, Juliet reflected with amusement. Well, why not? Everyone was at it. London was a writing mass of copulation, from couples in smart hotels, to damp shelters and in the back of cars. The city was rocking with sex. That's what war did to the human race. There was no greater aphrosisiac than the threat of imminent death.

*　　　*　　　*

Juliet left the house at nine thirty the next morning to go back on duty. She tapped on Rosie and Charles's bedroom door, to say good-bye.

'Happy birthday, Charles. You're going to paint the town red tonight, aren't you?'

'We are indeed,' he replied cheerfully, from the large double bed.

Rosie, propped up against the pillows beside him, looked relaxed and serene. 'We thought we'd go to see *The Dancing Years* this afternoon, and then dine at the Café de Paris tonight.'

'Good idea. I've asked Dudley to put a bottle of champers on ice, for you to have before you go out this evening.'

'Thanks, Juliet,' Rosie said, appreciatively.

'I like the uniform, Juliet,' Charles teased. 'Thick black stockings are . . . very sexy!'

'Flat heeled lace-up shoes . . . not quite so!' Juliet quipped, pulling her uniform cape closer. 'This should be mink lined. It's brass monkey weather, and I freeze to death in this blue cotton dress and apron. I might have a word with Norman Hartnell.' And with that she made a comical face and hurried off.

'Isn't she a scream?' Charles laughed, when they heard the front door slam.

'She does manage to enjoy life. Talk about black-market, though! Granny would be so shocked.'

'With her job, I think Juliet deserves all the fun and comfort she can get.' Then he told Rosie some of the things Juliet had told him the day before.

'God, I couldn't do what she does,' Rosie admitted. She put her cup of early morning tea on the side table, and slid down in the bed again. 'I must say it's wonderful not to have to get up at seven in the morning, to see to the children. I could do with a bit more of this spoiling myself.'

Charles lay down close beside her, one of his legs straddling hers, his hand stroking her stomach. 'Last night was wonderful,' he whispered, burying his face in her neck. 'Could we do it again, d'you think?'

'Yes, of course,' Rosie said generously, thinking that when his leave ended, she might not see him again for months. She found it strange, but their love-making the previous night, after the lively dinner party Juliet had given, was the only time she'd found sex with Charles quite bearable. She was no longer repulsed by him. It helped that they'd both had a lot of wine, a convivial evening with Juliet's merry friends, no money worries, and no crying babies, either.

In retrospect, she realized, it had been almost enjoyable. Not wild and thrilling, of course, as it was with Freddie, when she cried out with ecstasy, but quietly satisfying in a spiritual way; and affectionate and reassuring too.

Perhaps, after all, she thought, as he started to make love to her again, we can make a go of our marriage. For the sake of the children. For our own sakes, too. It warmed her to think it might be possible. It would avoid all the unpleasantness of a divorce, not to mention the scandal.

She began responding to his kisses, stroking his hair as she did so.

'I love you . . .' she heard him say amid the commotion of consumation.

She held him in her arms, accepting him as her husband. 'I love you, too . . .' she whispered, and it was almost true.

They made a strikingly attractive couple as they set off for the Café de Paris that evening. Rosie wore a romantic-looking red velvet evening dress, which had been a part of her trousseau, with her pearls and white fox furs, and Charles, elegant in his uniform, looked dashing and virile for the first time in his life.

'I can't believe it!' Rosie exclaimed, as their taxi shuddered down Park Lane, on their way to Leicester Square.

'What can't you believe?'

She pointed to the throngs of débutantes in white ball-gowns, and men in uniform or white tie and tails, entering Grosvenor House.

'It's Queen Charlotte's Ball. I never thought they'd hold it, in the middle of the Blitz. I read somewhere that a thousand people are attending.'

Charles peered out of the taxi window. 'Amazing! You wouldn't think there was a war on, at all, would you?'

'Juliet says she's never played so hard; not even when we Came-Out.'

'It does show that the British refuse to be bowed by Hitler, doesn't it?'

Rosie pulled her furs closer. 'In spite of everything I've got a feeling that everything's going to be all right.'

Charles looked at her, wondering if she was referring to Britain winning the war. Or their future as a married couple?

The air-raid siren sounded just as they reached the Café de Paris.

'How lucky it's underground,' Rosie observed, as they left their coats and walked down the curving staircase, into the restaurant.

They were shown to a table near the dance floor. The famous bandleader, 'Snake Hips' Johnson, was conducting a lively rendition of Cole Porter's hit song, *Just One Of Those Things.*'

'. . . just one of those crazy flings,' Rosie sang along softly.

The place was packed. She waved to a couple of people she knew. Charles grabbed her hand. His eyes were sparkling.

'This is great, Rosie. The best birthday I've ever had.'

'And it's not over yet . . . by a long chalk!' she said, smiling gaily, her eyes flirtatious. The champagne at Juliet's house had given her an extrordinary lift, making her feel anything was possible.

When they were seated, she took a tiny leather case out of her evening bag and laid it before him on the table. 'Happy Birthday.'

His eyes widened. 'Rosie . . .! I thought the pyjamas you gave me, which probably cost you most of your clothing coupons, were my present?'

She remained silent, smiling with pleasure.

Charles opened the case, revealing a pair of mother-of-pearl and platinum cuff-links. 'Oh, they're beautiful,' he exclaimed in delight. 'Thank you, darling. They may not go with my uniform, but I'm going to wear them tonight!'

When he returned from the cloakroom a few minutes later, he was wearing them with touching pride. He leaned forward to kiss her on the lips.

'I love them. Thanks awfully, Rosie.'

Later, as they danced, she was reminded of the summer of '35. She and Charles had danced like this night after night. She'd thought she was in love then. She'd been so young and naïve, and innocent. Charles had seemed like a knight in shining armour, and she'd felt so excited when he'd taken an interest in her.

Rosie wanted to recapture that feeling of youthful excitement now. To roll back the years to when she'd been a tremulous débutante, and her future had lain before her like a white vista of sparkling virgin snow, untrodden by human feet.

She pressed herself closer to Charles and his grip tightened, as they danced cheek to cheek.

Suddenly something was terribly wrong. The air seemed to shimmer and tremble. There was a blinding flash. Then with a surge of terrifying velocity, a great weight was crushing them, roaring like an avalanche, pressing them down, down, tearing them apart. She lost her grip on Charles It was dark. The music had stopped. Gritty dust swirled around, choking her, clogging her lungs, blinding her. A moment later the sound of hideous screaming rent the air.

It was nearly ten o'clock. Juliet and Laura were making cups of cocoa in the rest room of the First Aid Post. So far it had been a quiet evening.

'Maybe Jerry's taken the night off,' Laura observed hopefully.

Juliet suddenly stood quite still. She looked at the regulation fob watch, pinned to the bib of her apron. The hands stood at nine fifty-five p.m.

'What's the matter?' Laura asked.

Juliet didn't answer. It was as if she were listening for something.

A moment later a loud bell rang from the Commandant's office.

Miss Stafford's loud voice called out. 'Number One Unit! Out now! Leicester Square. The Café de Paris has had a direct hit.'

For a moment Juliet sagged, her face blanching. 'Oh, God, I knew it,' she gasped. 'Oh, Christ!' She grabbed her cape and tin hat and was running as fast as she could to the ambulance, where Dr Gearing was already on board. Laura and the other nurses followed. Sixty seconds later, they were off, careering up the steep ramp, their bell ringing with a deafening peel.

There was little traffic about and they shot along Knightsbridge to Hyde Park Corner, then on to Piccadilly, round the Circus, and down Coventry Street. Once in Leicester

Square they drew to a halt with a squeal of brakes and looked with horror at what had happened.

Where there had once been a building with a smart street level entrance to the Café de Paris, there was now a mound of rubble, dust rising from it like yellow steam.

Light and heavy rescue squads, with cutting and lifting tackle, were already at the scene, assessing the damage with one of the council architects, before they dare lift a beam or move any of the débris. More ambulances and fire crews were arriving, while the civil defence workers were cordoning off the area and setting up a Incident Enquiry Point. Amid the confusion and sense of urgency, German planes still droned menacingly low overhead, and every few moments there was an earth shuddering CRUMP as more explosives fell.

'There won't be many casualties,' Juliet overheard a policeman observe. 'The ruddy bomb went straight through the building and exploded in the restaurant.'

'Stand by,' Dr Gearing was told, by a member of the ARP. 'I don't know when we'll be able to get in, under that lot. A wrong move and the whole thing could collapse on top of us.'

Dr Gearing nodded. 'I'm worried in case there are any survivors who need immediate attention.' He turned to Juliet and the others. 'There's nothing you can do at the moment. Wait in the ambulance. There's no point in you standing around getting cold.'

A sharp east wind swept across Leicester Square at that moment and Juliet remembered it as it had once been, brightly lit and filled with couples in evening dress, drifting out of the Four Hundred at dawn, the sound of their carefree laughter floating on the air.

Now it was pitch dark and forbidding, with Civil Defence workers shouting instructions against a background of exploding bombs as they worked with frenzied activity to get to the trapped victims. Those days of revelry seemed to belong to another age, Juliet reflected, as she watched, stiff with anxiety.

'Quiet everyone!' a voice suddenly shouted.

In the deathly silence that followed everyone strained to listen intently for any sounds coming from under the rubble, but all Juliet could hear was the pounding of her heart. She gritted her teeth, forcing the panic to subside. Why, on God's earth, had she suggested Rosie and Charles go to the Café de Paris?

Then they heard a faint tapping, distant, muffled, buried deep.

'Keep going!' yelled the voice. The clamouring activity started again, like a thunderous wave crashing on to rocks.

'Over here!' Someone else shouted 'I can hear a faint cry.'

'Is where a back entrance?'

'Go round and bloody *look*!' screamed someone else.

Nerves were jangled, tempers fraught. Anxiety held everyone in its agonizing grip. The rubble looked unstable and shaky. A dozen men would be killed if it collapsed now. And time was of the essence. Every second counted if there were casualties with severe injuries.

Juliet watched, feeling helpless, as the men scrabbled feverishly to remove bricks, mortar, roof tiles, doors, window frames and heavy beams under the supervision of the architect, amid the swirling, choking dust that was settling on them, so they began to look like ghostly figures. She started pacing to and fro, gripped by frustration. To hope that Rosie was still alive was to court inconsolable grief, but she was desperate to *do* something, desperate to know the worst.

'Are you all right?' Laura asked worriedly. Juliet was usually the calm one at these incidents; tonight she seemed demented by apprehenson and nerves.

'How long are they going to *take* to get to the people, for Christ's sake?' Juliet retorted, wildly and abrasively.

Laura shrank back, shocked. 'I don't know. Sometimes it can take ages.'

'But we haven't *got* ages,' Juliet raged. She drew a dry sobbing breath, and strode over to the head of the Civil Defense team. 'Is there no way we can get in there? I'm quite thin. I've climbed through small gaps before to get inside a building.'

'And bring the whole lot down on the rest of us?' he jeered.

Dr Gearing came up to them. 'Is there a problem?'

Juliet spun on him her eyes were flashing dangerously.

'Yes. There *is* a problem,' she retorted fiercely. 'My sister and her husband are under that lot, and I've got to get to them. They may be . . .'

'I'm sorry. I didn't know,' Dr Gearing said swiftly.

At that moment a heavy beam was being expertly lifted,

exposing part of the doorway leading to the stairs down to the basement restaurant.

'We might be able to get in now,' he said hopefully.

Juliet pressed her hand to her mouth, struggling with her emotions.

It seemed an eternity before they were told a gap down one side of the curving stairway was clear enough for a First Aid unit to clamber down. A fireman led the way with a torch. followed by Dr Gearing. Clutching her case of emergency equipment, and crouching low, Juliet stepped forward gingerly, clinging to lumps of brick and plaster to steady herself. In the pitch dark, and choking from the dust that hung in the air like a veil, she followed the beam of light, until they were in what remained of the restaurant. Then she looked around, frozen with horror.

The balcony where people had been drinking as they watched others dancing below, had collapsed, instantly killing all those who were seated downstairs, having dinner.

'This way,' Dr Gearing said, shuffling cautiously forward.

Amid the débris, dead bodies were strewn, some half hidden. There were also body parts scattered about; a man's arm still in a sleeve, a woman's foot in a silver kid high-heeled shoe. Broken glass scrunched under their feet as they stumbled, fearful of standing on a face, or a hand, or a torso.

The girl who had cried out was miraculously unhurt except for a broken arm and some minor cuts because she'd been in the cloakroom when the bomb had fallen. Laura guided her out to the street to receive attention.

Juliet looked around wildly, finding it hard to breath. She noticed a man, lying crumpled on his side, bleeding heavily from a head wound. Another man was trying to get up, but one of his legs was trapped under some masonry.

Dr Gearing moved forward to attend to the first man while one of the rescue squad said, 'Wait there, mate,' to the second man, 'we'll get you out in a mo.'

'Where are you . . . ?' Juliet heard a woman scream. She was scrambling wildly towards them from behind a cascade of brickwork and plaster, stepping and tripping over the bodies, her clothes torn off her body, her arms and legs cut, and her face scarlet with blood. 'I can't find my husband,' she moaned, brokenly.

Juliet started with a mixture of horror and relief. '*Rosie!*' she shouted above the din.

Rosie fell into her arms, almost bringing her to the ground. 'I can't find Charles . . . we were dancing, Oh, God! Where is he?' she sobbed. She was turning her head this way and that, trying to see through the blood and mortar dust that covered her face.

Without answering, Juliet put her arm around Rosie's waist, and led her forcibly up the half shattered staircase, out through the narrow gap and into the cold night air.

'Come along, Rosie. Let's get you cleaned up,' she said, amazed by the professionalism of her tone.

But Rosie swung away from her, clawing at the rubble, trying to go back into the ruins. 'I can't leave Charles,' she screamed, hysterically. 'I've got to find him. I've got to go back and find him.'

Juliet hung on to her tightly. 'The others will do that. They'll bring him out,' she said, knowing it was probably a lie.

Once in the ambulance, Juliet saw that Rosie had a deep gash on her head, from which the blood was flowing down her face and running in rivulets down her body.

The doctor examined her scalp. 'No sign of broken glass,' he said. 'See she has a compress on the wound, and then bandaged tightly. We'll get her to casualty in a few minutes.'

'We will?' Juliet questioned in a whisper, following him out of the ambulance while Laura saw to Rosie's injuries.

Gearing nodded. 'I'm just going to check but I don't think there are many more survivors.'

Juliet hurried over to the team who were already carrying bodies to the mortuary van.

'My brother-in-law was in there,' she told him. 'He'd be in Guards uniform and his name is Padmore. Which mortuary are they taking them all to?'

'Wherever we can get them in,' he replied grimly. 'There's been a lot killed tonight, and not only at this incident.'

She nodded, sick at her understanding of what he'd said, and then hurried back to the ambulance, which was ready to leave for St George's hospital.

'Don't leave me, Juliet,' Rosie wept. She lay in one of the cubicles.

'Rosie, I'm still on duty. I may have to go out again, tonight. I'll telephone Daddy as soon as I get back to the Post, and he'll come to you. I have to go now, darling.'

'Will they bring Charles here, too? How shall I find him?'

'Don't worry. I'll leave all his details at the desk. Now, you stay here to get your head seen to, and as soon as I come off duty in the morning, I'll come straight here, and take you back to Park Lane with me.'

'Will Charles be there?' Rosie pleaded.

'I don't know, Rosie. Try not to worry. Now I must get back to the ambulance. I'll see you later.'

'Dads?' It was long after midnight, but Henry answered the phone immediately.

'Juliet, darling! I was just having a nightcap with Ian, before we turn in for the night.' He sounded relaxed and delighted to hear her voice.

'Dads, I've got some bad news. Rosie and Charles were celebrating his birthday at the Café de Paris tonight, and it got a direct hit. Rosie is hurt, but she'll be all right, but I think Charles may have bought it.'

'Oh, no.' Henry sounded deeply shocked. 'That's terrible. Where is Rosie?'

Juliet told him. 'If you could go to her. She's in a terrible state.'

'Is Charles definitely dead?'

'It's always possible he's still alive and severely injured, but I don't think so . . .' she paused, and took a deep breath. 'It was carnage, Dads. Total carnage.'

'Dear God.' Henry groaned. 'You shouldn't be doing this job, Juliet. A young woman like you.'

'Someone has to,' she said drily. 'I've got to go now. I think we're about to be called out again.'

Henry strode into the entrance of St George's Hospital. A scene of chaos met his gaze as his eyes swept around the rows of casualties waiting to be seen. Some were crying; others sat white-faced, in deep shock.

'I'm looking for my daughter, Rosie Padmore,' he told one of the harassed nurses at the reception desk. 'She was brought in from the Café de Paris, a short while ago.'

'You'll find her through there.' She pointed to a doorway, without looking up.

Henry walked into the next section. Through gaps in the green-curtained cubicles he saw people lying on beds; some looked half dead, others were covered in blood, most were moaning in pain, at the sheer misery of what had happened to them.

A stressed-looking nurse barged past him, a handful of bloodied bandages in her hands.

'Excuse me,' Henry said politely, 'I'm looking for my daughter, Rosie Padmore.'

The nurse looked at him for a moment. He noticed her eyes had a blank expression, as if she were determined to deny the bloodbath and suffering that lay behind the curtains.

'I think she's in the end cubicle,' she said, her voice expressionless.

Henry found Rosie lying quite still, her eyes shut and her face caked with drying blood. Her head was still roughly bandaged. The blanket she'd been wrapped in had fallen open, revealing her battered body and ripped clothes. She was covered in plaster dust and gore.

'Rosie, darling?' he whispered gently.

Her eyes flew open, bloodshot and startled. 'Daddy!' She started to cry, great wrenching sobs. 'Have they found Charles yet? Is he here? We were dancing . . .' Her hand, scraped and bruised, covered her mouth, to suppress the sounds.

Henry took her other hand. 'I'll find out as soon as I can, sweetheart. It's always chaos after a bomb's fallen. People get scattered, taken to different hospitals. Try not to worry. Have you seen a doctor yet?'

She shook her head. 'I hurt all over, Daddy.'

'I'm sure you do. You've been through a terrible ordeal. I'll stay with you until the doctor comes. Perhaps I can take you home to Hartley, when they've patched you up,' he added hopefully.

She spoke with panic. 'I can't go until I know Charles is all right,' she said.

'Of course you can't, darling. Now rest. There's nothing to be done until they've seen to your injuries.'

Rosie refused to leave London. As soon as she'd been treated she insisted that Juliet and Henry take her back to Park Lane.

'How can I leave when we don't know what's happened to Charles?' she demanded.

Juliet, coming off duty, helped Rosie into a hot bath, filling the tub way beyond the regulation six inches deep and only once a week, as the government had stipulated. Her skin was ingrained with dirt and blood, and under her bandages, a section of her hair had been cut off and her scalp shaved.

'Charles may still be trapped under the rubble,' Rosie opined hopefully, rubbing the pre-war bar of luxurious soap into her arms.

Juliet said nothing. She'd heard seventy-nine bodies, including 'Snake Hips' Johnson, had so far been recovered; and many of those, because of their injuries, were going to be difficult to identify.

'Would you like me to ask Dudley to prepare another bedroom in the house, for you?' Juliet asked perceptively. 'You might not want to . . .'

'No.' Rosie sounded decisive. 'I'll stay in the same room.'

'Mummy's on her way. She can stay here for a couple of days. Then you can go back to Hartley together.'

'Only if they've found Charles!' There was a note of hysteria in her voice. 'I'm not going back to the country without him.'

'That's all right,' Juliet said soothingly. 'You can stay as long as you like. Dudley will adore to have someone else to fuss over.'

Exhausted, Juliet went to her own room as soon as Rosie was settled, and, stripping off her filthy and bloodstained uniform, had a bath and crawled into bed herself. She'd been on the go, under the most terrible strain, for the past twenty-four hours. Within moments she'd fallen into a deep but troubled sleep.

At six o'clock that evening, a tall burly policeman arrived, asking to see Lady Padmore.

'Come in and wait here, please,' Dudley said. The policeman crossed the threshold, looking as out of place in the elegant hall, as if he'd walked on to the set of a Noël Coward play.

Dudley hurried up the stairs. In the drawing room Rosie was lying on the sofa, with Liza and Juliet sitting nearby.

'What is it, Dudley?' Juliet asked, but she'd guessed the reason the moment she'd heard the ring of the front door bell.

117

'It's for Lady Padmore, Your Grace. It's a policeman.'

Liza have a little shriek. Rosie sat upright, her face a painful mixture of hope and fear.

'Have they found my husband?' she whispered. Dudley didn't answer.

Juliet rose, as if bracing herself for bad news. 'Send him up, please, Dudley,' she said, authoritatively.

With his helmet held in the crook of his arm, the policeman entered the room awkardly. His tired eyes scanned the three fashionably dressed women will ill-supressed anxiety.

'Which of you ladies is Lady Padmore, please?'

'I a-am,' Rosie croaked, getting to her feet.

He breathed heavily, and held forth a small Cellophane envelope. 'Would you be able to tell me if this belonged to your husband, Lady Padmore?'

Rosie looked at a single mother-of-pearl and platinum cuff-link, as if it might jump out of his hand and sting her. She recoiled violently, and drew a deep jagged breath. 'I gave them to my husband for his birthday. Yesterday. Where's the other one?'

The policeman swallowed, but did not speak. Juliet guessed this one cuff-link was probably all they had with which to identify Charles.

Rosie's legs buckled and she gave a low moan, like an animal in pain, as she, too, realized the significance of only one cuff-link. Between them, Juliet and the policemen caught her, and half carried her to the sofa.

'Does that mean . . . ?' Liza asked stupidly.

Juliet silenced her with a fierce look. 'Thank you, Constable,' she said. 'Let's go downstairs.' She led the way from the drawing room, down to the dining room on the ground floor. There were things that had to be said, but not in front of Rosie.

'Captain Padmore was my brother-in-law,' she began. 'I was a nurse on one of the ambulance at the Café de Paris last night. You'd better give me all the details, because I don't think my sister is up to it.'

Consulting his notebook, he told her all he could. Charles's remains, such as they were, had been taken to Mortlake Cemetery, along with the bodies of the other eighty-two people who had, it was now confirmed, been killed.

When he'd gone, Juliet remained in the dining room for a

few minutes, wanting to be alone; assessing what had to be done.

Charles's regiment would have to be informed, his mother and sister told, and his death registered. Announcements would have to be put made in *The Times* and *Telegraph*. Then there'd be the funeral to arrange.

Dudley slipped quietly into the dining room, and placed a glass of brandy at her elbow.

'Your Grace, I've already taken the liberty of taking up some brandy to the drawing room,' he said. 'Is there anything else I can do?'

Juliet shook her head. 'No thanks. I'll need you to look after my sister and mother tomorrow, because I'm back on duty in the morning.'

'Yes, Your Grace. May I offer my most sincere condolences to Lady Padmore and yourself, Your Grace.'

'Thank you, Dudley.'

It was two o'clock in the morning, and Rosie was still talking. Unable to sleep, she was wound up like a clockwork doll as she sat on the edge of Juliet's bed, able to speak more freely to her sister than their mother.

'. . . The strange thing is, we were so *happy* during the last two days,' she rambled on, 'I think we'd come to a sort of understanding. We realized we *could* make our marriage work. I suddenly wanted that so much, Juliet. And even though I've been having an affair, I really wanted to create a proper home, with Charles and the children, after the war.'

'Will your lover be able to comfort you?' Juliet asked curiously.

'I never want to see him again,' Rosie replied decisively. 'It would be disloyal to Charles, now, much more than it was when he was alive. Charles had really changed, hadn't he?'

Juliet nodded.

'I couldn't believe how much he'd changed. I suppose Army life and all that discipline suited him. Anyway, I think we'd both, sort of, *grown up*, you know? He seemed more mature.' She paused for a moment, her brow puckering. 'What a good father he'd have made, too, wouldn't he?'

The weight of longed-for sleep pressed down on Juliet's head and eyelids, as if she'd been drugged, making her feel like screaming: stop talking! But she nodded again in silent agreement, propping herself up on her elbow, to try and stay awake.

'. . . We made love the previous night,' Rosie continued, almost dreamily. 'For the first time I really enjoyed it. I was no longer repulsed by him. He asked if we could do it again in the morning, and I said yes. I knew he was longing to, and we'd no idea when we'd see each other again . . .' her voice faltered, and she stopped talking for a moment. Then she said in a small voice. 'I almost felt love for him, that second time. He said he loved me, and . . . I'm so glad now I told him that I loved him, too.' She turned to Juliet, tears overflowing again. 'What am I going to do without him?' And she covered her face with her hands, sobbing piteously.

It's strange, Juliet reflected, closing her eyes, how death beatifies a person. The newly deceased instantly become heroic; pronounced as good and kind, remembered for their love and loyalty, praised for their unselfishness and awarded almost iconic standing.

Rosie had loathed Charles before the war. Couldn't wait to get away from him. Hadn't a good word to say about him. Seriously thought of divorcing him, and even had an affair with another man.

Then Charles comes home on leave, looks good in his uniform, and after a few days of having fun together, he's killed. And suddenly he's a saint.

Juliet's last thought as sleep finally overtook her was: how much more noble and dignified it would have looked if Charles had died on the battlefield, instead of on the dance floor of a popular restaurant.

The next day Rosie's sense of shock had faded, and reality had kicked in with a vengeance. While Liza fluttered uselessly, weeping as she watched her eldest daughter being torn apart with grief and guilt, it was Dudley who called the doctor.

Rosie was ordered to stay in bed for a couple of days, and the doctor prescribed bromide, to be taken every three hours.

'For how long?' Liza asked. She feared drugs in any form, but had herself taken to knocking back large amounts of gin, to alleviate what grief she felt for her late and unsatisfactory son-in-law.

'For as long as she needs it,' the doctor said firmly. 'Take her back to the country by the end of the week; see she gets lots of rest. Remember, she's been through the ordeal of being injured, as well as losing her husband.'

It was several weeks after the funeral, and Rosie, a scarf hiding where her hair had been shorn, walked slowly through the village to Speedwell Cottage.

When she'd first returned to Hartley, Freddie had tried to talk to her on the phone, and when told she was unavailable had written to her, expressing sympathy over Charles's death. The letter was laced with phrases like, 'I long to show you how much I love you,' and, 'You can count on me to look after you in future.'

This was the first time Rosie had felt strong enough to go and see Freddie, face to face. She wanted to tell him she couldn't see him again. He'd try and persuade her, of course. Be deeply disappointed and hate the rejection; beg her to reconsider when she felt better.

Only Rosie didn't think she'd ever get over Charles's death. Every time she looked into the sweet little faces of Sophia and Jonathan, she saw their likeness to Charles. And she felt wrenched with pity that they would have to grow up without a father.

When she pushed open the front gate, she noticed Speedwell Cottage had a closed look, as if there was no one there. Perhaps Freddie had gone out, now he had his false leg and could walk with crutches.

Rosie walked up the narrow path with its over-blown borders of lavender and put her key in the lock. As soon as she stepped into the tiny hall, she knew the house was not only empty, but had the cold air of desertion; Freddie was long gone, she thought, shocked.

Two envelopes addressed to her were on the mantelpiece.

One was a note from the farmer's wife who came to clean: 'Not wanting to bother you, My Lady, but I'm owed fifteen shillings for the last two months, for cleaning and laundry . . . at your convenience . . .'

The other one was from Freddie. Rosie sat in the bleak little room, scene of her unhappy marriage, and read his note several times, stunned with disbelief.

Darling Rosie,

I've done my best to get in touch with you, but you never replied to my letters. I am sorry about Charlie, but you were never happy with him, were you?

To my surprise, a girl I was engaged to, who is in the WRENS, has been unexpectedly sent back to England on leave, from Malta! to cut the proverbial long story short . . . ! – I've left for London, where we're getting married by Special Licence, on Friday! Imagine me? A married man!! Happy days, and take care of yourself.

Love,

Freddie

The bastard . . . ! Rosie thought as silent tears rolled down her cheeks. She'd betrayed Charles for an utter rotter, who had, in turn, betrayed her. The insensitivity of the letter stung her to the core. This made what she'd done doubly bad.

She hurried back to Hartley, wondering how she could have been so wicked. And stupid. Once back at home, she rushed to her room to take a large dose of bromide. It was amazing how it softened everything, like a soft-focus photograph, blurring the edges, making the world a warmer, rosier, almost bearable place. She held up the bottle of brown liquid to see how much was left. What ever happened, she must get another prescription from Dr Musgrove.

Five

Louise couldn't sleep. In her room on the top floor of Hartley Hall, she wriggled around, consumed by thoughts of Jack.

It was spring and an owl was hooting eerily in the woods, as if he too wanted something. But what, exactly? Louise felt confused and uncomfortable with her body these days. Her burgeoning sexuality was like a heavy burden, making her ache with a strange longing.

Jack had kissed her a few days ago, a quick kiss, his full-lipped mouth brushing hers, taking her breath away, and making her long for something more. And she was sure there must be something more.

Not having brothers, and being brought up in a home where nothing of an intimate nature was ever talked about, she'd taken to poring over books with pictures of sculptured figures. The trouble was, whatever it was she wanted to look at was mostly covered by a fig leaf. The figures of women bored her, but the figures of men, with muscular shoulders and thighs and flat stomachs sent the strangest sensation shooting through her own stomach . . . But *why*?

Juliet was working in London, and she couldn't in a million years ask her mother or her grandmother. Or Nanny. What about Rosie? On reflection she decided this was not a good idea. It might remind her how much she now missed Charles. It was all too embarrassing, but at the same time, dreadfully urgent.

I wonder if Jack knows? Louise thought in desperation, as she pummelled her pillow into shape, then realized she couldn't possibly ask *him*.

The next morning she was up early, pottering around with aimless activity, not knowing what to do with herself. She looked out of her window and saw that the soft buds of tender green hung like a veil over the dark branches of the trees. Spring was on its way, and her heart suddenly felt like bursting with joy. Today was Sunday. Jack had suggested they meet by the bridge, after lunch. Only he hadn't said 'lunch'. He'd said, 'After me dinner.'

Louise smiled indulgently at the memory. He was so honest and sweet, and so anxious to 'talk proper'. When she'd looked genuinely puzzled and said, 'But's that's awfully late, I'll never be allowed out then,' he'd asked her what time she had *her* dinner?

'Eight o'clock. We have lunch at one o'clock,' she giggled.

'Ta for that,' he said cheerfully. 'I'll remember next time.'

'You don't have to,' she protested, embarrassed. 'It doesn't matter in the least.'

'Does to me,' he replied.

Jack, she realized, was out to improve himself. He listened to the radio, so he was more up to date than her about current events, and every book she lent him was studied and analysed.

123

'Whatcha got there?' he asked, when she arrived at the bridge, clutching something in a brown paper bag.

Louise had sneaked a leather-bound book out of the library, struck by the likeness between the author, whose photograph formed the frontispiece, and Jack. They had the same blond wavy hair, straight nose, direct eyes and sensitive mouth.

'Poems!' he exclaimed doubtfully, when he looked at the spine. 'Cor! I don' know about that.'

'Beautiful poems,' she said firmly, too shy to tell him he resembled Rupert Brooke. 'Let's go some place where we won't be spotted; Mummy thinks I've gone to the village hall to work out the lunch rota for the Easter holidays.'

They walked along a tree lined avenue, the tall branches meeting overhead, reminding her of being in a cathedral. At the end was a five-barred gate, and the open countryside beyond.

Jack suddenly darted to a mossy bank, where primroses were already showing their pale faces. Plucking a few, he brought them back to her.

'Somethin' for your button-'ole,' he said, stopping to thread the delicate green stalks through the opening in the lapel of her jacket.

Louise blushed and grew hot at the nearness of him. She could feel his breath of her neck, and see the golden down on his cheek as he leaned forward, intent on what he was doing.

'Thanks,' she said awkwardly.

He helped her over the gate and then they looked for a place to sit.

'Over there will do, won' it?' he asked, pointing to a sheltered spot under a hawthorne tree.

'It might be a bit damp,' Louise said, and instantly felt she'd sounded like Nanny. 'But I suppose . . .' she added quickly.

'We can soon solve that.' In an instant he'd tugged off his worn jacket and laid it tenderly on the grass. 'There! That'll do you, won' it?'

Louise smiled with sheer happiness, dropping on to the ground and smiling up at him. 'But what about you?'

'I'll be fine.' He sat down beside her, close to her, and took the book from her hands. 'Let's 'ave a look at this, then.'

He opened the volume, with its gilt edged pages, at random.

124

'I like this,' he said positively, after a few minutes. ''Ere, read this one aloud.'

'You read it.'

'No. You'll do it better than me.'

Louise cleared her throat. Her face was flaming when she'd finished, and she didn't dare raise her eyes from the page.

Jack broke the agonizing silence for her. 'That's right, innit? You and me, I mean. How we feels.' He reached for her hand and held it tightly. She knew he was looking at her, and slowly she raised her head, to meet his piercing gaze.

'You . . . you look like Rupert Brooke,' she said falteringly, not knowing what else to say.

His mouth tipped up at the corners. 'An' there was I, thinkin' I looks like me.'

'I mean . . . yes. You do. It was a compliment.' Her clothes were sticking to her back with sweat, and as much as she longed for something more from him, so was she also filled with fear.

On the edge of something exquisitely dangerous, she pulled back, not wanting to offend him, but afraid of what might lie ahead.

He looked away then, a hurt and puzzled expression on his face. 'We can be friends, though, can't we?' His voice was diffident.

'Of *course!*' Louise exclaimed, tears of vexation springing to her eyes. There was nothing more in the whole world she wanted than to go on seeing Jack.

'But you ain't ready yet?' His blue gaze was directed on her again, and seeing her tears, he asked, concerned, 'Wot's the matter?'

Louise shook her head, giving a watery smile. 'Nothing's the matter. Look, let's go for a walk. It's getting chilly.'

He rose to his feet in one graceful movement. 'Can I borrow that book, or is it special?'

For a second she hesitated. It belonged to her father and she should never have taken it in the first place, but it seemed like a stepping stone between her and Jack now. Not at all certain where the steps would take her, she nevertheless knew she had to find out.

'Of course you can borrow it,' she said, with largesse.

'There's a lovely poem about the spring, and several about death.'

Jack grunted, pleased. The status quo between them had been regained and they were in comfortable waters once more.

'Where on earth have you been?' Liza demanded, when Louise returned to Hartley in the late afternoon. She was standing in the kitchen, talking to Mrs Dobbs, when Louise slipped into the house through the back door.

'I told you we were working out the lunch rotas for the holidays,' Louise replied, avoiding eye contact. 'Then we all got talking and I lost track of time.'

'I wish you wouldn't go off like that. There's such a lot to do here. We don't have masses of servants any more, you know. Daddy's invited Candida for supper tonight, so we've all got to pull our weight. We can't expect poor Mrs Dobbs and Warwick to do everything,' Liza added irritably.

'So what are *you* doing to help?' Louise snapped rudely.

'Don't be impertinent,' Liza retorted, wishing Nanny wasn't upstairs helping Rosie put the babies to bed. Both Louise and Amanda were becoming dreadfully insolent, and she simply didn't know how to control them.

'One extra person for supper can't cause that much extra work,' Louise pointed out. She'd had such a lovely afternoon with Jack, walking through the woods and across the fields, embarrassment at Rupert Brooke's apt poem temporarily forgotten as they planned to have a picnic, next Sunday, on the banks of the river. Now her mother had spoilt it all, making her feel put-out and cross. She turned pointedly to Mrs Dobbs.

'What can I do to help you, Mrs Dobbs?' she asked charmingly, whilst ignoring Liza. 'Would you like me to prepare the vegetables? Or make a pudding? I can do an Apple Charlotte, if there are any apples left in the larder?'

Mrs Dobbs, who had known Louise since she'd been born, smiled fondly at her. 'It's all done, m'dear. Warwick has laid the table, and he's even brought up the wine from the cellar.'

'If I didn't have to go to school tomorrow,' Louise said earnestly, 'I'd do the breakfast for everyone, and you could stay in bed and have a bit of a rest, Mrs Dobbs. But I can do it next weekend.'

'Aren't you a good little one,' Mrs Dobbs declared.

Liza stood watching this mutual admiration between the cook and her third daughter with frigid aloofness. Louise was actually being extremely manipulative. She'd have to talk to Henry about her. It was bad enough that Amanda was turning into a rabid socialist, without having Louise being nicer to the servants than she was to her.

Liza stalked out of the kitchen in a huff. She didn't count in her own house, and it made her feel small and superfluous.

The trouble was Henry should never have let his mother stay on when he got married. Hartley was still Lady Anne's house, looked after by *her* servants and gardener, occupied by her son and his children, loved by the whole village, and respected by the county.

Nobody likes me, I don't count here, Liza reflected, overcome with self-pity, as she stormed upstairs to her bedroom. She felt like an outsider from a different background. And the trouble was the servants knew it.

In the privacy of her room, she wept copiously. Henry was in London during the week. His mother bored her, the children despised her and the servants tolerated her. Life wasn't fun any more and she missed the gaiety of pre-war days. That evening she didn't come down for dinner, saying she had a bad headache.

'Oh, bad show!' boomed Candida, not sorry in the least. 'Hope it's nothing serious?'

'She's been over-doing it,' Henry said loyally.

They gathered in the library before dinner, to save lighting a fire in the drawing room. 'Sherry, Candida?' Henry asked.

'Dear old boy, you *know* how I detest the stuff; haven't you a drop of whisky?'

'For you . . . of course,' Henry replied. 'Water or soda?'

'Just pass the water jug over the top of the glass, Henry. Listen, I've got the most riveting piece of news to tell you.'

He looked at her with raised eyebrows, his expression quizzical. 'Sounds like a piece of scandalous gossip.'

'No, no. It's nothing like that, but this is absolutely confidential. Not a word to a living soul. I mean it.'

'Go on.' Henry's interest quickened. Since Candida had been working as one of Winston Churchill's secretaries in the War Cabinet Offices, she'd been at the heart of government, privy to everything that was going on.

127

'I'll try to be brief; if Mother, or anyone else, walks into the room, I'll have to stop. A secret organization called the Special Operations Executive has been set up, linked to Military Intelligence Research; in fact it's to do with guerrilla warfare. Code breakers from M15 will be involved, and trained people will be dropped behind the German lines, to carry out acts of espionage.'

Henry looked stunned. 'What does the regular Army think about that?'

'They're not delighted, but a British Lieutenant-Colonel is to set it up. He's recruiting people to spy on military bases, munition factories, aerodromes, and they will be given transmitters so they can radio back information to England. They'll also be blowing up bridges, disrupting transport, demolishing electrical plants; anything, in fact, that will impede the Germans. But I'm warning you; not a word.'

'You're not telling me . . . ?' he asked aghast.

Candida looked at him, and burst out laughing. 'No, I'm not going, Henry. Don't be ridiculous. I'm so heavy I'd drop to the earth like a stone, even *with* a parachute.'

'Thank God for that.'

'But I'll tell you who *has* volunteered, and who is training for his first drop, as we speak.'

'Who?' Henry asked blankly.

Candida lowered her voice. 'Gaston.'

'*Gaston?*'

'Yes. I bumped into him in Baker Street last week. When you think about it, he's perfect for the job. He's French, and of course he'll pretend he never left France. He's got a perfect alibi for being there. Nevertheless, it's extremely dangerous.' She looked grave. 'He'll be shot on the spot if the Germans pick him up. That's what happens to spies. He's a very brave man.'

'He certainly is,' Henry agreed soberly. 'God, you've quite shaken me, Candida.'

She leaned towards him, her voice very low. 'I've invited him to stay next weekend, just for a night, because I'm pretty certain he'll be off during the following week.' She looked apologetic. 'You don't mind, so you? I feel our old Dad might have been very proud of him, and I'd like him to know that – in case he never comes back.'

'Is that Gaston you're talking about?'

Henry and Candida spun round, guiltily. Lady Anne was standing in the doorway.

'I'm sorry, my dears,' she continued, 'but I couldn't help overhearing you talking about Gaston. He's staying with you for the weekend, is he?' she enquired diplomatically, taking in the guilty expressions of her son and daughter.

'Yes. That's right, Mother,' Candida said quickly, looking flustered.

'Why don't you bring him over to lunch on Sunday? I think you're right to keep an eye on him; I'm sure it's what your father would have wanted.'

Henry and Candida exchanged looks.

'Are you sure you wouldn't mind?' Candida asked.

'Not at all, my dear.'

'I know he'd be thrilled.'

Lady Anne smiled. 'Then that's settled. He is after all Papa's son and your half-brother, Henry. Don't look so anxious, my dear. Passions have cooled, mine especially. Common sense prevails. Hopefully Gaston's mother made Frederick happy for a little while and for that I'm now quite content. We must make Gaston realize how much his father would have thought of him, if he'd been alive today.'

Candida leaned towards Lady Anne and gave her a bear-hug, almost knocking her back against the cushions on the sofa. 'That's the stuff, Mother! You're a real brick! I know it will mean the world to Gaston to be accepted as one of the family.'

'What? That bastard's coming here? To the family seat?' Liza exclaimed loudly. 'That's a bit rich, isn't it?'

Henry turned on her with a pained expression. He never thought the day would come when he'd be tempted to break his early promise to be loyal to Liza, no matter what.

'Firstly,' he said, crusty as a barnacle, 'Hartley is *not* a "family seat". It's an old house, surrounded by a mere sixteen acres of land, that my great-grandfather bought, for a song, in 1876. Mother has a perfect right to invite anyone she likes to luncheon . . .'

'. . . In *our* house, then,' Liza shot back.

'. . . Anyone she wants,' Henry continued, ignoring her

protestations, 'and if she's generous enough to want to see my father's son, then it is a noble action on her part, that I, personally, applaud.'

Liza sat at her dressing-table, blinking rapidly, shocked by the vehemence of his manner.

'But what will everybody . . .' she bleated.

'*Think*?' Henry cut in roughly. 'Liza, I don't give a *damn* what anyone thinks. If Mother can accept the situation with graciousness, I fail to see what's bothering *you*.'

Tears ran down Liza's freshly rouged cheeks. 'You've changed,' she wept. 'You were never like this before the war.'

'It's times that have changed, not me.'

'No, you've changed – towards me. You used to back me up, Henry.'

'I used to let you have your own way,' he growled, frowning. 'The issues were trivial before the war, too. Do we accept Lady Diana Cooper's invitation to a party? Or do we dine with some boring couple, whose invitation we've already accepted? Hardly life or death decisions,' he added drily.

'You're so beastly these days,' Liza sobbed. 'I don't believe you love me any more.'

Henry opened his mouth to say that might well be true, but then he checked himself; there was no need to be cruel and of course he loved her; he was just losing patience with her.

'I'm going for a walk,' he said instead, walking briskly out of the bedroom and shutting the door with unusual care. No need for the whole family to know they'd been quarrelling.

It was Lady Anne who casually informed Louise, Amanda and Charlotte that a relative of their grandfather's was coming to lunch on Sunday. She would happily have told them the truth, but she considered them too young to understand, and confusion in a child's mind could be very disturbing.

Louise, of course, was careful not to give away that she already knew who Gaston was.

'You're right, Granny,' Rosie, who'd been let into the family secret, agreed. 'Is he going to be living permanently in England now?'

The next morning, Juliet telephoned to say she'd be down for the day, on Sunday.

'Juliet's such a gossip the whole of London will know

Henry has an illegitimate half-brother,' Liza moaned but not in Henry's hearing. They hadn't spoken since their quarrel.

Candida and Gaston, with Sebastian and Marina, arrived shortly before one o'clock. He'd been kitted out in a decent tweed suit and brown lace-up shoes, courtesy of Candida's late husband, and with it he wore a cream shirt and a maroon tie. Shaven and with his hair cut, he looked more like Henry than ever.

Lady Anne emerged from the house and stood on the worn stone front door steps as the car came up the drive, with Candida honking a friendly greeting on the horn.

'Welcome,' she said to Gaston, smiling as she extended her hand in greeting. 'I'm so glad to meet you, and glad you were able to come over today.'

Gaston looked taken aback and slightly scared. *'Madame,'* he said formally, bowing and shaking her hand.

'The whole family is here,' she continued, kissing Candida. 'Let's have a drink before luncheon.'

Henry was in the hall, warmly courteous and correct, anxious to do the right thing after the way he'd banished Gaston on his previous visit. 'Come and meet the rest of the family, Gaston,' he said, leading the way into the library.

Like a lioness who had gathered her cubs together, Liza sat very upright on a sofa, with Rosie, Louise, Amanda and Charlotte gathered around her. Only Juliet stood poised, one elbow resting on the mantelpiece, as she smoked a cigarette in a long holder.

Henry made hurried introductions to ease any awkwardness.

'What can I get you to drink, Gaston?' he asked. 'Sherry? Gin and French? Whisky and soda?'

'I 'ave zee *vin blanc*, if eet possible.'

'Gaston only drinks wine, the wise fellow,' Candida observed robustly, seeing Liza's sneering look.

'It's much healthier than spirits,' Lady Anne agreed.

While the older members of the family talked, Louise rose and went and stood beside Juliet.

'He looks like Daddy, doesn't he?' she whispered.

'Very much so,' Juliet agreed, grinning. 'You must be relieved it's all out in the open now.'

131

Louise gave a deep sigh. 'I can't tell you how thankful I am, and knowing that Granny doesn't seem to mind either is such a relief.'

'Never underestimate Granny. I wish Mummy was being more amenable, though.'

'It's the usual thing; she's terrified of what people think.'

Conversation was not exactly sparkling as they all tucked into Mrs Dobbs's chicken casserole. This was because Gaston's knowledge of English was very limited, and the others didn't want to talk among themselves, leaving him out in the cold.

However, Candida held forth in a mixture of both languages, seemingly carrying on several different conversations at the same time, so that in the end Gaston became increasingly relaxed, and ended up laughing and smiling.

Only Liza remained isolated, resentful that her mother-in-law and sister-in-law had taken over the role of hostess. They were making such a fuss of this French bastard, too. When the war was over and they were once more in London, his existence was going to be a total embarrassment.

Henry rose at the end of lunch, and held up his glass of wine.

'I would like to propose the health of Gaston, to welcome him into this family, and to wish him luck in the future.'

They all rose, charged glasses in hand, with the exception of Liza who rose lethargically and with a glass of water instead of wine.

Henry was the only one to notice and he glared at her accusingly. With a little shrug, as if she'd made a mistake, she put it down again and picked up her wine glass.

'To Gaston!' everyone chorused, drinking his health. He reddened and looked very moved, as he bowed his head in acknowledgement.

'We are very happy you are here today.' Lady Anne spoke with sincerity, looking him straight in the face.

Gaston raised his own glass. 'I *salute* ze family!'

Henry returned to London with Juliet that evening, Gaston having gone back to Hampshire with Candida, prior to their return to the city the next morning.

'Daddy, what's the matter with Mummy?' Juliet asked, as

they left Shere behind and she drove swiftly and surely along the main road to London.

'She's fine, darling,' Henry replied vaguely, pleased to have this quiet couple of hours with his daughter.

Juliet darted a quick look at him out of the corner of her eye. 'Dads, she's furious about something. I've never seen her so disgruntled – except when Alastair committed suicide and she blamed me.'

'I don't think she was too keen on having Gaston to lunch today.'

'What?' Juliet took her eyes off the road to look at him. 'There's a war on, for God's sake. Surely she's not still worrying about what people might think?'

'Your mother's a very loyal person,' he said carefully. 'It upsets her to think something might harm the family.'

'Why has Mummy got this terrible fixation that everything must be proper? Fuck what other people think, that's what I say.'

Henry looked shocked, 'Really, Juliet, you mustn't swear like that.'

She burst out laughing. 'Oh, come on, Dads. You do, because I've heard you. When Mummy's not around you curse and swear like a trooper.'

Henry sneaked a guilty smile. 'But you're a young lady, and it's not attractive in a woman.'

'Dads, I only swear in front of my nearest and dearest,' she said lightly, 'and right now, you're my dearest. Do you think,' she continued carefully, 'that Mummy has got a thing about her background being different to yours?'

Henry was silent for a moment. 'I think Mummy is very proud of being a Granville, and very loyal to the family; that's why she wants everything to be perfect,' he said eventually.

Juliet didn't answer, but sighed deeply.

Henry looked at her beautiful profile sympathetically. 'I'm afraid you've had a bad time, haven't you, sweetheart?'

Juliet nodded, suddenly feeling emotional.

'I'm sure you'll find the right person one day,' he continued sympathetically.

She took a deep rasping breath. 'I *did* find the right person.'

'Really?' He seemed surprised. 'And it didn't work out?'

'Mummy would be delighted by that, if she knew,' she said bitterly.

He looked puzzled for a moment. 'Was it that Jewish man who was already married?'

She nodded silently.

'But the fact that he was married must have made you realize it wouldn't work, darling?'

'I *can't* think beyond how much I love him. You've no idea, Dads. I love him with every particle of my being.' She paused, blinking back the tears. 'However, he doesn't want to have anything more to do with me.'

'My darling, I'm so dreadfully sorry. What a terrible time you've had. And losing the baby, too.'

'It was his, you know.' She was openly crying now. 'Daniel's baby, not Cameron's. But Daniel never even knew I was pregnant; I lost the only thing I had left of him . . .' She couldn't continue. Plunging her foot on to the brake, she pulled the car over and stopped by the roadside, covering her face with her hands.

Henry put his arms around her. 'My poor lamb,' he whispered. 'I can't bear to think how you've suffered. Did Cameron know it wasn't his child?'

She shook her head. 'He was so pleased . . . I couldn't take that away from him.'

'And now you're out in all these air raids, doing that dreadful job.'

Juliet rested her head on his shoulder. 'It helps take my mind off my personal problems. Seeing such terrible sights makes me realize how lucky I really am.'

He kissed the crown of her head. 'You should have told me all this before. Instead of bottling it all up. You must feel so lonely at times.'

She didn't answer. How could she tell him that during her off-duty hours, she buried her heartache in drink, the occasional line of cocaine, and sleeping with whoever she'd gone out with?

Her old demons kept reminding her that that was all she was fit for. Her nightmares had returned, taunting her about her utter worthlessness.

'I have a lot of good friends,' she said vaguely, blowing her nose on the snowy handkerchief he'd handed her. 'And Dudley spoils me to death, with his black-market goodies, including extra petrol for this car.' She sat up and gave her father a watery smile. 'Come on, Dads, let's get going or we'll never get to London.'

'Wouldn't you like me to drive?'

'No, I'm fine now. I'll drop you off at your flat on the way home.'

When she drew up outside Campden Hill Court, Henry begged her to come and have a drink.

'Just for a few minutes, darling. Ian was saying the other day that he hasn't seen you for ages.'

In the darkness he couldn't see the expression on her face.

'Thanks, Dads, but I really have to get home. I'm on duty again in the morning and I have things to do,' she said, her voice suddenly as dry as cracked ice.

'What's wrong, Juliet?'

'Nothing, really. See you very soon. 'Bye.' The car moved swiftly away, and Henry stood on the pavement, watching it disappearing into the black-out.

''Ow was your weekend?' Jack enquired, when he and Louise met at their new secret rendezvous, the sheltered grassy bank where they'd read the poems of Rupert Brooke.

'It was all right, but I was sorry to have to postpone our picnic because we had people to lunch.' Louise sat down beside him.

'I 'aven't finished the book yet. I 'ave to do a lot of 'omework when I gets back from school. I ain't got a light in my bedroom, neither. I'm going to 'ave to get a torch or somefink, so I can read in bed.'

She noticed there was golden hair on his forearms as well as his cheeks. For a moment her head swam, as she watched his strong hand pluck absently at the grass.

'I could lend you a torch,' she suggested in a small voice.

'Ta! You do a lot for me, don't you?'

Louise blushed. 'Not really.'

'I got somefink to lend *you*.' He reached into his battered old haversack, and pulled out a dog-eared paperback.

'*Crowned Love*,' she read aloud. 'It looks like a historical novel. How interesting. Thank you very much.'

'It's a marvellous book, but it ain't 'alf long. A bloke at school lent it to me, and I thought you'd like it. There's a lot about King Charles in it. Keep it under yer 'at, though. It ain't no children's book.'

'That's fine, because I'm not a child,' Louise retorted, slightly offended. 'If you can read it, so can I.'

They were still talking when the first reddish glow of the sunset sent long shadows across the grassy bank. Jack had been telling her how the war was progressing, which he'd gleaned from his avid newspaper reading.

'And it ain't good,' he summed up. 'If it wasn't for Winston, we'd all be a gonner.'

Louise sped home on feet light as thistledown, clutching Jack's book under her arm, inside her coat. To hold a book that he had held, to read the pages he had read, and to absorb the meaning of the words that he'd digested was the most intimate act she'd ever experienced with a boy.

Slipping back into Hartley without running into anyone, Louise sped up to her bedroom, and quickly stuffed the book under her knickers and vests in the chest of drawers. She'd plead a stomach ache after supper, so she could get to bed early and have a good read.

A shining new day, glittering with dew under a vividly blue sky, met Louise's gaze as she opened her curtains the next morning. She hadn't slept a wink, but she'd never felt more alive and imbued with the strange feeling she'd experienced in the past, when she'd been thinking of Jack.

And now she understood why. How could she have been so naïve . . . so *blind*! Nearly sixteen, and it had taken '*Crowned Love*' to tell her what 'making love' meant. She felt astounded. Amazed. Astonished. And terribly excited. So *that* was what happened.

'Oh, my God,' she murmured to herself several times. Was that why Jack had said, 'But you ain't ready yet,' that time he'd first held her hand? She blushed at the memory. Rosie and Juliet, she supposed, must have done it with their husbands, though she simply couldn't visualize her sisters partaking in such a thing.

If the facts themselves were delightfully surprising, nothing surprised her more than her own innocence. She was sure neither Amanda nor Charlotte had the faintest idea about the 'facts of life', either.

That thought made her feel terrifically grown-up.

It was only as she was walking home from school the next

afternoon, knowing that Jack would be waiting for her by the smithy, that she was suddenly overcome with the embarrassment of facing him. Had he lent her *Crowned Love* on purpose?

One thing was certain. The childish days of innocence had been swept away in one night, and now she was faced with the reality; wondering if she'd ever have the courage to go through with it.

Jack was standing gloomily, hands in pockets, scuffing the toe of his boot against the old cobbles. Behind him the smith was hammering on his anvil as he forged a shoe for a grey gelding that stood tethered to one side.

'Hello,' Louise called out gaily, shouting above the noise.

'Hello,' Jack replied, looking up. He was frowning and Louise looked quickly away, thinking he must be embarrassed, too.

'Had a good day?' she asked.

He fell into step beside her. 'The news is bad.'

'Is it?'

'The war's not goin' well.'

'We're going to win, though. In the end. Granny says Mr Churchill is a wonderful leader.'

They were both gazing at the ground as they walked, lost in their own thoughts.

'I wish I could join up,' Jack grumbled fretfully.

That made Louise turn to look at him, startled, a terrible sinking feeling clutching at her heart.

'Join up?' she croaked, appalled.

He nodded. 'Sooner the better. I can lie about my age, 'cos I'm tall. I wanna fly planes; Spitfires that knock Jerry out o' the sky.'

'Do you?' Louise drew out the words in anguish. Everything was going terribly wrong. She was seized with panic. Jack would go away. He'd be killed, and never come back. She'd never see him again. It would be the end of the world for her. She'd never get over it.

'They won't take you for some time yet,' she pointed out, her voice wobbly. 'By then, the war could be over.'

'Not a bloomin' chance,' he retorted fiercly. 'Wot good am I doin' 'ere?'

Privately, she had to admit that he wasn't doing any good for the war effort, stuck in Shere. But she needed him. Meeting him after school every day was all she had to look forward to. Seeing him on Sundays, at their secret rendezvous, was the highlight of the whole week.

Louise turned her face away, so he wouldn't see the tears trickling down her cheeks. How was she going to exist without Jack?

''Ere, wot's all this?' He stepped in front of her, blocking her way.

She drew a shuddering breath and stared at the ground. 'Nothing.'

''Course there's somefink wrong,' he said impatiently. 'This ain't like you, Louise.'

She sniffed and bit her lip. 'I don't want you to go to war,' she burst out, with sudden passion.

Jack's expression changed and a look of wonder filled his eyes. 'I'll be all right,' he said gently. Then he put his arm around her shoulders and she leaned against him, her face crumpling.

'Come on, now,' he chided gently. 'I'm not goin' off this minute.'

'I won't be able to bear it without you,' she confided, searching her pockets for a handkerchief. At last she found a tiny, lace-edged one, with which she dabbed her eyes and wiped her nose.

Jack watched her in silence. No one in his life had ever said anything so nice to him. On the contrary, his Dad, when he wasn't in prison, used to yell at him and hit him all the time, and his auntie had regarded his arrival on her doorstep as a burden that had been wished upon her by an interfering government.

'I'll come back on leave, an' all that,' he said to comfort her.

Louise looked up at him, her eyes red and her mouth drooping with misery. 'Promise?'

''Course I promise,' he said stoutly.

They started walking again, her feet dragging reluctantly.

'I didn't think you'd be bothered at my goin' away.'

'I'll miss you terribly.'

'Really?' They'd reached the bridge, and as if her legs couldn't carry her any further, she sank on to the stone ledge, hunched up in her brown winter coat.

'Yes, really.' Her tone was adamant. 'You know that, Jack,' she added almost accusingly.

For a moment Jack hesitated, then he sat down beside her, and reached for one of her hands. 'No one's ever bothered much about me before,' he confessed, shaking his head.

'Oh, *Jack*.' A wave of tender love swept through her, almost maternal in its intensity. Jack deserved to be loved. It was a cruel world that didn't recognize that. She squeezed his hand, then felt quite dizzy as their eyes locked.

Mesmerized, she gazed at his smooth fresh face, felt the heat of his skin, took in the curve of his young lips and the golden down on his cheeks, and felt something deep inside herself tremble in surrender. Closing her eyes, because the feeling was so strong it overwhelmed her, she felt his mouth brush hers, lightly at first, and then with the growing desire of youthful excitement.

When she opened her eyes again, she saw his were shut, as if he was concentrating intently on reaching some secret goal.

'Jack,' she breathed through her open mouth, as she put her arms around his neck, and felt him pull her close. His tongue was darting into her mouth and across her bottom lip. Oh, my God, she thought. This is how it starts.

'Dads?' Juliet lay on her silver bed with her white telephone beside her.

'Hello,' Henry answered, sounding pleased but guarded. He was at his desk in the bank, about to dictate letters to his elderly secretary; all the young ones had left some months before. 'How are you, Juliet?'

'I'm fine, but I'm afraid I've got some bad news.'

'Oh? What is it? Are you OK?'

'Yes, Dads.' She managed to keep her voice calm, because she knew her father was going to be deeply upset by what she had to tell him. 'It's Green Street. Our house had a direct hit last night. I walked round the corner when I came home from work this morning, and I'm afraid there's nothing much of the inside left. The front it still standing, you can even see fragments of the curtains hanging from the blown-out windows. There's also some furniture still perched high up on bits of remaining floor, but basically the place has been gutted. It's a heartbreaking sight.'

There was a shocked silence on the line before Henry spoke.

'I was afraid this might happen. That's why all the good stuff is stored at Hartley.' His voice was flat and weary.

'I'm so sorry, Dads darling. Thank God we'd all moved out. If there'd been anyone in the building last night, they'd never have survived. Mummy's going to be devastated, isn't she?'

'More upset than you know. The building wasn't insured, either,' he added gloomily.

Juliet sat upright in bed, 'What? Why not?' she demanded.

'Is your house insured against a direct hit?'

'Well, no, I suppose not. I think I've only got a normal policy. Oh God, I better get on to Lloyd's at once.'

'Don't waste your time, Juliet. No one is giving an insurance cover for London buildings at the moment.'

Although they'd lived in the building, which belonged to the Westminster Estate, on a long lease, this was nevertheless a great blow.

'Mummy's going to go mad,' she observed. Forty-eight Green Street represented everything Liza had ever wanted in terms of social status, fashion and desirability.

'I'll wait until the weekend to tell her,' Henry mused.

'Where will you live, Dads? After the war?'

He sighed. 'That depends on a lot of things. Don't mention this if you talk to the family, will you?'

Bidding her father good-bye, Juliet replaced the receiver.

A moment later the telephone rang. She picked it up quickly. 'Hello?'

'I'd recognize that voice if I heard it in a rain forest, on an Arctic floe, by the pyramids or in a Paris night-club,' said an attractive male voice.

Juliet burst out laughing. 'Eddie darling! How marvellous to hear from you. How are you? *Where* are you?'

'Waterloo Station,' he chuckled. 'I've got twenty-four hours leave. Can I see you?'

Juliet thought quickly. She was supposed to be lunching with Dick Henage at Le Caprice, having cocktails in the American Bar of the Savoy with Peter Osborne, and then she'd promised to dine with Gerald Knight before he returned to his ship; but on the other hand . . .

'I'm as free as a bird for the next twenty-four hours,' she said blithely 'Come around right away, if you like.'

By the time Juliet heard the front door ring, she'd cancelled all her engagements, and as Dudley opened the front door, she appeared at the top of the black carpeted silver staircase in a ivory satin negligée, trimmed with lace. Her smile was as scarlet and wicked as ever.

'Come right up, Eddie,' she said. 'Dudley, bring us some champagne, will you?'

Eddie, throwing his cap and greatcoat on to a hall chair, bounded up the stairs two at a time, to be enfolded in Juliet's welcoming embrace.

'Oh, God, darling, it's so good to see you again,' he groaned, burying his face in the white scented perfection of her neck.

Liza was waiting for Louise when she slipped through the back door.

'Where have you been?' she demanded shrilly, her face flushed with anger. 'And don't lie to me, Louise. I know you're up to something.'

Louise swallowed, determined not to panic. 'Sorry I'm late for tea, Mummy. I got talking to Janet and Elsbeth on the way home, and I'd no idea it was so late. I'll wash my hands and come for tea, right away.'

As she tried to duck into the hall cloakroom, Liza grabbed her by the arm. 'You're lying, Louise. You've been seen walking through the village with some common boy; one of those dreadful evacuees. I've said, over and over again, that you're *never* to have anything to do with them.'

'I did stop to say hello to one of the people I dish out luncheon to,' Louise admitted, lying glibly. 'We see *all* the evacuees in the holidays, and we can't be rude to them if we happen to meet them in the village.'

'You were seen by Mrs Dobbs. Just you and some boy, so don't try and lie your way out of it. Don't you realize these people are the lowest of the low?'

Louise had never seen her mother as angry as this. 'I can't be rude if someone says hello to me in the street,' Louise protested. Inside she felt chilled with fear. Her mother might try and stop her seeing Jack altogether. She might even find out where Jack lived, and go and tell *him* never to come near her again.

'Don't be impertinent,' Liza scolded. 'You are not to speak

141

to this ruffian, or any of the other scum from the East End, again. Do you understand?'

Like a whirling dervish, Amanda came streaking down the staircase at that moment, pigtails flying, and the lenses of her glasses enlarging her short-sighted eyes.

'You *cannot* talk like that, Mother,' she exploded in fury. 'It's not Christian. There's nothing wrong with the evacuees, and at least the government realizes that, if you don't. They've been sent to the country, the poor things, to prevent them being killed. When I'm an MP I'm going to make sure they have the benefits we all have. I think it's very democratic and *right* of Louise to talk to them and make them feel welcome.'

Liza's jaw dropped as she regarded her fourteen-year-old daughter with blank horror. The child was a monster. Where had she picked up all this ghastly socialistic stuff? Really, Henry would have to do something.

'Amanda's right,' Louise said, shooting her sister a grateful glance. She'd told Amanda all about Jack . . . well *almost* all, and Amanda was encouraging their friendship.

'You will both be punished for this disgraceful behaviour,' Liza said in a high-pitched voice. 'Wait until I tell your father . . .'

'Dear me, what ever's going on?'

Lady Anne came slowly down the stair, regarding them all with disapproving concern.

'The girls are being extremely rude,' Liza began defensively, but under the level stare of her mother-in-law, her spirits flagged. 'I really do think it's time they both went to boarding school, you know,' she added, turning and hurrying up the stairs, in an attempt to conceal her emotions. Tears of vexation sprang to her eyes. Louise and Amanda were beyond her control. Why, oh why, were they turning into bolshie rebels? Hadn't she expounded her belief that women should be sweet and non-confrontational? Hadn't she tried to prepare them for marriage to the right man? To be chatelaines of nice country houses? Hadn't she prepared them to take their places in Society?

Liza lay on her bed, utterly defeated. Her youth had been ruined by the Great War; now her ambitions for her girls were being ruined by this second wretched war. No one would ever know, or understand, how she missed Green Street, too. Everything was changing and not for the better.

142

Below, in the hall. Lady Anne was speaking to Louise and Amanda in a quiet but firm voice. 'There is never a need to be rude, and there's certainly never a need to shout.'

'But Mummy was saying *horrible* things about those poor evacuees,' Amanda protested pleadingly. 'She really was, Granny. Calling them all sorts of things. Louise and I *always* say hello, if we see them in the street, and some of them are really *sweet*.'

Lady Anne knew only too well what Liza thought of the influx of sad children from under-priviledged homes.

'Your mother is allowed to have her own opinion,' she said diplomatically, 'I think you'd both better go and apologize to her . . .'

Amanda looked enraged. 'Never!'

'You must, Amanda. Both of you must say you are sorry you were rude to her. And maybe, in future, you should both avoid going on about how sweet you think the evacuees are,' she added, trying to control her twitching lips. 'Political opinions are often best kept to oneself.'

Louise said nothing, but a desperate feeling of protectiveness towards Jack made her want to weep.

'But Granny,' Amanda argued, '*you* don't believe the Torys are right, do you? You think everyone should have the same opportunities in life, don't you?'

'I have three rules in life, darling, and I've always stuck to them.'

The girls looked at her hopefully.

'I never discuss politics, religion or money,' she told them firmly. 'You will get much further in life if you keep your thoughts to yourself.'

Liza knew she must assert herself, so when she came down for dinner that evening, having accepted Amanda's apology – 'Sorry I was rude to you, Mummy, but I still think we should do something to help the poor' – she commanded Louise to follow her into the library.

'In future,' she said crossly, 'you're to come straight back from school; you're to stop going for walks on your own, unless a grown-up goes with you, and if you're seen talking to some lout of a boy again, you'll be sent away to boarding school.'

Louise looked at her mother, bemused. The merry, vivacious woman of her childhood, who had looked like a fairy queen in beautiful ballgowns and glittering jewellery, always on her way out somewhere, had been replaced by a discontented shrew, whose faded prettiness was marred by inactivity.

It only took Louise a few seconds to decide on how to react to the situation tactically.

'I'm sorry, Mummy. I was only being polite, as you've always told us to be. It won't happen again, though. Do you think I should stop helping serve luncheons at the village hall?'

Wrong-footed, Liza blinked. 'Erm . . .' she hesitated. All the girls who helped do the luncheons were from local upperclass families; one was even the daughter of Sir Christopher Boyd, Conservative Member of Parliament. She didn't want Louise to lose these friends, who might be useful when the war was over.

'I think you should continue to help, Louise,' she said. 'After all, it's only at weekends and when you're on holiday and it might look strange if you dropped out now, but avoid *talking* to the evacuees.'

'Very well, Mummy.' Louise smiled primly.

For a fleeting second, Liza was reminded of Juliet when she'd been fifteen; underhand was the unfortunate word that seemed to spring to mind to describe them both.

'How did you get caught?' Amanda whispered to Louise that night, after they'd supposedly gone to bed. They were curled up on the window-seat of Louise's bedroom, the only light coming from a moon that seemed to drift behind banks of clouds from time to time.

'Mrs Dobbs.'

'The *traitor*!'

'Ssh-h-h.'

'But you're not going to stop seeing Jack, I hope?'

'Of course not, but I've got to get a message to him, to tell him what's happened.' Louise hugged her knees to her chest, and buried her face. '*Damn* Mrs Dobbs.'

'Why don't you write him a note? I can slip it to him while he's waiting for you after school. You'd better go home another way, though. Just until the dust settles.'

Louise looked up, brightening. 'Would you really? Thanks awfully. But how am I going to meet him, now?'

'Slip out of the house, when everyone's gone to bed?'

'Golly!'

'Tell him, in the note, where you want to meet him, and when.'

'I know where.' Louise's voice had a yearning note, as she thought of the grassy bank, under the hawthorne tree. 'This is like Romeo and Juliet, isn't it?' she continued, dreamily.

Amanda wasn't sure about that, but she was game for anything that cocked a snook at their mother.

Eddie cupped Juliet's face in his hands. 'I wish I could stay here for ever.' They'd stayed most of the day in bed, but now he was taking her to dine at the Berkeley. It was the last night of his leave and he was having to rejoin his regiment the next morning.

She slid her arms around his waist. 'I wish you could, too,' she whispered, pressing herself close to him. Edward was the only person who could blot out the memory of Daniel for a few hours, and she was going to miss him like hell when he returned to his unit in the morning.

Today, for the first time, she'd actually felt happy. They'd drunk champagne, licked caviar from mother-of-pearl spoons, and made love, again and again, as the sun rose over the trees in the park before sinking in a glorious blaze, tinting her silver bed ruby red.

Then they'd shared a gardenia scented bath, and she dressed in a clinging primrose yellow evening gown, with a matching ostrich feather cape.

Edward couldn't take his eyes off her. 'Let's not make it a late night, so we can go back to bed,' he murmured, gazing into the depths of her pale blue eyes, 'I have to leave so damned early in the morning.'

Juliet nodded, her scarlet mouth promising him one more night of passion.

As they enjoyed their dinner, and the small band played loud enough to muffle the sound of distant dropping bombs, Juliet refused to even think about what had happened to the Café de Paris. The Berkeley Hotel, she told herself, was a stout building, not as big as the Ritz opposite, but nevertheless high and well built. Even so, as she clung to Edward on the dance floor, she had a strange feeling of dread.

'When are you next on leave?' she asked, as they went back to their table for coffee.

He shrugged. 'God knows, darling. I'm being posted "somewhere abroad", as they say, so I don't know when I'll be home again.'

'Will you write?'

He took her hand and held it tightly. 'We should have done all this years ago,' he said regretfully.

'You weren't interested in me years ago, except as a friend,' she replied, smiling.

Edward's eyes widened. 'I must have been *mad*! I'll never forget how wonderful you looked at your Coming-Out Ball, and all those parties we went to.'

'Not to mention the ones we gate-crashed.'

He laughed. 'God, those were good times, weren't they? And we had no idea what lay ahead.' He looked serious again. 'I should have asked you to marry me then.'

Juliet looked startled. 'I wonder if I'd have accepted? It would certainly have spared me the nightmare of my marriage to Cameron,' she added thoughtfully, 'but we were different people then, weren't we? So young. Inexperienced. It was, after all, seven years ago.'

Edward took a gulp of his wine. His face was suddenly pale.

'Juliet?'

'Yes?'

'Would you say "yes" now, if I asked you to marry me? On my next leave?'

Marry Edward? she thought, taken aback by his seriousness. The idea had never occurred to her. He'd been a chum, a pal, someone to have a laugh with when she'd been seventeen. But now? Yet today, she had to admit she'd been really happy, so maybe it wasn't such a crazy idea? They got on together, he was a tender and inventive lover, and he had a sense of humour. He was nice looking, especially in uniform, they liked the same things, and perhaps . . . perhaps accepting his proposal would stop her present rackety existence. Her constant obsessive yearning for Daniel. Maybe Edward could become the focus of her love life?

146

'Do you mean it?' she asked, stunned.

'With all my heart, darling. I'm crazy for you. I should have asked you years ago; what the hell was I thinking of?' He shook his head, bemused. 'My darling one, I want to marry you more than anything in the world. When this damned war is over, we'll have such a good time. It'll be like the old days, only better. Please say you will, Juliet.'

She smiled slowly. 'I'd really love to, Eddie,' she said softly.

'You will? My God, you will?' He was almost shouting.

Juliet nodded, feeling quite light headed with the relief of knowing she now had a plan for living, a future with someone who loved her and would care for her.

He gripped her hand so hard it hurt. 'Let's get out of here and go home,' he said, flushed with happiness.

Their love-making for the rest of the night was rapturous, as if the promise of a future together gave their relationship new meaning.

'I love you ... I love you ... I love you ...' he said passionately, as the dawn came up, and it was time for him to leave.

'I love you too,' she said, holding him close for the last time.

'I want you to have this.' Edward took off his gold signet ring and put it on her finger. 'Next time let's announce our engagement properly. We might even get married if my leave is longer.'

'I hope it's soon,' she whispered. 'Write to me, Eddie. And I'll write to you and hope you get my letters.'

His last kiss, before he hurried away down the front door steps, left Juliet bereft. It had been the most marvellous and extraordinary few days. She'd found love with an old friend, of whom she previously been merely fond. Now she could feel happy and secure for the first time for ages.

Louise stole down the stairs, keeping close to the wall, groping her way until she reached the hall. Pausing, she listened intently, but there wasn't a sound. The grandfather clock chimed a quarter past midnight; Jack would be waiting for her at their meeting place.

Once through the green baize door to the kitchen area, it only took her a moment to unlock the back door, and slip into the garden.

The night was warm and starry. Hurrying along the grass verge that bordered the drive, she was out of the gates, hurrying down the lane to the bridge. A dark figure suddenly stepped from the hedgerows. She gave a little yelp of fright.

'It's only me,' Jack whispered, reaching for her hand.

Louise's heart thudded. 'I didn't expect to see you here. I thought we were meeting under the hawthorne tree.'

His arm slid round her waist with such ease she felt it might always have belonged there.

'Ta for the note,' he said, as they walked over the bridge and then turned right along a tree-lined path that led away from the village. 'I'm sorry you got grief from your Mum; she don' like me, does she?'

'Mummy doesn't like anyone who doesn't fit her picture of the perfect man,' Louise retorted.

Jack gave a soft chuckle. 'A snob, is she? Cor! No wonder she finks I ain't good enough for you.'

'And it's rubbish. Amanda and I had quite a row with her. I think Granny secretly took our side, but of course she couldn't say so. It's what someone's *like*, not where they come from, that counts,' she added robustly.

'I like your sister. Gutsy, ain't she?'

Louise spoke with pride. 'She wants to be a Member of Parliament when she grows up. She's a *dedicated* socialist.'

Jack's chuckle deepened. 'Know wot I read somewhere?'

'No. What?'

'It said: "A person who ain't a socialist when they're eighteen, ain't got no 'eart. And a person who's still a socialist when they're forty, ain't got no 'ead".'

Louise turned to look at him by the soft glow of the stars. 'I don't think I agree with that.'

'Oo cares about bloomin' politics?' He threw back his head and laughed. 'It's now that counts, 'aint it? This minute. An' meetin' you, like this.'

She felt hot and trembly. They'd arrived at the grassy bank, and Jack gently pulled her down, and then tipped her back, so they were lying side by side in the long dark grass.

'Jack . . .' she began nervously.

'It's all right,' he whispered, leaning on his elbow, and looking down into her face. 'You don' 'ave to do anyfink you don' want to.'

148

She smiled at him, trying to make out his features under the shadow of the overhanging branches. Twigs were sticking into her back, and she was sure the ground was damp, but a great wave of happiness flowed over her. For answer she reached up and put her arm around his neck. A moment later she felt his mouth on hers, kissing her deeply.

They lay for a long time like that, though it only seemed like seconds to her, and then through her jumper, she felt his hand cupping one of her breasts, and squeezing it gently.

She gave a little gasp of intense pleasure, and wriggling closer to him, became transported by the most exciting sensations she'd ever felt. She'd no idea it would be as wonderful as this, and yet they hadn't even . . .

Jack sat up slowly and carefully after a while. 'Time I got you 'ome,' he said in a throaty whisper.

Louise felt a pang of the bitterest disappointment. 'Really?'

'You don't want to get caught, sneaking back into the 'ouse, at dawn, does you?' Jumping up, he grabbed her hands, and pulled her to her feet.

'I suppose not.' Her whole body ached strangely, and she felt resentful, as if she'd been deprived of something she'd desperately wanted.

'When can we meet again?' she asked, as they walked slowly back to the bridge.

'Saturday night? 'Alf-past twelve OK?'

'Yes. If I'm late, it means not everyone's gone to bed. Daddy's home at weekends, and sometimes we have people staying.'

'Right-o.'

They walked on in silence, holding hands. On the other side of the bridge, Jack took her in his arms again, and hugged her so that they stood close together.

'Are you OK?' he asked.

She whispered, 'I'm fine,' forgiving him for leaving her so unsatisfied, but knowing she'd see him again in three days.

'Bye then.'

To her surprise, the clock in the hall chimed four as she crept stealthily up the stairs, and back into her room.

The next morning she had to surreptitiously shake her jumper out of the window, to get rid of the tell-tale twigs embedded in the wool.

'You're looking very pleased with yourself,' Rosie observed curiously, at breakfast.

Louise felt herself turning crimson. 'I can't think why,' she said haughtily. 'Except the summer holidays start soon.'

'And,' Amanda added brightly, 'there's a school trip to the local tannery this afternoon, which makes a nice change from maths.'

'Fascinating,' Rosie remarked drily, as she picked up the *Daily Express* to read the latest news on the war. Since Charles's death, she'd withdrawn into herself, and her life had narrowed down once more into looking after Sophia and Jonathan, and helping in the house and in the kitchen garden.

There were no more visits to Piltdown Court, Speedwell Cottage was a thing of the past, and she hadn't been to London for months.

'Give her time,' Lady Anne observed, when Liza fretted about Rosie 'letting herself go'.

'She should be getting out and about,' Liza pointed out. 'She's losing her looks, and have you seen her hands? All that gardening is terrible for the nails.'

Lady Anne ignored this, as she clicked away with her knitting needles. 'When Rosie's ready, she'll get into the swing of things again. Meanwhile, I think Sophia and Jonathan are greatly benefitting from being with her all the time. Especially now they have no father.'

'But Rosie's too young to be buried down here,' Liza argued. 'I'm trying to get her to go and stay with Juliet for a few days. The air raids have died down recently, and it would do her the world of good. I want to go up to town myself next week,' she added restlessly.

And that, reflected her mother-in-law, was the crux of the matter. Rosie was doing fine under the circumstances, conducting her recent widowhood with dignity while she put her children first. It was Liza who was desperate to get back to town.

'My darling one. I miss you more than words can say. I can't wait to have you in my arms again . . .'

Juliet read Edward's love letter once more, before placing it with the others he'd written, in a silver casket by her bed.

She had no idea where he was, and certain lines of the letter had been obliterated with a thick blue pencil by the Army censor, cutting out clues as to where he was stationed. But he wrote constantly of his devotion, his longing for the day they could be together again, and his plans, once the war was over, to leave the army and get a job in the city.

'. . . *We're going to have a blissful life,*' he'd written in one of his letters, '*going to all the places we've never been to, like Africa and America. I wish we hadn't wasted all those years before the War, when we could have been in Paris, or Venice, or Rome. Darling Juliet, I want to see the world with you, and everything that's in it. God knows when I'll next get leave. I think of you all the time, and long for you every night.*'

Sometimes, when she was off duty, Juliet lay in bed at night, reading and re-reading Edward's letters. Quiet nights now, except for the occasional air raid.

Morale in London was good, though not relaxed. The intensive bombing could start again at any time, and everyone continued to take precautions.

'How does this compare to the Great War?' Juliet asked her father, as they lunched in the city, near Hammerton's Bank, one summer's day.

'It was quite different then,' Henry replied thoughtfully. 'This time, civilians are in the firing line as much as the armed forces. Ian reckons nearly thirty thousand people have been killed so far.'

'How much longer do you think it will last?' she asked, realizing after the first mouthful that her tomato omlette was made from dry powdered eggs.

'Darling, I haven't the faintest. Thank God America has joined in to help us, after the terrible disaster of Pearl Harbour, and Russia is on our side, too. It's going to be a long hard slog, though.'

'Amanda's mad about anything Russian. She thinks their communist state is wonderful.'

Henry grinned at the thought of his rebellious daughter. 'If Amanda has her way when she's grown up, she'll *insist* we're all equal, even if that means becoming a communist herself!'

'Mummy must be having fits!' Juliet observed, laughing.

Something hard appeared at the back of Henry's blue eyes. 'When are you coming down for the weekend, again?' he asked abruptly.

'Soon,' she promised.

He looked at her closely. Her face was thinner, so her cheekbones were more sculpted, and her pale eyes looked larger than ever. Although she was a year younger than Rosie, Henry realized she looked much older; not in terms of age, but because experience and the terrible sights she'd seen had matured her way beyond her years.

'I hope you have someone nice in your life at the moment?' he asked gently.

'Yes, I have Daddy,' she said, looking confidingly into his face. 'Do you remember Edward Courtney? I met him years ago. He's in the Army. Somewhere overseas.' She sighed. 'We manage to get letters from each other, which is something.'

'Is it serious?'

'He asked me to marry him when he was last on leave. And I said I would. But we're not engaged or anything, so don't tell Mummy. When he returns, we'll probably announce it publicly.'

'I'm so glad, darling,' Henry said warmly. 'You deserve some happiness. My God, is that the time? I must fly. I've got meetings all afternoon. Come down to Hartley, soon, won't you?' he said wistfully. 'I miss you, you know.'

'Oh, Dads.' As they said good-bye, Juliet hugged him tightly. 'What would I do without you? I'll come down for a weekend, as soon as I can. And remember . . . not a word to anyone.'

'I promise.'

It was a promise he kept, which, looking back afterwards, he was to bitterly regret.

The moon was so brilliant, Louise was terrified they'd be seen. By now it was late July, a hot balmy month that was making her feel languorous and dreamy. She'd been able to creep out of the house on several occasions during the last few weeks to meet Jack by the bridge, before they hurried off to their secret place, where they lay on the grass in each other's arms, kissing and talking in whispers.

Tonight something was different. In the bright moonlight, Jack was staring at her, his mouth half open, his cheeks ruddy. Instead of taking her hand as he usually did, he just stood, quite still, his eyes wide, almost as if he were scared of something.

'Hello,' she said diffidently.

He went on staring at her. Then he gulped. 'I want you so much,' he blurted out suddenly.

Louise looked back at him, shocked, realizing what he meant. It was as if a dark, forbidden but terribly grown-up and exciting world was opening up before her, and she started trembling. But there was also a mysterious feeling, tugging deeply inside her, longing to be assuaged.

'Do you?' she whispered.

He nodded. 'I've wanted you for a long time. Don' you want to . . . ?'

'Oh! Yes.' Standing, looking frail and vulnerable in her little cotton frock, she reached out for his hand.

'Come on then.' He led the way in silence to their special place. Louise followed, clutching his hand, thrilled by the way he was taking control, being commanding like a grown-up. Only the back of his pale neck, visible above his shirt in the moonlight, wrenched her heart with tenderness, because it was the neck of a boy.

When they reached their secret spot, Jack knelt on the grass, pulling her down so she was kneeling opposite him and they were face to face.

'You're beautiful,' he whispered, slipping his hands around her waist. He looked feverish as if he had difficulty in breathing.

'So are you – handsome, I mean,' she murmured, quaking with fear and desire. She reached up to stroke his face, which looked strangely intense, and he turned quickly to kiss the palm of her hand.

'Have you ever . . . ?' he whispered throatily, his hands gently tracing the outline of her breasts through her cotton frock.

'No, never.'

He hung his head and spoke softly. 'Neither have I.'

Louise felt glad about that. It was going to be the first time for both of them; just like Romeo and Juliet.

Pent up passion and nervousness made Jack clumsy as he took of his shirt.

'Shall I take off my dress?' she asked shyly.

His kiss was hurried and rough. 'I want to see all of you.'

In that moment, she realized she'd see all of him.

As she lay back on the grass, the impulsiveness of Jack's

youth swept him forward, wanting her now, quickly, urgently, driving him on to seek fulfilment. At first she felt pain and was scared. He had become a stranger, not the gentle boy who just kissed her. But then she heard him groan, as if in great pain, too; 'I love you,' she whispered, and in a rip tide of feeling and a moment of blinding delight, she experienced an almost unbearable sensation of pleasure.

Jack lay panting afterwards, as if he'd run a hard race, and won. Louise felt energized, wonderful, as if she could keep on running.

'I never knew it would be like that!' she whispered with awe. 'Did you?'

His face was buried in her neck. 'Sure I didn't hurt you?'

'Only a little. At first. But not afterwards.' She moved her hips beneath him as if to recapture the moment, and almost immediately a searing, desperate need for him filled her again.

'Jack?' she whispered. 'Can we . . . ?'

As he moved once more, the feeling became stronger, there was no pain and only pleasure now, and she would have been happy to have died at that moment, as long as the sensations lasted for ever.

'What's wrong?' Peter Osborne asked, coldly.

'I just don't want to,' Juliet retorted. 'Taking me out to dinner doesn't mean you can automatically go to bed with me afterwards, you know.'

He crushed the remains of his Woodbine cigarette into the ash tray the waiter had placed on their table.

'It hasn't stopped you in the past,' he said nastily.

She drew herself upright, deeply offended. 'How dare you talk to me like that,' she exploded. Gathering up her furs and evening bag, she rose from the table.

'I didn't mean . . . !' Peter pushed his own chair back and got to his feet. 'Don't be like this, Juliet. You know I think the world of you.'

'Forget it,' she snapped. 'And don't bother seeing me home. I'd prefer to go on my own.'

He followed her across the crowded restaurant of the Savoy. People turned to watch their progress with amusement; was there anything as fascinating as a lovers' tiff?

But Juliet was serious. She'd promised to be faithful to

Edward, and that was what she was doing. If her men friends couldn't accept inviting her to wine and dine, without the expectation of having sex with her afterwards, then she wouldn't go out with them again.

'Come on, Juliet,' Peter coaxed. 'We've been good together in the past, haven't we?' As he spoke, the fumes of whisky on his breath assailed her.

'I'm not discussing this any further,' she protested angrily, hurrying to a waiting taxi.

He grabbed her arm, pulling her back. 'You know you love it. You know you want it,' he growled. 'It's too late to be playing hard-to-get with me, old girl. I know you too well.'

Juliet spun round, eyes blazing, wrenching her arm from his grip as she spoke. 'I never want to see you again,' she snarled. 'Get the hell out of my life.'

As she yanked the taxi door open, he yelled drunkenly, 'You're a cock-tease, Juliet, and goddam you.'

It took her a long time to get to sleep that night. It wasn't just Peter Osborne's behaviour that had been atrocious in the past month or so. Gerald, Hugh, John, Andrew, and all the others had turned nasty because she wouldn't sleep with them any more.

Now, in the darkness of her room, she felt deep shame as she realized she'd been behaving, when drunk and after a line of coke, like a tart.

How had it happened? Her feelings had been that as long as she didn't have to sleep alone, she'd be all right. At the beginning it had to do with blotting out the pain of losing Daniel.

The trouble was these chaps, these admirers, were no longer her friends. They despised her and were angry that she wouldn't sleep with them any more, and they were making her feel like a whore. But wasn't that what she'd always felt at heart anyway? Wasn't she really worthless? Nothing but an object of lecherous male desire?

No! No, she mustn't think like that, or the demons would come rushing back, she thought in panic.

What would Daniel think of her if he knew she'd slept around? Or had he guessed, and that was why he didn't want to have anything more to do with her?

There was no sleep for Juliet that night. She padded around her room, looking out of her window at the park, dark and silent tonight, before going down to the dining room for some brandy.

What must even Dudley think of her? she thought with sudden horror. Then with a shudder she realized how hurt and bewildered her father would be if he knew.

The next morning she phoned Henry at the bank.

'I was thinking of spending a few days at Hartley,' she told him. 'I've got some leave owed to me. Can we travel down together on Friday evening?'

'I can't think of anything nicer, darling,' he replied, his voice filled with pleasure.

Dad's so trusting, she reflected as she hung up, unable to explain to anyone why the tears were streaming down her face as if her heart would break.

'Are you all right, Louise?' Nanny asked, her eyes dark with suspicion.

Louise was sitting in the nursery, doing her homework at the small oak desk Henry had given her for her birthday when she'd been small. She looked up vaguely, as if she'd been awakened from a dream.

'I'm tired; I can't think why. I could sleep for a week.' She stretched her arms above her head, and yawned.

'You *look* tired.' Nanny frowned uneasily. Something wasn't right and she wondered whether she should say something to Mrs Granville. The girl was lethargic and had shadows under her eyes. Perhaps she was having trouble at school? Perhaps she wasn't eating enough?

Nanny's worries shot into overdrive when she was checking the contents of the bathroom store cupboard. Beside rolls of loo paper, rationed soap and tins of sticking plaster, she kept packets of Kotex. She stared long and hard at the shelf. Hardly any had been used, and now that both Louise and Amanda had started, she was required to replace the stocks every month or so. Mrs Granville wouldn't have taken any, having her own bathroom, and Lady Anne was long past needing such things.

Nanny, shrugging off the mystery, got on with the ironing, and temporarily forgot about it. Until the next morning.

She was putting on the kettle for her first cup of tea, when she heard retching sounds coming from the bathroom. Creeping into the passage, she paused by the door, which was ajar. Peering through the narrow slit between the hinges, she saw Louise on her knees, head bent over the lavatory bowl.

Everything instantly fell into place. Nanny leaned against the door lintel, weak with shock and horror, her plump hand clapped over the mouth.

Dear Mother of God! How had it happened? *When* had it happened? Louise was chaperoned every minute of the day when she wasn't at school. Nanny took her out for walks herself, although she loathed both the countryside and walking. And during the holidays, Louise was either with Lady Anne or Mrs Granville, or maybe Mrs Dobbs in the kitchen, from morning till night.

'I want to talk to you, Louise,' Nanny said harshly, when Louise emerged into the passage, looking washed out.

'Not just now, Nanny,' she pleaded. 'I've eaten something that's upset me.'

Beady eyes bore accusingly into Louise. 'I don't think that's true.' She took Louise by the shoulder and shoved her roughly onto her bedroom, and pushed her down on to the bed. Then she turned to shut the door.

'I want the truth now, mind. Have you been seeing that ruffian of a boy?'

Louise's head fell forward, and a crimson flush suffused her face.

'Answer my question, Louise.'

Her voice was barely audible. 'A few times.'

'I thought so!' There was a triumphant self-righteousness in her tone. 'You've been behaving like a filthy little slut, haven't you?'

Louise looked up at her, shocked and hurt. 'I don't know what you mean, Nanny?'

'You know what I mean all right, so don't give me that. You've been doing dirty things with that boy, haven't you? Wait until your mother hears about this.'

Louise had never seen Nanny so angry. Her face was red and ugly, and she seemed beside herself with rage and fear.

'Please don't tell Mummy,' she begged. 'There's no need to tell Mummy.' Tears plopped down her cheeks on to her cotton nightdress, and she started trembling.

Nanny spoke scornfully. 'So how do you suppose you're going to have a baby without your mother knowing about it, young lady?'

'A *baby*?' Bewilderment and disbelief flooded her face.

'Why else haven't you come on for the past two months, then? And have morning sickness, too?'

Louise seemed to shrink, subsiding into a quivering heap as she curled up on her bed, in a foetal position.

'I can't be,' she whispered, too shocked to cry. 'I didn't think . . .'

'It doesn't matter what you thought, you're pregnant. You know what that means, don't you? You're a disgrace; your whole family will be shamed by what you've done. It wouldn't surprise me if they don't kick you out, and mark my words, if they do, it'll be your own fault. You're no better than a gutter-snipe!'

'Nanny!' Louise wailed, deeply frightened now. Nanny had always been so jolly and cosy, a warm comforting figure in her life ever since she could remember. Why was she being so hateful now? She leapt to her feet and headed for the door.

'Where do you think you're going?'

'I want Rosie,' Louise sobbed. But Rosie had taken the babies for a walk and, pursued by Nanny, Louise found herself being propelled into her mother's bedroom.

'What's going on?' Liza demanded, looking up from her breakfast tray. Nanny stood over Louise, who had her hands to her face and was crying hysterically.

'Louise has something to tell you, ma'am. Go on. Tell your mother what you've gone and done.'

Louise, unable to stand, collapsed on to her knees by the side of her mother's bed, unable to speak.

Nanny continued venomously, 'She's only gone and got herself pregnant by that lout in the village.'

Liza stared, stunned, at Louise's ruffled blonde hair and shaking shoulders. Then, even to her own surprise, she turned on Nanny. 'Why didn't you keep an eye on her?' She hissed furiously, her first instinct being to make sure neither Warwick nor Mrs Dobbs overheard them.

Nanny spoke defensively; all along she'd guessed she'd be blamed, because Mrs Granville had always passed on the responsibility of looking after the girls to her, and in her heart she couldn't help feeling a tinge of guilt.

'What was I to do, ma'am?' she roared. 'Lock her in her room at night? I'm not her jailer.'

'Will you leave us, please, Nanny,' Liza asked coldly. 'I want to talk to Louise. And do not tell *anyone* about this, and that includes the rest of the staff.'

Louise waited for her mother to explode with anger, and accuse her of being bad and wicked. Instead, something much worse happened. Liza started crying.

'I'm sorry, Mummy,' Louise said in anguish, when she saw how upset her mother was.

'You're just a baby yourself,' Liza said, wiping her eyes with a tiny handkerchief. 'I can't believe this has happened to you. You're only fifteen.'

'Jack and I can get married,' she ventured tentatively. 'He's a wonderful person, Mummy. I know you'll like him when you get to know him.'

Liza didn't answer, but lay back against her pillows, feeling quite ill as she tried to take in the enormity of what had happened. Louise was ruined; that was a certainty. If she ever got married, how could she go to make her vows at the altar in a white dress, with her virginity gone and an illegitimate child somewhere in the background? It was a total calamity.

'Stay in bed today, Louise,' her mother told her. 'Don't tell *anyone* about this and I'll say you've got a touch of influenza. I've got to think about the best way to handle this.'

When Louise sped thankfully away, Liza set about making plans.

'Amanda,' Louise called out, in a stage whisper. 'I want to ask you something.'

Amanda, back from school, breezed into her sister's bedroom. 'Are you feeling better?'

'A bit, but Mummy said I was to stay in bed,' Louise replied.

'Poor you. What do you want?'

Louise signalled her to come closer. 'No one must know,' she breathed, handing Amanda a sealed envelope, 'but could you possibly give this to Jack? We were going to meet tonight . . . You know where he lives, don't you? But give it to him in person. Don't give it to his aunt, or leave it for him.'

'OK. I'll go after tea. I'll pretend I'm going to check on

the rabbits.' She stuffed the envelope in the pocket of her cotton dress.

'Don't put it there; everyone can see it.'

Amanda whipped it out, lifted up her skirt, and stuffed it into her knickers, which had elastic round the legs.

'Do you want me to bring back a message from him?' she asked eagerly. She was enjoying this. She'd pretend she was on a secret mission, taking plans to a Russian spy on behalf of Mr Churchill.

Louise shook her head vehemently. 'Just give it to him. Then come straight back.'

Henry, who arrived with Juliet from London, lowered himself on to a garden bench on the terrace, knocked sideways by the news.

'I can't believe it,' he kept saying in anguish.

Juliet, perched on the wooden arm, still in her hat and gloves, was more practical. 'Has she seen the doctor? It may be a false alarm.'

'She can't go to the local doctor,' Liza said. 'No one must find out about this. I was wondering, Juliet . . .' her voice trailed off uncertainly and she shifted uncomfortably on the bench.

'What?'

'Would you happen to know of somewhere she could go . . . to get rid of it?'

'An abortionist?' Henry exclaimed, horrified.

'Hush! Keep your voice down,' Liza scolded, glancing anxiously towards the house.

'I've heard of a couple,' Juliet replied evenly, 'but I wouldn't send a dog to them for an operation.'

'Then she'll have to be sent away somewhere, and have it adopted as soon as it's born,' Liza said resignedly.

Henry glanced at his wife in surprise. When it came to guarding the good name of the family, she was certainly ruthless.

'That boy should be horsewhipped. I'd like to get the police on to him,' he said with growing fury. 'She's only fifteen, for God's sake. He could go to prison for this.'

'He's only fifteen himself,' Liza retorted, 'and what's been done, has been done. We don't want the police involved, for God's sake. The important thing is to *contain* this disaster.'

160

'Does my mother know? Or Rosie?' Henry demanded.

'Only Nanny knows, and I've a good mind to sack her. She was beastly to Louise this morning, and very rude to me. If she stays I bet she'll start telling Mrs Dobbs, and then the whole county will know.'

'Oh, God,' Henry groaned.

'I'd definitely sack Nanny,' Juliet observed. 'It's not her business to be judgemental. Shall I take Louise back to town with me when I go? While we decide what should be done?'

'What about the air raids?'

'I have a shelter in the basement if necessary and at least I could keep an eye on her.'

'That's not a bad idea,' Liza said thoughtfully. 'It would get her away from here, before anyone suspects . . .'

'Get her away from that damned young man, that's more to the point,' Henry interjected heavily.

'I know.' Liza now found herself in the most agonizing position. She needed time to think.

Louise must be sent away and cared for by someone qualified, until after the baby was born. Liza knew someone but it could cost her her own social credibility if anyone found out they were related.

Liza had an aunt, whom she hadn't seen or spoken to for nearly thirty years. Tegan Williams was her late mother's sister, and when last heard of was living in a cottage on the outskirts of Aberystwyth. Aunty Tegan (Welsh for beautiful, which she'd certainly never been) had never married, and she'd been a district nurse until she retired a few years ago.

Although Henry knew the truth about his wife's background, or most of it, Liza had never wanted her daughters to realize that her beginnings had been so humble. Her parents had been dead for years now, so it had been easy to adopt the style and manners of the Granvilles, leaving the details of her own early life behind, lost in the mists of vagueness; however, it would all come out if they ever met Aunty Tegan.

Liza lay awake most of the night, tormented as to know what to do for the best. Her aunt was obviously the perfect choice; Wales was far away, she was a trained midwife, and she could surely be trusted to be discreet, in return for a handsome remuneration.

What kept Liza from sleeping was the thought of what her

daughters would think when they realized their mother didn't come from the same background as their father. They might despise her, and accuse her of that most despicable gaffe of all, according to Lady Anne: social climbing.

Liza whimpered into her pillow with anguish. Did she really have to relinquish her so-called social standing in order to ensure Louise was going to be looked after by a member of her own family? Wouldn't she perhaps be better placed in a convent? Where the nuns would be forgiving of her sins, and would find a nice home for the baby?

'Of course she must go to your aunt,' Henry said the next morning, when she tentatively put forward the suggestion. 'I just wish she could stay here, with all of us,' he added wretchedly.

He was heartbroken and very worried that Louise seemed to have decided, overnight, that having a baby was the most wonderful thing that had ever happened to her.

'Jack and I love each other,' she kept saying, her eyes starry, her expression radiant. Amanda had given her note to Jack, telling him she had to see him, urgently, 'tomorrow night, at the usual place'.

In a few hours now, she'd be with him, and she longed to see his expression when she told him the exciting news. Visions of a white wedding in the local church danced around in her mind.

Once married, they were going to live happily ever after, with their dear little baby, and no one could stop them now, she reflected dreamily.

Louise insisted on Lady Anne and Rosie being told. 'Why not? she demanded. 'Amanda should know, but maybe Charlotte is too young at the moment.'

Juliet backed her up. 'This is a family matter. We must all support Louise.'

'I'm so afraid of it getting out,' Liza mourned, hoarse now from whispering all day. 'You don't seem to realize what a disgrace this is. Poor woman are institutionalized, and shut away in disgrace, for being unmarried mothers.'

'That's right,' Henry agreed sadly. 'It is regarded as a terrible sin. Only the rich can arrange a cover-up. If there hadn't been a war, Louise would have been sent abroad, under the pretext of learning the language, and had the baby adopted on the Continent. And no one would have been the wiser.'

Telephone calls had been made, and a family conference had been held in the library, while Louise, Amanda and Charlotte had been ordered to help Spence in the kitchen garden.

Lady Anne had said very little, but her face had been etched with sadness, and her mouth had worked as if she'd had a problem concealing her feelings. Henry looked as if he'd aged ten years overnight as he outlined Liza's plans to send Louise to be looked after by her aunt in Wales.

'We've both spoken to Aunt Tegan, and she's very happy to have Louise to stay,' he said.

'But she'll come back here, afterwards, won't she?' asked Rosie, her face blotchy with crying. She couldn't think of anything more tragic than having to give away your baby as soon as it was been born.

'Louise will be sixteen when it's all over,' Liza observed. 'It might be better if she went straight to London to stay with Juliet when she leaves Wales, and then after her seventeenth birthday enrol in the Red Cross, or something.'

'I wouldn't want her to do what I'm doing, or see the sights I'm seeing,' Juliet said grimly.

'Oh, God,' Rosie wept. 'We should let her stay here. The baby could be brought up with Sophia and Jonathan.'

'Sooner or later it will get out that it's Louise's child,' Henry pointed out, 'and I have to agree with Mummy, hard though it is, that having an illegitimate child will ruin Louise's future.'

'When will you tell her?' Rosie asked, her voice quivering.

Liza spoke. 'Daddy and I will talk to her after tea.'

Liza, having decided to make the sacrifice of allowing her daughters to know about her background, now felt risings of anger towards Louise for causing this revelation. Things were never going to be the same, for either of them, in the future. There would always be that tinge of fear, lurking in the shadows of her mind at every social gathering they went to, that she was from common stock and that her daughter had had a bastard child.

There was the added humiliation of Nanny having to know the truth about Aunt Tegan. Already Liza thought she detected a difference in her attitude. Should she sack Nanny? No. Keep the enemy within the walls, she decided dramatically. If Nanny left, she could tell her future employers all about the Granville scandal. And anyway, who was going to do the ironing?

Oh, God, why did this have to happen, Liza fretted despairingly, as she led Louise into the library, followed by a depressed-looking Henry.

Louise looked hopefully from one parent to another; were they going to ask Jack to come and meet them? To discuss the future? He still didn't know she was expecting his baby; did they want to be the first to tell him? Adding he must marry her, as soon as they were both sixteen? Her heart thumped uncomfortably, and she felt slightly sick.

'Now,' began Liza, sitting down opposite her, her voice falsely bright and nervous, 'everything's organized, and you're going to be staying with my aunt, in Wales, until after you've had the baby. Daddy and I . . .'

'*Wales?*' Louise croaked, aghast. 'I don't understand . . .' Tears stormed her eyes, and her breath came in dry sobs.

'Darling,' Henry interjected sympathetically, 'you must understand that this boy has committed a serious offence, for which he could go to prison, for . . . for taking advantage of an underage minor. Because we want to avoid everyone knowing, for your sake, I'm not going to go to the police.'

'Daddy, we're in love, he didn't take advantage. I wanted him to . . .' her voice broke, as she covered her face with trembling hands.

'Whether you allowed this to happen or not,' Liza pointed out in a hard voice, 'you certainly can't keep this child. Aunty Tegan is a trained midwife. She will look after you and when the baby's born, she will give it away to someone who wants a child. Don't you *see*? Then you can come home again, without anyone knowing, and hopefully you can be a débutante, like your sisters, in three years time . . .'

Henry silenced her with a filthy look. 'For God's sake, stop all that nonsense, Liza, and concentrate of what's happening now.'

'Give it away—?' Louise shrieked, half rising from the sofa. 'Give it away? But I want this baby. It's Jack's and my baby, and I want to marry him. The minute we're sixteen.'

'Don't talk rubbish,' Liza said angrily. 'You'll do as you're

told. You've already brought shame on us all by your wickedness.'

Louise collapsed back into the sofa, crying hysterically. 'I
won't go! Mummy, *please* don't send me away. Jack will look
after me, I know he will. You've no idea how much we love
each other. I've got to see him . . . tell him . . .'

Henry, his own face crumpled with distress, rose and went
over to her, putting his arm around her shoulders. 'Sweetheart,
it really is for the best,' he murmured gently. 'I know how
terrible you must feel, and I'd have done anything to prevent
you having to go through this, but you're too young to get
married, and it would be a stigma you'd have to bear for the
rest of your life if you kept the baby.'

'Then Jack and I can get married when we're older,' she
protested, wiping her cheeks with the back of her hand.

'But he's an East End evacuee,' Liza protested, as if that
settled the matter. '*How* could you have got yourself into this
predicament? How many times have I impressed on you girls
that you must never let a man do anything, before your wedding
night? Decent men expect their brides to be virgins. Not unmarried mothers, for God's sake!'

At that moment the library door was flung open, and Rosie,
who'd been listening in the hall, came hurtling angrily into
the room.

'—And look where that advice got me!' she exploded. 'My
honeymoon was a nightmare. I couldn't, at that time, bear
Charles touching me! But that's all right by your book, is it,
Mummy? As long as one's a virgin bride and everyone knows
it, a lifetime of unhappiness doesn't matter?'

'You were happy with Charles – at the end,' Liza shot back.

'Yes, for a few brief hours. But I think that was because
I'd been having an affair with a man who I was attracted to.
He taught me what it was all about; something I wish I'd
known before I got married,' she added, more quietly.

There was a shocked silence, as Rosie regarded her parents
with defiance. Then she looked at Louise, curled up on the
sofa, looking like a whipped dog, cowering under her mother's
verbal onslaught.

'Darling, I'm so sorry,' Rosie whispered, hugging her. Then
she turned back to Liza, her anger spent, but not her critical
faculties. 'You've got your priorities all wrong, you know.

All you care about are appearances, conventions,' she started ticking off on her fingers, 'what other people think, with their bourgeois values . . .'

Liza sat very upright, her knees and feet pressed tightly together, her hands clasped in her lap.

'Don't speak to your mother like that,' Henry said sharply. 'She's done a wonderful job bringing you all up, and she's only ever wanted the best for you. You're being very hurtful and rude, Rosie, and I want you to apologize to Mummy, at once.'

Rosie stared at her father in surprise, then knew, by looking beyond the words and into the depths of his blue eyes, that he spoke more with a deep sense of loyalty to Liza than anything else.

'I'm sorry, I apologize, Mummy,' she said obediently, her eyes lowered. 'I shouldn't have spoken to you like that.'

Liza nodded fridgidly, knowing that Rosie had meant every taunting word she'd said.

Rosie continued, 'It's just that I'm so terribly upset that Louise is being sent away. If only she could stay here, with all of us. Surely we could bring up the baby ourselves? I wouldn't mind pretending it was mine, if it helps?'

'That's impossible, you've been a widow for five months,' Liza snapped. 'Louise has to go away to have this child, and we'll tell everyone she's gone to boarding school, and that's where they'll think she is. Your father agrees with me that this is the best way. You'll all thank me one day, you know, for protecting Louise's reputation.' She rose, and stood looking down at Louise. 'Daddy will take you up to London, tonight, and in the morning, he'll put you on a train to Aberystwyth.'

'But Jack . . . !' Louise sobbed. 'I've got to see him . . .'

'This is the best way,' her mother said firmly. 'A clean cut is less painful that long drawn-out goodbyes.'

While Rosie and Juliet help a distraught Louise do her packing, Henry walked down to the village, to face the most painful confrontation of his life.

The boy looked touchingly young and vulnerable, with his thin pale wrists sticking out from the sleeves of his shabby jacket, and his blond hair curling wildly.

What struck Henry most of all, though, was the open honest

face, the steady gaze, and the bracing of the shoulders, in an effort to appear manly.

'You must be Jack?' Henry began, when the cottage door opened.

'Yes?' The voice, questioning, hadn't broken yet.

'I'm Henry Granville, Louise's father . . .' Henry began gently.

'I know.' Jack frowned, suddenly worried. 'Is Louise OK?'

'Can we talk? In private?'

Beyone Jack was a dark passage leading to a kitchen. 'Yes. Me Aunty's gone to Guildford for the day.' He opened the front door wider.

Henry stepped over the threshold and smelled rank poverty. 'I shan't keep you long.'

'Wot's up?' Jack asked anxiously, leading the way into a small dark sitting room.

Henry seated himself on a hard wooden chair, determined to sound matter-of-fact. Jack perched on the edge of a saggy armchair, covered in worn crettone, watching him warily.

'I'm afraid it's not good news, Jack. I'm taking Louise up to London this evening, and then she's going to be staying in Wales for the foreseeable future, which means, I'm afraid, you won't be seeing her again.'

Jack blinked several times, never taking his eyes off Henry's face. Then he spoke without rancour. 'So you've found out about us? And you don't think I'm good enough for your daughter, is that it?'

Henry was finding this class business very embarrassing. 'She's too young, Jack,' he explained. 'Did you know she's only fifteen?'

Jack nodded, his expression intolerably sad. 'Same as me. But that ain't the real reason, is it, Mr Granville? I'm not posh like her. That's the trouble, ain't it? We loves each other, though. I've never met anyone like her. Lends me books, she does. Tells me about fings.' He was looking down at his feet now, in their battered lace-up workman's boots.

Henry gave a faint smile, imagining Louise, so gentle and helpful, explaining things to Jack. 'She's a good girl,' he heard himself say, impulsively.

Jack looked up, hopefully now. 'Does she 'ave to go away, Mr Granville? Suppose we promise not to see each other again?' There was a desperate plea in his tone.

'She can't have the baby here, can she?' Henry reasoned.

Jack stiffened, and his pale face turned bright red. 'Baby?' he croaked.

Oh, God, thought Henry with a pang, the poor lad doesn't know. 'Yes, Jack. We've just discovered she's pregnant. That's why she has to go away. My wife's aunt is going to look after her, and arrange for the child to be adopted when it's born,' he added, his voice trailing off, when he saw how Jack was struggling with his emotions.

The boy's hands were clenched, his shoulders hunched, and his face screwed up, as he fought back tears.

Then he rallied, lifting his chin, and spoke firmly. 'I'll stand by 'er, you know. I'll get a job, and wotever 'appens, I'll look after 'er, and the kid, too. We could get married next year, an' get a council 'ouse. They reely 'elp you if you 'ave a kid.'

'I'm terribly sorry, Jack.' Henry suddenly felt emotional himself. In all the drama of the past twenty-four hours, no one had thought that this was his grandchild who was going to be given away. 'It's for the best, old boy,' he muttered, wondering if that was true.

'Can I . . . can I say good-bye to her, before she leaves?'

'I think it would be better if you didn't. I'll explain to her that I've seen you.'

Henry couldn't remember when he'd last felt so utterly wretched. It brought back to him his own youth, and the un-requited passion he'd suffered more than once. Jack was such a decent lad. In a sensible world he'd have been proud to have had a chap like this as a son-in-law.

Henry rose to go, knowing he couldn't comfort Jack, and unable to bear the pain of watching another human being suffering like this. 'Take care of yourself,' he said gruffly, patting Jack on the shoulder. 'It's true what they say, you know. Time heals.'

Forlornly, Jack dragged himself to his feet and shuffled to open the front door. 'Fanks for comin'.' His voice was muffled.

'If there's anything I can do . . . you know, when you join up in a couple of years, and you want to get into a good regiment . . .'

'Ta.'

The door closed quietly behind Henry, as if a chapter in all their lives had ended. Then he walked slowly back to Hartley, knowing they were doing the right thing, but wishing it could all have been so different.

Juliet simmered with rage. People were dying in the air raids as fast as the armed forces were being killed in action, so why on earth couldn't her parents have been happy at the thought of a new life in the family? Instead of banishing Louise to the back of beyond, in as much disgrace as if she'd robbed a bank.

'It's all wrong, Granny,' she said to Lady Anne, heatedly. 'One would think Louise had committed a crime. She could easily have stayed with me, in London, and had the baby there. Then no one in the village need have known. I can't believe she's been shipped off to Wales, like a criminal.'

Lady Anne continued knitting without saying anything. Age and experienced had broadened her narrow moral standards, giving her a more lax attitude towards sexual emotions than her son and his wife. It was easy to be judgemental, she reflected, when one had never been faced by temptation in the first place. Dear Frederick was the only man she'd loved or ever wanted; although the reverse had not been true for him. The existence of Gaston had hurt her deeply, but she'd come to realize that Frederick's affair with the French woman had not lessened her husband's love for her, and that was what mattered.

She put down her knitting and looked sympathetically at Juliet. 'Darling, perhaps your feelings arise not so much from Louise being sent away, but from the tragic loss of your own baby. That would be quite understandable.'

'I can't help identifying with Louise,' she admitted. 'I know what it's like to lose the child that has been fathered by the one man you love, but my baby died. I didn't have a choice. I was going to love her and bring her up myself, no matter what. That choice is being taken away from Louise, and I think that's barbaric.'

'It's very hard,' Lady Anne agreed sadly, as she picked up her knitting again. 'But your parents feel the rest of her life will be ruined if she keeps this baby and in many ways I agree. She's still a child herself. The father is an uneducated boy, from a very different background. It wouldn't be fair to burden him with a child or Louise either, at his age.'

Juliet sat brooding as she gazed out of the window, her mouth drooping at the corners. Then she sighed deeply. 'I think I'll go back to London tomorrow. This is becoming an unhappy house, and I don't like it.' She rose, and leaned down to kiss her grandmother. 'You're the best thing about Hartley, Granny. Without you, I doubt if I'd want to come back again.'

'Don't say that, sweetheart.' Lady Anne caught her hand. 'You must keep coming back, because I'd miss you terribly if you didn't.'

'How was your weekend?' Ian enquired amiably when Henry got back to the flat on Monday evening. 'Want a drink?'

Henry sank exhausted into an arm chair in their cheerful little sitting room. 'It was probably the worst weekend I've ever had in my life, and yes, please, I'll have a large whisky and soda – if we've got any whisky left?'

Ian smiled and raised a bottle of Johnnie Walker triumphantly.

'How did you manage to get that?'

'Ask no questions and I'll tell no lies,' Ian quoted. 'So what happened?' He looked at Henry's grey face curiously. 'You went down with Juliet, didn't you?'

Henry nodded. 'For once, the drama had nothing to do with Juliet. Thanks.' He took the crystal tumbler from his friend, and took an appreciative sip.

Ian grinned. 'Oh, really? So, tell all.'

Ten minutes later Henry had filled him in, his voice gruff at times with suppressed emotion. 'I don't know which was worse; putting Louise on the train to Wales this morning, or seeing the absolutely naked grief on the face of the boy. I actually liked him.' He took a gulp of whisky. 'Bloody wretched business altogether.'

'How did Liza react to all this commotion?'

Henry shrugged. 'She's very upset, of course,' he replied vaguely.

'Are you all right, old boy?'

'It's this bloody war. I think it's getting us all down. There's no end in sight, either, and this has been the last straw.'

'Henry, cheer up, for God's sake! Why don't we go out for dinner? At least we wouldn't have to cook ourselves.'

'Maybe you're right.' But Henry still looked miserable. All

he could think about was Louise's face when he'd said good-
bye to her. She'd clung to him like a frightened child, weeping
copiously, begging him not to send her away.

'You're right, let's go out to eat,' he said, jumping to his
feet, 'and I don't know about you, but I intend to get very,
very drunk.'

Juliet was drowning her sorrows with a group of friends,
going to see Noël Coward's *Blythe Spirit* at the Piccadilly
Theatre, before going on to the Berkeley to dine.

'Champagne!' she said, with forced merriment, desperate
to block out the painful events of the weekend. 'Let's order
champagne before we do anything else.'

She'd collected some new friends in the past few months;
two RAF fighter pilots called Mark Taylor and Glen Fraser,
who came with their girlfriends, a naval captain, David Harris,
with his fiancée, and dear old Archie Hipwood and Colin
Armstrong, who could always be relied upon to help her paint
the town red if they were on leave.

To boost her spirits she was wearing a sexy black dress
she'd bought when she'd been married to Cameron. It had
been Daniel's favourite, too, and she knew she looked good
with diamonds sparkling in her ears and around her wrists.
Determined to put Louise's plight and the horrors of the war
out of her mind for a few hours, she proposed a toast.

'Here's to all of us!' She raised her glass.

'To all of us!' everyone chorused, laughing cheeringly.

The band started playing Cole Porter's 'You're the Tops', and
Juliet pushed back her chair and, rising, grabbed Archie's hand.

'Come on,' she commanded, swaying her hips, 'let's dance.'

Archie swept her on to the floor, his arm encircling her
waist. She seemed to float, skirt flaring out around her ankles,
her high heels skimming the polished dance floor.

'You're on good form, Juliet,' Archie remarked, his body
pressed to hers. 'Anyone special in your life these days?'

She gave an enigmatic smile, her scarlet mouth tipping up
at the corners, her eyes half shut. 'Maybe.'

'Do I know him?'

She paused for a moment before answering, wanting to
keep her secret to herself, until it was official. 'Maybe,' she
hedged, flirtatiously.

171

'I bet it's another Duke, or at least a Marquess,' he teased.

'Sez you! Come on, let's eat. I'm starving.'

Wine was ordered and dinner was served. Juliet danced with every man in the party, as if she could never stop dancing. She felt restless, feverish in her quest for distraction, almost over-excited now, as the drink went to her head. When she'd been like this as a child, Nanny had warned, 'This will end in tears.'

Back at the table after dancing a tango with Glen Fraser, she saw Colin telling Archie something. Archie looked across at her.

'Did you hear that, Juliet?' he half-shouted, above the loud music.

She leaned towards him, her cigarette in its long holder, held in the air. 'What?'

'Colin said he heard two days ago that Edward Courtney had been killed in action.'

'I'm all right, Dads. Really I am,' she protested, pale and dry-eyed, as she lay in her silver bed.

Juliet had fainted when she'd heard about Edward, and although she'd come round after a few minutes, Archie and Colin had brought her home, woken up Dudley and demanded he telephone the doctor.

The next morning Archie had phoned Henry to tell him what had happened.

'Darling, I really think you should take some sick-leave,' Henry begged, sitting by her bed. 'The job you're doing is a killer, and then to hear your boyfriend had been killed . . .'

'I just wish this bloody war would stop,' she burst out, passionately. 'So many people killed. All I can think about, dream about, talk about is war, war, war. When is it going to end, Dads?' She was crying now. 'I don't think I can bear it for much longer. And now I've lost Eddie; I was going to be so happy with him.' She scrabbled under her pillow for a handkerchief. 'This will never do. I must pull myself together. I should have gone on duty this morning, but I promised I'd go on tonight. Laura's ill, so they're one nurse short as it is.'

She blew her nose, pushed back her hair, and started getting out of bed.

'You cannot go on duty like this,' Henry implored her.

'You'll have a nervous breakdown. I'll ring your Commandant and explain. You need peace and quiet, and a complete rest, Juliet.'

She reached for her blue satin negligée, her expression determined. 'Dads, I've got to carry on. Carrying on is the one thing I'm good at. There will be people tonight who will be crying out for help, because they're in pain, terrified, and may have lost a loved one. I'm not in pain, and I'm no longer frightened of anything. And loss is something I've learned to get used to,' she added fiercely.

'You know that boy Miss Louise used to know? Well, he's done a bunk,' Mrs Dobbs remarked, as she prepared Lady Anne's breakfast tray one morning.

'Done a bunk?' Rosie stirred the children's porridge without looking up.

'Run away from his Aunty's house in the village. Couldn't stand the gossip, no doubt,' she added darkly.

Rosie ignored this. She knew people would suspect the worst, when Louise had left Hartley so suddenly.

'He hasn't gone back to his home in London, either,' Mrs Dobbs continued, undaunted.

'It's no business of ours,' Rosie spooned the porridge into two bowls decorated with pictures of Peter Rabbit.

Later that day, Rosie told her grandmother what had happened. 'You don't think he's found out where Louise is and gone to see her, do you?'

'No one but us knows where Louise is,' Lady Anne pointed out. 'Maybe he managed to join the Army by saying he's seventeen. Quite a few chaps have done that.'

'Poor Louise.'

'Have you heard from her recently?'

'Yes. Oh, Granny, she's so unhappy. Mummy's aunt is really religious, and makes her go to chapel *twice* on Sundays, and she has to read the Bible, and repent for her sins! It all sounds too Dickensian for words. She lives in a cold cramped cottage, and she makes Louise work quite hard.' Rosie shuddered at the thought of what her sister must be suffering.

Lady Anne looked grave. 'Is it really as bad as that?'

'It's bad because we've always had such a cushy time at home, haven't we? We've all been brought up in luxury, and we've taken it for granted. Even now, with rationing and every-thing, Hartley is still extremely comfortable, and we've basic-ally got everything we need here. It must be dreadful for Louise. Away from all of us, as well.'

'Perhaps she should have gone to stay somewhere else,' Lady Anne fretted, racking her brains. From what she'd heard, though, unmarried expectant mothers could be treated like criminals, wherever they went. Sometimes, their families rejected them for ever, and never let them forget their shame. At the time, staying with Liza's aunt had seemed the perfect solution, but now she wondered if it was.

'I'd better talk to your mother,' Lady Anne murmured. 'I'd no idea things were that bad.'

It wasn't only Louise she was worried about. Her heart also bled for Juliet, losing the young man she'd apparently planned to marry. The poor girl seemed doomed as far as men were concerned. Henry had said he feared Juliet was heading for a nervous breakdown.

The baby was the only person she had to talk to. Lying curled up on her side in the freezing bedroom under the eaves, Louise clasped has hands around her stomach, and talked to her baby, who now kicked and moved around, and even had hiccups.

'Precious lambkin,' she whispered, so Aunt Tegan wouldn't hear. 'You're all I've got at the moment, aren't you? I don't know where your Daddy's gone, but Rosie thinks he may have enlisted. I know he'll be wondering about you, though. And thinking of both you and me, and wishing we could all be together. I love to picture you, curled up, asleep. I bet you look like your Daddy, with blond curls and lovely blue eyes. And I want you to be born, so we can meet, and I can see you . . . but I'm dreading it too . . .' Here her tears started to fall, as they did every night, once she got to the part when she knew she had to warn the baby that she wouldn't be allowed to keep him. Then she rocked herself with grief. 'I'm going to miss you, miss you terribly,' she murmured brokenly. 'My precious baby . . .'

There were nights when she didn't sleep at all. Aunt Tegan wasn't unkind or anything, and she got enough to eat, but it was the unrelenting accusations of having sinned, having acted wickedly, of being irreligious, shameless, brazen and immoral ... that kept Louise awake. Especially as none of these words had anything to do with the love she and Jack had shared.

'Push! *Push!* Come alone, Louise,' Aunt Tegan said in her bossy it's-time-you-went-to-church voice. 'A few more pushes and you're there.'

'I c-can't,' Louise screamed. Sweat made her hair stick to her neck, and she wanted to die. The pains had been ripping through her young body for nearly thirty hours now, and her great-aunt was frazzled with impatience.

Small, plump, with curly grey hair, she bore an alarming resemblance to Liza and how she might look in another few years; the once pretty face deeply lined, the unintelligent blue eyes sunk into folds of loose flesh. There was something prim and waspish about her too, reminding Louise of her mother when she didn't get what she wanted. But Tegan was a woman with rough hands, her only jewellery a crucifix on a chain round her reddened neck, and as much fashion sense as a scarecrow.

Louise was plunged into a hell of pain again, casting everything else from her mind. 'No-o-o!' she cried out, as the pressure increased, and she felt as if she was being split in half. 'Oh, God, please ...'

'Come *on*, Louise! You're not trying hard enough.' Aunt Tegan forced her knees further apart. '*Push*, you lazy girl.'

Louise had never known such agony existed, but with that last ounce of effort to push, she was rewarded by a thin wail, and a feeling of her insides dropping out.

'At *last*, and thanks be to God,' her great-aunt said triumphantly, scooping up a mewling, bright red infant. 'You've had a boy.'

Louise opened her eyes, hardly able to believe it was over.

'Is he all right?' she asked anxiously. He looked awfully odd, with a crushed looking little face, and a slippery body.

'He's perfect,' Aunt Tegan said sternly. 'We'll soon find a home for him.'

Louise watched as she wrapped the baby in a piece of sheeting, before cutting the cord.

'Don't lie back and think it's all over,' she warned Louise, nastily.

'What do you mean?' She felt so tired she wanted to sleep for a year.

'You've still got to expel the afterbirth.'

'Oh, God . . .'

'And don't you go taking the name of the Lord God in vain, you wicked girl.'

When she was finally tucked up, and the baby was sleeping in an old wooden rocking cradle next to her bed, Louise couldn't help marvelling at what had happened. To think that the little boy had come from Jack and herself was the most extraordinary feeling. They'd made a child between them. But then the tears flowed, because Jack wasn't here beside her, as any other father would have been. And already Aunt Tegan was looking forward of 'finding a home for him', as if he'd been a kitten or a puppy.

'I don't think I can bear it,' Louise wept. She was worn out and brokenhearted. In the lonely little room in the isolated stone cottage, she cried herself to sleep.

When she awoke, Aunt Tegan was standing by the bed, and she held the squawking baby in her arms.

'Feeding time, Louise. We'll start him off on you. He'll have to go on to the bottle soon enough, but it'll give him a good start.' She dumped the baby unceremoniously in to Louise's arms, before stomping downstairs again.

Louise hadn't been prepared for this. Wasn't sure exactly what to do, but once the baby was in her arms, he nuzzled his way with determination, tiny arms flailing, rosebud mouth opening and shutting like a bird, until he latched on to her nipple with the instinct of all newborn creatures.

Louise was transported with delight and contentment. He was so sweet. So adorable, nestling close to her as if that was where he belonged. She noticed now he had soft fair hair; just like Jack. The nails on his tiny fingers were like a film of mother-of-pearl, and his skin was unbelievably soft and silky. After a few minutes he stopped sucking, opened his eyes and looked up at her.

For a strange, almost frightening moment, it seemed as if he knew her. There was recognition in his expression, and she held her breath, holding his gaze, almost expecting him to say something. Then the moment was gone. His gaze shifted and his face creased up as he started crying. Deeply shaken, she moved him so he could suck on the other side.

Was it possible he knew she was his mother? Reason told her she was being ridiculous, but she felt uneasy now, and filled with the most terrible sense of guilt. He was going to be given away to strangers, and there was nothing she could do to prevent that happening. Yet the connection she'd felt in those fleeting seconds had been strong and binding.

Louise lay awake all that night. Unable to sleep, she listened to every little grunt and sniff from the cradle, anxious not to miss a moment of being with her son. Yet, at the same time, she felt torn apart, because she knew that was what was going to happen.

For four days and four nights she watched over him, feeding him whenever he cried, and changing the rough towelling nappies Aunt Tegan had produced, along with some second-hand baby clothes she'd bought at a jumble sale.

Louise had even given the baby a name: Rupert, after Rupert Brooke. Jack would approve of that, she thought, wishing more than anything in the world that he was here to share these moments with her.

Then the blow fell with brutal suddenness on the fifth morning.

Aunt Tegan stomped into her bedroom at eight o'clock, just as Louise had finished feeding him, and put him, sleeping, back into the cradle.

'Come along, young man,' she said briskly, lifting up the baby. 'Come and meet you new Mum and Da; they've come to fetch you.'

As she walked out of the room, she turned to a stricken looking Louise. 'Nice couple. Got a farm. Looking for a boy who can help them when he's older. He'll be well looked after.'

The last Louise saw of Rupert was his tiny head, covered with a sheen of blond hair, as Aunt Tegan whisked him away.

'God dammit, it's inhumane,' Juliet swore furiously down the telephone, as she talked to her mother. 'You've no idea how Louise is suffering. I hardly recognized her when I met her off the train yesterday. And she's in great pain, too. She's flooding with milk, because that old witch made her feed the baby. I had to call the doctor. And now she's strapped so tightly she can hardly breath.'

Juliet remembered the pricking pain of rising milk from when her own baby had died. She also remembered, only too well, the anguish of her loss, the unspeakable distress and suffering she'd felt, followed by a sense of despair so black that she didn't think she'd ever get over it.

Yet Aunt Tegan had seen fit to put Louise on a train back to London the day after the baby had been taken away, as if she'd gone through something no more serious than having a tooth removed.

'There was nothing else we could do,' Liza responded defensivly. 'If Louise had behaved herself, none of this would have happened. It was very good of my aunt to look after her, and find a couple who wanted a baby.'

'Mother, you've no idea what you've done,' Juliet retorted, feeling desperate. In the space of less than a year Louise had lost her baby, the boy she loved and the security and comforts of her own home, and she'd only just turned sixteen.

'Can I stay here, with you, for a while?' Louise begged, when they arrived at Juliet's house. 'I won't get in your way, and I've got my ration book; it's just that I don't think I can go back to Hartley just yet.'

Juliet put her arms around her sister and hugged her. 'Sweetie, you can stay here for ever, if you like. I'm worried about your safety though. We're having random air raids, and at any time of the day or night.'

Louise looked at her, dry eyed and strained, as if she had no more tears to shed.

'Honestly, I don't care if I'm killed. My life is unbearable. What's the point of carrying on?'

Juliet held her sister firmly by the shoulders. 'You must *never* talk like that,' she said fervently. 'Believe me, darling, everything eventually passes. Granny once told me that God never throws at you more than you can handle, and it's true. You'll get over this, in time, I promise you.'

'I might get over Jack, though I'll never marry anyone else now. But I won't get over Rupert being taken away. He *looked* at me, Juliet, as if he knew me. It was extrordinary. I even half expected him to *speak*!' She paused, shaking her head. 'The dreadful thing is I feel as if I've let him down.'

'When he's grown up he'll understand you had no choice.'

'I could have run away from home. Jack wanted us to

178

get married when we were sixteen. I should never have listened to Mummy and Daddy.'

She'd started crying again. Great wrenching sobs of despair that wracked her body, and took away the bloom of youth from her face.

Juliet was supposed to be on duty at ten o'clock the next morning. Dudley was standing in the hall, as she came hurrying down the stairs in her uniform. 'Your Grace, is there anything special you would like me to do today?'

'There is, indeed.' When she'd finished giving him instructions, she added, 'Keep an eye on Miss Louise for me, will you, Dudley? She's been ill, and she needs feeding up and rest.'

'Certainly, Your Grace.'

The shrill penetrating wail of the air raid siren sounded just before noon. Dudley, back from running errands, hurried up to Louise's bedroom and knocked on the door.

Her voice was so quiet he could barely hear her. 'Come in.'

He found her, dressed in a baggy skirt and sweater, sitting on the window seat, looking out.

'Miss Louise, Her Grace told me I was to take you down to the shelter if there was a raid,' he said in alarm.

'I'm fine here, thank you,' Louise replied with dull politeness.

He spoke urgently. 'You must come away from the window.' As he spoke there was a series of heavy explosions as a stick of bombs landed several streets away. The house trembled.

'What was that?' Louise craned her neck to look down Park Lane. There was hardly any traffic now, and the streets were deserted, as people vanished to shelter in nearby buildings.

'Come along, Miss Louise. Those were bombs dropping. It's really dangerous for you to be up here.'

'I don't mind.' She looked up at the sky as they heard the menacing THRUM-THRUM-THRUM of low flying aircraft. 'Are those German bombers?'

Dudley had a swift look. 'Yes – and here come our Spitfires,' he added, pointing proudly and forgetting his own fear. 'When enemy aircraft are approaching London, the order is given to "scramble". They can be airborne in a matter of minutes.'

By now Louise was practically hanging out of the window,

looking up with horrified fascination. 'They're attacking the German's plane!' she exclaimed.

A dog-fight had started above the city, as the Spitfires, dodging and swooping, their engines screaming, attacked one of the Messerschmitts. Spitting machine-gunfire, outwitting the enemy with their speed, mobility and skill, they resembled a swarm of angry silver gnats.

Suddenly black smoke and flames started streaming from the tail of the German plane as it dived, headlong, towards the ground.

'Blimey, they've got one!' Dudley shouted, forgetting himself in the heat of the moment. 'That's one less Jerry!'

Louise watched, reminded of the pheasants as they were shot out of the sky when she'd stayed with Juliet at Glenmally.

'They'll be killed, won't they? The German crew, I mean,' she asked with a catch in her voice.

Dudley glanced at her stricken expression. 'Please come downstairs now, Miss Louise. Her Grace will be really angry if I let you stay up here. It's not safe.'

Louise turned to look at him over her shoulder. 'I'm not afraid of dying, you know.'

'Maybe not, but if you stay by that window, you risk having your face cut to ribbons by flying glass,' he said firmly, adding slyly, 'I was about to cook lunch, Miss Louise. Would you like some chocolate pudding?'

Louise hesitated for a moment, torn between her inner childish self and the new person she'd become.

'Yes, please,' she said, finally, following him obediently down to the basement, where he settled her in the shelter. He turned on the wireless. 'Music While You Work' was on, a programme lasting several hours every day, for the benefit of the young women working in munitions factories. Glenn Miller and his band were playing 'In the Mood'.

Dudley whipped up a tomato omelette, thanks to the supply of vegetables and eggs Juliet had brought up from Hartley. There was also a portion of chocolate mousse in a glass dish, and cheese and biscuits,

'I hope these are not your rations?' she asked, amazed, as soon as he set the tray before her.

'Don't you worry about that, Miss Louise. I have a few contacts, you know? I can obtain most things for Her Grace,' he replied gravely.

'Really?' Louise was fascinated. 'Can you ever get oranges? Or bananas?'

'They present a certain difficulty, because they come from abroad. But I will certainly find out if there are any available.'

'I can hardly remember what an orange tastes like. Aren't you having lunch?' She looked around to see what he had cooked for himself.

'I'll have mine later, Miss Louise,' he said diplomatically. His Army life had been good training for this new lark of being a butler, he reflected. Troops never sat down to eat with officers; likewise, servants didn't eat with the gentry. Even if the bombs were dropping all around and the THRUM-THRUM-THRUM of the German planes was getting on his wick.

He looked at Louise again, as she sat eating at the small table he'd put in the shelter. He'd guessed from the beginning she'd got herself into trouble. Judging by her figure, she'd only just given birth, too. Her expression was the picture of misery, and he could only guess at the upset such an event must have caused in a family like the Granvilles.

Later that afternoon, Dudley went up to the drawing room, carrying a basket. 'This has arrived for you, Miss Louise,' he announced primly, setting it on the floor in front of her.

Louise put down the book she'd been reading. 'For me?' she queried. 'What is it?'

At that moment there was a tiny yelp from the basket. Bemused, she lifted the lid, and found a little scrap of a puppy looking up at her, with two round black eyes, and a tiny blob of a black nose.

'Where did this come from?' she demanded.

'It's a present from Her Grace. She asked me to find a puppy for you, which is quite a problem at the moment, seeing as so many dogs were put down at the beginning of the war, but I managed to get this little bitch, through one of my contacts.'

Louise froze, aghast. How could Juliet, of all people, have been so insensitive as to imagine a puppy could take the place of Rupert?

'Take it away ... !' she exclaimed, bursting into tears. 'I don't want a dog. I want my baby.' She threw herself sideways along the sofa, sobbing dementedly, tugging at great handfuls of her hair with both hands. 'How dare she think . . . I want Rupert . . . it's my baby I want . . .'

Dudley quickly closed the basket and hurried out of the room. When he returned a few minutes later, he placed a cup of camomile tea on the table beside her. Then he left her again, still crying, to make a telephone call.

Juliet rushed back to the house an hour later, having got permission to take the night off, to look after her 'ill' sister.

By then Louise had gone to bed, worn out with grief, pining for her baby.

'What do you want?' she asked in a flat voice.

Juliet sat on the side of the bed and spoke directly. 'Dudley says you thought I'd got you a puppy, to take the place of Rupert. How could you get such an idea? You know that's not what I meant, Louise. Remember, I'm the only one in this family who understands what you're going through. When my baby died, I wanted to die, too. I felt I had nothing to live for.'

'Then why did you get me the dog?' Louise asked angrily.

'Dogs need exercising, and I thought it would get you to go for walks in the park, which would be good for you,' Juliet lied. In fact, she *had* thought it might divert Louise's maternal feelings, giving her something small and dependent to look after, but that had obviously been a mistake.

'It's insulting to the memory of Rupert to think he could be replaced by a dog,' Louise snapped. Her face was blotchy and swollen, her eyes dulled by grief.

'I never thought that, for one moment,' Juliet assured her. 'And you shouldn't talk about Rupert as if he's dead.'

'He's dead to me. I'll never see him again, and I don't think I can bear it. I loved him. He was so exquisite. How could I have let him be taken away from me?' She lay down again, and pulled the covers up over her head. 'Go away,' she said harshly, her voice muffled. 'There's nothing you can do.'

Louise awoke in the middle of the night. She'd refused to have dinner, and now she felt hungry. Slipping out of bed, she pulled on the silk dressing-gown Juliet had lent her, and slipped down to the kitchen. In the house of plenty, she was sure she'd find some bread and cheese in the larder, and maybe some fruit.

Switching on the light, the kitchen was immediately filled

with brilliance, and she found herself looking into two button bright dark eyes, and a little black nose.

'Oh, my God!' she gasped. She had forgotten about the puppy, who was now making friendly little squeaks, and trying to climb up her ankles. Lifting it up, Louise realized it was the smallest and lightest little dog she'd ever seen. It had soft silky grey and tan hair, feathering around her face and legs, and a tail that wagged furiously.

'Are you hungry?' Louise asked matter-of-factly, and slightly resentfully. She looked around for something to give the puppy, and found Dudley had also acquired everything a dog could need, from a bed to sleep in, to a collar and lead. She took a small biscuit out of one of the packets, and placed it, with the puppy, on the floor, while she raided the larder for herself.

When she'd eaten, she went to leave the kitchen, but the puppy followed her, and although she tried to shut it in, it was too quick for her. Irritated, she stomped back up the stairs to her room, with the little creature trailing at her heels. One thing was certain. She was not going to have this unwanted, un-asked for and unwelcome creature sleeping with her.

Again the puppy was too quick. The minute Louise opened her bedroom door, it shot ahead of her and, with a feisty leap, jumped on to the chaise longue that stood at the foot of the bed. From here it scrambled up on to the bed, and headed for the down pillows, where it proceeded to scrabble for a moment, before making a comfortable bed for itself.

'The cheek of it . . . !' Louise muttered crossly, too tired to take it down to the kitchen again. 'You'd better not make a mess.'

'Your Grace, shall I take Miss Louise a cup of tea, or shall we not disturb her?' Dudley asked the next morning, as he placed Juliet's cup of lapsang souchong on her bedside table.

'Leave her to sleep for the moment, Dudley.'

'Very well, Your Grace.'

But when he'd gone downstairs again, she got out of bed, worried about Louise. If she was as distraught as she'd been yesterday, she'd have to call the doctor again. Barefoot, she crept along the corridor, and opened her sister's door very quietly.

Two silky ears pricked up from the pillows, and a pair of

bright dark eyes looked at her enquiringly. Curled up against Louise's bare shoulder, the puppy was luxuriating in the warmth and comfort of human contact and a downy bed.

Louise was still fast asleep, her face turned towards the dog.

Juliet tip-toed away, closing the door soundlessly again. Perhaps the puppy, after all, was going to help distract Louise from her deep sense of loss. It had to be better than the path Juliet herself had chosen, which had, at times, been deeply decadent and self-destructive, to say the least.

PART THREE

Into the Light
1943–1945

Six

'Henry, is it all right if I bring Gaston to lunch again on Sunday?' Candida asked. 'He's got a few days off and I'm going home for the weekend. I feel like a troglodyte. I don't think I've seen daylight or breathed fresh air for *weeks.*'

'You poor old thing,' Henry sympathized, from the comfort of his fairly opulent office at the bank. 'Are you having to sleep in the cabinet rooms?'

'Mr Churchill keeps us all sleeping in those wretched cellars. He's even brought his own bed! The rest of us sleep on bunks in a corridor, in an even deeper cellar, which we have to reach through a trap door in the floor. I can tell you, Henry, there are times when I feel like getting out and running naked around Whitehall, bombs or no bloody bombs, just to get out of the wretched place!' she boomed, with a loud laugh.

'It'll be nice to see you and Gaston again.'

'You don't mind if I bring someone else as well, do you?'

'Of course not.'

'Good. He's called Andrew Pemberton. He's at the War Office. We've been seeing a bit of each other, bombs permitting,' she added with sudden coyness.

'Goodness!' Henry sounded surprised but pleased. 'I'll look forward to meeting him.'

'See you Sunday, then. Oh, God! The red alert phones are flashing; got to go.' There was a click and she'd hung up.

For once, the whole family was gathered together for lunch that weekend.

Lady Anne was delighted at the prospect of seeing all the family, while Liza's excitement at having an opportunity to entertain knew no bounds. Rosie, Mrs Dobbs and Warwick were rather dismayed though. The leaves would have to be put back in the dining table to enlarge it, rations would have to be stretched, and ingenuity brought into play.

Spence was instructed to bring in all the garden vegetables

he could find, and to kill three of the chickens. But only when Charlotte wasn't around.

It was the first time Louise had been back to Hartley, clutching her puppy, Bella, and feeling full of trepidation. Not that she need have worried. Her arrival was somewhat overshadowed by the carload of food that Juliet brought with them.

'How do you get all this stuff?' Rosie asked jealously, as the kitchen table became piled up with supplies, including caviar.

'I've got a present for you,' Juliet countered, whipping a flat package out of her suitcase.

'Stockings!' Rosie gasped with delight. 'Silk stockings? I haven't had any for years.'

'I've got some for Mummy and Granny, too,' Juliet added nonchalantly.

'Where did you get them from? And all these chocolates?' Rosie asked, suspicious.

'You do know the Americans have joined the war, I suppose?' Juliet asked scathingly.

'So . . . ?'

'London is flooded with GIs. They're lonely, and they're loaded, and they're lovely boys.' She saw Rosie's expression of horror. 'I didn't have to sleep with them, stupid. They're naturally generous, and when I give a drinks party, to introduce them to some of my friends, they bring me all these marvellous presents. If you don't want the stockings, give them to someone else,' she added tartly.

Rosie clutched the precious package to her chest. 'No, no. I love them. Thank you very much. I've been reduced to painting my legs brown, and drawing a line up the back with an eyebrow pencil.'

In the end, thanks to Juliet's contribution, it was quite a feast, with smoked salmon to start with, and a ripe Stilton to have after Mrs Dodd's apple pie. To add to the festivity, Henry brought up some precious bottles of wine from the dwindling stock in the cellar.

'I know a friend of yours,' Gaston said to Juliet in much improved English, as they gathered for drinks in the library before lunch.

'Oh, yes? Who was that?' Juliet asked, uninterested.

Gaston looked terrible today; unshaven, dirty, and dressed

like a French onion seller. It was an insult to her grandmother, she reflected, not to have made an effort.

'Daniel Lawrence.'

The blood drained from Juliet's face and for a moment the room seemed to spin around her. She stood quite still, letting the shock waves ricochet through her body and settle before she spoke.

'Daniel?' she repeated hoarsely. She was trembling so much she had to put down her glass. 'How do you know him?'

He shrugged elaborately. 'How you say . . . ? Talk costs lives. I cannot tell. He ask me if I know anyone in England, and I say the Granvilles . . . then he ask if I know you.' He gave a garlic-laden laugh. Juliet stepped back, feeling nauseous, whether from shock or the pungent smell she wasn't sure.

Gaston continued, 'I said we were related; he was very interested.'

'How is he?' Her voice sounded strange to her ears.

'How is anyone in this war? Over-worked. Very tired, I'd say. Have you known him long?'

Juliet wondered if she was dreaming. *He knew Daniel.* She realized he was looking at her, waiting for an answer.

'I've known him for some time,' she croaked. 'Is he still working in London?'

Gaston spoke cautiously. 'Sometimes. I cannot say more.'

'Luncheon's ready,' Liza trilled at that moment. 'You're sitting next to me,' she said archly to Andrew Pemberton, Candida's new beau. 'I want you to tell me all about yourself.'

Candida cast her eyes to the ceiling. 'I hope you've put an intelligent young girl, like Juliet, on his other side, Liza,' she remarked.

Liza gave a silly giggle, ignoring the remark. She never knew how to cope with Henry's sister; never knew whether she was joking or not. Candida was so loud, so bursting with what people called personality, but Liza privately thought was bumptious-ness. And she seemed to take up half the room with her large bosom and broad beam. Liza patted her own flat stomach with a self-satisfied smile as she led the way into the dining room. Norman Hartnell was always saying what a marvellous figure she had for someone who'd had five children.

'What's the matter, Juliet?' Louise asked, as they sat, side by side, at the table. 'You look as if you've seen a ghost.'

189

'I feel as if I have,' Juliet admitted, wondering if Daniel had said anything about her. And what type of war work were they doing that could possible bring them together?

She gave a wobbly smile. 'Gaston has just told me he's met Daniel.' Apart from Henry, Louise was the only person she'd confided in about her baby being Daniel's child.

'That's good news, surely? What's to stop you seeing him again?'

Juliet shook her head. 'He thinks I'm a bad lot. He thinks I just use men, and in a way I suppose he's right, although I've never used *him*.'

'What are you going to do?'

'He knows where I live and he knows where I work; it's up to him, really. I can't go chasing after him.'

Rosie leaned across the table. 'What are you two hatching?' she asked, hating to be left out of anything.

'We're making plans for when Louise starts to train to be a VAD,' Juliet replied airily.

'Is that what you really want to do, Louise? It sounds dreadful,' Rosie remarked critically.

'I want to work in a children's ward in a hospital,' Louise replied. 'St Stephens said they'd take me on, once I'm qualified. And Juliet says I can go on living with her, which means I can have Bella with me.'

'Bella's a great hit with Dudley,' Juliet agreed, then added laughingly, 'not that he doesn't adore Louise, too, so it's going to be fun.'

'I bet,' said Rosie bitterly, flushed with vexation. Now, not only was Juliet having an exciting and luxurious life in London, with a butler who had black market contacts, but Louise was going to be sharing in all the luxury, too. Why did nothing nice ever happen to *her*? Why did she have to be stuck down here, with two small children, helping Mrs Dodds cook for everyone, and doing most of the house-work, because Warwick was too decrepit, and her mother was too lazy?

Rosie had got over Charles's death, and Freddie's betrayal, and now she longed to *live* a bit. Find someone else to love her and take her out, and offer her an exciting future. It simply wasn't fair that Juliet always got everything, and now Louise was following in her footsteps. They'd both behaved terribly badly, causing scandals within the family, while her affair with Freddie had been the essence of discretion. It seemed, she reflected bitterly, that bad girls had a much better time than good girls.

Gaston, sitting between Lady Anne and Henry, watched the family with whom he now had a tenuous link, and felt much more at ease this time. Brought up on his own by his mother and step-father, he'd often wondered what it would be like to have siblings. Looking around the table now, he felt almost glad he'd been an only child. The atmosphere bristled with rivalry and discontent between the Granville sisters, who were all so different. Charlotte seemed the most uncomplicated one. In contrast, Amanda was a bossy little fire-cracker, squinting through her glasses with a critical expression, and tossing her head with irritation every time her mother spoke. Louise looked sad and quenched, and Rosie, who he remembered as an English-rose type of beauty, now resembled a frustrated, harrassed housewife.

Then he turned to look at Juliet. She was the star. She was stunning, chic, and totally fascinating, and he wondered why her pale blue eyes had the haunted look of someone who seeks redemption.

'Is everything all right, darling?' Lady Anne asked Juliet, as they all retired to the conservatory for cups of bitter camp coffee after lunch.

'I'm fine, Granny. I just . . . erm . . . just had a shock when Gaston told me he knew Daniel Lawrence.'

Her grandmother raised her eyebrows, a shadow falling across her face. 'I see. I suppose they're involved in the same organization.'

Juliet looked startled. 'What organization?'

Lady Anne hesitated. 'I can't be sure, because of course Gaston couldn't tell me what he's doing owing to the Official Secrets Act.'

Juliet looked over at Gaston, wondering if she could persuade him to tell her more. But he was deep in serious conversation with Andrew Pemberton. They sat close together, talking so quietly she couldn't catch a word. Gaston was gesticulating wildly with his expressive hands, while Andrew, a typical Englishman, from his neatly clipped moustache to his polished lace-up shoes, sat with his hands folded on his lap, his observant eyes never leaving Gaston's face.

Juliet ached to know what they were talking about, but as she rose and went over to join them, they stopped and the conversation became general.

At that moment the party started breaking up.

'We've got to get back to town tonight, Mother,' Candida told Lady Anne, gripping her shoulders and kissing her robustly on her wrinkled cheek. 'Take care of yourself. I must say you're looking grand. Come on, boys,' she called to Andrew and Gaston. 'Time we were off.'

'Can I give you all a lift?' Juliet suggested, seizing the opportunity to be with them on her own.

'Thanks, but I've got my car,' Candida replied, enveloping Juliet in her ample arms. 'You need to put on some weight, dear girl. You'll fade away at this rate.'

'Candida?' Juliet drew her to one side, and spoke in a low voice. 'Do you know what Gaston's doing? I have a friend who may be working with him. I'm afraid he might be involved in something dangerous . . .' Her voice faded away as she met the suddenly cold and disapproving gaze of her aunt.

'I'm surprised you should ask such a question,' she said briskly. 'You know Talk Costs Lives.' Turning away, she said good-bye to the rest of the family, before climbing into her ancient Daimler.

Then she revved the engine, and shot off down the drive, waving jauntily.

Juliet couldn't get the idea of Daniel being in acute danger out of her mind. Candida wouldn't tell her, and Juliet could under-stand why, and she'd no idea how to get hold of Gaston, so she arranged to meet her father for lunch the following week.

'I have to know, Dads,' she said directly, as they sat drinking apertifs at a discreet little restaurant in the city. 'What is Gaston actually doing? It's one thing if he is part of some secret operation, but quite another if Daniel's involved because of being Jewish.'

'I've absolutely no idea, darling,' Henry said sympatheti-cally. 'Because Gaston and Daniel have met, it doesn't mean they're doing similar jobs, does it? Are you sure you're not just panicking? Why don't you ask Ian? He might know, although he might not be able to tell you much, if it's top secret information.'

Juliet stiffened. 'I don't want to talk to Ian,' she said mutinously.

Henry frowned. 'What have you got against him? He may be a bit indiscreet, but he knows he can trust me not to repeat what he says. He'd trust you, too, if you asked him something.'

'Oh, yes. He knows he can trust *me*.' There was sudden bitterness in her voice.

'What *is* it?' Henry asked, annoyed. Ian was his best friend. Witty, intelligent and possessing great charm. 'I simply don't understand what you've got against him?'

She shrugged. 'It doesn't really matter. I'll find out about what Gaston's doing another way.'

'Why on earth don't you telephone Daniel, direct if you're so worried about him?' Henry asked, in a maddeningly reasonable voice.

Juliet took a cigarette out of her gold case and placed it in her long holder. Her hands were shaking. 'I can't possibly do that,' she retorted dismissively. 'Let's order.'

They talked about other things, but a barrier had suddenly sprung up between them that had never been there before.

Henry chatted cheerfully about how the RAF had bombed Nazi harbours, industrial plants and rail junctions, in daring low-level daylight raids, which had forced the Germans to withdraw from the Russian front.

'With the help of America and Russia, I think the end is in sight. Maybe not for another year or so, but things are going well in North Africa, and in the South Pacific, and once we're in a position to invade France and push the Germans back, we'll be on the home straight. It's the Might of Right, against evil,' he added, pleased with the phrase.

Juliet nodded, but Henry found her *distraite*. He stretched out and laid his hand over hers. 'I wish you could get a real break, darling, away from the First Aid Post.'

She looked up in surprise, her eyes dazed, as if she'd just awoken. 'What? Oh, there's no need, Dads. There's been a lull in the raids. Anyway, I like having something to do. I don't know how Mummy can bear to carry on as if there wasn't a war.'

'I don't think Mummy knows quite *what* to do,' Henry replied carefully. 'It's so peaceful down at Hartley, the war seems a million miles away.'

193

'Why don't you let her come back to London?'

Henry hesitated. He couldn't admit to Juliet that he'd grown to relish his time away from Liza. It was wonderful not to have to go out every night, to have to dress up, to make small-talk to people who frankly bored him, to keep a social diary. He'd grown used to grabbing himself something to eat after a long day at the under-staffed bank, and then, if he wasn't fire watching, reading the newspapers and listening to the wireless.

'I might suggest it,' he replied unconvincingly. 'The flat's rather small for three of us on a permanent basis, though.'

Juliet didn't press the matter. It would drive her crazy to have her mother living with her, too.

'I've had enough of this,' Rosie exploded, throwing Jonathan's dirty nappy into the bucket of cold water. 'I'm sick of being a drudge.'

Nanny looked up from cleaning the wash-hand basin. 'Now, now. It's not an easy time for any of us,' she said reprovingly, as if Rosie were still a six years old.

'But it's different for me. I'm still *young* . . . though only just!' Rosie slammed the lid down on the white enamel bucket in disgust, and stormed out of the nursery bathroom.

She was fed up that there was no one in her life these days. No one to love her; no one to make her feel good. The future was like looking into a bottomless pit. She was tired of wearing the same old clothes month after month, and not even having shampoo to wash her hair. Soap was rationed, make-up was hard to get, and nail varnish and lipstick impossible. She couldn't remember when she'd last been to a restaurant, or received a bunch of flowers.

The trouble was she never even got to meet anyone interesting stuck at Hartley, because all the young men were in the armed forces.

Thoroughly disgruntled, she poured out her vexation to her mother that evening.

'Well, I don't know what you can do about it,' Liza said rather firmly. In spite of Nanny, she dreaded the idea of being landed with the grandchildren, if her daughter were to go to London.

'I'm twenty-*six* this year,' Rosie protested. 'I don't want to be a widow all my life.'

Privately, Liza wondered why not. Rosie had been married, got a title for life, and had had two children; surely that was enough?

'Anyway,' Rosie fumed, 'the children need a father figure. Daddy is the only man they know.'

'I'm sure you'll meet someone after the war,' Liza pointed out. She'd had more than enough of being stuck in the country herself.

'I'm going to ask Juliet if I can stay with her for a bit,' Rosie said, determinedly. 'I don't see why she and Louise should have all the fun.'

'What about the babies?' Liza shrilled, appalled.

'Mother, they're hardly the Lost Babes in the Wood,' Rosie mocked. 'What has Nanny done for the past thirty years, but look after babies? They'll be fine with her. And you'll be here, to keep an eye on them.'

Liza suddenly saw her daughter as an obstacle between herself and the party circuit. It had been one thing to bring out a fresh, beautiful, youthful creature who did her credit; quite another to find a twenty-six-year-old titled woman blocking her own path to an enjoyable life.

'I'm not going to be down here myself much, this summer,' Liza said coldly. 'The King and Queen are going to Royal Ascot for the first time since 1939, and I want to go, too.'

'I might go as well,' Rosie said thoughtfully.

'But who could you go with?' Liza asked querously.

'My mother-in-law,' Rosie retorted, eyes flashing. 'She usually gets invited to tea in the Royal Box, too.'

'So? Daddy and I are always invited to lunch at the Jockey Club,' Liza retorted, pettishly.

Lady Anne, walking past the open drawing-room door at that moment, paused and looked in at them, her eyes steely blue.

'I think we should remember that this country is fighting for survival, and thousands of lives are being lost on both sides, every day,' she said coldly. 'If I may say so, I really don't think Ascot race meetings feature very high on a list of priorities, do you?'

'I will *not* have her talking to me like that,' Liza fumed sulkily, when Lady Anne had gone to her sitting room. 'Who does she think she is? This is *my* house, and I'll damn well do as I like.' Then she stalked off to her bedroom, filled with determination to go to London. And so was Rosie.

Liza's shrill voice could be heard all over the house.

'Our lives are being destroyed because of this wretched war, Henry. We're missing out on everything!'

Henry, sitting at his desk in the library, closed his eyes wearily for a moment. Then he spoke, his voice flat. 'I don't know what you expect me to do about it, but this is the reality of war.'

She looked bewildered, her usually neat blonde hair ruffled and untidy. Her expression filled with discontent.

'But all our friends are in London, Henry. Lady Cunard is entertaining every night, in her permanent suite at the Dorchester. The Duke of Westminster and Chips Channon . . .'

'You're talking about exceedingly rich people, Liza,' Henry protested. 'Multi-millionaires.'

She stopped short, stunned. 'But we're rich!' she bleated.

'We were very well off before the war, but we're not any more.' His voice was steady. 'I shall be fifty-five next year, and as soon as the war's over, I'm going to retire.'

'Retire?' she asked in a small terrified voice. She still thought of Henry as the young Army officer she'd married in 1914, when he'd been twenty-five. Apart from greying hair he didn't seemed to have aged much, either. *Retire?* Was he as old as that? Was *she* as old as that?

'Why do you want to retire, Henry?'

'I'm tired. I'm on the roof of the BBC, fire watching, every other night. I work up to sixteen hours a day at the bank. I can't wait to get back here at weekends, and be able to go for long walks with the dogs. Breath the fresh air. Wake up to the sound of the dawn chorus.' As he spoke, he leaned back in his chair, gazing through the windows to the garden beyond.

'Yes, but . . .' Liza panicked, her face quite white with anxiety.

He turned at looked straight at her. 'When the war is over, this will be our permanent home, my dear. I don't intend to get another house in London, nor one of those beastly new flats.'

Liza shrunk like a balloon left over from a children's party.

'You can't do that . . . !' she exclaimed, bursting noisily

into tears. 'We *must* live in London. All our friends live in London . . .'

'. . . Social acquaintances,' he corrected her.

'No, Henry. Friends. Before the war we were out every night.'

'I know,' he said hollowly.

Liza spun round, angrily. 'What do you mean?'

'It was a superficial existence, Liza. And then bringing out Rosie and Juliet, both of whom made disastrous marriages. I'm not going through all that again with Amanda and Charlotte, whatever you say. We're going to stay down here from now on,' he added firmly.

'I won't! I won't!' she wailed. 'You can't do this to me. What am I supposed to do with myself, buried down here?' She slumped down on the old leather sofa, holding a handkerchief to her mouth.

Henry sat immobile, looking out of the window again, the fingers of his right hand thrumming lightly on the arm of his chair. He'd spoilt Liza, of course, so he was partly to blame for this. But they were both getting on now, and he, especially, was aware of the passing years.

The idea of getting another town house and doing it up and going back to things being the way they were before the war appalled him. Made him feel quite sick with exhaustion just to think of all those late, champagne-fuelled nights.

'Anyway,' he continued, 'no one will be able to get the staff. People like Parsons and Mrs Fowler will be too old, and the younger generation, having found a living away from domestic service, are not going to want to go back to it.'

'Juliet's going to go on living in town, in that grand house of hers,' Liza pointed out, sitting up and blowing her nose.

'Cameron very generously made sure Juliet will always be rich,' Henry commented.

'What about the flat you share with Ian?' she asked, clutching at straws. Even a basement flat in Campden Hill would be better than *nothing*.

'It's Ian's flat and I think he's going to go and live in the country, too, when the war ends.'

With a yowl like a cat that's been trodden on, Liza jumped up and rushed out of the room, slamming the door behind her.

*   *   *

197

'They had a fearful fight,' Rosie informed Juliet, with a certain relish. 'Especially when I said that I was going to stay with you for a while. It is kind of you to have me,' she added, with a sudden wave of genuine gratitude.

Juliet shrugged. 'God knows, the house is big enough, and Dudley seems happy, which is the main thing.' She grinned. 'As long as you and Louise realize that you're both out the door if Dudley finds it all too much. He's more important to my life, right now, than anyone else.'

Rosie laughed. 'As long as he doesn't end up in prison. Where does he *get* all that extra food and petrol from?'

'I don't dare ask. Listen, I've got some American friends coming to supper tonight. Louise is out, meeting some girls from her First Aid Course, but you'll be in, won't you?'

Rosie's eyes widened. 'Yes, I'll be here. What shall I wear?'

Rosie was expecting a bunch of gregarious GIs, bearing gifts of stockings and chocolates, who would want to paint the town red as soon as they'd eaten, and dance until dawn, but instead, Juliet's friends were connected to the American Embassy: two charming couples in their forties, who'd been in London for several years; a lawyer called Salton Webb; and Colonel Rourke Zimmerman.

'I've put you next to Salton,' Juliet whispered, as she led the guests down to the dining room after they'd drunk several White Ladies. 'He's single.'

Rosie looked askance at her sister. 'And Colonel Zimmerman isn't?'

Juliet pursed her scarlet lips. 'We don't enquire about his wife,' she said with mock primness. 'She's somewhere in Iowa.'

Salton Webb was in his thirties, with a deeply tanned face, crinkly hair and a light-hearted approach to life. It was obvious Juliet had told him about Charles's death, for he questioned her sympathetically about her children, and asked her how long she was staying in London. She enjoyed talking to him, but beside Juliet she felt increasingly inadequate.

In the past few years she'd only seen her sister down at Hartley for occassional weekends, but now, in the magnificent setting of ninety-nine, Park Lane, Juliet seemed to have metamorphosized into a woman of starry sophistication and confidence. Able to hold her own with anyone. This was an altogether different Juliet, who was engaging in serious discussion about politics and the state of the country, entrancing the men because she now had the art of appealing to them both cerebrally and physically.

Rosie watched in awe; and this was her *younger* sister, acting as if she was an equal of these older intellectual guests. Where were the flushed-faced boys she used to go out with? The debonair escorts who whisked her around the town, bringing her back as dawn was breaking, as were their hearts, because she'd led them up the garden path?

By comparison, Rosie was now feeling like a naïve country bumpkin, frumpy and plain, only able to talk about different ways of making jam without fruit or sugar, and teaching her children to speak.

'How long are you staying in town?' she heard Salton ask.

'I'm not sure,' Rosie replied diffidently, her self-confidence low. That was the galling part of it: being the eldest sister but feeling like the youngest, in need of a perm and wearing a dress she'd had for years.

'Do you like the theatre?'

She nodded, sipping her wine.

'I hear Noël Coward is doing a tour of England with his plays,' Salton continued.

'Really?'

This was dreadful. Rosie felt ashamed of her lack of small-talk, and her total inability to fit in.

'What part of America do you come from?' she asked in desperation.

'Washington, DC,' he replied, pride in his voice. Then, as if she'd turned a key in a lock to open a door on to a great vista, Salton started talking about himself. He told her about his humble beginnings, living in a trailer park with his widowed mother, and with hardly enough to eat; then his aptitude at college, and how he went on to get a degree in law, and finally how he'd set up his own practice in the capital, where he now handled a lot of work for the White House.

'So – you don't live permanently in London?' Rosie asked, amazed at the sudden feeling of disappointment she felt at the thought of him returning to America.

He shrugged, grey eyes looking into hers with something like regret. 'Sadly, no. I'm here for a few months, doing stuff for our embassy, but I'll have to return to the States, sooner or later.'

'I see.' Rosie drank some more wine, determined to keep up with this attractive man, and only by getting slightly tipsy did she think she'd have the confidence to do so. She loved his American drawl, and his easy and relaxed manner. She loved the way he spoke to her, as if he'd known her for years.

'Meanwhile,' he was saying, turning to smile warmly into her eyes, 'would you like to see a film one evening? And perhaps have supper out, afterwards . . . air raids permitting, of course?'

'I'd love that,' she replied, more quickly than she'd meant to. Blushing deeply, she picked up her near-empty glass again.

'Allow me,' Salton suggested, reaching for the wine and topping up her drink.

From the head of the table, Rosie was aware of Juliet's watchful yet slightly amused glances.

Damn Juliet, Rosie reflected, drinking more wine. *She's* not the only one who is attractive to men. They used to flock around me, too, when . . . when . . . Sudden tears sprang to her eyes. *When I was young and beautiful*, she reflected, engulfed by a wave of self-pity.

She wished now she hadn't come to stay with Juliet. It had been madness to think it would work. Juliet was always going to upstage her, make her feel inferior, and whisk the best men from right under her nose.

It had seemed like a perfect idea to stay with her sister, especiallly as Louise was already here, but now she knew it was a great mistake. Once again, as had happened when they'd been girls, Juliet would undermine her confidence and spoil her chances of success.

Rosie put down her empty wine glass, and Salton once again refilled it, with an easy smile and a vague remark about Juliet giving such wonderful parties.

'Yes,' Rosie agreed loudly, fighting back tears. 'Well, she can afford to, can't she? With the generous settlement her ex-husband gave her.'

Silence entombed her remark in the ether, so the words remained hovering over the dining table like a banner flung up in a declaration of enmity.

Juliet's smile was sweet and deadly. 'You're right, Rosie.

200

Cameron was *so* generous, and so *kind*. I shall always be grateful to him. Shall we go upstairs and have coffee?'

The other women murmured agreement, rising from their seats, while Juliet led the way out of the dining room, leaving the men to enjoy their port and cigars.

Once upstairs, Juliet dragged Rosie into the spare room.

'How dare you behave like that,' she hissed, giving Rosie a shake. 'You're drunk for a start! What the hell do you think you're doing?'

'I hate being here, and I hate you,' Rosie wept.

'Fine. Go back to Hartley then. You abused my hospitality tonight, Rosie. I invited a really nice single man to meet you, a man who was obviously taken with you and would have asked you out, and then you go and make bitchy remarks about me . . .'

Rosie drew herself up, so furious her tears suddenly stopped.

'I don't need you or anyone else to find a man for me,' she stormed, flushed with anger. 'How *typically* patronizing of you. Just because you're rich you think you can lord it over everyone else . . . but then you were always like that, weren't you? You ruined my year as a débutante . . . !'

'Oh, for God's sake, that was eight bloody years ago! How you harp on, always bearing grudges. It's time you grew up,' Juliet growled in a low voice so her guests wouldn't hear. 'You've had much too much to drink and I think you'd better go to bed, before you embarrass yourself any more.'

With that, she marched out of the room and shut the door, praying Rosie would go to bed. They'd been close for a short while, after the tragic bombing of the Café de Paris, but now Rosie had reverted to being jealous and petty once again, and as far as Juliet was concerned, life, especially in the middle of a war, was too short for such nonsense.

The next morning, Louise came into Juliet's bedroom, as she was getting dressed into her uniform.

'What's up with Rosie?' she whispered, mystified.

'Why, what's happened?'

'She's packing her things. She says she's going to stay with someone called Lady Sonia Musgrove.'

'Oh, really?' Juliet chuckled. 'Sonia Musgrove is also a war widow, but immensely wealthy, and lives in Eaton Square.

She's an extra Lady-in-Waiting to the Queen, and she knows *everyone*. I'd forgotten she was a friend of Rosie's.'

'Why is Rosie going to stay with her?' Louise asked, amazed.

Juliet's smile broadened. 'Because I think our sister is about to turn into our mother.'

Liza joined Henry at the Campden Hill flat two days later.

'I'm meeting Rosie and Lady Sonia for lunch at Claridges, tomorrow,' she told Henry, when he returned from the bank that evening. Her voice was estatic. 'This is the best thing that could have happened to Rosie. Juliet knows such bizarre people; I gather her whole dinner party the other evening was made up of Americans.'

Henry looked pained and remained silent, every word Liza said grating on his nerves.

'What's the matter, Henry? Why don't we dine at the Dorchester tonight? We might drop in to see Lady Cunard; just a courtesy call, you know, to let her know we're all back in town.' As she spoke, she was unpacking a large suitcase, full of evening dresses, pushing his suits to one side on the rail, to make room for her things.

'I would have thought, Liza,' he said slowly, 'that with one of your daughters a Duchess, and another the widow of a Baron, you'd have felt you'd arrived.'

'Oh, Henry, you're such a stick-in-the-mud,' she laughed humourlessly. 'The trouble is, you've no ambition.'

He raised his eyebrows. 'I've never felt the need, my dear,' he replied quietly.

The Granvilles were now maintaining a divided front on the London scene.

Juliet and Louise continued to live in friendly harmony, Juliet helping her sister with her First Aid and Home Nursing studies, in the build-up to her exams, while herself working twenty-four-hour shifts, at Kingston House. There had been a definite lull in the air bombardments and so, when not on duty, Juliet continued to entertain, while Louise formed friendships with girls of her own age.

Rosie, on the other hand, was leading a flighty and gregarious life, as she continued to stay with Sonia Musgrove.

As if there was no war, apart from Sonia constantly grumbling at lack of staff, they went out every night to meet Sonia's rather grand friends. Sonia liked Rosie's company, because she was sweet and acquiescent, and happy to fall in with her plans. Rosie, from her point of view, began to secretly dream that Sonia might put her name forward to be another extra Lady-in-Waiting to the Queen.

Meanwhile, Liza flitted around the perimeter of their lives like an old cat, watching, with envy, the kittens at play.

Henry observed with growing dismay that his wife's previous pride in her elder daughters, as appendages to her, had now turned to furious jealousy because they were young women in their own right, with their own lives. Lives in which she was no longer included.

Henry decided it was time to issue an ultimatum.

The wailing sirens suddenly pierced the air with a note of alarm, just as Liza was walking down Piccadilly. This wasn't the first of the day-time raids, but from the first menacing THRUM-THRUM-THRUM of the German bombers overhead, to the sickening SCHER-RER-RER-RER . . . BOOM of the falling bombs, it looked like being the most severe.

She started running for cover, hindered by her high heeled shoes. Shrapnel PINGED as it hit the pavement around her like hailstones. Sticks of bombs, raining down on nearby buildings, made the ground shudder. Never before had she been out in an air raid, and she felt enormous relief when she flung herself through the doors of Fortnum & Mason, safe in the knowledge that even if the large store suffered a direct hit, she'd be safe in the beautifully presented delicatessen department.

Other people had run in for shelter, too, and were being advised by the uniformed commissionaire to stay in the centre of the ground floor, away from the glass windows.

To her surprise, Liza realized she wasn't scared; there was a pleasant feeling of camaraderie. And here, in this exclusive store, strangers were talking to each other, no matter what their background.

When the All-Clear sounded, Liza took a taxi back to Campden Hill, no longer in the mood for shopping – not that the shops had much to sell, unless one had masses of coupons.

The telephone on the hall table was ringing, as she let herself into the flat.

'Hello?'

'Mummy?'

'Oh, hello, Juliet. I've just got in this moment. I was in Piccadilly when the bombing started . . .'

'Mummy, I'm on duty, so I have to be quick. Have you heard from Daddy?'

'I told you, darling, I only got in this minute. Why?'

'I've just heard Leadenhall Street has been heavily bombed.' Juliet's voice was harsh with worry. 'We're on stand-by, in case they need more ambulances . . .'

'Leadenhall Street . . . ? Oh, God, the bank!'

'I'm afraid so. A direct hit, from the reports we're getting.'

'Oh, my God! Oh, Juliet, what shall I do?' She'd slithered down on to her knees on the hall floor, weak and overcome with shock and terror. 'They have a shelter, don't they? In the vaults?' she croaked.

'Yes, if they had time to get everyone down. I've tried phoning them, but all the lines are down, so I can't get through.' Juliet sounded as desperate as Liza felt.

'What shall I do?' Liza wailed. She was trembling violently by now, more frightened that she'd ever been in her life.

'Stay by the phone, whatever you do,' Juliet commanded. 'Then if Daddy tries to contact you, you're there to take the call. I'll keep in touch. I've got to go now, Mummy. Talk to you later. Bye.' There was a click, and she'd gone.

Liza shivered her way restlessly around the dark basement flat, drinking the last of the brandy, and trying to make up her mind whether to phone her mother-in-law or not. Lady Anne was with the two younger children, and Nanny was looking after Sophia and Jonathan; better to say nothing for the moment, she reflected.

Then Liza, unable to bear the solitude of being on her own at a time like this, decided to phone Rosie, at Sonia Musgrove's house.

Rosie burst into tears when she was told. 'Oh, Mummy . . . ! I can't bear it. How can we find out of Daddy's all right?'

'Juliet says I must stay here, in case he phones me. I was in Piccadilly when the raid started. If I'd known . . .' her voice caught and she was unable to continue.

'I'll start ringing around the hospitals, as we did when Charles . . .' Rosie sobbed.

Liza's terror increased. 'If anything's happened to Daddy—Oh, God, what shall I *do*?'

'Stay by the phone, Mummy. Stay there, like Juliet said. I'll let you know if I find out anything.'

'All right.' Falteringly, and reluctantly, Liza replaced the receiver. Without anyone to talk to, she was distraught. What was happening? Was Henry buried beneath the rubble? Were they digging to get him out, right now? Supposing . . . supposing he was never found at all? Juliet had told her some people were never found; not even bits of them.

Weeping uncontrollably, she stumbled into their bedroom.

'Henry . . . Henry,' she sobbed, so overwhelmed by grief that she feared she'd go out of her mind. This nightmare can't be happening, she thought, during moments of agonizing clarity. Henry *must* be all right. He had to be.

'Please God,' she vowed fervently, 'let Henry be alive. I'll do anything if only he's alive. Anything.' And then she fell to weeping again, for the husband on whom she depended totally, but might never see again . . .

Liza awoke later to hear a key turn in the front door of the flat.

'Ian?' She scrambled to her feet in panic 'Ian? Have you heard anything? Is Henry . . . ?'

Henry stepped quietly into the room. He was grey from top to toes. Plaster dust caked his hair, frosted his eyelashes, was streaked on his exhausted face and embedded in his clothes.

'Hello, Liza.' He looked steadily at her, his shattered expression telling her more of what he'd been through than words could ever have done.

'Oh, Henry, darling.' Liza flew to him, putting her arms around him, holding him as if she could never bear to let him go. 'Thank God you're safe. Thank God. Thank God,' she kept murmuring, her wet cheek pressed to his grimy one.

'How did you know?'

'Juliet phoned me as soon as she heard. I'd just got back from Piccadilly; it was a bad raid, wasn't it? What can I get you, darling? A drink?' She remembered she'd finished the brandy. 'A whisky and soda?'

'What did you say?' He shook his head. 'I'm temporarily deafened. The noise was terrible.' His voice cracked as he lowered himself painfully into a chair.

'Would you like something to eat? There are a couple of eggs, and some tomatoes. I could make you an omlette?'

'I'm not hungry. I just need to sit quietly for a while. And I'd like a glass of water.'

Liza phoned Juliet and Rosie, thankful she hadn't alerted Lady Anne. Then she sat quietly by Henry's side, remembering her promise to God. She would keep her word, no matter what.

Things would have to change. She was going to have to change. Henry deserved a better wife.

After a hot bath, Henry dragged his bruised and tired body to bed. He'd told Liza briefly about his lucky escape, in which the blast of the bomb, as it exploded on hitting Hammerton's sturdy stone building, had thrown him down the steep stairs to the vaults, where everyone else in the bank was already sheltering.

'We were all stuck down there for several hours before the rescuers could get to us,' he said briefly, 'but no one was injured, and so it wasn't too bad.'

As she lay beside him that night, she held his hand tightly.

'Are you going to retire, now that Hammertons has gone?' she asked softly.

'Only the building's gone,' he replied in a reasonable voice. 'Hammertons has to go on, and tomorrow we're having a directors' meeting at the Savoy, to see how we're going to manage.'

'I only asked,' Liza said carefully, 'because if you are going to retire, a couple of years before you'd planned, I'd be perfectly happy to leave London, and live at Hartley, on a permanent basis.'

Henry lay in silent amazement. So Liza's swollen and blotchy face and solicitous manner really had been because she'd thought he was dead. 'Are you sure you want to live in the country?' he asked doubtfully.

'Absolutely sure, darling,' she said with touching sincerity. 'Oh, Henry, I wanted to die today, when I thought something had happened to you. I'll do anything you want as long as we can be together. I love you so much,' she added, wistfully.

Henry turned to her in the darkness, gathering her to his sore and bruised chest. 'I love you, too, Liza. I always have, and I always will. Thank you for saying you'll stick by me, whatever I decide.'

'I will, Henry. I really will. And if you decide to stay in London a bit longer, I thought I'd join the WVS; they were so wonderful during the raid today, offering tea and hot soup to people in distress. I think it's something I could really do.'

'The Women's Voluntary Service?' Henry tried to keep the astonishment out of his voice. 'That's an excellent idea, darling. They desperately need all the help they can get. It'll be pretty gritty, you know. Sometimes you'll be dealing with people who have lost everything. Their homes, all their possessions, and maybe a loved one, too. You see them wandering the streets clutching their worldly possessions with nowhere to go.'

Liza lay in shocked silence, and Henry knew she was weeping.

'It's pretty rotten, isn't it, darling?' Henry murmured, reaching up to stroke her wet cheek in the darkness.

'This is the most terrible war,' she agreed brokenly, as if she'd only just realized it.

There was something familiar about the fireman, as he rolled up one of the hoses. When he took off his brass helmet, to rub the smoky grime off his face, showing his blond curling hair matted to his head with sweat, Juliet knew for certain it was him.

She hurried over to where he stood, her own uniform crumpled and streaked with smuts.

'Jack?' she asked questioningly.

He spun round, his expression blank. 'Yes?' he grunted uncertainly. Beneath the dirt, she was struck by how young he looked, still a mere boy.

'I'm Juliet, Louise's sister. I thought I recognized you.'

Jack flushed crimson, his dark eyes flashing with recognition. ''ow's Louise?' he asked instantly.

'She's all right. She's living in London with me. She's a nurse now, working in a children's ward, at St Stephen's Hospital.'

'And . . . ?' He paused, inarticulate and tongue-tied with sudden anxiety. 'Did she . . . ?'

Juliet nodded, understandingly. 'She had a little boy. A beautiful healthy little boy. She called him Rupert.'

A range of expressions shadowed Jack's face; delight,

profound regret, and finally sadness. Juliet could have wept. 'And what 'appened to 'im?'

'He's been adopted by a farmer and his wife. They live in Wales, so he'll have a good life, Jack.'

'They wouldn't let Louise keep 'im, then?' he asked bitterly, as if he were referring to a family of which Juliet was not a part.

'This was the best way for everyone's sake,' she said gently, wishing she believed it. 'Of course Louise was terribly upset, but we do know he's all right, because my great-aunt lives nearby.'

Juliet looked at him speculatively, liking the open honesty of his face and his serious eyes.

'Your disappearance caused a stir in the village, you know, Jack. Don't you think you should tell your father and your aunt that you're OK, and that you're in London?'

'Me aunty knows, now. I just 'ad to get away. By lying about me age, I was able to join this lot.' He indicated the fire crew, with a hand blackened with soot. 'I felt the war was 'appening without me. And it was the shame, you see. Everyone guessing wot 'appened, 'ating me for gettin' a young girl, from up at the big 'ouse, in the family way . . .' He shook his head, and gazed with unseeing eyes at the still-smoking ruins of what had been a terrace house. He continued: 'But Louise and me, we loved each other. It seemed natural-like, wot we did. Just like the birds and the bees.' His boyish mouth drooped at the corners. 'I'd liked to 'ave seen me son. Just once.'

'Better not, perhaps?' she suggested. Her heart bled for this youth, who, because of the war, had strayed into the path of both the rigid upper-classes, and the morality of the age.

Juliet didn't tell Louise she'd bumped into Jack. She thought it better not to bring up the past. They'd avoided mentioning Rupert for months now, and Louise seemed to be settling into her nursing with calm efficiency. How she could bear to work with small children, after what had happened, Juliet didn't know, but that was up to her.

Juliet and Louise were having a late breakfast, a few mornings later, both having been on duty the previous night, when Dudley announced there was a visitor to see them.

'Who is it, Dudley?' Louise asked.

'It's me, darling,' said Liza, marching into the dining room, looking very neat in the dark green uniform of the WVS.

'Mummy!'

'*Mummy* . . . ?' Louise echoed in astonishment. Then they were all laughing and hugging each other and Bella was yapping and bouncing around their feet.

'What a scream! I didn't know you were going to do this?' Juliet exclaimed. 'Mummy, you're amazing.'

'The uniform suits you,' Louise giggled.

'Daddy and I are making several changes,' Liza said, accepting the offer of a cup of coffee, as she joined them at the table. She seemed brighter and more cheerful than she'd done in years, and her attitude was refreshingly positive. 'We're going to rent a tiny pied-à-terre, just for the two of us, until Daddy retires,' she continued, 'and then we'll be based permanently at Hartley.'

Juliet's mouth fell open. 'Aren't you going to miss London?'

'I'd rather miss London a bit than miss your father altogether,' Liza responded bravely. 'I realized, when Hammertons was bombed and I feared your father had been killed, that socializing isn't what really matters.'

'So you're not going to share a flat with Uncle Ian any more?' Louise asked, still surprised by her mother's determination to change her life.

'Thank God for that,' Juliet observed acidly.

Liza frowned. 'You never want to see him, do you? And he used to give you such lovely presents when you were small.'

Louise jumped to her sister's defence. 'He's not really our uncle, though, is he? He's just Daddy's friend.'

'His oldest and best friend,' Liza reminded them, 'and he *is* your godfather, Juliet.'

Juliet looked away, mutinously, her mouth tight, her expression veiled. 'I hate him,' she said coldly. 'That's all there is to it.'

'University?' Lady Anne exclaimed, in delight. 'Amanda, I think that's a wonderful idea. What do you want to read?'

'Politics, of course.' Now that Amanda had turned seventeen, and passed her School Certificate exams with flying colours, she was more determined than ever to have a career. Tall for her age, and more curvaceous than any of her sisters, she wore her glasses unashamedly, and had her hair cut short, with a side parting. Her wardrobe consisted of tweeds, flat shoes and thick stockings. She said *yuck!* to make-up and perfume, and absolutely refused to 'get dressed up like a dog' for any occasion whatsoever.

'You've always been interested in politics, haven't you?' Lady Anne observed, ready to back this bright young woman, who was bound to face family opposition by becoming a bluestocking.

'The thing is, Granny, I absolutely abhor and *detest* the class system in this country. It's so bloody . . . sorry . . . so unfair! I've had a much better education than the village children, but only because Daddy could afford to send me to a private school. How unfair is that? And we can afford to have Dr Musgrove when we're ill, while the poor have to queue up at the panel doctor. It's a disgrace! People can go *hungry* in this country, and nothing is being done about it. And all the time the rich aristocracy are living in grand houses, with dozens of servants . . .'

'Not any more, darling,' her grandmother said, mildly, 'the war has put a stop to that. And with food rationing, even the very poor are having a healthy and balanced diet for the first time in their lives.'

'For the time being!' Amanda insisted, refusing to see any point of view except her own. 'Eventually, I want to be an MP but even if I have to start by being a Parliamentary researcher, or even a secretary in the House of Commons, I'll be happy,' she told her grandmother, earnestly.

Lady Anne smiled. 'It's what you've always wanted, isn't it?'

Amanda nodded. 'Especially since everyone in this family thought Jack was so beneath Louise, they couldn't possibly continue to see each other.' She leaned forward, her intelligent blue eyes filled with firey ambition to right the wrongs of the country. 'If Jack had been the son of an Earl, things would have been handled absolutely differently. Louise would have been *urged* to marry him when she was sixteen, and she'd have been absorbed into his family, probably hailed as a heroine for producing the next son and heir!'

Lady Anne sat listening, her clacking knitting needles quiet for once. 'I think the point you're missing, darling,' she said carefully, 'is that, if Jack had been the son of an Earl, a marriage between him and Louise would have worked, because, in simple terms, they'd have spoken the same language. They'd have been brought up in the same way. Shared the same culture, values, possibly religion and politics. As it is, if she'd married Jack, the difference in their backgrounds would have grated, sooner or later. This doesn't mean there is anything wrong with Jack. From what I've heard, he's a thoroughly decent, polite and honest boy, but he and Louise come from very different homes.' Lady Anne paused, reflectively. 'It is hard enough as it is to make a marriage work, to make it last when the first ardour dies down, but people have a much greater chance of making it work if they start off by coming from similar families. That's all I'm saying.'

Amanda frowned, pushing her glasses higher up her nose. 'But love should overcome any differences,' she argued, unconvinced. 'I'm sure Louise would have been happy with Jack. And she'd certainly have liked to have been able to keep the baby.'

'The baby, yes,' Lady Anne agreed, reflectively. 'But sadly, young women who have babies without being married are pilloried for being immoral, which is a very unforgiving attitude.'

'And *that*,' Amanda exclaimed, 'is something else I want to change, Granny. How old does one have to be to join the Labour Party?'

'Lady Padmore! How nice to see you again. How are you?'

Rosie turned to see Salton Webb, smiling down at her. She flushed, remembering how drunk she'd got at Juliet's dinner party.

'Very well, thank you,' she replied with cool crispness. They were at a drinks party given by Lady Diana Cooper in her beautiful suite at the Dorchester.

'Are you still staying with your sister?' Salton asked.

Rosie's features hardened, her thin face resembling a whippet with long mascarered eyelashes. 'I'm staying with Sonia Musgrove. In Eaton Square,' she explained, grandly.

Salton shook his head. 'I don't know her.'

'*Lady* Sonia. She's the Queen's Lady-in-Waiting.'

'The Queen has a whole bunch of Ladies-in-Waiting, doesn't she?' he remarked, in his unimpressed, easy-going American manner. 'I suppose they work in shifts.'

She looked at him reprochfully. 'It's a very high position.'

211

'Can't be much fun, though, can it?' He grinned, showing even white teeth. 'Anyway, what are you doing with yourself, these days?'

Rosie shrugged her shoulders. 'Seeing friends. Going to the theatre.'

He gazed expectantly at her, eyebrows raised, as if waiting for her to say more.

'What?' she asked, defensively.

Salton looked around the crowded cocktail party, where the air was blue with cigarette smoke, and the chatter of voices was giving him a headache. 'I wondered if you'd like to come out to dinner with me. This is a bit of a bun-fight, isn't it? How about supper at the Savoy Grill?'

Rosie could feel her animosity towards this arrogant Yank dissolve. Supper at the Savoy Grill sounded divine. After the years of being stuck down at Hartley, she was ready to go out with almost anyone, especially if it meant supper at a restaurant like the Savoy.

'I *suppose* I could,' she drawled, with faked nonchalance.

'What about the friend you're staying with?' he glanced around the room. 'Are you with her? Should we ask her to join us?'

'You mean Sonia?'

He nodded.

'*She's* dining at Buckingham Palace this evening.'

Salton's grin broadened, and his eyes danced with amusement. 'Can't quite equal that,' he murmured, 'but I bet we have a lot more fun.'

As it turned out, Rosie couldn't remember when she'd last enjoyed herself so much. Or laughed so much. Salton turned out to have a dry wit and an amusing turn of phrase. She almost, *almost*, didn't mind that he was not a member of the Englishman aristocracy. She wasn't sure what Mummy was going to say, but meanwhile she was finding his soft drawling accent incredibly sexy. When he placed his hand on her arm, wanting to stress a point he was making, she felt a delicious shiver tingle down her spine.

Rosie was beginning to look at Mr Salton Webb through different eyes. Maybe, in time, he'd become more than a pleasant escort, she reflected, as he signalled to the waiter to top up her glass of champagne.

'You and your sister are quite different, aren't you?' he remarked, looking at her thoughtfully.

Rosie stiffened, expecting a flow of complimentary remarks about Juliet to come next, *as they usually did.*

'We are rather,' she said casually.

'I wouldn't like to get on the wrong side of Juliet,' he continued, 'I mean, she's no cupcake.'

Rosie dissolved into laughter, feeling much better. 'You're right. I've never heard that expression before.'

Salton had a habit of raising his eyebrows when amused, as well as when surprised. 'Do you get on with each other?'

'Most of the time.' She didn't want him to realize she was jealous of Juliet. 'There are five of us, you know. And we're all different. I suppose I'm most like my mother. Louise takes after Daddy. I don't know *who* Amanda takes after, she's a rabid socialist. Charlotte is a little angel, she's fourteen and incredibly pretty and sweet.' Rosie thought about it for a moment. 'I think she takes after our grandmother, actually.'

'And Juliet? Who does she take after?' Laughter lurked behind his eyes; she knew he realized they didn't get on.

Rosie raised her chin, and gave a little shrug. 'I don't know, really.' Her tone was lofty.

'But you're . . . erm . . . not close, are you?'

His manner was so warm and intimate it broke down some of her defences. 'We became very close when my husband was killed,' she admitted. 'Juliet looked after me and had me to stay because I'd been injured. We're basically incompatable, though.'

'You won't be for ever,' Salton said astutely.

'You don't think so?' she asked mockingly.

'Once you're *both* happily married, you'll feel differently about each other.'

Rosie blushed in spite of herself. Salton seemed to be seeing right into her soul. And it was true that neither she or Juliet had been happily married, because they'd both married for the wrong reasons.

They'd wanted status, position and money. Each of them competing for the biggest catch. Becoming deadly rivals. And every time Juliet had won – but had it made her any happier?

It had all seemed so important at the time, Rosie thought, gazing into the black depth of her tiny cup of coffee. Or was it that their mother had *made* it seem so vital to make a 'good match'?

Rosie looked up at Salton, who'd been gazing at her in silence.

'I think both Juliet and I have been burdened all our lives by our mother's expectations,' she said slowly, as if it had just occurred to her.

'A familiar story, the world over. I was driven to succeed by my own mother. It all depends whether one is fulfilling one's *mother's* ambitions, or one's own.'

Her eyes widened. No one had ever spoken to her as wisely or as perceptively as Salton. His words seemed to gather together the scattered pieces of a jigsaw and place them so they fitted perfectly, exposing the picture with clarity. And the picture wasn't very attractive.

'So what does one do?'

'Follow your heart,' he said in a low voice. 'There's no other way.'

When he dropped her off at Sonia Musgrove's house, he held her hand, and then kissed her softly on the cheek.

'Will you come out with me again, tomorrow night?' he whispered.

Instead of saying, as she usually did, 'I'll have to consult my diary . . . I've got *so* much on,' she replied unhesitatingly, 'I'd love to, Salton.'

He swooped down to kiss her other cheek. 'That's swell. I'll call you up in the morning.'

A few weekends later, Rosie invited Salton down to Hartley.

'I want him to meet Sophia and Jonathan,' she told Liza, her voice tight with excitement.

'Is it that serious, darling?' Liza asked in surprised.

'Mummy, it's very, *very* serious,' Rosie admitted. 'You've no idea how wonderful he is. So kind, so gentle and clever. Such a *man*.'

'What do you mean?'

'He's not like the average Englishman. He talks openly about his feelings. If we go to see a sad film, he'll cry, too. His emotions aren't buried as they were with Charles. And his interest in me isn't just sexual, as it was with Freddie. It's hard to explain, but he seems like a *real* man, compared to them.'

A few months ago, Liza would have bristled at the suggestion that an American was superior to an Englishman. She'd have been shocked at a man who showed his feelings, too. But she was beginning to see that she'd changed more than she'd realized.

Becoming a member of the WVS had had a huge impact on her. She was having to deal, first hand, with people from all walks of life, and finding to her surprise, that under the skin, everyone was much the same; hurt when injured, frightened of dying, inconsolable when a loved one was killed, hungry, thirsty or tired. Most of all, she realized with astonishment, everyone *counted*. They mattered. They were all human beings, too.

How had she become so blinkered? Then she began to wonder how she'd treated Parsons and Mrs Fowler, and the other servants at Green Street, as anything but efficient slaves to carry out her wishes? And her poor lady's maid, Miss Ashley? Who'd had to sit up, sometimes until four in the morning, to help her undress and return the family jewels to the safe; only to have to reappear again at eight o'clock with a her cup of Lapsang Souchong. Now, after nearly five long bleak years of war, the profligate extravagance of the Thirties seemed obscene.

It was just so sad, she reflected, that it had taken a terrible world war to make them all wake up to reality. And to make her aware she wasn't required to impress anyone; and by just being herself she wasn't letting Henry down, after all.

'Do you love him, Rosie?' she asked gently.

'With all my heart.' Rosie had regained the bloom on her cheeks, and her features were softer. 'You wouldn't be too disappointed if ... ?'

'... All I want is for you to be happy.' Liza's eyes were over-bright with emotion. 'That's all I ever wanted for you and Juliet, and I really believed the path to happiness lay in having a lot of money and a good position in society. Now I realize those things don't matter so much.'

'They *did* matter though, when you thought them,' Rosie replied generously. 'It's the war that's changed everything. As Salton says, there's no greater leveller than impending death, and let's face it, we've all faced *that* in the last few years, haven't we?' she added, without bitterness.

There was no bitterness in Juliet's voice either, when Rosie told her some weeks later, that she'd become engaged to Salton.

'I'm really happy for you, Rosie,' she said, giving her sister a kiss on the cheek. 'And to think I introduced you to Salton! I'd no idea I was a matchmaker.'

Rosie laughed, basking in the contentment of this new and wonderful relationship. 'I know. You usually keep all the best men for yourself, don't you?' she added, jokingly.

A shadow passed over Juliet's face. 'I *had* the best of the bunch, once, and I lost him.'

'You mean Edward? Daddy told us when he was killed that you'd planned to marry him. That must have been dreadful for you.'

'No, I don't mean Eddie. He was the second best. I mean Daniel.'

Rosie frowned, perplexed. 'But that was *years* ago. You can't still be in love with him? When did you last see him?'

'Two or three years ago. We were in the same restaurant and he was lunching with his wife. We didn't speak; in fact he cut me dead.'

'But didn't you say Gaston had met him?'

Juliet nodded

'And you're wondering why he hasn't been in touch? Maybe,' she continued earnestly, 'if you saw him again, you'd realize you weren't still in love with him, at all. Are you sure you're not clinging to the past?'

Juliet's pale eyes were filled with pain. 'I'm in love with him, Rosie, and I always will be. We were so close. I'll never stop missing that closeness. We were like one person, at times. No one has ever matched up to him, and no one ever will. It was his baby I lost, you know. That was the last straw.' She paused and took a deep breath. She'd never tell anyone how many men she'd slept with in order to try and recapture the intensity of passion she'd experienced with Daniel. 'I'll never find another man like him,' she said instead.

'I'd no idea it was *his* baby you were having. Was he the love of your life?'

Juliet grimaced. 'God, how I loathe that expression! It's the ultimate cliché.'

'Sorry.' Rosie looked abashed. 'It must have been terrible for you.'

Juliet lit another cigarette. 'It's probably God's Punishment for the way I treated Alastair, causing his suicide,' she said drily. 'Nevertheless, I still literally *pine* for Daniel. The longing never leaves me. My heart practically stops when I think I've seen him in the street; and then I feel sick with disappointment when it turns out to be a stranger. I dream of him, sometimes, too.'

Rosie looked concerned. 'You sound obsessed.' Her tone was anxious.

Juliet closed her eyes for a moment. 'Maybe I am,' she said in a small voice, defeated for once. 'All I know is that I still love him more than anyone else in the world. What else can one do?' she shrugged, removing her cigarette from its holder, and stubbing it out in a glass ash tray. 'No one's interested in a Moping Milly. It helps to pass the time to go out with lots of friends, but it doesn't stop me remembering.'

Rosie looked at her sister, trying to quell her secret satisfaction at realizing that Juliet's *didn't* have an enviable life, after all. She might be a great beauty, and a Duchess, with a fantastically fashionable and beautiful home, lots of money, and masses of friends and admirers, but she wasn't happy.

Not that Rosie wanted her to be unhappy, but it did somewhat redress the differences there had always been between them.

'How diabolically clever,' Louise exclaimed in horror. 'Now they can bomb London, without any loss of life to themselves?'

Dr Shane Hunter nodded. 'The V-1 is a pilotless plane, filled up with sufficient fuel to reach London and no further, and stuffed with bombs. When it runs out of fuel, it plummets to the ground and explodes.'

They were on a brief break from the children's ward of St Stephen's Hospital in Fulham, and were having a cup of tea in the hospital canteen.

Louise thought about this. Then she asked, 'How do they get the plane to take off, if there's no pilot?'

Shane grinned. He was a lean twenty-nine-year-old, with an engaging smile and laughing eyes. 'I haven't the faintest! The navigation instruments are obviously pre-set.'

'Then that must be what I heard last night. My sister and

I were asleep when the siren went, and we were discussing whether it was worth going down to the shelter or not ... because the raids have been quite light recently ... and then we heard what we thought was an aircraft in trouble. The engine was spluttering and just about to conk-out. A minute later there was that horrible whistling sound, and then an explosion.'

'That was a doodlebug, all right,' Shane replied, nodding vigorously.

Louise giggled. 'A *what*?'

'A V-1. They're called doodlebugs. Listen, are you doing anything on Saturday night? I rather fancy going to the cinema. They're showing *For Whom The Bell Tolls*, at the Kensington Odeon.'

'Oh yes, I'm longing to see that,' she replied eagerly, enjoying this new relaxed and easy relationship, liking the way Shane treated her with his friendly banter and teasing. She admired him as she might an elder brother, and at times she was deeply moved by his tender manner when dealing with a sick and frightened child, and his compassion, one day, towards a mother whose little girl had died.

His friendship was important to her, too, for she still sorely missed her own beloved Rupert. There were moments when she felt like flinging herself on a train and heading off to Wales in her desperation to see him again, but she knew she mustn't. For one thing, she could never go through the agony of parting from him a second time.

Aunt Tegan had written to Liza, to say the boy was well and happy, and greatly adored by his adopted parents, who had called him Tostig, which was Welsh for 'sharp'.

The letter, though reassuring, had plunged Louise into a tearful depression for several days, and she almost wished her mother hadn't shown it to her. Torn between being glad that Rupert was well and happy, and secretly devastated that he could be so without her, her arms literally ached with emptiness.

Mixed up with thoughts of Rupert was Jack. She wondered endlessly where he was and what he was doing; no doubt he'd joined the armed forces by now. There were frightening moments when she couldn't remember his face; what had he looked like? There were no snapshots to remind her. She had

218

no pictures of Rupert, either. If she wasn't careful, she feared they'd both disappear into the past, and then she'd only have vague memories to comfort her.

One evening, Shane took her to supper at the Blue Cockatoo restaurant, on Chelsea Embankment.

'I think we deserve a treat,' Shane announced, 'after the terrible week we've had.'

Louise nodded in agreement. A little girl had died on the ward, as the result of her injuries from a doodlebug landing on a row of terraced houses where she'd lived, and there were other children who had been badly hurt in similar incidents.

'Let's have a drink, or two!' he added, eyes twinkling conspiratorially, as if he'd suggested something naughty.

Louise smiled, feeling relaxed. 'Good idea.'

'Shall we make gin our choice of poison? With lime?'

'Definitely.'

'The food's not great here, but it's nice to be able to sit in this little garden, isn't it? Especially as it's such a warm night.'

The menu was limited so they settled on carrot salad, with hard-boiled eggs, as their main course, and rhubarb tart with custard to follow.

Shane looked up at the clear sky, still pink from the sunset. 'Let's hope Jerry doesn't want to join us,' he remarked. 'I've had enough of air raids, this week.'

'Me, too,' Louise replied fervently. 'I never knew I appreciated silence until I came to live in London.'

'Have you always lived in the country?'

She described her childhood to him, realizing that they knew nothing about each other. 'Then we all went down to Hartley in 1939, and it's still the family home,' she concluded.

Shane looked interested. 'So why did you come to London? Surely you could have worked in a hospital in Guildford, or Dorking? It's much safer than being here.'

Louise felt the blood draining from her face. No one had asked her that question before. 'I – I just wanted to,' she stammered awkwardly.

'Why?' His probing eyes were studying her face closely. 'Don't you get on with the rest of your family?'

'Oh, yes. Of course I do. We're all very close. But my eldest sisters are in London, and so I decided to come up here, too.'

'Do you like being in town better than the country?'

'No,' she replied vehemently, and realized, too late, that she'd already said too much.

His eyes were sharp pin pricks of curiosity. 'That doesn't make much sense, Louise.'

'That's . . . well, that's just the way it is,' she floundered, flushing deep red, now. She was sure if he knew the truth he'd no longer want to be her friend. This secret shame was something she was going to have to bear for the rest of her life, except with those she was truly intimate with.

But Shane was a doctor, experienced at patients pretending they were fine, for fear of being told there was something wrong with them. He could tell Louise was hiding something, and as long as that barrier was there, he knew their relationship could never move forward.

He chose his words with care, his eyes never leaving her face. 'We haven't known each other very long, Louise, but I hope, one day, you'll feel close enough to me to tell me the secrets of your heart. As I shall tell you the secrets of mine; whenever you want. Do you think, one day, you'll be able to trust me? I'm a very good listener, you know. And I trust you implicitly.' A grin spread over his face.

Louise looked down at the table cloth, her eyes brimming, unable to speak.

Shane reached over and very gently laid his hand over hers. 'You don't have to tell me anything, if you don't want to. I've no right to try and invade your privacy, and I apologize for trying.'

'It's not that,' she murmured, dashing a tear away as it spilled down her crimson cheek. 'But you're not going to want to know me any more.'

His grip tightened. 'That will never happen,' he said firmly.

'You'll be nice because you're a doctor, and *trained* to be nice,' she burst out brokenly.

His mouth tipped up at the corners. 'Forget I'm a doctor and try me as a man,' he suggested.

Louise took a deep jagged breath. Then she looked at him defiantly, her words coming out in a rush. After all, what did she have to lose? His respect? His friendship? That would hurt her more deeply than she suspected, but it would be a great relief to talk to someone who was not a member of the family.

'When I was fifteen I fell in love with a boy in our village, who was also fifteen,' she began, her heart thumping. 'I was naïve and foolish . . . I'd only just learned the facts of life by reading a novel . . . and I had a baby, a little boy. He's been adopted by a couple in Wales. And *that's* why I can't go back home, except for the odd weekend. My family sent me away, to avoid a scandal, but Jack . . . he ran away and then everyone guessed what had happened between us.'

Shane held her hand tighter than ever, and his expression was filled with such compassion, her tears flowed faster.

'Louise, I'm so dreadfully sorry. It must have been heart-breaking for you.' He shook his head. 'I think it's barbaric the way unmarried mothers are treated. Just when a woman needs love and support, she's treated like a criminal and I believe that's absolutely wrong.'

'You don't think I was wicked?' she blurted out through her tears.

'Of *course* I don't. Mark my words, Louise, in twenty, thirty years time, it will no longer be a sin to have a baby out of wedlock,' he said fiercely.

'That's the way it is now, though,' Louise said, sniffing. 'My mother was furious. As if she hated me. Saying I'd ruined my life. Daddy was sympathetic, but he wouldn't let me keep the baby.' She gazed into Shane's face with a woebegone expression. 'You know, I don't think I'll ever stop missing him. I called him Rupert, after Rupert Brooke, but he's called Tostig now.'

'I'm sure a part of you will always miss him, but at least you gave him *life*, Louise. Be thankful that no one pushed you into having an abortion.'

She nodded slowly. 'It was talked about, but my sister, Juliet, put her foot down.'

'Good for her. I like the sound of your sister. How are things with your family now?'

Louise had stopped crying, leaving her young face blotchy and vulnerable looking. 'Fine. It's all been swept under the carpet as if it never happened. That's what my family's like.'

'That's what most English families are like. How about another drink?'

'Yes, please,' she said gratefully.

When he'd ordered more drinks, he took her hand again.

'Do you think, now that everything's out in the open between us, that we can become – more than friends?'

Surprised, Louise looked into his intelligent face, and the sharp grey penetrating eyes that didn't miss a thing. Shane made her feel safe, and maybe something more.

'Yes, I think we can,' she replied, smiling shyly.

Sunday, June the nineteenth, 1944 was a beautiful summer day, all blue and golden and glittering, without a cloud in the sky.

Louise and Shane were off duty, and he'd picked her up from Juliet's house after breakfast and they'd taken a bus to Kew Gardens, carrying between them a picnic luncheon prepared by Dudley.

Meanwhile, Rosie and Salton, spending the weekend at Hartley, sat in the garden with Lady Anne, while Sophia and Jonathan played on the lawn, and Liza helped Mrs Dobbs cook roast chicken for lunch. Over on the tennis court, Henry was giving a tennis lesson to Amanda and Charlotte, occassionally shouting, 'Hold your racket *up*, Charlotte. Not hanging around your ankles.'

It was a day when Juliet had gone on duty at ten a.m. As she walked down the steep Kingston House ramp to join the rest of her unit, she wished she could have stayed at Hartley. It seemed all wrong to be spending the day underground when it was so warm and sunny.

When the siren sounded an hour later, their unit was the first to be called out. There was a surge of energy as everyone scrambled on board, but still she had no premonition of what they were about to face.

'Where are we heading?' she asked the others, hanging on tightly to her seat, as they driver headed east, swerving around bends in the road and racing on the straight, bells clanging.

Dr Gearing replied. 'The Guards' Chapel. Wellington Barracks.'

'Very near Buckingham Palace,' she observed.

'That's not the point,' he said grimly.

'What's up, then?'

'The chapel's had a direct hit from a doodlebug.' He paused, before adding. 'It was packed for Morning Service,'

'Oh, my God,' Juliet said slowly.

It was worse than anything she could have imagined.

The four walls were still standing, but the roof had collapsed on to the congregation.

Buried under great mounds of masonry and a glittering glaze of broken glass were bodies. Three hundred of them.

Afterwards . . . after the hopelessness of trying to help, after seeing the severed limbs and lakes of blood, Juliet was left with flashback memories of the worst catastrophe she'd attended.

A woman in Army uniform, one of the still barely alive, was calling for her friend. 'She was right next to me,' she wailed. Juliet blocked her view as best she could as the rescue team lifted her on to a stretcher; the friend was still right next to her, but she was headless.

Then there was the body of a man, buried into the brickwork high up on one of the walls; his arms outstretched, as if crucified.

They did all they could, working for hours alongside other ambulance units. Numbed from the sheer horror of it all, Juliet forced herself to carry on, knowing that the hideous images would be imprinted on her brain for ever.

'If it had been hit an hour earlier or an hour later, the chapel would have been empty,' a member of the Civil Defence Service mourned, as he strived to coordinate the police, the Fire Service, and ambulance units, while at the same time directing people wanting information to the Incident Enquiry Post.

With her uniform covered in blood and filth, and her eyes rimmed with grime, Juliet eventually emerged from the scene of carnage, amazed that a normal world still existed. The All Clear had sounded and streams of volunteers had come to help; even civilians, coming out of shelters, offered to help clear away the débris.

Stretcher parties worked in shifts, entering the scene of devastation to collect more bodies. The WVS were handing out cups of hot sweet tea and biscuits and Juliet was relieved her mother wasn't there to witness one of the worst atrocities of the Blitz.

The glittering morning, so fresh and clean, had turned into a blood soaked Sunday afternoon.

With her head bowed, she walked slowly back to the ambulance. Suddenly a strong hand gripped her elbow. Thinking it was Dr Gearing wanting her back, she spun round and looked up.

Straight into the face of Daniel.

Henry came out of his study, looking grave. 'Ian's just telephoned,' he announced to the rest of the family as they sat in the garden after lunch. 'The Guards' Chapel's had a direct hit, during Morning Service.'

Lady Anne gave a little cry of distress. 'Oh, it's wicked if people can't even pray in safety.'

'I was supposed to have been on duty this morning,' Liza exclaimed, 'but Cynthia Askey wanted to swap weekends with me, because her daughter's getting married next Saturday. How dreadful! I feel I should be there to help.'

'Juliet's on duty today,' Rosie observed, nervously.

'Do you want me to take you back to town, darling?' Salton asked, stroking her shoulder. He looked at Liza. 'I could give you a lift, Mrs Granville, if you'd like to go back, too?'

'There's no point in you all rushing back,' Henry pointed out. 'In fact, with these damned doodlebugs, London's become distinctly unsafe again.'

Amanda stretched her bare tanned legs, as she lay on the grass, sunbathing. 'I'm old enough to enrole next week. I'm thinking of joining the WRENS.'

Henry looked at her doubtfully. 'I'm afraid, darling, as you're so short-sighted, you'll never pass the medical, for any of the armed forces.'

She stuck out her bottom lip. 'I want to do something more interesting than nursing; that's for sissies. What about a job in the War Office? That might be a good start to my political career.'

'I'll talk to Ian, if you like. He might have some good suggestions for what you could do.'

'Daddy, do stop talking to me as if you're trying to humour me,' she grumbled. 'It's so patronizing. I'll find myself a job.'

'When can I do something to help the war?' Charlotte asked. 'Even Mummy's doing war work; can't I be a Fire Watcher, like Daddy?'

'You're only fourteen,' Rosie pointed out. 'I hope the war will be over by the time you're old enough to join in.'

*   *   *

Louise had invited Shane back to supper, after their day at Kew. As it was Sunday, and his day off, Dudley had left some cold cuts and a bowl of salad for them, in the dining room.

'I'd forgotten Juliet was on duty and won't be back tonight,' Louise remarked, as they helped themselves to the supper, while Bella looked up at her, hopeful of being fed some scraps.

Shane laughed. 'I suppose it is more peaceful without her; she's a live wire, but good fun.'

'She's marvellous, isn't she? I just wish she had a really nice boyfriend. Do you suppose it's because she's so beautiful? And that attracts the wrong sort of man?'

Shane considered this for a moment. 'I think she's probably just been unlucky. She'll find the right person, one day.'

'As I have,' Louise said, in a small shy voice.

Shane's thin face broke into his quirky grin. 'I'm glad you think so,' he rejoined, 'because I've definitely found the right person.'

'Have you?' She looked at him, and something clutched at her insides, a half-forgotten yearning that reminded her of being with Jack.

'Absolutely.' He reached across the formal table, and planted a kiss on her mouth. 'I love you, Miss Louise Granville.'

Louise giggled, turning pink. 'Me, too.'

'You love yourself, too?' he teased. 'Well, that's a good start, anyway. Do you think, in time, you could get around to loving me?'

'I could try!' she retorted playfully.

He thumped his chest with his fist. 'Try?' he repeated. 'That's not good enough, Miss Granville. You've got to do better than *try*.'

'Perhaps I'll try very hard.' Her blue eyes were sparking with fun.

'Very, very hard?'

Louise nodded silently. 'Perhaps.'

Suddenly the mood changed from flippant to serious. Shane had stopped grinning and his eyes drilled hers, almost with anguish.

'I love you.'

'I love you, too,' she whispered, hardly able to breath.

He rose suddenly, and came round to where she was sitting.

'I don't think I can bear this much longer. Louise, will you marry me?'

She looked up at him, shocked. 'Marry you? But you barely know me.'

'I know that I've found what I've been looking for, all my life,' he said softly. 'If there wasn't a war I'd say we should wait. But there *is* a war and none of us knows if we'll even be alive this time tomorrow. Let's try and grab all the happiness we can, before it's too late.'

Louise's head was in a spin. It was true; people were marrying after the briefest of courtships these days. But could she really . . . ? It was the most exciting thought, and he was right; they could be killed at any time. She also knew she loved him, in a way she'd never loved Jack.

'Yes, I will,' she said slowly, her face filled with wonder.

Shane dropped down on to his haunches in front of her, so their faces were level. 'You're quite sure?' he urged. 'I'm only an impoverished doctor, while you're . . .'

She silenced him by placing the palm of her hand across his mouth. 'I love you, and I always will,' she whispered, 'because you're my friend, as well.' Overcome by emotion, she bowed her head and leaned forward, so their foreheads were touching.

'Are you all right?' she heard Daniel ask in his deep rumbling voice. He was looking anxiously into her face.

Dazed, Juliet wondered for a moment if she was suffering from delusions brought on by exhaustion. Was it really Daniel standing before her, in grey flannel slacks, and an open neck shirt, looking at her with a concerned expression?

'I'm fine,' she said, raising her chin. 'It's my job; we're all in it together.'

His dark eyes never left hers. 'You're very brave, Juliet.' Then he glanced over at what had been the entrance to the chapel. 'It must be hell, in there.'

'Dante's Inferno has nothing on this,' she heard herself say, her voice hard and harsh, her pale eyes narrowed as she looked defiantly into his, as if challenging him.

'I didn't know you were still a VAD.'

'There's still a war on, isn't there?' she shot back, stung by the surprise in his voice. 'What are *you* doing here?'

'When I heard what had happened, I came along to see if there was anything I could do to help.'

She nodded briefly, her bloodied hands smoothing her crumpled and filthy apron. In that moment she felt vastly superior to him, as he stood, immaculate in mufti, whilst all around them doctors, nurses, wardens and the rescue services toiled away, reduced now to collecting body parts.

'I must go,' she said briskly. 'I've got to get cleaned up. We're on stand-by until tomorrow morning, in case of further incidents.'

Then she walked away, her head held high as she climbed into the ambulance with Dr Gearing and the others. She even managed not to look back, as they drove towards the Mall, on their way back to Kingston House.

Only then did she start shivering and crying; weeping for the victims of the slaughter she'd witnessed, weeping from tiredness and horror, and weeping most of all because of her own confrontational manner every time she saw Daniel.

Why did she do it? What possessed her to ruin any chance they might have had of even being friends? Some demon inside her always had to keep twisting the knife as soon as she saw him. Punishing him for the hurt and pain she'd suffered from his rejection of her . . . Or was she really punishing herself for ever letting him go, in the first place?

'I don't believe it!' Rosie sounded quite put out. 'Louise getting married?'

'She *is* nineteen,' Liza protested. 'That's a normal age for a girl to get married, surely?'

'I suppose so, but it makes me feel so old, to have my little sister getting married.'

Henry laughed. 'That's what I felt when you made me a grandfather. Shane Hunter is a great chap. He's clever, and now he's decided to specialize in paediatrics, he could go far. Medicine is a fine profession, and one that Louise understands, as a result of her experience at St Stephen's.'

Rosie said nothing. Privately, she was sure her mother had welcomed Shane into the family because she was relieved that Louise had found a husband at all. Not everyone would be willing to marry a girl who'd had an illigitimate baby. Especially not the young men they'd met when she and Juliet had Come

Out. One was expected to be a virgin. Rosie groaned at *that* memory, and the hell of her honeymoon with Charles.

At least, thanks to Freddie, she was now a woman of some experience. Perhaps rather more experience than Salton realized, she reflected with a secret smile, but no matter. They were having a wonderful love life; though she did rather wish he'd set a date for their marriage.

'I think it's marvellous,' Juliet enthused, when Louise told her the news. 'You deserve some happiness, after all you've been through, darling, but I'm going to miss you terribly when you move in with Shane.'

'I'll miss you, but we'll still be in London, and Juliet . . . ?'

'Mm-hm?'

'Thank you so much for everything. You've saved my life, you know. Looking after me when . . . you know,' her voice caught, '. . . and letting me live here with you, and giving me Bella . . .'

'Frankly, I don't know what I would have done without you,' Juliet replied bluntly, averted her face to hide the anguish in her eyes. In the past week she seemed to have lost even more weight, and her cheek bones, carefully roughed, stood out so her face looked almost skeletal.

Sleep had eluded her since last Sunday. Flashbacks of the unbelievable horror of that morning blazed across her tired mind, and they were always accompanied by images of Daniel taking hold of her arm. Looking down at her. Talking to her.

Then attacks of pure panic would swept through her, so that she could hardly breath, didn't dare move, waited for death to strike her too.

Louise and Shane's wedding was to take place at St Paul's, Knightsbridge, with a small reception afterwards at the Hyde Park Hotel.

'We must do the best we can for her, as we did for Rosie and Juliet,' Liza pointed out, and Henry agreed. The hotel promised to provide sandwiches, biscuits, and the wedding cake, for a hundred guests. Henry, who'd moved the contents of his wine cellar down to Hartley at the beginning of the war, brought up several cases of his best champagne.

'I don't need a wedding dress,' Louise assured her mother. 'I mean it would be hypocritical for me to wear white, wouldn't

228

it, and it would be silly to use up our clothing coupons for a dress I'll only wear once.'

'White stands for purity, darling, not necessarily virginity,' Liza said staunchly. 'Let's see what we can do.'

It was decided it would be bad luck to borrow the exquisite dresses Norman Hartnell had made for Rosie and Juliet, and Liza's own wedding dress was too small for Louise, and a very unbecoming 1914 style.

'I have something to show you,' Lady Anne announced mysteriously, when they were all at Hartley the following weekend. She led the way to her bedroom, a still sprightly, upright woman, who reminded people more and more of Queen Mary.

'There!' she said, with a sweep of her hand. 'What do you think?'

Hanging on the outside of her wardrobe was an exquisite white lace wedding dress, with long sleeves, frilled at the wrist, and a full skirt flowing into a train.

'Granny . . . !' Louise gasped. 'It's exquisite. Look at the little bands of pleated organza between the layers of lace! And all those tiny silk buttons down the back!'

'Paquin made it for me in Paris, when I married your grandfather in 1882.' She turned to Liza. 'What do you think, my dear? With one of the family tiaras, and a plain tulle veil . . . ?'

Liza was as entranced as her daughter. 'Mama, it's beautiful. Quite beautiful, isn't it, Louise?'

But Louise had flung her arms around her grandmother, almost knocking her over. 'Thank you, thank you, thank you,' she said, beside herself with delight. 'With all the coupons in the world, I'd never be able to get a dress like that.'

Lady Anne beamed. 'I'm glad you're pleased, darling.'

They took the dress back to London with them that night, hanging it in Louise's bedroom, so Shane wouldn't see it before the big day.

'You're all set now,' said Juliet. 'Happy?'

'Happier than I ever thought I could possibly be,' Louise replied dreamily. 'The past is behind me now, and I've got such a wonderful future with Shane to look forward to.'

'Quite right, darling. Never look back . . . unless you want to be turned into a block of salt like Lot's wife!' Juliet quipped.

*   *   *

Two days later, Louise, having just arrived home after a night on the children's ward, was still in the hall when the front door bell rang.

'It's OK, Dudley. I'll answer it,' she called out, striding across the black and white marble floor and opening the heavy door.

''Ullo, Louise.' Jack was standing on the front door steps, his expression eager. 'I 'ad to come and see you. Ain't you goin' to ask me in?'

Then his smile faded as he saw the look of shock on her face.

Seven

He'd grown into a man compared to when she'd last seen him. Taller, bigger, brawnier and with a roughness about him that surprised her. He sat stiffly and awkardly in Juliet's stylish Art Deco drawing room, and she noticed his black boots seemed enormous.

This was not the Jack she'd known. That Jack had been a gentle boy with a bloom on his cheeks and an honest gaze, who'd liked to listen to her reading Rupert Brooke's poems. She'd even thought, at one time, that he resembled the great writer, with his sensitive mouth and beautiful features.

Where had that boy she'd loved so much gone? This was a thickened, coarsened version. Stubble bristled through his skin. The large splayed hands resting on the knees of his shiny grey suit were the hands of a labourer, not a poet.

The thought *My family was right . . . It wouldn't have worked* flashed unwillingly through her mind.

'So, what are you doing these days, Jack?' she asked, wishing Juliet was at home to help her conduct this embarrassing visit.

He looked astonished. 'Didn't your sister tell you we'd met?'

This caught her unawares. 'No? Which sister?' She wondered if he'd been back to Shere and had seen Amanda.

'The one wot's a Duchess. That's 'ow I knew where you lived. I looked 'er up in the telephone directory.'

230

'Juliet?'

'Didn't she tell you? I'm a fireman, see. We saw each other at one of them bomb incidents. She wos in 'er nurse's uniform, an' all. Told me you'd 'ad a son, too.'

It was all happening too fast. Louise felt bewildered. Why had Juliet never mentioned any of this?

'Th-that's right,' she stammered. 'Rupert, except that he's now called Tostig.'

A look of deep sadness settled on Jack's face like an imprint of grief. 'I wished I'd seen him. 'oo did he look like?'

'He had your blond hair . . . but he didn't look like anyone, particularly,' she said lamely. She was finding this painful. Any mention of Rupert still hurt deeply. Even if she and Shane had a dozen children, there would always be Rupert; the empty space in her life.

Jack was watching her closely. 'So wot about us? That's why I came to see you. I'm bringing 'ome a steady wage now. Got meself a room over a shop in Peckham. I suppose we can't get Rupert back now, but 'ow about us. Lou? I still loves you, you know.'

'Oh, Jack . . .' She was crying openly know. Crying for the love they'd lost, and the child they'd lost, along with their innocence. They'd been children themselves back then, as they'd lain in the long grass in a secluded field in the summer of their youth.

'I love you too, Jack, but not in the same way,' she said, dabbing her eyes. 'We had something special, but that was over four years ago and we've both grown up since then.'

Louise couldn't bear to see the disappointment in Jack's face. Fleetingly, it made him look like a young boy again, the corners of his mouth drooping, a sudden bright sheen in his blue eyes.

'I'm so sorry,' she said diffidently, averting her gaze. 'I wish it had all been different. And I wish we'd been able to keep Rupert.'

Jack stayed silent, unable to speak.

What had Juliet told him? Desperate to soften his fall from hope to reality, she continued; 'We were too young, Jack. It would have been different if we'd been older, but we've both changed.' She kept staring out of the window at the red buses going up and down Park Lane, so as to avoid having to look at him.

'So, that's that, then,' he said at last, in a flat voice.

She nodded, her mouth a tight line of suppressed anguish. 'At least we know that Rupert is well and happy, and being looked after by a couple who adore him.'

'Yup. And you've got someone else, too, 'aven't you?' he added grimly.

Louise looked at him, startled. 'Yes. How did you know?'

He pointed one of his strong fingers to her left hand. 'I just seen you got a ring.'

She turned crimson. 'Oh, yes. He's a doctor. We met at the hospital where I work.'

'A doctor?' he asked, surprised. 'I thought wiv a family like yours, you'd *want* to marry a toff, like your sisters.'

'We can marry who we like, Jack,' she replied, knowing it was a lie, and yet at the same time true.

He raised his thick eyebrows. 'So you ain't turnin' me down, 'cos I ain't good enough?'

'Of *course* not!' she exclaimed, distressed. 'That doesn't come into it. Like I said, we were too young. First love and all that, you know?' she said, wanting to do anything to lessen his hurt.

'Right then.' He rose, and stood awkardly. 'I'd better be off, then. Got to meet some chaps for a game of snooker.'

Louise stood up, not believing him, and walked with unhurried feet to the door, as if she was reluctant to let him leave.

'Thank you for coming to see me, Jack.' God, she sounded like her mother bidding an acquaintance good-bye. 'Take care of yourself, won't you? Will you stay in the Fire Brigade after the war?'

She didn't even hear his answer. He looked crushed, as he ambled in his big boots down the black stair carpet, clattering on the marble floor when they reached the hall.

'Ta-ta, then,' he said, without looking at her.

'Good-bye.'

A moment later he was gone, running down the front steps, and turning right to head for Marble Arch.

'Oh, my God,' she murmured, closing the door and leaning against the wall for support. She closed her eyes. 'That was terrible,' she muttered aloud. It was as if a ghost from the past had come to claim her, bringing back bitter-sweet memories of that summer, when she'd been a romantic young girl, her head filled with poetry about love.

The front door swung open at that moment, and Juliet stepped into the hall.

'Hello! What on earth are you doing standing there? Are you all right?'

Louise opened her eyes, and peeled herself away from the wall. 'Jack came to see me. Why didn't you tell me you'd seen him?'

'I thought it would upset you.'

'It upset me more to have him turning up like that. He's changed so. I'm not sure I'd have recognized him if I'd seen him in the street.'

Juliet led the way upstairs. 'He's grown up, darling. Like you have.'

Louise followed, her legs still shaky. 'I don't think I've changed, though. Not much, anyway. It was awful. He wanted us to get back together.'

Juliet looked at her sister curiously. 'Would you have gone back to him, if you weren't for Shane?'

'No, never.'

'Really? You're sure of that?'

'Absolutely! Is that terrible of me?'

'Of course it's not terrible, sweetie. Are you going to tell Shane?'

Louise nodded. 'We've already made a "no lies" pact.'

Juliet smiled at her sister's youthful naïvety. 'Really darling? Don't you think it might unsettle Shane?'

In her experience, the odd lie, albeit a white one, was *vital* in a marriage. There were certain things husbands didn't *want* to know. Confessions could be the death-knell to any relationship, in her opinion.

'Shane will understand,' Louise replied confidently. 'After all, it's him I've chosen to marry, isn't it?'

Shane did understand, and two months later their wedding took place, witnessed by their family and friends. Little Sophia was a bridesmaid and Jonathan a page. Amanda refused to 'get tarted up' for the occasion, saying photographs of her in a picture hat and flowery frock would ruin her career in years to come when she was the first woman Prime Minister.

As at Rosie's wedding, nearly seven years before, the bride was outshone by one of her sisters, whose outstanding looks caused heads to turn and people to whisper, in awe-struck admiration. Only it wasn't Juliet this time who stole the show, it was Charlotte, who showed a promise of beauty far greater than any of the others.

'What are we going to *do* with Charlotte?' Liza asked Henry nervously, as they lay in bed that night, in their small new Knightsbridge apartment. Experience had taught her that exceptionally beautiful daughters weren't necessarily a blessing.

'Keep her at school and in the country for as long as possible,' Henry advised. 'Anyway, I don't think she's interested in boys yet, do you?'

Liza rolled on to her back, her hands cupping the back of her head. 'Not that I know of. Lady Diana Cooper told me at the reception that she could be a film star, with her looks.'

'Oh, God!' Henry groaned. 'I hope Charlotte didn't hear? She'll be off to Hollywood the minute the war's over.'

'Yes,' Liza replied thoughtfully. Charlotte Granville . . . the next Veronica Lake? The next . . . Betty Grable? A blonde edition of Hedy Lamarr? Liza turned quietly on to her side again. 'Anyway, it was a lovely wedding, wasn't it? Louise looked really happy.'

'Yes, she did.' Henry sounded slightly mollified, 'I wish Salton would get on and marry Rosie, though. I don't think long engagements are a good thing.'

'Why not?'

'They're rather working class, aren't they? You know, waiting until the couple have saved up enough money, and that sort of thing.'

'Henry, you're actually being snobbish,' Liza giggled, prodding him in the back. 'I thought that was my department?'

He grunted amiably. 'Maybe it's an American custom?'

'Should we say something?'

'Definitely not,' he replied firmly. 'He'll marry Rosie when he wants to.'

A week later there was an unexpected bombing attack, unexpected because there'd been no warning, no siren, nothing to prepare people for what was to happen.

The first V-2 had landed. This was not an un-manned aircraft like the doodlebug, but the first of many rockets, launched from the other side of the Channel.

234

Juliet, writing letters in her study, heard the explosion and suddenly she had the most dreadful premonition. It was so strong and frightening that she sat rigid for a moment, almost unable to breath.

Daniel! She could picture him in her head as vividly as if he stood before her. She felt an over-powering desire to see him again. He was rarely out of her thoughts, and she dreamed about him almost every night; but this was different. She must go to see him now, no matter what.

Grabbing her handbag, she flew down the stairs, shouting to Dudley, 'I've got to go out. I'll be back later.'

Then she ran along the pavement towards Marble Arch, and turned right into Green Street, where she'd parked her car opposite the now boarded-up ruins of her old home.

With shaking hands, she put her key in the ignition. Minutes later she was speeding down Park Lane, free of traffic at this time in the morning. At Hyde Park Corner, she headed in the direction of Chelsea.

Juliet knew, even before she'd reached Bywater Street, that her worst fears had been realized. The road had been taped off. Air Raid Wardens, the police, several ambulances and the fire brigade were out in force; it was a scene she knew only too well.

Abandoning her car in the King's Road, she climbed out, her legs almost giving way beneath her as she crawled under the cordon.

'Sorry, Miss, you can't come here,' an Air Raid Warden told her. Under his tin hat, his weary face was covered with grime, and his eyes had the look, as did the eyes of all the rescue workers these days, of having witnessed sights that were too hideous to bear.

'I'm a nurse on an ambulance unit at Kingston House,' she explained, her heart thumping in her rib-cage, her throat dry with terror. She looked beyond him, and then she crumpled, bending over as if she'd been punched in the stomach.

Daniel's house had been destroyed. Dust, sand, concrete, plaster and earth had coalesced in a hovering cloud above the ruins. On one side the party wall was left standing. There was even a painting of a landscape still hanging high up on what had been the wall of his bedroom.

The Warden stepped forward, gripping her elbow in his strong hand. 'Are you all right, Miss?'

'Was . . . w-was th-there . . . ?' she stammered, unable to continue.

'Anyone in the house?' he prompted, gently. 'Yes. A man and women were living there. We got them out, but there was nothing we could do for them.'

The world was a dark frozen place, devoid of feeling, hope, or love. Juliet continued to go on duty, tend to the injured, meet her parents for dinner, play bridge with her friends, all in a soulless vacuum; along with Daniel, something inside her had died.

Eddie's death paled now to a mere regretful sadness in her mind. So did everything else that had happened to her since she'd been a child. What was real, the *only* thing that seemed real, was that Daniel was no more.

In her numbed state, she was able to go through, almost dispassionately, every moment of the times they'd been together. While she longed to cry, to grieve, to lose control, to *die* from a broken heart, all she could summon up was a calm clarity. She recalled his deep rich voice which had thrilled her from the beginning. And his almost black eyes piercing hers and in so doing making her feel she'd known him for ever. They had been a part of each other.

She even played gramophone records of their favourite dance music, and remembered the feeling of his hands as they'd held her tightly. The whispered words of love, in bed. The closeness that was like nothing she had ever known before. And the baby daughter she had borne him, who had died unknown and unloved by him.

But still, her heart was empty, her mind a blank screen where there should have been emotions. The tears simply refused to come.

'I'm worried about her, Daddy,' Rosie confided to Henry, when she finally found out what had happened. 'It's three weeks since she found out he'd been killed, and I don't believe she's broken down once.'

'It's shock, sweetheart. Nature's way of protecting people from the pain of their own feelings. It won't last. Juliet will suddenly start to feel again, the emotions will thaw and then she's really going to need all our support.'

'Oh, dear, I feel so sorry for her,' Rosie lamented. 'Especially as Daniel seems to have been with a woman at the time. Juliet must wonder if it was his wife or a new girlfriend, mustn't she?'

'She didn't go to the funeral, did she?'

'From what I can gather, she refused to even read the death columns in the newspapers, far less go to his funeral. In fact, she didn't even *tell* me about it for over a week. Then she got cross with me one day, about something trivial, and mentioned, almost in passing, that Daniel had died when his cottage was bombed. It's as if she's pretending nothing dreadful has happened. I can't even talk to her about it. I don't think she'll ever fall in love again, after this.'

'I know.' Henry sighed, feeling wrenched with sympathy for his secretly favourite daughter.

'How long will this shock last, Daddy?'

Henry hesitated. Sometimes people never recovered from something like this. Juliet, though, was strong. She had guts. He felt sure it was only a matter of time before the barriers of shock gave way.

'It could last weeks or months. We must all keep an eye on her.'

'Yes. Thank goodness we're all in London. I don't know what we'd do without you, Daddy,' she said softly.

'At least you're happy, my sweet,' he replied, smiling.

'I'm *so* happy, Daddy. I never thought I'd be happy again, but Salton is the most marvellous person in the world.'

'Let's hope one day someone marvellous comes into Juliet's life, too,' Henry replied, fervently.

Rosie, shaken by Juliet's loss, felt compelled to get Salton to marry her, before anything could go wrong in their relationship.

'We're winning the war, aren't we, Salton?' she asked, as they strolled in the garden at Hartley, one Sunday afternoon. 'Why don't we get on with it and have a quiet wedding, down here? I don't want another white meringue "do". And we could have a luncheon party in the house afterwards; what do you say?'

Salton hesitated. 'I want to make sure it's right for you, and also, that your children are prepared to accept me as a stepfather,' he replied slowly. 'When the war ends, we'll be living in Washington. Do you really think you'll like that? Won't you miss your family? And what about Jonathan? One forgets, because he's so small, that he's actually Lord Padmore now. You'll want to send him to Eton, I imagine? All these things have to be taken into consideration, Rosie darling.' He slipped his arm around her waist, and pulled her close to his side.

'Jonathan doesn't *have* to have an English education,' Rosie protested. 'And I'm sure I'd adore living in Washington,' she added, a note of panic entering her voice. She was going to die if he changed his mind about marrying her now.

'As you say, we're winning the war.' Salton looked into her eyes with such earnestness, she knew he was being truthful. 'I think it will be over in another twelve months, God willing. What I suggest then, is that as soon as we can, we fly, with the children, to Washington, and we all stay in my apartment.' He leaned forward and kissed her, to still the alarm in her expression. 'It'll be all right, honey. I'm sure you'll love it. You'll get to meet all my friends, and you can check out schools. Of course, you might want to run, screaming, to get on the first plane home,' he said jokingly. 'But, if you and the children like it, then we'll think about actually getting married.'

Rosie hung her head, unhappily. 'I know I'll like it, Salton. I want us to be a proper family.'

He turned to face her, looking at her squarely. 'Trust me, sweetheart. In the last three years, I've seen dozens of English girls getting married to Americans and already many of those marriages are on the rocks. The divorce rate is going to rocket off the Richter scale when some of those English brides actually *arrive* in the States. About all we have in common, in reality, is the same language, and even *that* differs when you get down to it. You may hate the American way of life, and not want to bring up your children that way. And you'll only find out if you come over for a while and see it for yourself.'

'I'd be happy with you in Timbuktu,' Rosie said coaxingly. 'I don't want to wait, Salton.'

He smiled, pulling her close. 'What I think you need is a romantic weekend away. Just the two of us. That will re-assure you that I love you, and want you, more than anything.' He kissed her gently on the mouth. 'What do you say? As we can't fly to Paris or Rome for the time being, how about a cosy, olde worlde hotel, in Gloucestershire?'

'I'd say you're boringly sensible,' she teased, clinging to him. 'I just hope the war ends soon.'

You're the top . . . you're the Colosseum . . .

Juliet gave a convulsive sob, as the little card fell out of one of the pigeon-holes of her desk. After all these years . . . ! She started scrabbling frantically amongst the letters and old postcards in the same compartment, wondering if she'd kept the others. All written in Daniel's hand. Every one an invitation to experience an affair of such extraordinary potency that the passion had never died for her.

You're the top . . . you're the Louvre Museum . . .

Those were the only two she could find. The others, in the tumultuous excitement she'd felt at the time, had probably been hidden or destroyed for fear her mother would find them.

'Daniel . . .' she sobbed now, overwhelmed with anguish and longing. There was anger, too, now the dam of pent-up grief had burst; who was the woman he'd been with? And why, why hadn't it been her? Then they could have died together as she'd told him she wanted, on that far distant day, when the war had broken out.

In an agony of thawing emotions, like frost-bitten fingers held to the heat, she doubled up, sobbing her heart out, inconsolable and desolate.

Hearing her distress through the closed drawing room door, Dudley entered the room quietly, and placed a glass of brandy on the desk. She didn't seem to notice, she was so demented with grief, so he left the room again quickly, and hurried to telephone Henry Granville.

'The tragic thing is, if Daniel Lawrence had lived she'd probably have got over him by now,' Henry whispered to Liza that night as they got ready for bed in Juliet's spare room, having insisted on staying with her for the next few days. 'By *dying*, Daniel's going to remain like an icon, never ageing, never having any faults, the perfect man,' he added drily.

'Don't you think she'll fall in love again one day?' Liza whispered worriedly.

'You've got to remember he had the fascination of being forbidden fruit from the start and I fear he's still got a grip on her psyche. I hope she doesn't turn into a sort of modern-day Miss Havisham,' he said gloomily, as he buttoned up the top of his silk pajamas.

'Oh, nonsense, Henry. She's just had a bad shock. Of course she's upset, but she'll get over it,' Liza replied robustly. 'I think she ought to get compassionate leave for a while and go down to Hartley. Your mother will cheer her up, if anyone can.'

When Henry suggested this to Juliet the next morning, as they had breakfast in the dining room, she flew into a tearful rage.

'What good is that going to do, Dads? Daniel wasn't just a boyfriend, you know. Someone whose death I'll get over in time. He was like the other half of me and he understood me and taught me how to *like* myself.'

Liza looked at her, mystified. 'What do you mean, darling? *Like* yourself?'

Juliet covered her face with her hands, her shoulders shaking. 'He took away my terror of sex. My fear of men, although I pretended to like them . . .' her voice broke and she couldn't continue.

Henry, watching her with narrowed eyes, frowned with concern.

'I don't understand, Juliet,' Liza said. 'Why were you ever afraid of . . . men?'

As if she hadn't heard, Juliet continued, 'Daniel made sex beautiful for me, not a disgustingly dirty act. Not something horrifying and painful that made me feel sick and gave me terrible nightmares for years and years. And now he's gone. I shall never find that special closeness again, that understanding. It's as if my life is over, and I wish I was dead, too,' she wept despairingly.

Henry got up from the table and put his arm around her shoulders. 'But *why* did you have these feelings in the first place, darling? Did Nanny tell you nasty things? Is that it?'

Juliet pushed him away, her eyes stricken with rage.

'Do you *really* want to know?' she asked, with hysterical fury. 'Do you really want me to tell you who robbed me of my innocence? Who ruined my life? Because I sure as hell wasn't able to tell you at the time, because you'd have said I was a wicked girl.'

Henry looked at her, appalled by her words, and Liza gave a shocked little cry. 'For God's sake, what *is* it, Juliet?'

Juliet suddenly subsided, like a rag doll with the sand draining out of its limbs. When she spoke her voice was small and thin.

'I was sexually assaulted by Ian when I was seven.'

The loudest noise in the room was the discreet ticking of a small silver carriage clock on the mantelshelf.

'Ian . . . ?' Henry croaked, his skin waxy white, his eyes wide with disbelief.

'What?' Liza demanded shrilly after a moment. 'Ian? Daddy's best friend, Ian?'

Juliet nodded, her head bowed, the tears dropping on to her folded hands in her lap.

'When?' Henry's single word flew like an arrow through the air, as he continued to look at his daughter in horror.

'You were going to send Meads to collect me from a children's party at the Mansion House, but the car broke down, and Ian . . . 'Uncle Ian', saintly godfather and your best friend,' Juliet raged with dangerous quietness, 'offered to pick me up in his car. You were both at a wedding or something. It was already dark. But instead of taking me back to Green Street he parked the car in a narrow alleyway. Then he said . . .' she faltered, her throat clogging with tears, 'he said . . . let's get into the back of the car and play a game.' Juliet closed her eyes, unable to continue for a moment. '. . . A game that he said was to be our little secret, because you'd be very angry with me if I told anyone. I was so frightened. Then he did these dreadful things to me.'

'Ian?' Liza repeated, dazed, as if the name was new to her.

'Oh, my God,' Henry breathed. 'Oh, dear Christ.'

'Do you know, I remember now,' Liza said, after a pause, 'when you got back from that party . . . it was a charity do, and you all had to present Queen Mary with a little purse filled with money . . . you said . . . Yes, I remember you complained of a stomach ache.' She looked at Juliet, her face strained. 'We kept you in bed for several days, because we thought you had 'flu or something. Oh, darling, if only you'd told us,' she said, breaking down in tears. 'I can't bear to think how much you've suffered.'

Henry rose stiffly to his feet, as if he'd aged greatly in the last few minutes. 'I'm going to call the police.'

'No, Dads. I simply couldn't bear to have to go through all

that,' Juliet said vehemently. 'I've kept it to myself all these years, and I'd rather it stayed that way. God, haven't I been through enough scandal in the past few years, without having this brought up?' she added pleadingly.

Liza nodded. 'She's right, Henry. This is the last thing she needs.'

'And it won't undo the damage Ian's done,' Juliet pointed out. 'It won't stop the nightmares or my feelings of being worthless. And it won't bring Daniel back,' she added brokenly.

Henry dropped back wearily into his chair. 'I'll deal with Ian myself then,' he added cryptically.

'Let me take you down to Hartley, dearest,' Liza coaxed. 'Just for a few days. You're not well enough to work, and I think some peace and quiet is just what you need. You know how Granny loves to spoil you.'

Juliet gave a deep sigh, as if some of the burden she'd been carrying for so long had been partly lifted. 'Maybe you're right.' She dug the heels of her hands into her eyes. 'I used to be terrified Ian would do something to the others. I was always watching out, to make sure they weren't alone with him.'

'I can't believe it,' Liza kept saying.

Henry said no more, but sat, silent and brooding, shocked to the core that he'd never realized what his lifelong friend had done. Everything was fitting into place, now. Including Juliet's refusal to be at Hartley if Ian was coming to stay.

This was the most terrible blow Henry had ever received in his life, for Ian had not only assaulted Juliet, he'd betrayed over forty years of close friendship and trust.

'I'm going out,' he informed Liza and Juliet stiffly, as he got up and walked to the door.

'When will I see you again, Henry?' Liza called after him.

'I'll join you all at Hartley, at the weekend,' he replied curtly. A minute later they heard the front door slam.

'Have you heard about Uncle Ian?' Rosie asked in a gossipy voice.

It was a hot June day, and once again various members of the family had drifted down to Hartley for the weekend, and they were having lunch on the terrace.

'What about him?' Liza asked crisply without looking up.

'Haven't you heard, Daddy?' Rosie asked. 'He's been in St George's Hospital.'

'Oh, dear, what's the matter with him?' Lady Anne asked with genuine concern.

While Henry continued to eat without saying anything, Rosie continued, 'He's been in some kind of accident. I bumped into Aunt Helen in Peter Jones yesterday and she seemed very worried. I don't know whether he was knocked down by a car or what, but she said his jaw had been badly broken, and it's had to be wired, and most of his teeth have been knocked out.'

'Fancy that,' Juliet remarked drily, sipping her wine.

Rosie looked deflated that her news hadn't caught her family's imagination. 'You ought to send him some flowers or something, Mummy,' she said sulkily. 'I suppose a basket of fruit would be no good, because Aunt Helen said he can only suck things through a straw.'

'What . . . like milk?' Charlotte asked, interested, as she waved away a bumble bee that was droning sleepily over the lunch table. 'I'd hate to have to live on milk. He'll get awfully thin.'

'I'm sure he'll survive,' Liza observed briskly, avoiding eye contact with Henry. 'Now, who would like some more potatoes?'

'The war news is much better, isn't it?' Lady Anne observed diplomatically, sensing the tension in the atmosphere.

Amanda looked up, alerted by the thought of a more intelligent topic than stupid social gossip. 'You mean we've landed in France? It could be the beginning of the end of the war, couldn't it?'

'The *Allied* forces have invaded Normandy,' Henry corrected, the colour coming back to his tired face. 'It *is* great news.' He paused thoughtfully. Normally he'd have been discussing the state of the war with Ian, and that was something he missed now. On the other hand, there were things Ian had told Henry over the years that were surely state secrets and should not have been repeated. Betrayal and untrustworthiness seemed to be his forte.

'Thank God for the Americans,' agreed Rosie enthusiastically. 'Without them I don't know what we'd have done.'

She was happier these days, because Salton was coming

round to the idea of their getting married in England at the beginning of the following year.

'We must be grateful to the Russians, too,' Lady Anne observed. 'For a dreadful moment in 1940, I really feared we'd be invaded, and that would have been it.'

'Will the war end this year?' Charlotte asked hopefully.

'We've a long way to go yet,' Henry warned, 'unless Germany surrenders, and I can't see that happening.'

'I reckon once the Allied forces get to Paris, we'll be on the home straight,' Juliet said.

Charlotte was determined to know more. 'And then what will we do?'

'Salton and I will go and live in Washington,' Rosie affirmed.

'I want to do a shorthand and typing course . . . if I'm not allowed to go to university,' Amanda asserted, giving her parents a reproachful look, 'and then I can get a secretarial job in the House of Commons.'

Henry looked at his fourth daughter with secret amusement, wondering how long this socialistic phase was going to last. Perhaps it would be cleverer not to oppose it.

'We never said we wouldn't allow you to go to university,' he remarked mildly. 'More and more young women go these days, and if you're still interested in a couple of years, why don't you try and get into Oxford, where I went?'

Amanda's face was transfixed with excitement. 'You mean it?' she gasped. 'You really wouldn't mind?'

'I want you to do what will make you happiest, darling.'

She leapt up from the table, and flung her arms around his neck. 'Thank you, Daddy. Thank you. Thank you. That's all I've ever wanted to do, instead of being a silly débutante in an absurd fluffy white dress!'

Rosie and Juliet exchanged glances. Then Rosie turned to Amanda. 'You won't miss much.'

'Oh, I don't know,' Juliet remarked quietly. Her face still had a pinched look, and her eyes were sunken, as if she hadn't slept for weeks. 'Was it all so ghastly?'

She might never have met Daniel if she hadn't Come Out.

'It's a cattle market!' Amanda asserted. 'It's a competition for who can nab the most eligible man first!'

Henry laughed, but Liza looked pained.

'You're being unfair, Amanda,' she said, hurt. 'I know

244

times have changed, but when I was a girl, and when Rosie and Juliet were eighteen, marriage *was* the best career open to a woman, no matter what her class or background. Being a wife and mother, and running a home was what women *did*.'

'And there's nothing wrong with that,' Henry said firmly. 'It's what most women want, in the end, anyway, whether they admit it or not.'

'It's certainly not what I want,' Amanda said sornfully. 'I hate the idea of having squalling runny-nosed brats, and a husband who expects dinner on the table every night.'

'Then it is certainly wiser if you have a career, my dear,' Lady Anne said calmly. 'I think university life would suit you very well.'

'I know what I want to do, when I'm older,' Charlotte remarked, her exquisite face suddenly sparkling. 'I want to be a film star.'

'Many a true word is spoken in jest,' Juliet quoted, with the hint of a smile. 'If Churchill's daughter Sarah can be an actress, why shouldn't you?'

Things seemed to be rushing more quickly towards peace than they had towards war six years previously.

On New Year's Eve, the atmosphere already seemed to hold a promise of peace. The Café de Paris had been restored to its former glory, although it was a place of entertainment for the troops now. Ivor Novello's *The Dancing Years* was playing to packed houses. Racing had been resumed at Newmarket, and Chips Channon, doyen of the social scene for over a decade, was once again entertaining on an unimaginable scale, as if food rationing was already a thing of the past.

What was different now was that people had changed, and in the Granville family the clock could never be turned back.

They were no longer rich, Henry having lost a fortune in overseas investments. He was deeply tired, too. The years of hard work and sleepless nights had taken their toll, and all he wanted to do was to retire and settle at Hartley.

As for Juliet, living alone in the enormous house in Park Lane, the future looked so frighteningly empty and lonely she almost dreaded the day when the war ended and she'd have to leave the camaraderie of the First Aid Post, for the last time.

'Everyone seems to have a future except me,' she said

wistfully when she was lunching with Henry one day. 'You and Mummy will soon be at Hartley all the time. Rosie is off to the States with Salton. Louise and Shane are buying a house in Chelsea, now that she's pregnant; and as for Amanda and Charlotte, one's going to become a bluestocking at Cambridge, and the other's planning to take Hollywood by storm!' she added, with a little laugh.

Henry smiled, glad to see her laughing again, although the pain had never left her eyes since Daniel's death.

'. . . And even Aunt Candida is marrying that old bloke she brought to lunch – what was his name? Oh, yes, Andrew Pemberton,' she added.

Henry chuckled. 'All we need now is for Granny to announce she's about to dash off with some heroic cavalry officer!' he joked.

Juliet's face softened. 'Granny's going to be seventy-five on May the seventh, isn't she? She's been so marvellous, right through the war.'

'Knitting for England!'

'Refusing to get anything on the black market.'

'Changing for dinner every night, even if we're only having a poached egg on toast!'

'Listening to our woes.'

'Keeping up standards,' Henry observed robustly.

'And never, ever, complaining.'

'You're right.'

'We should give a party for her birthday, Dads.'

'Yes. I think she'd like an elegant, formal dinner at Hartley, black tie and all that, don't you? Like we used to have in the old days.'

Juliet nodded. 'And black market or no black market, if Chips Channon can get hold of oysters, lobsters, salmon, venison, and God knows what else, so can Dudley! I'll be responsible for the food, Dads, if you do the drink.'

Henry grinned, his face lighting up so that for a moment he looked like the handsome young man he'd once been. 'Vintage champagne, of course.'

'What else?'

Events were overtaking them as March quickly merged into April. The dinner party was to be a surprise for Lady Anne, and Warwick was secretly cleaning all the silver that had been packed away for several years, while Liza unpacked the Crown Derby dinner service, which had been kept in boxes in the stables, since it had been brought down from Green Street.

'Let's hide it in the pantry cupboard,' she whispered to Warwick, 'We don't want Lady Anne to see it until the night of the party.'

Even Nanny got involved, washing an Edwardian white damask table cloth that seemed as big as a tennis court when it came to ironing it. Two dozen damask napkins also had to be laundered.

'What shall I *wear*?' Charlotte kept bleating. 'And am I old enough to borrow some of your diamonds, Mummy?'

'A string of pearls, perhaps,' Liza replied judiciously.

There was a growing feeling of excitement in the family as the date drew nearer. And when they heard Winston Churchill, President Roosevelt and Stalin had held a secret summit of the Grand Alliance at Yalta, to discuss the last stages of the war and the plan to share power after it, everyone became estatic.

After the long dark tunnel of fear and apprehension, they were moving towards the light; peace was in sight,

Then Juliet, asleep in her bedroom, with the Blitz seemingly over, was awakened one night when a rocket dropped near Marble Arch, causing great damage.

'Can you bloody believe it?' she raged on the telephone to Henry the next morning. 'I've been in this house throughout the entire Blitz, without even a cracked pane, and now this goddamn rocket had blown in all my front windows!'

It was, in fact, the last bomb ever to fall on London.

Events moved so swiftly that, apart from worse food shortages than ever, the emotional suffering of the war seemed to recede with astonishing haste as peace drew ever nearer.

In April the blackout came to an end, and a few days later it was announced that Hitler was dead.

The whole Granville family decended on Hartley, wanting to be together at this historic moment. They hadn't long to wait.

On the morning of Lady Anne's birthday they gathered in the drawing room to listen to Winston Churchill's announcement to the nation on the wireless. His great voice, which had brought inspiration and assurance to everyone for the past five years, boomed no less dramatically.

'The German war is at an end. The evildoers now lie prostrate before us . . .'

Lady Anne sat very upright, blinking back the tears; it was the first time she'd allowed herself to show any emotion since the outbreak of hostilities. She'd heard earlier, from Candida, that Gaston was home, safe and well, from the dangerous but successful espionage work he'd been doing behind the German lines with the Special Operations Executive. She was proud of him and she longed to tell him his father would have been very proud of him, too.

Liza wept quietly, a tiny lace edged handkerchief pressed to her mouth. 'Thank God it's over at last,' she murmured at the end of Churchill's speech.

'Not quite,' Henry reminded her. 'We're still fighting in the Far East.'

'At least there'll be no more bombing,' Louise pointed out as she sat holding Shane's hand.

Rosie looked hopefully at Salton. 'And we can fly to Washington, soon, can't we?'

'I was going to tell you,' he said grinning, 'we're not going to Washington, after all.'

She blanched nervously. 'What do you mean?'

'We're staying put. I've been offered a swell job in London, as legal adviser to the American Embassy . . .'

Rosie flung herself at him before he'd finished speaking.

'That's the best news *ever* . . . !' she squealed with excitement. 'Mummy, Daddy, did you hear that? Salton and I are going to be living in London!'

Juliet asked Warwick to serve champagne – 'Yes, Charlotte, you can have some, too, darling' – and they toasted the end of the war.

'And here's to Mother!' Henry said, raising his glass again. 'Happy Birthday . . . and what a wonderful day to be celebrating it on.' Amid a feeling of ecstatic euphoria, they all toasted Lady Anne, and made her promise she wouldn't go near the dining room.

'We have a little surprise for you this evening,' Henry told her fondly.

*　　　*　　　*

248

That night Juliet played her part to perfection; she was the loving daughter, granddaughter and sister, the twenty-seven-year-old beautiful Duchess, who lived in a magnificent Mayfair house and had a fortune in money and jewels. She played the part so well she fooled her immediate family into thinking she was back to her happy carefree self; independent, adventurous, and out for a good time.

It was only when she returned to London the next day that the veneer cracked, splitting wide and exposing the depths of her grief and loneliness.

She cried as she had never allowed herself to cry before. She sobbed over the death of Daniel, of their baby, of all the people who had died in the Blitz, and the heart-rending scenes of horror she'd witnessed. She felt scarred, broken and devastated, because for too long she'd suppressed her emotions, for too long she'd gone back on duty and been forced to face yet more scenes of carnage.

Inconsolable, she refused to take any phone calls and stayed in her room, wanting to shut herself away from the world, which had become a cold and bleak place.

Trays of delicious food were returned untouched, and Dudley began to worry that she was having a nervous breakdown. She hadn't left the house for weeks, hadn't even bothered to get dressed, or put on any make-up.

Hour after hour she lay on the chaise longue in her bedroom, gazing out at Hyde Park.

One day Dudley tapped on her door. 'Your Grace, I'm sorry to disturb you, but there's a gentleman downstairs who insists on seeing you.'

'I'm not seeing anyone,' Juliet replied shortly, without even looking at Dudley. 'I don't care who it is, send him away.'

'Your Grace, I don't think he'll go away.' Dudley sounded flustered.

'You're quite right,' said a deep voice behind him. 'I'm not going anywhere until we've talked, Juliet.'

Daniel was standing in the doorway, his dark eyes glittering, his powerful presence filling the room.

Juliet's heart contracted painfully, as if it was being squeezed by a strong fist, and for a moment her body seemed to hover, suspended between life and death, so that she thought she was going to pass out.

'Daniel . . . ?' she croaked, her mouth dry. She felt paralysed with shock, unable to move. Her eyes were fixed on his face, hungrily taking in every feature while her mind was spinning . . . *it can't be . . . how can it be?*

He strode forward, broad shouldered and strong, and dropped into a chair near where she was sitting. He was frowning anxiously now. 'Are you all right?'

Juliet nodded, still unable to speak.

'I saw Gaston yesterday,' he said. 'He told me you thought I was dead?' he asked abruptly.

Her face was still ashen, and she looked fragile. Somehow she found her voice and she spoke bitterly. 'So you and your girlfriend *weren't* killed when your house was bombed? The Warden told me . . . he said they'd taken out a man and a woman, and there'd been nothing they could do for them.' She felt queasy and jarred from the impact of his sudden appearance, and her head ached.

'Oh, *Juliet!*' Daniel sounded both angry and compassionate at the same time, as if he'd picked up a child who had stepped off the pavement and almost got knocked down by a car. 'After we stopped seeing each other I rented the house to a friend of mine and his wife. Tragically, they were killed in the bombing. Not me. Didn't you *check* with someone?'

Stung by his criticism, she rallied. 'Like who? I could hardly telephone your wife to ask if you'd been killed, could I? And no, before you ask,' she continued feeling strangely rattled, 'I did not look for the announcement of your death in the newspapers, and I did *not* try to find out when your funeral was being held. I did what I had to do. Went back on duty and kept bloody going,' she added, suddenly bursting into angry tears.

'Oh, darling.' He leaned forward and looked tenderly into her face. 'I'm so sorry.'

'It's a bit late to be sorry now. You obviously didn't want to have anything more to do with me,' she dashed the tears from her cheeks with the back of her hand. 'So why should I have wanted to go to your funeral? Why should I care what happened to you?'

'That's not what Gaston told me,' he said softly, 'and I don't believe it's true. I've always loved you, Juliet. Always wanted you. It was your choice to marry Cameron Kincardine.'

'Because you were already married. And it was obvious you were so wrapped up in your family, you couldn't even telephone me, or drop me a line,' she retorted.

Daniel reached out for her hand, clasping it tightly, holding her fast. 'It was true that I was moving my family away from Kent, but what I couldn't tell you, and I can't give you the details even now, is that I was in Norway, setting up a network for SOE, which Gaston also happens to work for. The difference is he gets dropped behind the enemy lines, while I sit at HQ thinking up codes. I've been with MI5 for years you see.'

Juliet's hand flew to her mouth. 'How did you get back from Norway – the war had already started?'

He shrugged. 'Ways and means . . . sorry, my darling, Official Secrets Act and all that. You'll just have to trust me. All I want now is to be with you. My wife left me for someone else four years ago and we're divorced now.'

'Daniel . . . why haven't you got in touch before?'

'Because I really didn't think you'd want to see me. Whenever we bumped into each other, you were so cold, so distant.'

'Oh! So I was supposed to fall at your feet, in adoration, was I? Even when I crawled out of the Guards' Chapel, covered in other people's blood? You could have said something then,' she flashed with the old fire alight in her eyes.

'Why do you have to put on this act of being an utter bitch?' He sounded angry again. 'Underneath all that brittle arrogance, you're a sweet girl, you know. Why don't you let that show? Why do you always end up trying to push people away? You do it every time. You're doing it now.'

Juliet levelled her gaze at him. 'To protect myself, of course. And the last thing I want is your pity.'

He looked mystified. 'Why should I pity you, for God's sake?'

There was a long pause before she answered. 'I was pregnant with your baby, some years ago. Then I had a bad miscarriage. The baby was too premature to survive . . .' her voice caught, and she fought for control, '. . . so she died,' she added in a whisper.

Daniel looked appalled, his eyes stricken. 'Why didn't you tell me at the time?'

'I wanted to tell you . . .' she said fiercly. 'I wanted to tell

251

you more than anything, but I could never get hold of you.'

'. . . You had a baby, all on your own? And she died?' he asked, horrified.

'Cameron was very kind, although we were getting divorced. He flew down from Scotland; he thought it was his child.'

'And you didn't disillusion him?'

'What was the point? He can't help being a homosexual and he seemed so thrilled to think he'd fathered a baby, even if it was a girl. I couldn't take that away from him.'

'Oh, my God,' Daniel groaned, dropping his head into his hands. When he looked up at her again, his eyes were wet with tears. 'Juliet, I've always loved you. It's you I've always wanted. You've got to believe me. Don't you love me any more?'

'Would you have come to see me, if you hadn't met Gaston?' she challenged. 'Are you only here, because he'd told you I'd been upset by your death?'

'Yes, I would have done,' he said firmly. 'But first, I wanted to get my divorce over and done with, so that I'd be free to ask you to share your life with me, as my wife. Of course if you're not interested . . .'

Juliet stared into his face. Not daring to believe his words. Wanting to show him she loved him, but frightened of being hurt, again. He was the other half of her, a soulmate, a lover, all she'd ever wanted and yet she felt scared. He was looking intently into her eyes, and his forceful personality was as magnetic as ever; would she be able to resist him?

Then she heard herself say, 'I've been half dead myself, since I thought you'd been killed.'

'So can I take that as a typical Juliet declaration of love?' he mocked gently, his mouth tipping up at the corners.

Suddenly her face had lit up and she was glowing. Stretching her arms towards him she wound them around his neck as he pulled her close.

'I suppose so,' she whispered as if she only half believed this was happening.